THE HARD SIDE OF THE MOON

HUGH A. D. SPENCER

Milton, Ontario

Brain Lag
Milton, Ontario
http://www.brain-lag.com/

ISBN 978-1-998795-02-4

First paperback edition 2023

Library and Archives Canada Cataloguing in Publication

Title: The hard side of the moon : a novel / Hugh A. D. Spencer.
Names: Spencer, Hugh Alan Douglas, author.
Description: Previously published: Milton, Ontario: Brain Lag, 2021.
Identifiers: Canadiana 20220443467 | ISBN 9781998795024 (softcover)
Classification: LCC PS8637.P47 H37 2022 | DDC C813/.6—dc23

Content warnings: Medical procedures, rape

To my friends at CKUL
Was there anybody out there?

BOOK ONE: INVASION OF THE CAPEKOIDS

Audio Transcript:
The Amazing Struggles Show, CKUB FM
October 1970-something

Sound:	*Paper being shuffled.*

Matthew: What is it that you're handing me here?

Eugene: Classic work of theatre.

Matthew: Really?

Eugene: Really. I'm sure you're familiar with it.

Matthew: (coughs) Uh, yeah.

Eugene: I'd like you to read it for the listening audience.

Matthew: (voice rises slightly) I'm not an actor. I don't do dramatic readings.

Eugene: Nonsense. You have a solid university FM voice.

Matthew: But *R.U.R.?*

Eugene: That's right, *Rossum's Universal Robots*, the 1920 play by Czech author Karel Capek.

Matthew: So?

Eugene: Did you know that the word "robot" comes from the Czech word "robota" which alternatively means "serf" or "grunt work"?

Matthew: I actually did know that.

Eugene: Well, as you know, issues associated with oppression and liberation are rather important on this show.

Matthew: Yeah, but how is this relevant to tonight's album? Are these guys in the yellow radiation suits supposed to be robots?

Eugene: Maybe, but I think you can interpret DEVO in a number of ways. There's a manifesto about human de-volution in the publicity package from the record company.

Matthew: Why are we talking about fictional Eastern European robots again?

Eugene: I detected some thematic similarities between DEVO and *R.U.R.*

Matthew: Okay…

Eugene: …and before I put on their latest single, I think you are the best person to set us up to appreciate the connection.

Matthew: Really?

Eugene: So, if you don't mind…

Matthew: More paper shuffling.

Eugene: Well, okay. (clears throat) "*Robots of the world! The power of man has fallen! A new world has arisen: the Rule of the Robots! March!*"

Music: (Voice wails behind blast of guitars.)

1.
Timmie (Part 1)

Where the hell had he come from?

By "he" I mean Timmie. a.k.a., The Evil One.

That question echoed through my head every broadcast day since that awful morning when first Timmie showed up.

Showed up.

Not the most accurate description.

Infection?

Invasion?

Infestation?

Yeah. All of the above work better.

Timmie was a sign. A symptom. An odious indicator. A slightly puffy, scraggly-haired harbinger of doom wearing a Bay City Rollers t-shirt.

Where do you get boring shit like that?

Timmie pretty much rolled into our radio station and took over.

At the time, I just couldn't figure it out. I mean, why us? We weren't anything particularly special. At least I didn't think so.

CKUB was just one of many excessively serious university FM stations in the 1970s that were just too cool and too sophisticated to care if we had an audience. Actual listeners would have been so gauche.

Also, I suspected that our transmitter was powered by two no-name penlight batteries so we probably never broadcast much further than the campus buildings, the Esso station on University Drive and the (in)convenience store on Highway Two heading out towards the town of Blinn (population 62,976—which was a pretty big city for southern Alberta back then).

If we offended or inspired anyone, the audience numbers were so small that we never heard about it. Hey, the interwebs were still just for elite units of the Military-Industrial Complex back then, so our non-existent fans had no way of telling us what they did and didn't like.

But somebody must have been out there. Otherwise there never would have been a Timmie.

Audio Transcript:
Pop Goes Your Evening!, CKUB FM
November 1976

Sound: *Click of a switch.*

Timmie: Hey there! Pop Goes Your Evening, what's the magic word today?

Sound: *Dial tone.*

Timmie: Gosh! Somebody must have forgot how to use the phone there!

Sound: *Another click of a switch.*

Timmie: Hey! What's today's magic word?

Voice: Is it "mellow"?

Timmie: Congratulations! You have just won a beer voucher at the S.U.B. Pub!

Voice: Free beer! Far-out!

Sound: *Switches off.*

Timmie: Just say "Pop Goes Your Evening" at the bar and they'll fix you up. And in honour of the magic word, it's going to be wall to wall Olivia Newton-John starting with "Have You Never Been Mellow"!

Sound: *Distant screaming.*

Timmie was a transfer student from the Southern Alberta Institute of Technology who was taking some liberal arts classes to round out his certificate so he might have a better shot at doing some broadcast journalism when he grew up.

From S.A.I.T.? What a toad. I mean, they actually taught useful things there.

So gauche on so many levels.

Toad-boy or not, within twenty minutes of his arrival he had a prime-time spot. Five to seven p.m. Top 40 no less! Barry, our station manager, created the slot by cutting Hairy Banjo Men music in half and dumping the Goon Show reruns and replacing them with the Norwegian Headache Concert that used to come on just after dinner.

S.A.I.T. Toad. Top 40.

Still more Norwegian Headache Music.

45 rpm harbinger.

2.
ARE YOU R.I.P.?

UNLIKE CRASS PEOPLE, TIMMIE for example, I was an intellectual and an artist. Well, sort of. I was more of a Bohemian-Lite.

But I did have kind of a muse and it came from two sources.

One no longer exists and the other may be on its way to extinction. The first was *Famous Monsters* magazine, or at least the back pages of *Famous Monsters* magazine. That was where you could find ads for all kinds of great things that you could order in the mail: posters taken from the paintings they used in *Rod Serling's Night Gallery*, three minute clips from old horror and science fiction movies on rolls of silent 8 millimetre film stock, and these incredible all-rubber, over-the-head creature masks from Don Post Studios.

The masks were what really interested me.

I didn't have a lot of use for the front part of *Famous Monsters*. The horror movies were of note from a technical point of view, but nothing produced by either Universal or Hammer Studios seemed to be terribly important artistic statements—nor did they scare me very much. And if a horror movie doesn't scare you, I mean, what's the point?

Although, I did sometimes wonder what a really arty horror film would look like. What if Bergmann re-made *Frankenstein* or Truffaut had collaborated with Roger Corman on *The Little Shop of Horrors*? Those movies would appeal to both ends of my aesthetic spectrum.

Some of the insect fear films were fun and the Japanese sci-fi films were both challenging and humorous but *FM* never gave them the coverage they deserved.

Speaking of critical analysis, the text of *Famous Monsters* was filled with dozens of brain-melting puns which meant that I couldn't read the magazine for more than thirty seconds at a time without risking a stroke.

This was not *American Cinematographer*.

Hell, it wasn't even *Starlog*.

My second source of inspiration was the mail. Or rather, the postal service was the vehicle for my inspiration. Some people have asserted that the main indicators of civilization in any society is the extent of its public transit system and its postal service.

I agree.

Every four weeks I would get a Creative Care Package from the Science Fiction Book of the Month Club and sometimes I would even order paperbacks directly from publishers. It was hard out on the western frontier and those services kept us going.

The deliveries from Don Post Studios were particularly important. I needed those materials for what I came to call the "*R.U.R.* Installation Project" or "R.U.R.I.P."

It started back in my last year at high school.

Ah, high school.

I pretty much hated every fucking minute of it.

That's too harsh. To be fair, I just pretty much hated *every other* fucking minute of it.

Here's the part that I didn't hate:

Thanks to my mother taking us on an unexpected vacation I was late enrolling on my upcoming year at high school, so I had to share a locker with a guy named Ross, who happened to have the same last name as me.

Ross was a good guy who was essentially everything I wasn't: polite, respectful and adept at fixing things. He was also very tidy and organized, which is *very much* not like me.

In addition, Ross was a very tolerant person. Early on, we split the locker space along a horizontal axis: he got the top and I assumed control of the bottom. There was no hierarchy involved here, we were just cooperating with gravity. The top shelves of the locker were always very neat with textbooks carefully stacked according to size and thickness. Under that there was another stack of extra notebooks and pads of graph paper and bundles of pencils (3B to 4H) and pens held together with completely flat rubber bands. Ross' locker territory looked like it belonged to a future aerospace designer or robotics engineer.

Funny that.

My section of the locker looked like some kind of mutant gene-splicing experiment had gone horribly wrong and escaped from the lab. This palpating green-grey mass seemed to get bigger and smellier every day. I'm not sure what was making the mess grow—whether it was the half dozen pairs of gym socks, the rotting papier mâché sculptures from art class or maybe a few weeks' worth of half-eaten lunches.

Every time I approached the locker the swamp-like smell reminded me that I needed to do something radical. Like clean up my half of the locker.

But how? They didn't sell flamethrowers at Blinn Hardware and the school janitor kept the snow shovels under lock and key.

Let's get back to the *R.U.R.* project.

The robots in Capek's play were scientifically engineered artificial humans, kind of quasi-organic in that they were grown in vats and "spun" rather than constructed machines manufactured from wires and metal by mechanical tools.

You don't believe me? Take a look at a bit of the play:

> "The pestle is for beating up the paste. In each one we mix the ingredients for a thousand Robots at one operation. Then there are the vats for the preparation of liver, brains, and so on. Then you will see the bone factory. After that I'll show you the spinning mill… For weaving nerves and veins. Miles and miles of digestive tubes pass through it at a time."

The manufacturing process that Capek describes has the twin virtues of being both interesting and disgusting at the same time. Good *Famous Monsters* material when you think about it.

So anyway, when I first read *R.U.R.*—back when I was sixteen and still believed science fiction was the way to solve all the World's Problems by taking us forward into a glorious technological utopia with floating cities, faster-than-light travel, a three-day work week and millions of beautiful women all anxious to have sex with horny teenage losers like me.

My powerful political convictions were probably inspired by looking at Nichelle Nichols' legs in her role as Lt. Uhura in *Star Trek.*

Of course, the play suggested none of these possibilities. Frankly, I found it rather depressing, a little boring and the love interest felt like the romantic side-story they would staple onto the early Marx Brothers movies when they had to give Zeppo something to do on screen.

But *R.U.R.* is regarded as an important work by lots of people who write, speak and think way better than me.

But…

Even though I wasn't crazy about the play, Capek's idea of a more efficient, more streamlined human being fascinated me. No, fascinated is the wrong word. Worried is more accurate.

Audio Transcript:
The Black Hole on Friday Night, CKUB FM
January 197ish

Sound:	*Words in reverse.*
Matthew:	Sorry about that. A little trouble cueing up the records.
Sound:	*More backwards words and music.*
Matthew:	There! As I mentioned, tonight's Made-for-Radio Movie is Kurt Vonnegut reading from his novel

Player Piano accompanied by the music of Scott Joplin which is, appropriately enough, rendered on an actual antique player piano.

Sound: *Pages being flipped.*

Matthew: But before we get into that I want to talk about a really interesting book, and by interesting I mean strange, that someone left in the studio. What's the title again, Barry?

Barry: (distant, off-mic) *The Young Man's Guide to a Successful Career in the Business World.*

Matthew: And it's written by who? Abbie Hoffman? Karl Marx?

Barry: There's no author listed.

Matthew: So, I want to read a passage because I think it might be really useful to our Management Arts students. The language might get a little salty but our station manager says that since it's after 10 p.m., it should be okay.

Barry: Just be careful.

Matthew: The book says: "Successful entrepreneurs and business leaders come from a variety of different backgrounds, have different abilities, different levels of education, and even widely vary in their IQ scores." Is that right, Barry?

Barry: Apparently so.

Matthew: Our anonymous author continues: "However, the one thing all these men have had in common was the ability to master their mental, emotional and physical processes to an extraordinary control. It almost goes without saying that all of these men disdained any activity even remotely resembling masturbation but what is truly extraordinary to many lay persons is the fact that they had absolute command over their bowels. Every one of these human titans were able to direct themselves to have a substantial movement at the same time every morning before they left their homes for work."

Barry: That is extraordinary.

Matthew: So boys and girls, the secret to a happy, prosperous and important life is to avoid touching your privates and above all teach yourself to poop on schedule!

Maybe what worried me about Capek's robots was that I suspected streamlining me would certainly make my mother's life easier. Who knows, maybe a simpler me would make a lot of people's lives easier.

Soon, probably to cope with this unexpressed anxiety, I started collecting toy robots. When I hit eighteen and was in my last year at high school I had a collection of over one hundred and fifty of the things. Most of them were just little tin or plastic apparatuses that you could pick up at Woolco or Zellers.

I didn't even buy a lot of them. Once people heard that I was interested in something small and relatively cheap, I had a fairly steady stream of them coming into the house.

Not that I complained; I liked getting all the toys.

Yeah, my therapist said exactly what you're thinking, divorce-traumatized adolescent uses toys to psychologically revert to a happier time in early childhood. The gifts become reassuring love-tokens from estranged family and friends.

Blah, blah, blah.

It's annoying because both of you are probably absolutely right. Although, I really don't remember my early childhood being all that happy.

I would also express my robot-pathology by drawing pictures of my toy collection. I used a lot of media: pen and ink, pastels, watercolours, acrylics. If I wasn't such a klutz in the fine-motor skills department, I would have even tried an airbrush. That would have made a real mess which would have really irritated my mother.

Good.

Okay, I'm in danger of getting to the point about something here, so back to the schizoid locker and my virtuous school-mate, Ross.

Ross and I were also in the same art class. Drafting class too.

Did I mention that Ross had near computer-precise drawing skills? And this was before we had computers that could do stuff like that. Back in the 1970s computers just typed things. Usually numbers. You could make simple shapes and even jerk those polygons across a TV screen but frankly you were going to get more joy out of an Etch-A-Sketch.

Our drafting teacher used to almost weep with joy when Ross would hand in an assignment. All the lines were the same thickness. They all matched up. No smudges or stains. A lot of what passed for skill back then was really more like being able to perform like an extremely reliable machine. Ross was a nice person and a good pseudo-machine.

I sensed that he would do well in later life.

One day Ross saw my sketchbook and noticed that it was filled with dozens of crudely rendered robot pictures. He didn't say anything nasty (he never did) just that he thought some of the detailing was kind of interesting.

"I like the way you've stacked the shapes."

What the hell? He was complimenting me?

On my drawing ability?

Ross was a trustworthy person (hey, reliable pseudo-machine), so I told him about my collection. I was flattered when he asked if he could do some sketches of them.

Then I realized that I had a problem. My mother would not be pleased to have someone over to "play" with my toys ("It's so infantile!") and I was way too embarrassed to bring any of the robots to art class. There were a few hockey and football players in the class who were looking for easy grades and I sensed that coming out as a robot fan would be kind of dangerous. To them, anything even remotely unusual was potentially "gay" and that meant instant punishment. It was like having giant stupid homophobic Gorts looming over the schoolyard. Except these robots were much, much stupider than that really cool silver robot from *The Day the Earth Stood Still*.

Ross and I came up with a great compromise. It was great because it would be a pretty credible expression of Capek's original vision of what robots were and because it did not involve getting the living shit beaten out of me for the rest of the semester.

We might also be able to submit it for extra course credit.

Win. Win. Win.

Ross and I would make some robots in class and sketch them there.

The school janitor had recently cleaned out the main storage closet and had retired two of his denim coveralls. He was also in the process of dumping all the out-of-date cleaning solvents down the sink.

This was the 1970s, remember? People who worried about toxic drinking water were just sissies!

The union suits were just too cool to be believed because they looked like something you might pick up at the Airstrip One Thrift Store on the way home from a hard day's work at the Ministry of Truth.

The empty solvent containers also had all kinds of possibilities. They were big shiny aluminum rectangles and once Ross and I steamed off the labels and warning stickers they looked just like… you guessed it… *robot heads*.

The janitor also gave us some old, massive vulcanized rubber gloves and Ross and I found some old winter boots we could use. That took care of the exterior elements. Now there was the problem of making our embryonic Capekoids three-dimensional.

In dealing with this challenge, Ross and I were equally disadvantaged. As I mentioned earlier, as far as precision operations go, I might as well have hooks for hands.

While Ross could draw perfect circles and polygons freehand, this was not something that would be happening on a flat surface. With the manipulation of raw physical materials, he seemed just as hopeless as me.

I feel badly that I found our shared handicap deeply satisfying.

Fortunately, our solution involved very little skill. We ended up lining the insides of the coveralls with chicken wire and stuffed the empty shells with over four years of newspapers—from the F.L.Q. Crisis to Ford pardoning Nixon.

Fun times!

Our art teacher was somewhat impressed; we had created two reasonably sturdy yet malleable humanoid structures and managed to free up a lot of extra space in the teachers' lounge. And we had our *R.U.R.* robots!

I would argue that even though our creations had no moving parts and they certainly could never pick up Anne Francis and walk around the surface of Planet Altair IV, they were still real robots… of a sort.

Here is my thesis: if you apply the definition that a robot is a construct intended to do the work of a human being, then that was precisely what our robots were doing. Instead of having actual people pose as models for us in art class, we had our denim-chicken wire-newspaper simulacra doing the job.

Maybe I'm stretching things a bit here.

Even so, Capekoids #1 and #2 were pretty successful. Not only did Ross do some fantastic ink-wash renderings of them, some of the other kids from other classes started to draw and paint them as well.

One student, we didn't know who at the time, did glazed ceramic sculptures of them. They were about ten inches high and the artist made them look as though they were melting. The title, which was printed in very precise handwriting, said: "*Mecha-Physiological Effects of Nuclear Fallout Case #114*". The label had the twin virtues of being very creepy and very cool.

To both Ross' and my amazement, no one ever tried to vandalize our stationary robots. We decided that the resident sport-thugs only like to hit things that moved or had the capacity to cry out in pain.

Then about three months after we built them, something very strange happened. Before our art teacher could ask us to dismantle Cs #1 and #2, they disappeared. They weren't in the classroom. Not in the hallways, not even in the janitor's closet or the dumpster by the loading bay.

They were gone. It was as though they had stood up and hobbled out the door on their chicken-wire legs.

Almost.

They reappeared the next day outside the guidance counsellor's office sitting in chairs and looking like they were waiting for an appointment. We later heard that the guidance counsellor was not pleased.

There was a brief announcement over the school's public address system but before Ross and I could collect the robots, they were gone again.

The next Capekoid manifestation was two weeks later at a school assembly. They were sitting dead centre in the front row. Ordinarily this would have just been a prank, stupid but harmless.

Except this was not a normal assembly.

There was a provincial election going on and the then-Premier decided to use our event as a photo opportunity to show all our voter parents how education friendly he was.

Education was good, would be the message, just as long as that book-learning helped those kids get good jobs and that they didn't pick up any fancy ideas above their station. Ideas like socialism. Or asking their employers for more money. Years later I learned that the then-Premier was actually something of an artist and a patron of the arts himself but he probably had been briefed on the psychographics of the voters and figured he had to play to his base.

In other words: simpler people are better. They are easier to control and they perform with greater consistency.

And there were our robo-guys. Right in our leader's face, looking like some kind of protest.

I was terrified but also impressed.

Our principal looked as though he was going to shit a brick of pure processed plutonium dark-star matter. The vice-principal's face was bright green, as though he was dying of the radiation poisoning from being close to interstellar plutonium.

But the Premier seemed totally cool with it all. If it bothered him that two of his greatest fans were a couple of tin-heads then he gave no indication of it. Maybe he thought a population of tin-heads was a good idea.

Things got worse after the assembly. A photographer from the local paper was there and the next day they ran a picture of Cs #1 and #2 in the audience with the caption: "*Does the Premier think kids are dummies?*" The images were accompanied with a couple of the editorials you might expect in a southern Alberta newspaper of the time: "Education standards are at the lowest they've ever been", "teaching evolution will cause earthquakes", and "we need to kill all the immigrants and teenagers before they kill us."

I think there was an unrelated column about how Prime Minister Trudeau was responsible for sunspots, UFOs and cattle mutilations but that sort of thing was pretty frequent in the local papers back then.

Audio Transcript:
The Alienated News, CKUB FM
December 197ish

Sound:	*Electronic music clip from* The Silver Apples of the Moon.
Eugene:	Time for Campus Current Affairs Announcements…
Sound:	*Rustling of paper.*
Eugene:	The Ayn Rand Society is holding a joint dinner-dance with the Friedrich Nietzsche Appreciation

Club. Only the strongest people will be allowed to eat and only the most attractive will be permitted on the dance floor. Apparently a live band will be playing polka arrangements from Wagner's Ring Cycle. (pause) There are promised ritual slayings.

Voice: (distant and indistinguishable)

Eugene: I don't know if this is serious or not. They just hand me the pages and I read what's on them.

Voice: (distant)…careful…

Eugene: There are two illustrated lectures this week. On Tuesday night in Room C-180, the Provincial Libertarian Party will be hosting designer Kelly Fry who will be talking about fashion mistakes by Soviet political leaders since the Korean War, and the Astronomy and the Religious Studies departments, on Wednesday night, will be exploring the "theological and psychopathological implications of Velikovsky's *Worlds in Collision*." (pause) That last one is a must-see in my opinion.

Voice: (distant) Brlagoshs.

Eugene: Wrap it up? Okay, one last one: for the entire week of February 7, the Campus Young Conservative Society will be drunk.

Voice: (angry) *BRLAGOSHS!*

Eugene: It's what the paper says! Their president brought it over himself.

As the creators of the offending humanoid objects, Ross and I were in as much trouble as possible without felony charges being laid.

We got called into the principal's office.

Which was inevitable, really.

Ross was a rock.

Unfortunately, while it was impressive that he refused to say anything, it also looked really suspicious. I knew Ross well enough to know that he was no prankster or rule-breaker, so he wasn't responsible. He was just pissed at whoever was messing around with our tin-heads.

Fortunately, I wasn't nearly as composed. Hell, I wailed and blubbered so much that I embarrassed everyone in the room, which disgusted Ross but convinced the principal that a crybaby like me couldn't possibly have the nerve to stage what might have been some kind of a political statement.

The principal and vice principal concluded that we were innocent. Irritating, but innocent.

This outcome helped Ross forgive me for my performance and we stayed friends. Also, he was still a nice person.

Another fortunately: after that, the Capekoids went away for a while. Which to me was an indicator that there may be occasionally merciful forces at work in the universe.

The only evidence that Cs #1 and #2 were still in operation came about two weeks later during the break between my 9:00 A.M. Typing class and my 10:30 A.M. Lit tutorial. A note and Polaroid photograph were taped to the locker door. The picture was a head shot of the robots and the note read:

> "Your half of the locker is an absolute mess! Nobody should have to put up with your crap! Clean it up or we shall strike again!"

Told you the stuff about the locker would bite me back.

Ross was standing next to me and reading over my shoulder. I didn't have to say anything before he shrugged his denial of all knowledge. I believed him. Ross never lied, so you just believed him.

I feared the wandering robots, even though I helped create them. Perhaps because I had helped create them.

Thank you, Mary Shelley.

I would do what they demanded.

I stayed after classes ended, and with the help of the assistant janitor, shovelled out the gross goo and disgusting detritus from the bottom of the locker. We sprayed the interior with massive amounts of ozone layer-destroying aerosol substances to remove the smell and destroy any traces of the Andromeda Strain that might still be lurking there.

After that there was nothing from the robots for months. I figured they were either in a local landfill or had been taken up by a flying saucer and been warped off to some Planet of the Androids in the Galaxy of the Weird.

Either possibility was just fine with me as long as I never saw them again.

But no.

On the final day of school, just after my last exam, I was walking towards the bus stop to get a ride home. I wasn't walking fast enough. The Number 7A was just pulling away.

Crap.

And crap again.

There they were.

The two Capekoids sitting in the back seat of the bus. I only saw them for a second before that big metal and diesel vehicle huffed and wheezed its way down the street.

The rogue Capekoids still lived. They still roamed the world.

This was not good.

Walking home, I stopped in on a second-hand bookstore and bought some back issues of *Magnus: Robot Fighter*. I liked Magnus. He was serious robot opposition. Right away, you knew what he was all about. I decided that in addition to some moments of escapism, I might pick up some good self-defence tips.

I got home safely and there were no more Capekoid manifestations for a few days.

But then…

That weekend the buzzer at the front door went off and I heard the words "special delivery" squawk through the intercom speaker.

That cheered me up. It might be a package of some cool stuff that I had ordered from *Famous Monsters*. It didn't occur to me to wonder why the mail was being delivered on a Saturday. Remember, this was the 1970s, you hardly ever got anything by courier.

When I opened the door, there they were. Leaning against the side of the house. A note was pinned to the chest of Capekoid #1 and there was a Polaroid on the chest of Capekoid #2. The photograph was another head shot—this time of a teenage girl.

Dark hair. An angry expression. Asian.

That wasn't a big deal. There were a lot of Asian people in Blinn because they had internment camps here in World War II and for various unfathomable reasons (to me anyway) some of these families decided to stay. I didn't know who she was, which was probably why she put it there. She wanted me to recognize her later.

A warning?

The note said: "I am returning your creations. Use them well. Or else."

Yeah. A warning.

I couldn't leave the stupid things just sitting there so I took them inside.

My mother wasn't terribly impressed when she found them sitting on the living room couch watching *Challenge of the Super Friends* on TV so I had to move them into my room.

Which is where they stayed. Ross, for some reason, was not keen on the idea of joint custody.

So now I had roomies.

I would move them around and change their postures every week or so just to make sure their newspaper stuffing didn't start sagging into one spot. One week C #1 would get to sit in my chair and C #2 would be propped against the bookcase. The next week their positions would be reversed.

At least I didn't have to walk them or empty a litter box.

By the end of the summer the boys had stopped creeping me

out and I started wondering what my critic/benefactor meant by "use them well". And what would that angry girl in the Polaroid do if I didn't find a way to use them to her satisfaction?

Ross was absolutely no help at all at this point. He had gone off to some exotic pre-engineering program out east where they probably immediately put him to work working up technical drawings of fusion reactors and neutron bombs (again, remember this was the 1970s, a mostly pre-CAD era).

So, I had to take on the mission alone. But what to do? What was that mission? As I often did back then, I binge-read my comic collection and came across a reprint of *Detective Comics* Issue One where the toned and trained Bruce Wayne sits in his mansion wondering the same thing. How best to avenge the death of his parents and fight evil in Gotham City:

> "Criminals are a superstitious, cowardly lot, so my disguise must be able to strike terror into their hearts. I must be a creature of the night, black, terrible... a... a..."

Then a big bat flies in through the window:

> "...a bat! That's it!"

And thus, Batman was born.

Then I remembered how this reprint inspired me to create a superhero of my own. A young married couple, the husband a successful inter-personal psychotherapist, the wife a leading researcher into human sexual response, are gunned down by an emotionally repressed NRA supporter. Their young son, like Bruce Wayne, trains himself to his physical and mental apex awaiting the right omen to inspire him in his mission and evil-resisting identity. Then one fateful February 14:

"Criminals are an unloved and alienated lot..." A stray card blows in through the man's window. "That's it!" And thus, the loving avenger Captain Valentine was born.

I never could persuade the high school paper to print that one and maybe it wasn't just the bad art.

Never mind, I was going to go with the same concept now. I decided that Cs #1 and #2 were going to be the conscience of our prairie community.

Immobile robo-mimes with a message.

3.
GOAT SACRIFICE

MY FIRST INSTALLATION PROJECT came around mid-term time in my first year at university. It happened downtown outside the Paramount Theatre.

For the past few weeks, the local Pentecostal kids from one of the high schools and the community college were getting pretty aggressive as they handed out religious literature to people lined up waiting to see whatever movie was playing.

From a marketing point of view, this time and location made a lot of sense. Friday night was the start of the weekend and that was the night of the week that the Paramount would premiere its first run features. And Blinn was a town without a lot of alternative entertainment options. Even when you had a lame movie like *Aloha Bobby and Rose* or *The Swarm*, you were pretty sure to have a good crowd out there coming up on seven and nine p.m.

Those Rollers had a pretty dim-witted view of the nature of the universe but they sure knew how to promote. But don't let my attempt at objective description be mistaken for any form of admiration. I thought the pamphlets they were pushing were stupid and it was pretty rude bothering people when they were just trying to have a night out.

I really didn't like it.

Further, it was obnoxious and arguably a veiled attack on, or at least a snub at, civil society. At least a part of civil society that I sort of cared about.

Something had to be done.

Audio Transcript:
The Black Hole on Friday Night, CKUB FM
November 197-er…

Sound:	*Electronic music fades.*

Matthew: That was Debussy's "The Engulfed Cathedral" as interpreted by Isao Tomita on the Moog Synthesizer and I'm afraid that because I received a grand total of one letter complimenting me on playing "Clair de Lune" from the same album, I will be playing tracks from *The Snowflakes are Dancing* every chance I get this term.

Sound: *Paper rustling.*

Matthew: A couple of arts and culture announcements before we listen to Vincent Price reading from Edgar Allan Poe: there's a petition out from the Western Canadian Friends of America to have the Sorel Etrog sculpture removed and replaced with a replica Remington piece. (coughs) Personally, if any of you actually sign that thing I hope you are the immediate victim of spontaneous combustion. I guess that that's the only way you can do that, there's no such thing as gradual spontaneous combustion.

Sound: *More paper rustling.*

Matthew: Hey! After that kerfuffle with Student Council, the University Film Society is back in business. There's been a few changes in the programming, however. The Ingmar Bergman retrospective has been replaced with showings of *True Grit*, *Dirty Harry* and *That Darn Cat*. (laughs) Well, there seems to be a new artistic philosophy at work with our projectionist friends!

So one night, I borrowed my mother's car and while things were relatively deserted mid-way through the early evening show, I propped the robots up against a telephone pole next to the entrance of the Paramount and put my own pamphlets in their hands. I included a sign that invited people in line to take one. It was inspired by those little display booths that the Jehovah's Witnesses sometimes put up when they are trying to distribute back issues of *Watchtower*.

The literature advertised the benefits of Paganism and invited everyone to a Druidic goat sacrifice social at a date and time to be later specified.

When they came back to hit on the people lining up for the nine o'clock show, the Pentecostals were too frightened to touch the robots. In fact, the kids never returned to that spot, possibly fearing some kind of satanic contamination might occur.

Cool.

Everyone else thought it was either stupid or funny.

They were right.

My work there was done.

4.
ICE LOBOTOMY

THE NEXT CAPEKOID INCIDENT was during the winter of the same year. Our school hockey bullies had grown up (at least physiologically) and some were now players in the local semi-pro league.

Yip. Fucking. Eee.

Well, it was a big deal to some people in Blinn. Okay, it was a monstrously huge deal to 99% of the population of Blinn, Alberta.

Audio Transcript:
The Amazing Struggles Show, CKUB FM
November 1976

Eugene:	So I have Assistant Coach Doyle here from the Athletic Department.
Doyle:	Good evening.
Eugene:	He's going to talk about some of the facilities available at the new gymnasium extension.
Doyle:	That's right, Eugene.
Eugene:	But first, we're going to explore why the Athletic Department is doing nothing about the recent sexual assaults on female students by members of the university hockey team.

Doyle: Ah—

It would be misleading to call what they were doing a sport. The ref's whistle would start the "game", the gloves would be off and those cretins would be slugging it out before the puck hit the ice.

Once again, attention must be paid (with thanks to Mr. Arthur Miller and Mr. Joe Mould, my Grade Twelve English teacher).

This time, I borrowed my uncle's pick-up truck and as one of the games was closing, I put the robots in the back and gave each one a hockey stick. I also gave them signs to hold as I drove the truck past the people who were coming out of the arena. I drove very slowly so they could read the message:

"ENJOY ICE LOBOTOMY! THE GREAT CANADIAN GAME! HATE IS GOOD IF IT WINS US GAMES!"

We didn't stick around but I think we made an impression.

5.
STUDYING WITH SUE

SUE CALLED ME ON the telephone.

That was how we communicated back then, but even so it was still a rare occurrence.

My friend Sue.

I would usually see her at the cafeteria or at the bus stop at the campus. We would catch up on things there and she would always offer to give me a ride into town in her ancient and giant Oldsmobile.

My good friend Sue.

I would always decline because the long bus ride home was an excellent time for studying away from the distraction of the TV and my high tech eight-track stereo.

Sue was short, skinny and had straight, shoulder length hair and theoretically she had a body but it was always completely undetectable under remarkably loose clothing. She also had a nose that was a little big and she almost never wore makeup.

She was gorgeous.

Although she was not a big person, there was something about her that told you that she was incredibly strong; in character and intellect anyway. Sue was also really interesting to talk to which was probably the most important thing to me.

I'm sure that some boring people are good and virtuous individuals and I would never deny the Chronically Dull their basic human rights. But I did find them very difficult to hang around with.

They were just so *boring*.

Even the pretty ones with really nice breasts.

I mean, we're going to be dead in a couple of decades, right? It is our responsibility to be bored for as little time as possible.

"What were you doing on Sunday night?" That was near the start of one of our bus stop conversations.

The first thing when asked a question by any young woman was to make the initial decision whether to lie (and try and sound cool) or tell the truth (and reveal that you were completely dorky).

"Watching TV." No sense in trying to lie to Sue. She'd see right through anything but the absolute truth. Besides, she already knew I was a dork and she talked to me anyway.

My precious friend Sue.

She laughed. "Let me guess. The ABC Sunday Night Movie."

I blushed a little. "It was the world television premiere of *Thunderball*."

A sigh. "James Bond is such a dick."

I blushed a lot. She was right but I liked those movies anyway.

"I'm watching for fashion tips."

Her very ordinary but very pretty eyebrow arched. "Do you even own a suit?"

"I might. (pause) Someday." I really didn't sound very convincing. "If I ever get a job or something like that." Even I wasn't convinced about that.

"I suppose that is a justifiable reason for watching that crap."

"Oh yeah, I hate all the fighting and shooting and the half-naked ladies." I tried to make that statement in a way that Sue knew I was *deliberately* lying. What's that called? Oh yes, irony.

"What did you think of the commercial at 9:30?"

Christ! I'd about forgotten that! This was an American election year. There was usually a big political ad after the first half hour of the Sunday night prime time movie. But the paid political message thirty minutes into *Thunderball* was a bit unusual:

"This time, vote for real change! VOTE COMMUNIST!"

I shit you not, as we used to say back then.

The American Communist Party had nominated candidates for, put all its mailed-in rubles together and bought what was probably some of the most expensive air time on the planet that week and suggested a rather surprising political option to the American people.

"It was bizarre!"

Sue laughed. "Wasn't it hysterical?"

"I thought that at the end of the spot, James Bond was going to appear and shoot them."

My remark made Sue laugh even more.

"Do you need a ride home?"

I shook my head and lifted my rather massive geography textbook. "I gotta read."

"Suit yourself."

I came to really treasure those conversations at the bus stop— sometimes they were the highlight of my day. Although that time, when I was riding home on the bus, I looked up from the explanation of the break-up of Pangaea and realized something. Sue had to be watching *Thunderball* to know about that commercial. And here she was dissing me for liking James Bond! Or maybe she was a communist and had never mentioned it.

Sneaky girl, that Sue.

I was quite smitten with her, although I sometimes wished otherwise. I knew that nothing romantic was ever going to happen between us. I suspected that Sue had some very definite ideas about the kind of man she was after in the serious relationship department and that I missed out on at least five of the three key criteria.

That was okay.

Good conversation was not quite as rare as good (or any) sex for me at that time. But talk like that was still pretty rare.

I miss my good friend Sue.

Anyway.

That was how things were between Sue and me and why she didn't call me up very much. Or why I didn't call her very much.

There was no need. The bus stop and the cafeteria were enough for us.

"Hello, Matt."

Sue's voice was very soft and careful. I could imagine her sitting with correct but relaxed posture in an inexpensive but still nicely designed chair.

"Hey Sue!"

Not me. I was wearing nothing but my Big Blue overalls, sprawled out over the old La-Z-Boy recliner we'd inherited from my long-departed grandfather. I had coloured inks and drawing charcoal smeared all over the denim of my overalls. I wasn't even wearing any underwear.

I wasn't being sexy, just lazy.

Audio Transcript:
Auto Shift, CKUB FM
March 197—

Sound:	*Click of switch.*
Drew:	We just got another request. Once again, this is from Matt and it's dedicated to Sue…
Sound:	*Music slowly rises.*
Drew:	A sexy song from a very sexy lady… Carly Simon doing the theme to *The Spy Who Loved Me.*

"Haven't seen you for a while, Sue. What's up?"

"Is your mother around?"

For some reason, Sue got extra careful when the subject of my mother came up. Maybe it was because in some ways Sue's life was very different than mine. Our mothers for example.

I lived with my mother and she was fairly busy making her unique mother-impact on my life. Some of it good, some of it not so much.

Sue's mother was dead. This meant that their relationship was rather subdued and there was less business involved.

Her dad lived in one of the nearby farm towns and as far as I could tell after giving her his used Oldsmobile, had no further role in her life.

She inherited a bit of dough from her mother and worked on highway construction crews during the summer months. The money was very good on those gigs, so every year she was able to rent her own little house and run the place as she wanted while she studied for her teaching degree.

In other words, Sue was almost completely independent. Even though she was an undergraduate student, she was essentially living the life of an adult.

This was a completely foreign concept for me.

The most assertive thing I was doing that year was walking the eight blocks to the variety store to buy the latest *Adam Warlock* and *Howard the Duck* comics.

Don't knock it. Those were very thought provoking narratives for the time. But if you said that to most folks in Blinn, you risked ridicule or a fist in your face.

Back to Sue's question about my mother being around:

"Naw, she's out on a date."

I think Sue, somewhat unfairly, felt my mother was partly responsible for my proto-slacker lifestyle.

"Is there something you want to tell me that she shouldn't know about?"

"Oh no, I was just wondering how you two were getting along these days."

Darn.

I briefly hoped that Sue might have sustained a head injury and wanted to drive over to my house and have sex with me. A guy can dream, can't he?

"We're fine, Sue."

Sue, unlike me, is better at getting to the point: "Did you take Upton's mythology class last semester?"

"Yeah, it was pretty good." Actually, I loved the class. *Myths to Live By* and *The Hero with a Thousand Faces* were two of our texts and they totally blew me away.

"Didn't the reading list include the Vantage edition of *Heart of Darkness*?"

"Yeah."

"Could I please borrow it?"

Of course.

6.
OTHER PEOPLE'S LUNCHES

Audio Transcript:
Sugar Shack Time, CKUB FM
December 197—

Sound:	*Recorded applause.*
Timmie:	Thank you! Thank you! *Thank you!*
Sound:	*More recorded effects: fireworks, sirens and cartoon bouncy springs.*
Timmie:	It is so great to be here in this new prime time spot. I'm having a great time and I know you're going to have a great time, too!
Sound:	*More recorded applause.*
Timmie:	We got lots of partying to get to with Paul Anka, The Captain and Tennille and some Donnie and Marie. But let's first get down with some Bay City Rollers!
Sound:	*Music.*

Eugene got sent to the hospital. More on that later.

Also, Barry, against almost everyone's protests, turned over the empty slot on the CKUB schedule to Timmie. "He works hard, he works fast and a lot of people listen to what he plays."

"A lot? As in more than ten?" I meant that as a put-down but everything is in context, right? Any ratings for CKUB involving two digits or more was a runaway success.

"It's Timmie's spot."

Thusly did Barry forever compromise the quality of our broadcast standards and alienate every one of us at CKUB.

Except for Timmie, of course.

If I hadn't needed to get out of the house on Friday nights I would have quit right then. Some of the DJs did quit. They must have had less needy lives than me.

It was interesting that the people who replaced the departing DJs were a lot more like Timmie in their programming than they were like Eugene.

Anyway, the result was that we had even more top forty to deal with.

Fuck. And *why?*

I really couldn't figure it out. Why were the local commercial stations letting Timmie and Barry get away with this? Prior to this, the only reason the real radio stations put up with CKUB was that we were pumping out stuff that none of their sponsors would pay for and that none of their audience demographic would listen to even if under the influence of truth serum and/or they were being held hostage.

I bet that our original playlists were part of the commercial stations' marketing strategy:

1. The average listener would tune us in.
2. Hear what we offered for about ten seconds and…
3. Scramble along the dial searching for just about anything else to listen to.

But what was happening with Timmie? He was definitely trying to eat the regular stations' lunches. Why wasn't someone from the local Chamber of Commerce writing angry letters to the editor of the *Blinn Bulletin*? Calling their Member of Parliament?

Making presentations to the Canadian Radio and Television Commission?

It was weird at all kinds of levels.

7.
I Don't Like Wednesdays

Wednesday.

It was a Wednesday.

Lots of people aren't all that keen on what they call "humpdays" so I'm not alone there.

But I have to tell you, Wednesdays really suck. I don't hate Wednesdays in the same way that the Boomtown Rats sang about Mondays, so everyone at the local MacDonnell's was pretty safe, but my loathing for Wednesdays was still pretty intense. Please note that I am not being cute with names here. The most popular fast food place in Blinn was called *MacDonnell's*. We were probably the only community with a population of more than 5,000 not to have a McDonald's. At the time I thought it was just weird, later I would appreciate the significance of the absence. It was all about competing corporate interests.

So back to Those Hideous Wednesdays.

First of all, everything on the six TV channels we had was absolute shit on Wednesdays. I mean, even shittier than usual. The only thing on offer were bad sitcoms that were staked out on the screen to die from neglect after two or three months, variety shows featuring pop stars that we'd forgotten about before broadcast date, and if we were lucky, one of the lamer Quinn Martin crime shows. The big "QM" logo and the gravel-voiced announcer would be the highlights of the evening.

Man, the networks really held us hostage before we had VCRs.

Out of an urge to avoid brain damage I might try and find some news or arts programming or maybe some drama on CBC Radio but more often than not Mr. Erdos next door would fire up his mega-ham radio which would pretty much reduce the signal to our house to complete static.

Once my mother asked Mr. Erdos about the interference and he said that he was just talking to his relatives in Hungary. I figured that the cranky old fascist had decided that our national public broadcaster was the vanguard of an invading ideological army and he was going to do whatever he could to prevent as many people as possible from falling sway to this sinister socialist wave of entertainment and education.

Asshole.

Audio Transcript:
The Amazing Struggles Show, CKUB FM
February 197—

Sound:	*Atonal chamber music. Probably something by Elliot Carter with strings and harpsichord.*
Eugene:	So, it's time for one of my favourite parts of the show, "Things We Should be Talking About But Aren't."
Sound:	*Recording of boos and hisses.*
Eugene:	I know, I know, you hate this stuff but you really have to know about it.
Sound:	*Paper rustling.*
Eugene:	Think of it as political cod-liver oil. It goes down yucky but it keeps you alive and healthy.
Sound:	*Recording of groans.*
Eugene:	Tonight's topic: Local High School Teachers Who Are Also Holocaust Deniers…

Now why, you might ask, wasn't I listening to the university radio station? Showing a bit of loyalty? Well, first of all the CKUB signal rarely made it to our part of town, and second, if I did manage to tune in, it would likely be Timmie playing the goddamned Bay City Rollers.

I could have tried to read something or listen to some eight-tracks or records but I was usually too stressed out from the first three days of classes to settle into something like that.

The only way for me to depressurize was to check over my lecture notes and do some highlighting of passages from my textbooks. Since I was too wired to actually read much of the type, my colourization of the books was more decorative and random than informative.

Thrilling stuff.

Speaking of which, the classes on Wednesday were particularly dire.

First there was a three-hour Macroeconomics marathon starting at 8:30 A.M. Our prof was a young woman from Scotland. I picked up on her origins from the first two (and just about only) sentences she spoke to the class. Then she shut up for the rest of the semester.

Every Wednesday morning, Dr. Sheena MacWhatever would walk up to the front of the lecture theatre, open a notebook on the podium and then copy out her notes on the blackboard.

This usually went on for just under 180,000 minutes.

We were free to copy along with her if we so desired.

I used to wonder why that particular class was happening to me. *What had I done?* Then I wondered how this prof managed to get herself in such a weird and stupid situation.

Maybe there was a romantic tragedy going on here.

Maybe she had developed a long distance relationship with an Albertan rancher which blossomed into a full blown passion. It was possible back then. We used letters and Polaroids.

So she broke up with her local fiancé, who she had probably dated since early teens, quit her job as an associate professor at Strathclyde University, and spent all her savings to get out to where the prairies meet the mountains.

As usual, my hand was getting tired from all the writing. At least Dr. MacW. had legible handwriting.

Back to my fantasy narrative: when our idealistic academic had the trauma of actually meeting a real Western Canadian rancher—gun rack in the back of the pick-up truck, empty beer cans all over the floor of the passenger seat (and not even Guinness!) as well as the appearance and manners of a bison bull dressed in flannel and denim.

I know I would have been disappointed but maybe she was into hairy guys. However, that kind of thing can only go so far. Most people like to have sex with members of their own species.

Now whenever I hear about the Gross National Product I think of that lonely red-haired woman and sad country music songs (and maybe some bagpipes).

Even so.

Dr. MacBrokenHeart was not the worst thing about the Wednesday curriculum.

No, that had to be the last class of the day, another time-distorting mind-fuck called Aspects of the Modern British Novel. Before I go on, I have to explain that I have nothing against the modernist tradition of social realism that emerged on the British Isles in the early decades of the 20th century. I actually really liked *Heart of Darkness* and from that experience read just about every-thing by Joseph Conrad that I could get my hands on. And I am really sure the experience of World War I and the collapse of the Great British Imperial Dream was really rough stuff to deal with.

H.G. Wells was also incredibly cool and that included some of the stuff that wasn't early science fiction. Although the professor for Aspects sneered at Wells every chance he got.

I was less thrilled with *A Portrait of the Artist as a Young Man* but at least I seemed to understand what was going on in that book. Plus, it was short. Unlike *Ulysses* and *Finnegan's Wake*, which made me feel like I was experiencing some kind of aphasia-inducing stroke whenever I turned the page. At least there was a bit of Pythonesque fun there sometimes.

Virginia Wolfe and D.H. Lawrence were even greater challenges. At five page intervals through *To the Lighthouse*, I wanted to scream at the author to *get to the fucking point!*

As for DHL. Well, I hadn't even had a girlfriend at that point in my life. How the hell was I supposed to comment on these tortured primal mammalian chokeholds?

I was way, *way* out of my psychosexual depth here. There should have been some sort of advisory or prerequisite. You shouldn't take the class if you were still a virgin and if you hadn't lived in a town with a coal mine in it. Actually Blinn did have coal mines once but they shut them down just after World War II.

There was another reason I was having a hard time with Aspects of the Modern British Novel. It turned out that Professor Larson was "William," a rather colourless guy my mother had dated for a few months the year before. He was so nondescript that it took me over a month to remember him. Unfortunately he knew who I was right away and by the time we had mutual identification going it was too late for me to transfer into a different class.

As soon as I started getting my essays back I realized that he was trying to work something out; he wrote some very interesting things in the margins of my papers:

"Fickle."

"Unfair."

"Insensitive."

By the second half of the semester I was expecting to read "SIZE REALLY DOESN'T MATTER!" in red ink on the last page of one of my submissions.

The best mark I ever got in that class was a C+. The asshole was too much of a coward to flunk me outright but he was going to do as much damage to my grade point average as he could get away with.

Sometimes my mother was a very accurate judge of the character of men. Other times not so much, but more on that later.

8.
ANYWAY

I HOPE I HAVE adequately explained the various shortcomings of Wednesdays during that period of my life.

This particular Wednesday, while not exactly better, was at least a little different. I received a letter but it was not from Don Post Studios, *Famous Monsters* magazine or the Science Fiction Book of the Month Club. Although any of those would have been good.

No, it was a letter from the rescuer of the Capekoids. The envelope held two things: one was another Polaroid of her face. I still had no idea who she was, or even if that was her face for that matter. The other was a small lined index card; it carried very precise cursive letters. They formed just one question:

"What are you going to do about declining broadcast standards in our community?"

I understood what the rescuer was getting at and it was a terrifying idea:

The rescuer wanted me to take out Timmie.

9.
THE WRETCHED OF THE EARTH PLAY THE TRUMPET

Audio Transcript:
The Alienated News, CKUB FM
March 197—

Sound:	*Organ passage from* Journey to the Centre of the Earth *(by Rick Wakeman).*
Drew:	Hello, I'm Drew Niven sitting in for Eugene Plotnik. It's time for Campus Current Affairs.
Sound:	*Paper rustling.*
Drew:	Incidents of violence in our community seem to be on the rise… (fades)

I had no idea how I was going to make a dent in Timmie the Indestructible DJ. It was a miracle Barry didn't give him all of Eugene's spots now.

I decided that I would go and visit said Eugene, who was still in the hospital. Maybe that would inspire me. Or at least make me feel less like a selfish little prick.

I figured that the poor guy must be pretty bored in there so I started to fill my backpack with books: copies of *The Wretched of the Earth* and *The Trumpet Shall Sound* from my political anthropology class. As my favourite (and only) known hard core commie in my circle of acquaintances, Eugene would probably enjoy an injection of applied dialectical materialism and the Marxist analysis in both books. They were also the closest spare textbooks I had on hand.

I also threw in a couple of Science Fiction Book of the Month Club editions of Joanna Russ and C. J. Cherryh that they sent to me by mistake. I felt good about passing those on because Eugene had decided to merge his commitment to feminism with his interest in popular culture and announced one day between tracks of Bulgarian heavy metal that he was now only reading science fiction written by women:

"The techno-patriarchy of the penis-bearing elite has dominated our collective speculative imagination for too long."

Even when he was sometimes not mistaken, Eugene had a talent for occasionally expressing his ideas in ways that were truly irritating.

I also decided to take a chance and throw in some back issues of *Creepy* and *Eerie* (no *Vampirella* though, way too much cleavage!). I also added a Del Rey paperback by some guy named Lucas. Real space opera stuff, not quite as brain-meltingly dumb as E.E. 'Doc' Smith or Ray Palmer but not far off. Something called *Star Wars*.

Apparently the Lucas book was going to come out as a movie in a couple of months. I just couldn't see how they could pull off the special effects for what was described in the book.

It was probably going to be one truly lame flick.

So off to see Eugene.

When I got down to the driveway I noticed a pair of feet sticking out the front door of Space Truck. Space Truck was a blue 1960 Austin Cambridge that I bought for $100 out of the honorarium I received for being a DJ on CKUB. The vehicle was a sedan but when my sister first saw it, she called it "Space Truck" and the name seemed to stick.

Now, why was someone laying under my near-archaeological automobile? I was more confused than alarmed because the idea of anyone taking the time to steal Space Truck simply exceeded the limits of my imagination.

UFOs? No problem.

Alien abductions? Absolutely, probably happen any day. Time travel? Of course!

Someone else wants Space Truck? Inconceivable.

"Hello?"

I decided to investigate and see if I could gather some clues to help solve this mystery.

"Hey Matt."

The frayed basketball shoes covering the feet started to looked a little familiar but the Austin's hefty dashboard muffled the voice.

"Uh… what's up?" I never knew what to say to shoes.

The body belonging to the shoes decided to unravel itself out from underneath the car.

It was Rob. "How did you…?"

He smiled. "I can pop the lock on anything built east of Halifax, bud." By that, Rob meant all foreign cars.

"Yeah, but why?" My confusion problem wasn't getting any better. "If you wanted to drive her, you just had to ask." But why would he want to? Rob owned way cooler British cars.

He shook his head, smiled and put a cream-coloured slab of plastic in my hand. "I wanted to surprise you."

I looked at the semi-small slab. It was an eight-track tape of the latest Pink Floyd album.

Animals.

"I got a new system for my MGB," Rob continued. "I thought you wouldn't object to some previously loved gear."

For a stoner, Rob may have been one of the greatest human beings on the planet. Not only was he trying to enhance my motoring experience, he was recycling old technology and thereby keeping it out of the local landfill.

He was amazing because he liked me and he loved the planet. And yeah, sometimes we did think about stuff like that back then, maybe not as often though.

I briefly wondered if Rob was such a great person *because* he was a stoner but the implications of that concept were simply too disturbing to me to think about for too long.

"Want to try it out?"

I made a great effort and held up the backpack full of books (I didn't have much upper-body strength back then). "I was going to go to the hospital and give Eugene something to read."

Rob nodded his head. "Excellent. Then it will be a mission of mercy."

So we drove to the hospital. But we went the long way around—down by the river and past Scenic Drive so that we had enough time to listen to some songs about pigs on the wing and how all the dogs were dead.

The music was incredible and the prairie side of the sky seemed to lay out into infinity as it does sometimes. Rob had the speaker balance and the volume set so that it almost completely cancelled out the ancient wheeze of Space Truck's deteriorating four cylinder engine.

Even though it was just 10:30 on a Sunday morning and we were just looking at some suburbs and foothills without much growing on them… with the music and forward motion, it was a pretty psychedelic, pretty magnificent experience.

The only bring-down was when the tape switched tracks. It sounded like a hostile secret agent had snuck into the back seat of the car and shot you in the temple with a silenced revolver.

Bit of a mood killer for a couple of seconds.

I once wondered if the reason that eight tracks died was because of the big 'thunks' that came in between, and sometimes in the middle of, the music.

Apparently, it made them very unsuitable as soundtracks for making out. You and your sweetie could be heavily into some serious rec-room canoodling, halfway through "The Great Gig in the Sky" or "Year of the Cat" when you hear this huge "KA-THUNK!" and you think it's your parents slamming the car door.

But this was just a theory. I had no practical experience to back me up.

Boy Virgin here.

10.
AWFUL BLACK CIGARETTES AND THE ABOMINABLE DR. PHIBES

EUGENE LOOKED LIKE SOMETHING from the cover of *Famous Monsters Magazine.*

Kind of a combination of The Invisible Man, Frankenstein's Monster and the Abominable Dr. Phibes. Maybe some Phantom of the Opera as well. (If you haven't seen *Dr. Phibes,* do so as soon as possible.) In other words, what we could make out beneath all those bandages on his face looked pretty bad.

Audio Transcript:
Wild and Wacky Wednesday, CKUB FM
March 197—

Sound:	*Music fades.*
Timmie:	April Wine! Not too shabby for a Canadian band.
Sound:	*Distant voice on the loudspeaker.*
Timmie:	Barry, our ever-groovin' station manager, is telling me that I gotta stop for a minute and make some PSAs.
Sound:	*Paper rustling.*

Timmie: Tomorrow at noon in Lecture Hall C–80 there will
               be a debate between the Chief Curator of
               Ethnography (is that really a thing?) from the
               Provincial Museum and Professor Basil Pocha from
               the Native American Studies Department about the
               ethics of displaying human remains in public.

Sound: *Crumples paper.*

Timmie: (laughs) Jeez, aren't they all dead? What do they
               care? Gosh, some people will get offended about
               anything!

Eugene's hands and shoulders were set in plaster casts; the
doctors left his fingers free so that he could still pick things up and
smoke those awful black Russian cigarettes—but only with great
effort.

Even so, Eugene seemed to be in pretty good spirits.

Partly because I think he liked the contents of my speculative
fiction care package.

"Cool, C.J. Cherryh!" was the first thing he said. Eugene then
went on to explain that while he had already read everything by
Joanna Russ, it was good to have these copies to refer to while he
was laid up.

He agreed that the Lucas book looked a little iffy but we
decided that we would suspend judgment until the film was
actually released. If they ever released something as obscure as a
space opera.

"What the fuck happened to you?" Rob, not being very
interested in the books, had decided on a direct approach to
changing the subject.

It occurred to me that there might be another reason that
Eugene was in such a good mood. As an urban communist from
the vast and sinister city of Northburg, at least 50% of the
population of Blinn hated his guts and 50% of that group would
have cheerfully drowned him along with the latest bag of

unwanted kittens.

I wondered if it was kind of reassuring to be loathed by complete assholes. Besides, Eugene had likely trained himself to expect pain and sacrifice as he dedicated himself to the *Struggle*. Getting the shit kicked out of him had vindicated him as a Class Hero.

Maybe Mr. Self-Righteous was right about that too.

"What the fuck happened to you?"

Rob repeated the question.

Or maybe Eugene was just enjoying all that Demerol they were injecting him with.

Eugene shrugged. Or rather tried to shrug with that big plaster glacier covering him.

"I was carrying my records, waiting for the Number 4A bus."

"Working on your playlist?" That was me talking.

"So you were standing out in front of Kresge's?" That was Rob.

We knew the routine. Buses that ended with numbers took you to the university campus and back. Buses that ended with letters took you in and out of the actual city. The big bus stop where Kresge's faced Woolworth's was Checkpoint Charlie between the learned and the unlearned communities.

"So they just jumped out and grabbed you?"

Eugene tried to shake his head but it obviously hurt him too much.

"Was it those assholes from the Longhorn?" Rob was a more worldly fellow than me, so it was natural that he would think of that scenario.

The Longhorn Bar and Grill was where a crowd of particularly nasty bunch of gun-rack-owning, pick-up truck-driving and cowboy hat-wearing thugs used to hang out. Every few weeks these testosterone powered Mistakes of Nature (and yes, they played hockey in the winter) would get really boozed up, jump into their trucks and do a street patrol looking for people who looked like Eugene.

You know, people who look like they might know how to read.

Or might be homosexuals.

If you were a homosexual reader, you were totally fucked.

Eugene winced as he tried to shake his head again. "No."

No?

How dare Eugene contradict my prejudices?! I already had this whole thing all worked out.

"What do you mean, Gene?" Rob was one of the few people who got away with using that name.

"There wasn't a truck." Eugene coughed and closed his eyes. "It was a van."

So it was a van! So what? Maybe the truck was at the shop getting fitted with a new gun rack.

"And it wasn't anybody from the Longhorn. It was guys in suits."

"Suits?" That was both Rob and me.

What the hell would people in suits want with Eugene? Even I knew that people who wore suits gravitated towards money. Just being within thirty feet of Eugene would melt your credit cards and evaporate all your cash.

Speaking from the perspective of my now advanced years I think I can safely say that's why people hate communism and communists like Eugene. They make them afraid they are going to lose their money. Not their lives or loved ones. Not their sense of decency, integrity or personal responsibility. No, just their money.

Now, I agree that such a thing can be annoying, however, much worse things can happen to you. Sometimes you can make more money later on. If you are crippled, you can't walk again, if you're dead, you're dead forever.

"What did they do? Did they show you any ID?" I was a little afraid to ask those questions but I couldn't stop myself. If those guys were RCMP or city police, then Eugene and maybe all of his friends (even those not all that close ones like me) were in the deepest shit imaginable. Even though violent student activism was pretty much over by the mid-seventies, there were still plenty of cops out there wanting to do a 1968 Democratic Convention reenactment.

"They didn't say who they were. They just grabbed me by the arms, pulled me inside the van and punched me while we drove out to Highway #2."

"They hit you?"

"And kicked."

"Yeah, kicked."

"Holy shit."

"They kicked me a lot."

"Really?"

"Seemed to enjoy it."

Eugene was completely calm while he said this; at that moment I thought he was the bravest human on the planet. If any of this had happened to me, I would have been a quivering mass of post-traumatic stress syndrome.

Rob leaned back in his chair and folded his arms. "So did they say why they were beating you up?"

Eugene sighed. "I've already told this to the police."

"What the fuck?" Yes, we had this saying back then.

"Three times."

"The cops were here?" Rob managed to look nervous but only just.

"Yeah, once it was the city cops and twice it was the Mounties."

That statement challenged my latest theory. The last time I looked, the police do not like to spend time investigating themselves unless they absolutely had to. The last time I also looked, there wasn't much public pressure to protect the safety and civil rights of Albertan socialist utopians.

It was wrong, but there you go, that was our reality back then in Blinn. I don't know if any similar thoughts were going through Rob's mind.

He just laughed. "Gene, I hate to surprise you but the local constabulary rarely copies us on their memos."

"True enough." Another sigh pushed itself through the bandages. "After I felt them break a couple of my ribs, they threw my records out the window of the van."

"Bastards."

Getting the living bejesus whaled out of you was one thing. But deliberately destroying somebody's music? That was extremely uncool.

"Then they knocked some of my teeth out and told me that I needed to get out of the radio business."

Get out of the radio business? My god, somebody actually was listening! This was wonderful news!

"But why go to all that trouble?"

"At that point they threw me out of the van." Eugene tried really hard to shrug. "I didn't think to ask questions."

Ouch.

"Did I mention that the van was still moving?"

More ouch.

"I landed on my face."

Ouch. Ouch. Ouch.

That was the only time I thought I heard Eugene's voice break a little. Who could blame him?

Rob and I were silent.

Audio Transcript:
Powerhouse Thursday!, CKUB FM
March 197—

Sound:	Brass band music.
Timmie:	Big news, folks! Thanks to a deal with the Phys-Ed Department we will be presenting live radio coverage of intermural basketball, baseball and hockey three times a week!
Sound:	Recorded cheering.
Timmie:	So, before that, let's hear the latest scores…

"Dude," Rob said eventually. "You're really lucky to be alive."

"It's not a question of luck." Eugene pulled himself forward and looked at us. The skin around his eyes was a deep, deep purple, almost black colour. The impact with the road surface must have pulverized his cheeks and eye sockets. "It's a question of being able to carry on with the Struggle."

Carry on with the Struggle. Struggle with a capital S.

If anyone but Eugene had made that statement, it would have come across as totally bogus. With him, less so.

Of course, we were hearing it from a person who would look in the mirror every morning for the rest of his life and see how that Struggle had changed his face.

We needed to change the subject.

The emotional temperature of the room was getting way too high for three heterosexual men. Well, at least two of us were heterosexual.

One? I dunno, I know I wanted to have sex with women. It was all theoretical with me but a very powerful concept/urge. Like the Theory of Evolution.

We unconsciously decided to talk about things that all three of us were likely to be at least mildly interested in but would generate almost no controversy. Rob was the only one who gave a rat's ass about sports so we decided to talk about where the storyline for *Howard the Duck* was going, why the second season of *Space: 1999* was even more disappointing than the first one and whether this guy Robin Williams was an absolute genius or a complete fuckwit.

Eventually a nurse came in and said that it was time for Eugene's injection of Demerol and that we had to leave.

Rob looked a little envious, although I'm not sure if it was because of the nurse or the drug. Both could probably make a guy pretty happy.

We asked Eugene if he needed anything.

"Yes."

Damn. I was afraid of that.

"I need a tape recorder and some tapes."

"Sure, Eugene. No problem." For the record, it was Rob who

said that.

"I'm going to do my show from here."

I remembered a quote from my first year English class: something along the lines of "no good deed goes unpunished."

11.
STALKED BY THE BANK BUILDING

A BLACK CADILLAC WAS following me down Fifth Street.

Here's another (hopefully brief) history lesson: back in the 1970s, Cadillacs were absolutely huge and they were always sedans. Essentially they were more like mobile buildings than any kind of an automobile. So having a big black Cadillac was a lot like being stalked by your local branch of the Bank of Montreal. I felt stupid. I had decided not to risk my life and leave Space Truck in the garage. Now I felt like my life was at risk because a mobile building was out to get me.

The Cadillac pulled up beside me a few minutes later. The morning had been going so well up until then. I had been to the Cigar Store and scored a couple of Ace paperback editions of minor Roger Zelazny and Philip K. Dick novels and the latest issue of that black and white *Unknown Worlds of Science Fiction* comic. I had been in escapist hog's heaven.

Audio Transcript:
The Black Hole on Friday Night, CKUB FM
April 197—

Sound: *Low drone of analogue synthesizer music. Continues underneath.*

Matthew: Tonight's Movie for Radio is a major cultural event. Courtesy of Cademon Records, Arthur C. Clarke will read passages from *2001: A Space Odyssey*.

Sound: *Synthesizer music rises.*

Matthew: And in a creative interpretation which I believe rivals Kubrick's cinematic vision we will be simultaneously playing Tangerine Dream's electronic tone poem *Phaedra*.

Sound: *Music gets very spacey.*

Matthew: So hang on folks, we're taking the Ultimate Trip.

One of the windows of the Cadillac rolled down. Back then electrically powered car windows were still rare enough to be impressive and slightly creepy.

A voice came from inside the car: "Matthew."

Okay, somebody in there knew my name.

Not good.

I kept on walking.

This was too much like the Eugene Incident for my liking.

"Matthew Bishop!"

Uncool as it was, this seemed like the right time to start running.

"Matthew!" The voice was now yelling. "Your mother said I might find you here!"

This was just getting embarrassing.

I stopped running, turned around and watched the giant black block roll to a stop by the curb.

"I hope I'm not interrupting anything important." The driver got out of the "car". He was about six foot, two inches tall, tanned and wearing a windbreaker, polo shirt and golf pants.

I hated him immediately. Whoever this guy was, his wardrobe was much too athletic for my tastes.

"I have an appointment." With my books anyway.

"I'm Ed."

Of course he was Ed. He looked a lot like the Six Million Dollar Man but he was still definitely an Ed.

Ed walked up to me and stuck out his hand. I told myself to relax; if this guy was going to give me the Eugene treatment, he would be approaching me with his fists, not an open hand.

"We should be friends."

"And why do you want to be friends?" I know, I sounded hostile. But as far as anything to do with my mother's social life, that was my default mode.

"I guess you could say that I'm your mother's boyfriend."

Fuck.

Now I had to shake his hand.

"Ed Wilson."

Hand pump. Hand pump. Hand pump. Easy, man, this may be Alberta but I am not an oil derrick.

Barf.

So he was Ed *Wilson*. Who else could this walking bag of teeth and handshakes be? I'm sure he had a big German Shepherd named King and they wrestled each other every night on the shag carpet in his bachelor pad; then they would laugh and listen to Percy Faith and Chicago on his quadraphonic stereo.

This guy needed to die.

"You seem to already know my name."

"Matthew? I don't suppose you might have lunch with me now?"

"Like I said, I have—"

"Couldn't you be a bit late? We're not far from the Big Steer."

I made a big deal of sighing before I finally said: "Well, I guess."

Dickhead factors aside, free steak is free steak.

My love of very rare, very bloody, almost quivering slabs of meat was the one thing I had in common with the mainstream of Albertan society. I understand that it's cruel, inhuman, environmentally irresponsible, and just not very nice—but although I was a virgin, I was so not a vegan.

It gets worse, folks.

I was now discovering that if someone put sixteen ounces of barely dead cow in front of me I was willing to sit still and listen to all kinds of high-octane horseshit.

"You know, your mother is a bit worried about you." Ed was also having a manhole-sized cut, also rare enough to be mistaken for zombie bovine.

It bothered me that we had this much in common.

"How would you know that?" The instant that question left my mouth, I knew that I really wasn't going to like the answer.

"Shirley..." Ed's teeth were smeared with beef-juice when he smiled. "I mean, your mother and I are very close, Matt. We share just about everything."

I was right. I didn't really like the answer. Even though the fullness of said answer was still in the process of emerging.

Time for more steak.

"So how come I've never heard of you?" I knew that it was rude to talk with my mouth full.

Good.

"My fault." Ed pushed a serrated blade into red-grey flesh. He seemed to enjoy the process of penetration. "I asked her if I could introduce myself."

In less than ten seconds he transformed the steak into a cluster of beef cubes. Amazingly, all the cubes were just about the same size. It's not easy to cut meat like that; this guy was even more precise than Ross.

"Face to face?" I asked.

"Man to man."

I was pretty sure that Ed didn't regard me as much of a man. Nobody else seemed to, why should he?

"So what's on my mother's mind?" Not that I noticed that she held back her opinions when we were in the same room together.

"She feels you don't have much direction in your life." Ed put down his fork and gave me a friendly sigh that I bet he had been practising all morning. "Some of your marks are above average but some definitely aren't."

"I guess art history was less interesting than I thought it would be." I really hated the idea that Ed might know my grade point average.

"What about geography?"

"What about it? Rocks, trees and water."

"What about psychology?"

Fuck. The one thing I was trying to forget for a few hours.

"Even if you had all As…" Ed picked up his fork and used it to tuck a few cubes into his mouth. "…what kind of degree are you going to get? English with a minor in Philosophy?"

So he could talk with his mouth full too. It was probably a ruse to make me think that he might have actual human failings.

"What kind of a job are you going to get with that?"

"I really don't know at this point." I decided that it was a good time to stare at my mashed potatoes. "They say you should follow your passions."

Ed shook his head. "From what your mother says, it doesn't sound as if you're particularly passionate about anything."

Who did this asshole think he was? I considered just getting up and leaving but I decided that the blowback at home just wouldn't be worth it.

Ed continued: "Have you thought about changing your major to something like Pre-Law or Business Administration?"

"I'd rather die, thank you."

"No head for commerce, eh?"

"You think I should transfer to the Community College?"

"Don't sell them short." My mother's latest boyfriend waved a finger at me gently. "They just started up a new computer skills program."

"So?"

"You're into science fiction, technology, things like that. You'd probably enjoy it."

"Computers are boring and ultimately unimportant." Okay, just because I liked science fiction didn't mean that I was particularly good at predicting the future.

"You really need to work on your attitude, Matt."

I had eaten just about everything on my plate, so I decided that this was a good time to set Ed straight about a few things:

"I don't know if you're trying to ingratiate yourself with all this free advice but you really don't have to bother."

Ed stopped chewing for a second.

"Since we moved here, my mother has one of the more active social lives in town."

Ed shrugged. "She's a very attractive woman, Matthew."

I just kept on talking: "My mother doesn't really care what people think and she makes up her own mind about who she dates and for how long—no matter what I, or my sister, might think."

Ed responded with another big bloody grin. "I don't think you get it, Matt. I'm not looking for your approval."

"That's good, because—"

"I want to help you figure out how to support yourself."

"I'll get a job after I graduate, like everyone else."

Ed shook his head. "Your mother and I are getting married in three months."

What the fuck?

"We're selling her house and she'll be moving in with me."

But Mom doesn't even like dogs! Especially big dogs named King.

"You and your sister aren't invited, I'm afraid."

I barely made it to the men's room before I puked out all that steak.

12.
TIME TO MAKE SOME NEW STATEMENTS

MY SISTER WAS WAITING for me when I got home.

"Ed find you?"

I kept moving once I got in the front door.

"Yeah."

Moving up the stairs and toward my bedroom.

"Did he tell you—"

"Fuck, yeah." I went inside. "Thanks for the heads-up, sis!"

I sprawled out on my bed and studied my Alphonse Mucha and Jim Sterenko posters. Then I turned my head a little and saw Capekoids #1 and #2. Both of them were leaning against the wall. Their big tin heads were making them lean forward, as if they were waiting for me to say something.

The boys were right, it was time for me to make some new statements. Or maybe I could just haul some of the magazines out from under my bed and masturbate until I felt better.

Maybe both.

Audio Transcript:
Auto Shift, CKUB FM
April 1977

Sound: *Click of a switch.*

Drew: Another request, folks. Once again, this is from Matt…

Sound: *Music slowly rises.*

Drew: The theme to *The Spy Who Loved Me*. (fades) Matt, do you think you might be in a bit of a rut?

13.
STATEMENT ONE

WESTBRIDGE MALL. THE TRAVEL agency my mother liked to use when she was arranging vacations with her latest boyfriend was located there.

It wasn't much of a stretch to conclude that the first thing Mom thought about when she agreed to remarry was where they were going to spend the honeymoon. I enlisted Rob, who used some of his supply to buy off the security guard on the night shift so we got access to the mall just after 0500. I was amazed that the sound of Space Truck rolling in the loading dock didn't wake up half of Blinn.

But hey. Maybe they were all stoned or drunk or otherwise sedated.

We went to work and by the time the Westbridge opened its doors at 0900, CP #1 and #2 were standing at the entrance of the travel agency. CP #1 was holding a sign that read: "*Visit Thailand: Support Sexual Slavery!*"

CP #2's sign said: "*Corruption and state-sanctioned murder really aren't your concern: Enjoy Beautiful Chile!*"

Take that Mom, Ed and everyone in the Evil Decadent Vacationing Class.

And because they were decadent (and lazy) the management at the agency didn't show up until just after lunch so the Capekoids got a good four hours to do their job before someone with any authority could show up and make security take my wonderful

dummies away. And since Rob had the self-same security personnel in his cannabis thrall, the Capekoids were in the back of Space Truck before the police showed up.
Audio Transcript:
Wake Up and Work!, CKUB FM
May 197—

Barry:	So today's topic is student mental health. And we have here Dr. Joel Brass, who is one of the councillors at Campus Services.
Joel:	Hey, Barry. It's good to be here to rap with you.
Barry:	Rap? (coughs) Sure, it's always really groovy when Campus Services wants to help out our listeners.
Joel:	Right on, brother.
Barry:	Is mental health a big issue among the student body? I mean, lots of the faculty are crazy…
Joel:	It is a big concern, Barry. Many young people are getting so stressed that they're starting to really freak out.
Barry:	Gosh, that's pretty un-hep.
Joel:	Well, I was going to say uncool but yes.

The next day, I was reasonably happy but I had a killer migraine. Probably the result of delayed stress from the mall operation. I was laying on the living room floor with the curtains closed, hoping that the Fiorinal Cs I had taken from my mother's medicine cabinet were going to do something besides induce a false state of euphoria.

The phone rang.

Ouch. Headache wasn't gone yet.

I answered, mostly to make the sound go away.

"Hello?

"Is that Matthew?" It was a young woman's voice. I wondered if it belonged to someone I'd only seen in Polaroids.

"Yeah." God, I sounded weak.

"Nice one."

She hung up.

14.
MORE MAGICAL WONDERS OF DIALECTICAL MATERIALISM

FRIDAY NIGHT AT CKUB. Your intellectual voice in Blinn.

I put ninety minutes of Pink Floyd and Tangerine Dream on uninterrupted play. At that point I figured that all four of our listeners were either asleep, completely stoned or in deep hypnotic trances. None of these states were likely to lead to any awareness of what I was about to play.

I cued up Eugene's tapes.

Audio Transcript:
Nova Express, CKUB FM
May 1977

Sound:	*Music—urgent electronic pulses and tones.*
Eugene:	(on tape) Welcome to *Nova Express*… a brand new program. *Nova Express*… unlike anything you're heard before. *Nova Express*… your one-way ticket to subversion and enlightenment…
Sound:	*Music rises.*
Eugene:	(on tape) On *Nova Express*, there is freedom and there is danger… (fades)

Eugene didn't come back to the uni after they discharged him from the hospital. Instead he moved out past Fort Stevens to a farm that one of his uncles owned. After a while Rob and I drove out in Space Truck to pick up his latest tapes and see how he was doing.

Eugene was getting around well enough with his pair of canes and it might have been the painkillers but he was smiling fairly often. The bandages were off but he still looked like raw shit warmed over.

"This place used to be a lot more back in the 1930s." Eugene pointed at the view outside the living room window. There were three rows of wood-planked cottages and clusters of rusting farm equipment that were just old and exotic enough looking that they might be mistaken for western Canadian installation art. Or they could just be abandoned junk.

Hard to tell sometimes.

"Really?" Rob was looking out the window too.

We had parked Space Truck across from the biggest, most ancient tractor that we'd ever seen. A man who was maybe even older than the tractor, decked out in a denim Chairman Mao suit, was circling my car, carefully studying it. I wondered if he was looking for parts that he might strip off and melt down in the small steel furnace he had probably set up behind the barn. It could be… maybe he hadn't heard that China's last Five Year Plan was over.

"My folks helped set this place up as a farmers' commune."

Eugene came from a family of prairie utopians? What a huge surprise.

"When World War II started the RCMP shut them down as subversives."

"Tough break." For someone who had a few run-ins with the Mounties, I figured that Rob could have sounded a little more sympathetic.

Actually, Eugene sounded proud. "Then the Feds came in and used our cottages as temporary housing for a Japanese internment camp." Okay, proud but angry. "When my parents got out of jail all they could do was watch those fascist pigs oppress those poor people."

"Maybe it would have been better if the government had used the farm to process German POWs." Rob's statement was kind of mischievous, the Nazis being real fascists and all—but I was impressed with his command of history. He was one of the few serious stoners I knew with a good memory.

Because he was pretty smart too, Eugene ignored Rob. "After the War some people from Regina bought up most of the farm and used it as a summer camp for socialist youth."

"That must have been fun." I was just guessing there. I had no idea what dedicated Trotskyites did to enjoy themselves. I wasn't even sure if it was okay for them to enjoy themselves. Even at summer camp.

"They went bust by the early 1950s."

Okay, so it probably wasn't okay for them to have fun.

"Then some Ukrainians from Saskatoon bought everything and threw my folks off the land."

"Bummer."

"Those people were crazy. They were putting kids through all kinds of military drills."

"What the hell for?" I didn't think Montana would be particularly easy (or productive) to invade.

"They were training them to defend themselves against a Soviet invasion."

"Sort of like Cub Scouts but with machine guns and hand grenades?" Rob was such as smartass sometimes.

"We still have some craters out back by the chicken coop."

"Craters?"

"Where the kids blew things up."

That sounded kind of impressive. Scary but impressive. I would try to check that out before we left for Blinn.

"It really pissed my uncle off that another crop of fascists had got hold of the farm."

"Mega-bummer." Rob sounded a little more sincere this time. He didn't approve of para-military types.

"Then about ten years ago my uncle had a brainwave and reported them to the RCMP for having all those illegal weapons."

"That was pretty smart."

"When the Feds put the land up for sale, my uncle had saved up enough to buy the place back."

"That was brilliant."

Yeah Rob, it kind of was.

Speaking of Uncle Mao, he was completely out of sight at this point. Maybe he was laying on top of a haystack, gazing at the patterns in the clouds and contemplating the magical wonders of dialectical materialism.

"Someday we're going to return the farm to its original purpose." Eugene sounded wistful. This was his dream too. "Once we get the right investors and the enough capital together."

I wondered if Eugene had any idea how ironic that last statement was.

"That's a great plan." Rob said that without any trace of his own irony, conclusively proving that he really was a good shit.

Eugene let out a very long sigh, one that embodied the continued broken dreams of generations of idealists. Or maybe it was just a randomly longer than normal sigh. Eugene was not the type to feel excessively sorry for himself.

"I don't have anything particularly good to share with you for lunch," Eugene said. "So I better let you get home." Then he grasped the handles on his aluminum canes, lifted himself out of his chair and pulled himself across the living room. He stopped in front of a large cardboard box that was sitting on the table. The box was open and we could see that it contained dozens of reel-to-reel tapes.

"I've been busy."

"Yeah."

"If you play one a week, you have enough programming to get you through to January 18th, 1984."

"That's over half a decade of shows, Eugene."

"Yes." Eugene smiled. "There should be clear signs of the Revolution by then."

15.
STATEMENT TWO

So BACK TO THAT Friday night at the radio station. I had stopped for station identification and couple of campus PSAs and Part #2 of Eugene Tape #1 was cued up and ready to go. I hit the play toggle.

Audio Transcript:
Nova Express, CKUB FM
May 197—

Sound:	*Musical interlude. First some banjos and steel guitars, then some percussion and finally a synthesizer. The music is lazy but bouncy… boingy… distressingly sexual.*
Eugene:	(on tape) Have you masturbated today?
Matthew:	(distant) *Gack!*
Eugene:	(on tape) You might even be masturbating right now. In fact, I can imagine you masturbating in my mind's eye.

The only thing you can do at a moment like that is fall out of your chair. That is what I did.

The voice on the tape continued: "I hope for the sake of World

Peace that you are."

I got back into my chair and thought about turning off the tape. Eugene just kept on talking about touching yourself:

"Most violence and conflict in the world has a foundation of sexual frustration which the ruling classes transform into aggression."

I moved my hand towards, then away, from the pause toggle.

"Every time you jerk off, you reduce the level of aggression in the human community."

I told Eugene I would play the tape and so I was going to play it.

"Every time you cum, you bring us closer to World Peace."

Okay, for the next hour or so, it was going to be Eugene talking very frankly about very explicit matters. Even so, none of what he was saying made me feel terribly aroused.

16.
"It's for you!"

My sister was screaming from the bottom of the stairs in the direction of my bedroom.

No wonder our mother wanted to get us out of her home.

I groaned and looked up at Capekoid #1. He was holding my alarm clock in his hands: 08:35.

Audio Transcript:
Wake Up and Work!, CKUB FM
April 197—

Drew:	Okay, how many of you tried the hypoglycemia experiment we suggested last night and ate an entire chocolate bar just before you went to bed?
Voice:	(Distant. Groans.)
Drew:	I bet you feel absolutely terrible right now. That's because paradoxically, you now have incredibly low blood sugar!
Voice:	(Distant. Groans.)

Too early. Much too early.

My show had continued on until 5:30 in the morning and it was pretty much wall to sonic wall Eugene. I once again considered turning off the tape and playing something else. And honour and all that nonsense aside, I hadn't prepared any alternative programming.

Eventually, Jennifer, an insanely cheerful drama major, showed up and started playing obscure medieval music as she did every Saturday morning for four hours. You had to be insane, cheerful or not, to listen to that crap every week.

I didn't get to bed until six and hadn't slept particularly well anyway.

"*Matt! Phone!*"

I pulled on my jeans and staggered out of my room. This had better be the most interesting telephone call in the history of human communication.

"Hello?"

"Monday morning, get over to the studio and collect everything that's yours." It was Barry, the studio manager.

"What?" Why did he have to phone me on the weekend? "Did I leave a mess?"

"You're banned from the station."

"Uh… banned?"

"Off the air."

I knew there had been lots of adult and political material in Eugene's program but the language was more or less four-letter word free and we were a university radio station! We were supposed to raise new ideas! Youthful controversy and all that shit.

"For how long?" How serious could this be?

"For the rest of your life, maybe longer." Barry hung up.

This was disheartening. But at least I finally knew that I had an audience of at least one more than me.

17.
HUNGRY SOUL

MY FAMILY WASN'T MUCH help in my time of crisis.

My mother was off "hunting elk" (i.e. having sex) with Ed and my sister just shrugged and suggested that having my Friday nights free might improve my social life. I didn't bother to explain that her line of reasoning was like multiplying things by zero; you needed something to start with before you can get more.

On Monday morning just after my first class, I went by the studio. Barry had packed up all my albums and books into a box. There were also a few roach clips and some girl-on-girl porn magazines.

"Those aren't mine."

Barry shrugged. "You seemed to be the best candidate."

Erin, who also did the glam rock show on Tuesday afternoons, looked over at us from the record library. If Erin had super-laser-vision powers I figured she would have set Barry's hair on fire.

It made a sick sort of sense though, after this arbitrary display of power and continuing to push Timmie into every possible slot, that the other DJs wouldn't have a lot of love for Barry. Not that the DJs did anything crazy, like threaten to resign or even object to my getting fired.

Big surprise.

The only person who understood the concept of solidarity was hobbling around an old farm house with pair of canes.

It was definitely time to blow that audio pop stand.

Audio Transcript:
Silver Echoes, CKUB FM
April 197—

Sound:	*Music. Close of "Breaking Glass".*
Erin:	Track off of one of Bowie's more recent works. It's off an awesome album and I love the cover art. Bowie looks gorgeous! What's that from?
Drew:	(distant) It's the poster for *The Man Who Fell to Earth*.
Erin:	(laughs) That was one freaky movie. Matt Bishop made me see that.
Drew:	(distant) Sounds like something he'd be into.
Erin:	I hear that Matt did his last show. *The Black Hole on Friday Night* is no more.
Drew:	(distant) What's the new show going to be?
Erin:	*Hits All Night* with Timmie McPherson.
Drew:	(distant) Aw, f—

At lunch time I was in the cafeteria, sitting by myself, checking to see if anyone at the station had ripped off any of my LPs. I was particularly concerned that they had taken my Kraftwerk albums. I wasn't sure what I thought about these new European synthesizer bands—interesting but no Tangerine Dream. Way too stripped down for my tastes but admittedly worth your attention. Apparently some of my fellow students had figured out a way to dance to the stuff, which was why my personal copies might have been at risk.

I found *Trans Europa Express*. That was good. It didn't matter that I might not ever listen to the album again but that wasn't the point. The record was my property and I was going to goddamned hang on to it. I'd dig around for *Autobahn* and

Radioactivity later.

"Great show on Friday," someone said.

"Last of its kind," I replied without looking up from my albums. "But I'm glad you enjoyed it."

"Of course, Eugene Plotnik did all the work."

I heard whoever it was sit down on the other side of the table.

"Yeah, but I got to take the hit."

"Maybe you deserved it."

I looked up.

Yeah.

It was the angry young woman from the Polaroids. I wasn't sure if I was surprised or annoyed. I narrowed my eyes and decided to go with annoyance: "So how do you figure that?"

"Oh…" Polaroid girl shrugged. "Maybe because you're a bit stupid and a lot complacent."

"Thanks." I hoped that my voice carried buckets of acid and ice.

"Nice to meet you again. I'm Colleen Jang."

Nice? I kind of doubted it from the way this person laughed and held out her hand.

"You can call me the Jag."

"As in shard of broken glass?" I was trying to be nasty but my question made her smile. Who was this wacko? "I know your face from the pictures you sent, but I don't think we've met."

"You really are a total moron." The person I now knew as Colleen Jang, a.k.a. the Jag, withdrew her hand. However, she was still smiling. In a slightly scary way.

"Thank you for your kind words of support in my time of difficulty."

The Jag rolled her eyes. "What else can I say? It's only that I've seen you just about every other weekday during the school year for the last five years."

"What are you talking about?"

"I was in your art class in grades ten, eleven and twelve."

I studied her. "Sorry, but no."

She sighed. "And I've been enrolled in this university for two years. We've ridden on the same buses, sat in the library less than ten feet away from each other and we're both in Bucagnani's behavioural psychology class."

I shook my head. "You are truly crazy."

She shook her head back at me. Then she spoke two words: "Hungry Soul."

I was shocked. I knew exactly what she was talking about.

Hungry Soul was a small ceramic sculpture that someone produced in my grade eleven art class. It was a damned disturbing work: a pair of incredibly detailed hands—hideous hands, actually—cracked, twisted and diseased with cuts, sores and cracks. Way worse than anything you might see in *Famous Monsters*.

These horrific hands were clutching a bleeding, ragged, and leprous heart. Long, root-like nails grew out of the ends of the fingers and these tore deep into the flesh of the ventricles, making the heart bleed all the more.

Ross and I, and the rest of the art class, immediately noticed Hungry Soul when our teacher put it in the shelf next to the kiln. We weren't sure if he wanted us all to see it or if he just wanted the glaze to dry without too much fuss.

The name of the piece was carved in the clay sand with very precise and very demented cursive script that looked familiar to me now.

Hungry Soul.

Diseased Soul.

Angry Soul.

Angry Artist.

Nobody knew who created this work and no one seemed very anxious to find out.

Jang/The Jag/the artist finally revealed, sneered at me some. "So we've been in the same rooms together for the last five years and you never noticed me."

"Uh… sorry?" Well, what can you say?

"So, let's consider this… as I have over the years…" The Jag counted off points on her fingers. "Are you vision impaired? Do you have some cognitive dysfunction that impedes facial recognition? Or are you just some dumb-ass racist who can't tell Asian people apart?"

This situation was getting almost as upsetting as her sculpture. "You're not going to try and hurt me, are you?"

She took the Kraftwerk album from me and studied the bicycle pictures. "I'm not a violent person, Matthew."

"Your art suggests otherwise." Jeez! I could never resist trying to sound smart.

Fortunately the Jag smiled. "I usually did pastels and watercolours of birds and flowers and butterflies and other harmless seeming shit like that." She handed the album back to me. "I just liked to shake things up once in a while."

"Thanks." I put the album back in the box.

"Are those guys any good?"

I shrugged. "It's electronic and apparently you can dance to it if you're in a bendy kind of mood."

"Interesting."

I couldn't tell from her expression if the Jag was the sort of person who liked to dance or not.

"So…" I decided to take another risk. "Why are we talking?"

The Jag raised one eyebrow. Very Vulcan. "You don't like to talk to people, do you?"

"Oh, really?" What the hell did she know? She hadn't tried to speak to me in five years!

"Or maybe you just like talking at people, through radios and big public statements."

I didn't have to put up with cheesy quasi-girlfriend analysis. "I like talking to the few people I like. Since you're not in that category, why are we talking? And why now after all this time?"

"Maybe you aren't such a racist."

"Just a dumb-ass?"

"Definitely a dumb-ass. And you might be more of a really, *really* self-absorbed individual."

"Maybe." Okay, she might be right there. "But you haven't answered my question."

She smiled and it was not at all ironic. "Your tin head people impressed me."

"The Capekoids."

"The what?"

"Capekoids is their proper name."

"Is that a reference to Karel Capek?" Her voice got a bit more animated. "The author of *R.U.R.?*"

"Of course."

I knew that we were thinking the same word: *impressive*.

We sat there for a minute and didn't say anything.

"You still haven't answered my question." The silence was starting to feel weird.

"Right." The Jag squinted at me and scratched her ear. "Are you familiar with the concept of critical mass?"

I nodded. "You mean how things keep building up and building up over time until it all gets too much and something incredibly huge happens? Like a nuclear explosion or a revolution or the Big Bang that started the universe?"

"Yeah." She nodded back at me. "That's just about where things are right now."

"What things?" I sincerely hoped this was not an attempt to recruit me into some fringe political party or fucked-up religion.

"The way life is."

"Life? Like life in general?"

"No, much more specifically." The Jag looked right through me. "The way life is right here. Today. In this city."

This sounded like conspiracy shit. I looked over her shoulder, calculated how quickly I could get to the nearest exit.

"This city as in Blinn, Alberta?" I remembered the still scary Hungry Soul. And the stalking. This person still might try and hurt me.

"Yeah." She smirked. "Has it ever occurred to you that we live in kind of a strange community, Matthew?"

Yeah, she might want to hurt me.

18.
WE HAVE SOME NEW PRODUCTS FOR YOU

"YOU CAN PICK UP your Conrad if you like."

It was Sue on the phone. I hadn't heard from her in weeks.

"No rush, I don't need it for anything."

"Me neither."

"You finished your assignment?"

There was a bit of a pause at the other end of the line. "I dropped out of the class."

"You got a job?" That was the only reason I could think why Sue would drop a class.

There was an even longer pause. "I'm leaving town, Matt."

Before she graduated? The sound she may have heard on her receiver would have been my jaw bouncing off the carpet.

"When are you heading out?"

"Next Monday."

"Do you need help packing?" I needed to know what was going on here.

Audio Transcript:
The Head Shop Show, CKUB FM
February 197—

Sound: *Recorded laughter. Fades.*

Art: Cheech and Chong in concert. Those guys never get old.

Sound: *Paper rustling.*

Art: Now it's time for listener mail. (coughs) Now I have to remind you folks that CKUB and Blinn University in no way endorse the consumption of any form of illegal or mood-altering substances no matter how beneficial and enjoyable they may be.

Sound: *Laughter, recorded and live.*

Art: The only materials we discuss on The Head Shop Show are Silly Putty and Chewin' Tabacky.

Sound: *More laughter.*

Art: So a listener who signs herself as "Ms. Head in the Clouds" is writing about her friend: "Dear Art, after a really heavy duty party last month my best friend became convinced that she was being followed by black helicopters and that red ants on the windowsill are taking nude pictures of her and selling them to *Hustler* magazine."

Voice: (distant, off-mic) What issues?

Art: Hey! Be good over there. Back to Head in the Clouds: "On Friday she came over to my room in residence and crashed on my bed and slept for three days. Now she just gets up to use the bathroom and empty my refrigerator. What the (pause) *heck* is going on here?"

Voice: (distant) Burn-out!

Art: We'll get to that later. Well, Ms. Head in the Clouds, to put this in context, it is important to remember that sometimes there can be impurities in your Silly Putty purchases and your friend should

not over-indulge in Chewin' Tabacky no matter
how much of a good idea it might seem to be at the
time…

It took fifteen minutes for me get Space Truck started and
another ten for me to actually drive from my house to Sue's place.
When I got there I discovered that she had managed to collect a
lot of cardboard boxes but she actually hadn't managed to put
very much into them. Plus she wasn't behaving much like the
super-competent Sue that I had come to love and slightly envy.
She seemed happy enough but kind of vague and fuzzy.

Sue but in slow motion.

I went to work right away and started putting plates and
Tupperware into boxes. Jeez, I was acting more like Sue than Sue
was. Yes, Tupperware. Sue was a student and she was that well
organized.

"So where you going? Northtown?" It was a natural
assumption at the time. There were buckets of oil money in
Alberta back then and the Provincial Government was growing
on steroids. Sue was good, they would be lucky to have her and at
the time, the Province was smart enough to know it.

"Baron."

"Baron?" My reaction was about the same as if Sue had said that
she was moving to the Eleventh Circle of Hell.

"Yeah." She looked at a paperback and put a cigarette in her
mouth. Sue smoked? I mean, she smoked *tobacco*?

"Isn't that where your dad lives?" I didn't look at her. I just
started putting rubber bands around cutlery.

She lit a match and inhaled. For some reason I really didn't like
it. I knew she smoked weed and hash to relax sometimes—I mean
someone who worked as hard as she did probably needed to do
something like that. But seeing her inhale tobacco? I really didn't
like it.

"I'm going to move in with my dad for a while." She took
another long drag.

I broke a rubber band. She *was* moving to the Ultimate Level of Hell.

"Why?"

Sue never gave me many details about her family life but my Failed-Boyfriend-Sense told me enough that I knew that this was an absolutely terrible idea.

"I'm kind of stressed out, Matt." Were her eyes tearing up? It was hard to tell through the blue haze. "I need to get some rest for a while."

I found another rubber band and created a nice neat cluster of forks. Normal Sue would have been proud. "So when are you going to graduate?"

"I don't know if that's in the cards now."

Sue looked very startled but I guess I made a lot of noise when I threw the forks into the box.

The doorbell rang.

I opened the door and saw Steve standing there. He was wearing what can only be described as a half-plaid/half-tweed sports coat and one of those knit ties they used to have back then. Nice haircut and a well-trimmed moustache. Too well-groomed for a student really.

I sort of knew Steve, he was in his last year in the Management Arts program. Usually he would be talking to Sue in the cafeteria or at the bus stop and would always excuse himself within thirty seconds of me showing up.

"Hey, Steve."

I didn't like him very much.

"Hey." He activated his X-ray vision and looked right through me. "Sue at home?"

"Come in, Steve." Sue sat down in front of her dining room table.

Steve pushed past me. He was carrying a metal-sided attache case which was very James Bond indeed.

This was not helping me to like him much more.

"I heard about your situation, Sue." Steve sat next to her and popped open his case. "I hope I can help."

The contents of the case were pretty remarkable: foam lining with shapes of different sizes. Nestled inside each indentation was a vial of something, a bag of something, some small containers of some kind of pills and various silver-lined implements for smoking, spooning or injecting somethings.

"We have some new products for you."

Sue didn't say anything. She just looked away from me and examined the contents of the briefcase.

Steve did look at me. And his expression suggested that if I ever mentioned anything about what was going on here, I was pretty much dead.

I'm not trying to make any big anti-reefer statement here; I'm just relating what happened. It is true that I was not much of a stoner; both Rob and Sue told me that occasionally ingesting some weed would probably do me a lot of good and although they never directly said so, help me grow up and stop being such an eternal boy-child. But why stop doing something once you've perfected it?

Because Sue was way cuter than Rob, I did agree to go to a party at their place where they were going to be smoking up. There was a big hash pipe and they were also passing around a little metal thing they called a roach clip. I tried whatever they gave me.

Didn't do much. I did realize that I couldn't stop smiling halfway through the evening (which I found kind of weird and a little creepy) and I was disappointed that it didn't make me any more attractive to any of the women at the party. When I thought about it later, I realized that the dope just made people act like themselves, only more so. That meant that the women who were attracted to six-foot plus hockey players or pre-med students would *not* suddenly undergo some quantum sexual paradigm shift and be filled with an insatiable urge to fuck some skinny 5'7" slacker humanities student. No, when these ladies were stoned, they would just be really, *really* attracted to six-foot plus hockey players and/or pre-med students.

Helpful to know, really. Disappointing but helpful.

The only interesting thing about consuming THC that night was that when I (very irresponsibly) drove home in Space Truck, I discovered that I was able to do an absolutely effortless and perfect parallel park in front of the house.

That was rather remarkable but actually not particularly useful.

So, I was not hugely anti-stoner but what was happening at Sue's place was really pissing me off.

"You've probably been having a bad reaction to some of the old supply," Steve was telling Sue.

What really got me was how commercial, how corporate, Steve, his product and his presentation were. If you squinted a little you might think he was selling Avon products or real estate instead of peddling dope. Clearly there was big money involved and Steve was working for a very large organization. I wondered if he was getting a salary or just commission.

Looked like he was doing well either way.

"These new strains are guaranteed to avoid similar problems and might even help your current condition."

Fucking asshole. Sue had gotten so burnt out she couldn't attend class. She didn't need anything Steve had to offer.

I found some parcel tape and started sealing up boxes. Maybe I should have said something. I would have liked to have kicked Steve in the crotch so hard his balls flew out his nose but I didn't that do either. Partly because I figured it would have embarrassed Sue and made her feel even worse. Also Steve could probably beat the living shit out of me.

I finished with the boxes and sort of waved at Sue as I headed for the door. She didn't acknowledge me as I left but then, she and Steve were still talking.

I never saw her again.

19.
Dead Aliens in the Basement

I WAS SPENDING TIME with the Jag that Friday night.

Something to do, I mean I didn't have a radio show anymore.

"Do you like your father, Matthew?"

We were driving in her Datsun B210 on the way to what she said was her studio. I was doubtful that she really had a studio and I even wondered if she wanted to take us someplace where we could make out in private.

No.

Not a plausible theory. She didn't look even remotely horny, emotionally needy or even crazy. Or at least crazy in the way that led to sex.

"My dad?"

I had to think about that for a minute. We were heading past the stockyards and cement factories. I briefly wondered if the Jag's family lived in a grain elevator. Or at least something industrial and concrete. That would seem to suit her.

"Haven't seen him in three years."

The Jag nodded. "Your parents had a pretty rough break-up."

Before I could ask her how she knew about Mom and Dad's divorce, we were interrupted by a big bump as the car drove over an old set of train tracks.

"Nice car."

I wasn't being completely ironic. The suspension on her Datsun wasn't terrific but at least, unlike Space Truck, it *had* suspension.

The Jag laughed. "My father was horrified when I got this car. He wanted to buy me a Jaguar or at least a 240Z."

"What a monster."

Up until now, the Jag had been bouncing back and forth on my 'Like-Dislike Scale' but the knowledge that she could have been *given* a car that would have cost more than our house put her pretty deep into the "D" range at that point.

"I hate my father." She might have been mentioning that it had started to rain outside.

The Jag turned the steering wheel hard and we went down a dark road lined with one storey garages and auto body shops. Rob territory.

Where the hell were we going?

"He knows that I loathe him which is why he's always trying to buy me off."

"Why do you hate your father?"

I wondered why I had just opened my mouth. Asking someone why they hate their father is usually going to result in a very long, very embarrassing and basically incomprehensible answer. The only question that's stupider to ask someone is why they hate their mother.

Audio Transcript:
This Week in Conservative Feminism, CKUB FM
February 197—

Karen: So it's pretty much agreed that everything that Freud ever wrote was completely wrong.

Arundhati: Well, perhaps not everything.

Karen: What?! I can't believe I'm hearing this!

Arundhati: Well...

Karen: His body of work is nothing but misogynist, patriarchal hate-mongering!

Arundhati: I don't know about the hate-mongering part.

Karen: You call yourself a feminist?

Arundhati: I call myself an intellectually honest feminist.

Karen: Deranged is more like it.

Arundhati: That was uncalled for.

Karen: So what is so "intellectually honest" about Mr. Penis-Envy Theory?

Arundhati: I don't know about Freud personally but he did say something that I agree with very much.

Karen: What? That sometimes a cigar really is just a cigar?

Arundhati: No, that may be true but wasn't what made an impression on me.

Karen: What then?

Arundhati: That the most important things in life were love and work.

Karen: Oh.

"My father is a microbiologist."

Okay, not really the answer I was expecting.

"Is that a bad thing?"

"He used to be Head of Research at the Westfield Base." So, it probably was bad. Probably very bad.

"You mean Hellfield?" That's what people who thought the Armed Forces were conducting germ warfare tests there called it.

"That's the place."

"Is it true that they—"

"Yeah, every fucking awful rumour you hear about that place is dead-on true."

That was a pretty extraordinary claim because the local conspiracy lore about Westfield included some really bizarre stories. Everything from dead aliens in the basement to cattle-mutilating robot drones to viruses so lethal they could reduce a hitchhiker to a puddle of goo right there in their Levis.

"My father loved working there."

So maybe he was a very bad man.

"But then that company, Progressive Apparatus, offered him more money to work for them."

Progressive Apparatus? I remember Boyfriend Ed mentioning that he worked there.

"I've heard of it."

"I know."

Of course. "Do you know what they do there?"

What could it hurt to ask, I thought stupidly. The Jag seemed to know everything else.

"I know that they have a mandate under the War Measures Act that gives them jurisdiction over all of Blinn."

"Jurisdiction? What does that mean?"

"They run the town."

"Why?"

"To do things."

"To do what?"

"Whatever they like."

Thanks for narrowing that down, Colleen.

"They pay my father a shitload of money to help them do it."

"Lucky you."

She pulled up in front of a large and rusting aircraft hangar. Now I knew where we were—the outskirts of the airport. The Jag had just taken a weird route to get us there. Maybe she didn't want us to be followed.

"Shitloads of money does give you some advantages." The Jag pulled on the emergency brake so hard it looked like she might yank off the handle.

"So what do you know about Progressive Apparatus?"

As we walked towards the hangar I gave her an abbreviated version of my lunch with Boyfriend Ed.

"He sounds like one of their typical management assholes."

"Unfortunately he is about to become a typical management asshole stepfather."

"That's pretty much according to program."

The Jag paused before she opened the side door to the hangar.

"What program is that?"

The Jag inserted a key into a padlock.

"Absorb or eliminate nonconforming phenomena to establish control."

"Oh good, that clears up everything."

She chose to ignore my statement.

"Are you familiar with the saying, imitation is the sincerest form of flattery?"

"Yeah, so?"

She pushed open the door.

"Prepare to be really flattered."

They were all hanging there. Strung up with ropes under the armpits of their coveralls.

About one hundred Capekoids.

20.
CONSIDERABLE DANGER

Audio Transcript:
Drivin' Time!, CKUB FM
April 197—

Sound:	*Recorded applause.*
Timmie:	Has anyone been watching *The Muppet Show*?
Sound:	*Recorded cheers.*
Timmie:	Isn't it like the greatest thing on TV next to *Hockey Night in Canada*?

The time in the Jag's warehouse was a little overwhelming.

She explained that it was pretty easy to secure the coveralls from the retired gear from her father's company and she picked up some extras from things she found in the dumpsters in the industrial park. That was where she got all the tin-heads a.k.a. canisters as well.

"But how did you make so many...?" And no, I wasn't flattered. I was more like terrified.

Capekoids #1 and #2, while odd, emerged through fairly sensible processes. Ross and I had a logical need so we employed reasonable means to create them. A sensible number of them. As in two.

One hundred Capekoids was just crazy shit.

The Jag must have picked up on my nervousness.

"It's not like I made them overnight."

No?

"I started replicating them after I stole them back at Blinn Collegiate."

That was supposed to make me feel better? The Jag had been making copies of my guys for over three years? I studied one of her Capekoids.

"This is really impressive, Colleen."

The articulation was much better than anything Ross and I were capable of.

"But isn't this just a little bit…"

"Obsessive?" The Jag shook her head. "No, my actions are completely normal."

Sure they are.

"…a distraction from your own art?" Yes, I was thinking "obsessive" but this seemed to be a much nicer thing to say and I really didn't want her to go batshit and hurt me.

"That is a really nice thing to be concerned about." The Jag smiled. "But no."

"That's good." What else can you say at a time like that?

"There are two alternatives here." She straightened the head of one of her creations. "The first, and the one I think is the correct one, is that we are in considerable danger. In which case these constructions constitute our army. Our primary means of protest and protection."

Considerable danger? I hated those words. Especially when they were put together. I wasn't very enthusiastic about us having to need an army of anything either.

I started to walk down the length of the warehouse, hands behind my back, like I was an admiral doing an inspection of a warship.

"So what's the second alternative?"

The Jag started walking with me.

"That I've been delusional for the last few years."

I was impressed that the Jag could discuss this possibility so openly.

"What will you do then?"

She smiled at me.

"Well, if you don't mind, then I will have enough material for art installations for the next ten or fifteen years."

I didn't mind and I doubted that Ross would have.

21.
THAT BUBBLE-EYED SPRITE

ROB AND I WERE having an animated discussion about Capekoids and Space Truck. We both needed the use of Space Truck, but for very different reasons.

Or rather Rob wanted to do something with Space Truck and I needed Rob to do something completely different with Space Truck. Neither of us was particularly keen on the other's plans so the exchange was getting pretty intense.

"I need the trunk room!" None of Rob's MGs had any carrying capacity and that cute bubble-eyed Austin Sprite was completely out of the question.

"So do I!"

I had Capekoids to deliver. And other stuff to do.

"You do know that what you want to do is highly illegal, don't you?"

Rob was right about that but the Jag had convinced me that it had to be done.

"As if your plans aren't?"

Rob's motives were more conventional than mine: profit and pleasure-seeking. He and some of his buddies from the auto-shop had set up a huge dope buy at a really good price. They needed a vehicle that could easily transport some large bags of pot and which the local cops wouldn't immediately associate with them.

"It's a question of degree and you won't be involved."

I kind of resented Rob asking me for this favour. While I didn't completely condemn cannabis-based recreation, I frankly just didn't get it. It never did anything for me and look how it messed up Sue.

Rob was aware of all of this so he should have known better.

"What if the cops trace the car back to me?"

"I'll just tell them that I didn't tell you what I wanted it for."

Audio Transcript:
Drivin' Time!, CKUB FM
April 197—

Sound:	*Recorded cheers. Fireworks.*
Timmie:	Aren't we having fun?
Sound:	*Recorded applause.*
Timmie:	Cars are good, right? Let's face it, you can't live around here without one!
Sound:	*Recorded—engines revving.*
Timmie:	So let's hear the Beach Boys and how they use their groovy wheels to get from Point A to Point B!
Sound:	*Music.*

I was pretty sure that Rob resented what I wanted him to do for me as well. If he and I, and the Jag, got caught… we could be looking at some serious jail time.

Maybe as bad, or worse, than dope jail time.

I leaned back in Rob's bean bag chair while he took a long drag off his (regular) cigarette and rested his elbows on the kitchen table. We didn't say anything for a while. Finally, Rob exhaled a plume of blue smoke and tapped a small heap of cinders into the 7-11 Superhero tumbler he was using for an ashtray. Adam Warlock never looked so grotty.

"Fine."

From the tone of his voice I could tell that it really wasn't fine but Rob was going to do it anyway.

"Fine," I replied. It wasn't fine for me either, but this was the only way past this one.

Tit for tat. I help him. He helps me.

"Yeah, it's just fucking excellent."

22.
PSEUDO-ANDROIDS IN THE TRUNK

Audio Transcript:
Pop Goes Your Culture!, CKUB FM
April 197—

Drew: So did you catch that new sci-fi show on NBC last Thursday?

Erin: *Fantastic Journey?* Yeah.

Drew: I noticed that some of the writers and producers were from *Star Trek*.

Erin: Really didn't help. You at least need a spaceship for a show like that to work. Plus you need a special effects budget of more than fifty bucks an episode.

Drew: So, change the channel?

Erin: Kill it before it spreads.

Drew: So what else have you been watching these days?

Erin: One of the super-stations in Spokane is re-running *Mission Impossible* after the late movie. That's been pretty decent.

Drew: I dunno, I've always thought it was kind of a dumb

show.

Erin: What are you talking about? It's classic spy TV!

Drew: It was dumb and all it did was convince Americans
               that they could do anything.

Erin: It was a great caper every week!

Drew: With a dangerous message.

So it's three days later, Saturday night is just about over and
we're driving Space Truck towards the Blinn University campus.
Rob is at the wheel, the Jag is riding shotgun and I'm in the back
sharing the bench seat with three Capekoids. We have four more
of the pseudo-androids in the trunk. The Jag packed them up
rather nicely.

Before I go any further in describing the events of that night
you have to remember that this was the 1970s. Security was
something you got from hugging a blanket or cuddling a warm
puppy. Nobody cared what we were doing there so we just drove
on into the campus grounds, turned down the road behind the
Student Union Pub (the only place on campus that had most of its
lights on), opened a chain link gate and sailed on into the main
building's loading bay.

Of course they had forgotten to lock the shipping doors and
the power to the freight elevator was still turned on.

I mean why not? What possibly could happen?

Why would anyone want to sneak into a university in the
middle of the night?

"Get your masks on."

The Jag pulled out the Don Post Crimson Skull mask she had
borrowed from me.

Rob and I groaned.

"If the cops find out that we tried to disguise ourselves, we are
just going to be in deeper shit."

Rob had already explained the legal realities of premeditated break and enter to the Jag several times. It didn't seem to be taking.

"It is vital that we cannot be identified," was always her answer. "Besides, you are assuming that we're going to be caught."

"It is a possibility."

Even at slackass Blinn U, it was. Through some astronomical combination of job descriptions and patrol patterns, some security guy might see us.

"We can't afford to be caught."

That was true, too.

Rob and I groaned again and put on our masks. Mine was a grey alien (of course) while Rob was wearing Nixon's face (back then, a classic).

I turned on the lights in the loading bay and found a hand cart. The Jag opened up Space Truck's trunk and started unloading the Capekoids.

"What the hell is this?!"

Rob was holding a long metal object in his hands, something he had found under the passenger seat.

"*Holy shit!*"

That was me talking. Well, more like yelping really.

The Jag threw a Capekoid over her shoulder. "It's a machete, what do you think it is?"

"*A fucking machete?!*"

That was me too. I was scream-whispering.

The Jag walked over to the hand cart. "Relax, I brought one for each of you guys, too."

Rob threw the machete onto the passenger seat and got back behind the steering wheel. "What the hell do we need machetes for?"

The Jag gently laid the Capekoid on the cart. "If we've been anticipated we could be up against some pretty serious opposition."

"Like what? The only security guard on shift is probably at the Students' Union getting tanked."

Rob turned the keys. "Get in, Matt."

Before I could move, the Jag ran over to Space Truck and turned off the ignition.

"What is wrong with you?!" She seemed genuinely surprised by our reactions.

"You're talking about creating a crime scene with lethal weapons in your possession." Rob wouldn't look at the Jag while he talked, or rather his Nixon nose was steadily pointing at the steering wheel which suggested he wasn't looking at her. "They will put all of us away. Forever."

"We must protect ourselves."

"Colleen…" I put my hand on the Jag's shoulder. "No machetes or no mission."

Rob turned and glared at her. "This is a deal-breaker." I swear you could see his eyes burning laser beams out of the holes in his mask.

The Jag let out a heavy sigh and looked like she wanted to punch out the windshield of the car.

Then, eventually: "Fine. Great. Leave the blades. Fucking excellent."

We loaded the rest of the Capekoids into the freight elevator without saying much. I don't know what fearsome menace the Jag was expecting but the rest of our operation was gloriously anti-climactic. My intelligence on the behaviour patterns of my ex-coworkers at the radio station turned out to be dead on. Erin Davis, the DJ for the Saturday Night-early Sunday Morning slot, "Jazz-Laxtion," was nowhere to be seen. He had a crush on one of the bartenders at the SU Pub so, as usual, he loaded up a four-hour tape and headed out there to get himself loaded. Which I'm sure he thought would make him vastly more charming.

Maybe the bartender had gone home with someone else and Erin was bonding with the security guard by now.

All wonderful news.

It meant that we could take off those stupid masks which in turn meant that we could work a lot faster. The Jag and I started in on getting the Capekoids in place—it was a complex installation that required a lot of stands and wires.

Meanwhile Rob had his wire-cutters and screwdrivers out and went to work in the control booth. In just over an hour we were just about done.

Rob's job was straight-forward but fiddly. He had to remove the control board and most of the guts for the station's transmitter. We were counting on the fact that all of the three people who were listening to "Jazz-Laxtion" had already fallen asleep and wouldn't notice the interruption of the broadcast.

I was extremely proud of our Capekoid piece.

We had positioned all seven of the figures so that they looked like they were dancing together. The label we mounted on the wall read: "Silent Disco".

This may have been the first use of the expression.

I took a few shots with my Instamatic and really wished that I could be there when Barry walked in the door.

But the Capekoid installation was just a statement, it was our actions that mattered. It would probably take months, maybe years, for the student body to come up with enough cash to replace the transmitter—that is if they ever bothered to. University politics were lurching very hard to the right this year. If it wasn't beer, weed or red-neck movies, students just didn't want to pay for it anymore.

It took another twenty-five minutes to get the electronics into Space Truck's trunk and pull out of the shipping bay.

"Good job."

The Jag seemed pleased.

I was just happy to get Timmie off the air.

Rob was just happy to get the hell out of there.

"But this is just Phase One," she added.

Hopefully Phase Two would not involve machetes.

23.
A Heck of a Lot of Sense

I HAD A DREAM about the Jag and the Capekoids.

It was pretty erotic and extremely terrifying. It was the Sunday night after the Silent Disco mission. Some of what she said was just a replay of what she told me and Rob on the way back into town. The sexy parts were probably just my constant level of horny frustration coupled with the fear that if I got caught I would either die a virgin or end up servicing alpha-convicts in a federal prison.

And no, the Jag and I never, ever, had sex in real life. This was a dream, folks.

We were humping away in the back seat of Space Truck while Capekoid #1 was driving us to a group of domes and rectangles out past Highway #2.

"Now listen very carefully, moron," the Jag whispered in my ear as I experienced a very brief but intense orgasm. I wondered why my fantasy-Jag also had to say mean things to me.

"I'm listening."

"Your Capekoids are really freaking them out."

"Really?" Even in my dream-induced, sexually excited state this seemed to be an unlikely scenario. "They're just home-made dummies."

Admittedly, in this dream one of those home-made robo-dummies was driving the car, but never mind.

"We're dealing with major control freaks here." The Jag bit the inside of my elbow. It felt incredibly good. "They like to think they can master all the variables in any community."

"What kind of variables?" I noticed that the lights lining the highway were getting brighter. We were getting closer to those buildings.

"Everything is a variable to those people." The Jag kissed the spot where she had bitten me. Now that felt *really* incredible.

"How do they control everything?"

"They can't but they are very good at tracking things."

This wasn't making a heck of a lot of sense.

The Jag was now on top of me and while I was capable of making sounds, I wasn't quite able to re-work those noises into actual words.

"They didn't like the messages you and your friends were sending out on the radio." It was impressive how the Jag was able to speak so calmly while she… ah, never mind. "That's why they had to drop Timmie in there."

Space Truck rolled to a stop. The Jag, however, was not stopping. "That's how they found out that you were the creator of the Capekoids."

I heard the trunk open. I pulled Colleen closer to me and looked out the window. Capekoid #2 was emerging from the trunk.

"They hate those things," she whispered in my ear.

Then another Capekoid got out, then another one and another one and another one… until it looked like Space Truck was some kind of clown car filled with home-made androids.

"Matthew?"

My mother was standing at my open bedroom door.

"We need to talk about the wedding arrangements."

I hoped she hadn't noticed my erection.

24.
SOCIALISTS IN SPACE

FOR THE NEXT TWO weeks pretty much nothing happened. Or at least things were happening but I wasn't aware of them.

That was completely fine with me. I figured that even in the cause of art and human freedom nobody should be required to break into a public building more than once a year. I was done for a while.

Besides I had exams to study for and essays to write. Most of what I was writing was absolute shit but I did a paper comparing religious cults to themes in *The Invasion of the Body Snatchers* for my Symbolic Anthropology class that I was pretty pleased with. I called it "An Alien Millennium"; a bit purple, but appropriate, and if I ever did manage to write a science fiction novel I figured I could use it for the title.

Okay, maybe I was hitting the books a little harder than usual; I didn't want my mom and soon to be stepfather to have any sort of window to throw me into business college. I had no desire to wear knit ties and sell dope to messed up young people.

I was just stapling the pages of my Body Snatchers paper together when the phone rang.

It was the Jag: "AM Frequency 940. Five minutes."

"Hi Colleen, how are things with you?"

"Shut up. Tune in."

Dial tone.

Strange that we never really dated.

I did what she told me.

Eugene, bless his heart, had found an old Syrinx album and was starting his first broadcast day with their saxophone and ARP synthesizer composition "Field Hymn". He had gone as local as he could manage given the state of musical technology and Canadian musical culture at the time.

Audio Transcript:
Rise Up Alberta!, Radio Free Blinn
May 197—

Announcer: Good morning, working people! And welcome to your day!

Sound: *Passage of music rises for a moment then fades.*

Announcer: Today is May Day! A suitable day for all of you to take pride in your collective achievements and respect your personal dignity!

Sound: *Recorded cheering.*

Announcer: If this sounds like a bunch of communist propaganda to some of you, then you are completely wrong! This is *super-communist propaganda*! This station is dedicated to *super-hyper-ultra-communism*! Not the feeble timidity nonsense you might pick up on the short wave from Moscow or Beijing! *No, this is the Socialism of the Future!*

Sound: *More recorded cheering.*

Announcer: This is Meta-Communism! This is Socialism that is actually fun and interesting!

Sound: *Heroic music slowly rises in volume.*

Announcer: Who am I? Who are we? It doesn't matter. Where are we broadcasting from? It doesn't matter. What does matter is that we are your comrades. We are an anonymous, nomadic flow of truth, ideas and inspiration that will always be there for you!

Eugene's manifesto was about 85,000 miles further to the left of any political position I was comfortable with, but he was doing all the work now and at least he wasn't Timmie. Besides, I kind of liked the idea that I had helped create "an anonymous, nomadic flow of truth, ideas and inspiration." It felt like I'd finally done something worthwhile, maybe even heroic.

The phone rang again and put a stop to that silly idea.

"This is pretty wild!" I thought I'd share my impressions right away.

"Oh, you're listening to Eugene?" This time it was Rob on the line. His voice sounded a little muffled. "How does he sound?"

"Like a classic episode of *Socialists in Space*."

"That sounds like it could actually be a show."

"Only in Saskatchewan, Rob."

His laughter was interrupted by a brief coughing fit.

"You okay, Rob?"

He took a deep, ragged breath. "Frankly, I have been better."

"What happened?"

"Listen, Matt, does your mother still have that prescription for Tylenol #3?" Like all house guests in the 1970s, Rob had made the obligatory examination of the contents of our medicine cabinet. It would be rude not to.

"I think so."

"Do you think I could borrow five or six tablets?"

Audio Transcript:
Rise Up Alberta!, Radio Free Blinn
May 197—

Sound: *Music ends.*

Announcer: That was Sun-Ra. Some people would say that it's pretty "trippy" stuff and I suppose it's a reasonable segue into this afternoon's topic, which is the mass narcotization of human populations—

As part of our Mission Impossible deal I had to lend Rob Space Truck for the weekend. When I got off the bus and walked over to his place I noticed some fresh dents in the side of my beloved quasi-tank. Nothing too serious, just additions to the many scrapes and scrunches I'd put in myself. Still a little upsetting. It was my job to wreck my car.

Rob buzzed me in and when I walked into his apartment I saw him sprawled out on his bean bag chair puffing away at what, I could tell from the air quality, was Cigarette No. 12.

"What the hell did you do to my car?" I know, not a great way to say hello, but like I said, only I got to tattoo Space Truck.

"I could fix the dents if you like." Rob took a long drag and looked away from me. "But if I did that then I'd have to fix all the rest of the dents, otherwise they'd stand out too much."

I dropped into the easy chair on the other side of the room. "Bullshit." I threw the little vial of my mother's prescription at him.

Rob snatched it out of the air with his free hand. "Not bullshit. And if I did everything necessary to clean up that crap car of yours, the bodywork would collapse."

I shrugged. "Well, maybe." It was hard to lie to Rob.

I noticed that Rob had his radio playing softly in the background.

It was Eugene reading passages from *The Young Man's Guide to a Successful Career in the Business World*:

"There is one primary key to making a lot of money: whenever you can and in every way you can, *act* like people who already have money…"

Speaking of Eugene, when Rob turned his head and looked at me I saw that much of his face was covered with bandages. The parts of his face that weren't covered in bandages were deep, dark patches of purple, blue and black skin.

"Good god!"

He looked almost as bad as Eugene did when we came to visit him in the hospital.

"…do not waste time or energy trying to figure why people with money are doing what they do. Do not think, *act*. Do not concern yourself about the values and beliefs that people with money may hold. They are wealthy, therefore their values are superior and admirable. Your understanding is not needed…"

Rob laughed. Not very much and not very happily. "I know, I look like shit."

"Well, you look worse than my car." Oh dear, maybe too soon for jokes.

"You moron." No, actually Rob was laughing again. A little bit more and he sounded happier.

"…you simply are not worthy to comprehend the needs, the aspirations and desires of the Wealthy. Magical and Godly forces are at work; if you surrender to your station, you may be caught up in these currents of power and prosperity…"

"So what happened?"

Rob took another drag and sighed. "The purchase of certain substances did not go as well as it could have."

There was a brief silence over the radio speaker. Then Eugene spoke again: "*Can you believe this utter horseshit?!*"

Rob reached over and turned off the radio. "Sure I can, buddy."

I shrugged. "Eugene's just going for an effect. He never talks that way normally."

"Well, he's going to be doing a lot of talking now." I could see Rob wince as he eased back into the beanbag chair. "At least for a while."

"You and Colleen set him up at his farmhouse?"

"Better." There was a look of satisfaction on Rob's face. "We set the transmitter up in his uncle's old van. Eugene can broadcast from anywhere in southern Alberta where rubber wheels can take him."

Hence, the 'nomad' proclamation. "But what kind of range can you get with a mobile antennae?"

"I did the mechanics but it was the Jag's idea." Rob stubbed out his cigarette and opened up the vial. "We set up a stationary transmitter on the farm, it boosts and rebroadcasts the signal from the van."

"But you need a huge ass tower for that."

"Or a windmill with an aluminum frame."

That Jag. Very smart. Crazy but very smart.

Rob scarfed three tablets. Anyone else I would have figured they were trying to get high. From the looks of those bruises I knew he was in a lot of pain.

"So what happened to you?"

"Well, I learned a very important thing about going to remote places to meet your new dealer."

"Yeah?"

"Don't ever do that. Even when you bring your friends." Rob put another cigarette in his mouth and lit it. "Because your dealer can bring his friends and they can bring their guns."

"Guns?" What the fuck was this, Montana? On second thought, maybe these guys were from Montana.

"They beat the shit out of us and drove off with all our money. Kicked Space Truck a few times too."

"Monsters." They must have been from Montana.

"We're actually lucky to be alive."

"There probably wasn't enough room in Space Truck for all your bodies."

Rob looked at me. Okay, it wasn't very funny.

"Anyway…"

I thought of turning the radio back on and hear how Eugene was faring with *The Young Man's Guide to a Successful Career in the Business World* but decided against it. It was kind of nice to sit here in the quiet for a few minutes.

Eventually Rob stubbed out the latest cigarette. "You talked to the Jag recently?"

"Not for a week or so."

"She's got something big for this weekend. Wants to know if you can help."

I sighed. "You can have my car but I can't make it."
Rob looked surprised. "What? You got a date or something?"
I sighed again. "My mom does."
"So?"
"She's getting married. I think I better show up for that."

25.
THE YOUNG AND THE RESTLESS

Audio Transcript:
Rise Up Alberta!, Radio Free Blinn
June 197—

Sound:	*Music:* The Silver Apples of the Moon. *Fades.*
Announcer:	Nothing like a little Morton Subotnick to accompany the sunrise.
Sound:	*Paper rustling.*
Announcer:	I see from this week's issue of the Blinn University paper that the Student Libertarian Society will be having a symposium with columnists Barbara Amiel, Conrad Black and yet another collection of Randian scholars from around the world. One wonders where these rugged individualists get the cash for these things at such an early age.
Sound:	*More paper rustling.*
Announcer:	Possibly like many self-made men they took care to be the children of financially secure parents. However, that's probably just my sour grapes.
Sound:	*More vintage electronic music rises slowly in the background.*

Announcer: However, our Objectivist friends have raised the interesting questions of self-determination and social responsibility which in turn made me think of Asimov's Laws of Robotics. I won't go into them here because you probably know them off by heart, and since you do, will recall that the tragedy of Dr. A's robots is that they are intelligent creatures who are compelled to do good without choice and probably very little moral awareness. That's sad because acting in the best interests of others is meaningless if you don't understand why you are doing it and how this connects you to them.

Sound: *Announcer pauses to let the music play for a time.*

Announcer: But before I continue along on this line of discourse, I want to clear up something. Much as I enjoy those robot stories, I feel the principles of the Asimovian Laws are divorced from reality and therefore fundamentally flawed. As many of you may know, I am very keen on reality. Therefore, permit me to share the Real Laws of Robots:

Law Number One:
A robot will always break down just after its warranty period has expired.

Law Number Two:
The instructions for the proper operation and repair of a robot will always exceed the understanding of its owner.

Law Number Three:
A robot will always be purchased on the basis of features and functions that the owner later discovers will never be used.

Law Number Four:
A robot rarely ends up doing what it was designed

to do anyway…

Sound: *Two-fingered typing.*

Announcer: And while we are on this topic, I just decoded a message from a very reliable source telling me that there may be some interesting robotic manifestations in the neighbourhood soon.

A lot happened on that particular Saturday in June and some of the events I had to put together after the fact. But here goes:

03:00

Rob and presumably some of his stoner and/or mechanic friends drove up to the Jag's studio warehouse. Because I wasn't going to need it that day, I loaned him Space Truck.

I was told that Colleen was waiting for them and if I know her she had a few dozen Capekoids neatly stacked up on a platter and ready to go.

03:30

I could hear my sister and my mother talking downstairs. I couldn't hear what they were saying but they sounded very happy and excited.

I was not in the same frame of mind as they were. My life was going to change big time and I had no idea how to handle this or what I was going to be doing or where I would be living six months from now. Hell, six days from now.

Plus the wedding was resurrecting some very old and deep-seated feelings of resentment in me. I was very angry with my mother. Also with my annoying sister but to a much lesser extent.

I guess I should tell you a few more things about my relationship with my mother. I wasn't the only one in the family who had a broadcast presence. Very soon after we moved to Blinn—about ten years ago—my mother landed a job hosting a daytime "human interest" show on local commercial television: *Your Perfect Life.*

They used to do shows like that back then. Usually she'd just get the movie critic from the paper, maybe a chef from the community college and some of her drinking buddies to sit and talk about stuff. The show had a huge cringe-factor for me so I hardly ever watched it. I was always kind of grateful when my course schedule meant that I was on campus at 2:30 in the afternoon. The slot just after the farm market report and before the rebroadcast of the soap operas from the USA.

Mom was a bit of a celebrity in town and when people found out what my last name was they would ask me if we were related. I always said no.

When I was feeling under the weather and was at home and wanted to catch up on what was happening on *The Edge of Night* I might accidentally catch a few minutes of my mother's show. Usually she was either talking about exotic vacation destinations or the importance of female orgasms. Like the editors of *Cosmopolitan* magazine, my mother was convinced that the power of a woman's orgasm could be used for everything from ensuring monetary wealth to healing broken relationships and keeping your bedroom dust-free.

The vacations I could understand. Mom liked to visit interesting places and the local travel agency was a regular sponsor.

Intellectually I could get behind the female orgasm thing, but it just didn't feel particularly comfortable hearing about them from my mother.

Worst of all, I just hated the way she looked on camera. Her skirts were too short or the tops on her pant suits were too tight or she had too much of that silver goop plastered on her eyelids and I never liked that platinum blonde colour she dyed her hair.

She looked like some bar-girl on Rigel-Seven that Captain Kirk might try to pick up.

04:00

Space Truck suitably loaded, Rob and the Jag parked my car in front of the main entrance of Blinn City Hall.

Rob, being very mechanically inclined, was able to open the big glass doors with a Robertson screwdriver with a minimum amount of damage to city property. The Jag was a little more aggressive with their security system. She used a pair of wire-cutters to make sure the police had absolutely no idea what we were up to.

They then started piling Capekoids onto dollies and rolling them inside.

Elsewhere, Rob's friends were doing similar things at the main branch of the public library.

04:30

My mother and my sister were still talking in a very animated fashion and now they were starting to move furniture.

They had to, I suppose. The wedding was being held here and people needed places to sit and stand and eat and be generally made happy by the wonderful ceremony.

"A lovely way to say goodbye to our old home," was how my mother put it.

Goodbye was right. Our home was also a good buy on the local real estate market and my mother and Ed had already sold the place. After the wedding I had two weeks to clear out.

My sister, who'd been working for six months now, was already moved in with some of her girlfriends. I, on the other hand, had neglected to make plans.

While we are on the subject of moving, or rather before we moved anywhere, my mother was also a TV star. When we all lived in Saskatoon, Saskatchewan, my mother was a very young, charming and pretty preschool teacher who successfully pitched an idea for a locally produced TV show.

Miss Shirley's TV Kindergarten. Every weekday at 4:30 p.m. There wasn't much traffic back then so mom could get from her school to our house to the TV station after her real job ended at 3:15. The format was pretty simple, she had some hand-puppets, she would play the guitar and sing a song, read a story and do crafts.

Seemingly harmless.

The only problem was that she wanted an audience for the show. Getting a studio audience of children was impossible, no budget for that kind of thing, so my mother and the producers decided that my sister and I would be her side-kicks.

That was why she had to drive around to the house before going to the station. Our babysitter had to have us dressed, pressed and ready to go every weekday.

My sister and I were my mother's audience for the song and the story and she would guide us through the daily craft. My sister was six years old. I was four.

I was a four year old boy.

Sitting still through the song and the story was absolute agony for me. Once when my mother told me to be as "quiet and still as I possibly, possibly could," I had to resort to digging into the cameraman's toolkit and tape my mouth shut.

The station got some mail regarding how that looked on screen.

The crafts were the absolute worst. My sister was just old enough to manage them with some direction from my mother. I was hopeless. I mean they were making fractally patterned paper birds less than two inches long. With my tiny, fat and clumsy fingers I could barely crumple paper into a ball.

Of course I would cry on camera and that would be beamed into living rooms all over the province.

What made it worse was the producer's brainwave that my competency meltdowns were "cute" and should be a regular part of the show. To keep me from crying all the time, my mother would feed me half of one of her Valium tablets, which of course made me even more of a craft-klutz.

So I got beat up a lot at school.

The Lord may hate a coward but the bullies of Saskatoon really hated a crybaby.

By the time my hand-eye coordination had matured to the point that I could actually do some of the crafts, my mother and father had split up and we were on the Trans-Canada rolling on to Blinn.

So, no chance of a televised redemption.

And things between my mother and I have never been completely easy ever since.

05:00

Team #B was heading out to Blinn's first mega-church. A hangar-sized brick structure that could seat over 1,000 of the faithful. Every Sunday there were four services. At 10:00 a.m. and 2:00 p.m., the Power-Faith Evangelical Church would be in action. At 8:00 a.m. and 4:00 p.m., a combination of about a dozen Asian faith communities who called themselves "The People of the Blessed Golden Shower" would be making use of the facilities. Multiculturalism, and reliable translation services, were still relatively rare back in the 1970s.

God knows what Rob's friends were going to do with all those Capekoids.

In the meantime, Rob and the Jag were heading out to a giant block of Brutalist concrete nestled in the foothills.

The western Canadian headquarters of Progressive Apparatus.

11:30

"Matthew?"

My mother was knocking on my bedroom door.

"Glurph."

"Are you up?"

Well, not really.

After about another hour of listening to my mother and sister happily hoot away, I padded into the bathroom, opened the medicine cabinet and ingested an uncertain amount of her Valium tablets. Hello, old friends.

Threshold to harmony, that medicine cabinet.

Next thing I knew it was all bright outside and almost lunchtime.

It probably wasn't a good thing but I had been scarfing more than my usual amount of my mother's tranquilizers. Partly it was the realization that after four years I was actually going to be out of university in a little over a week with not a terribly impressive academic record and not the most marketable set of skills. On top of that, my mother had been on my case about what I was going to do after she sold the house and moved in with Ed.

"You can't stay with us."

Frankly, I would rather die than live with my mother and my new step—*her* new husband. I might get Management Cooties off Ed, and Jesus, what would happen if I actually heard them humping and sloshing away in that big water bed? I actually had no idea if Ed had a water bed or not but somehow I figured it was a pretty safe bet that he did.

"You can't expect Ed to pay your way."

I probably could find some way to take money from Ed but I also figured it was a pretty safe bet that such an offer was never going to happen. It wouldn't be good for my character and the fact that it saved him a few bucks would just be a bonus.

"Have you spoken to your father?"

Yeah, I had. His position was pretty much the same as Ed's and my mother's.

I felt a little like I was being staked out on a rock and left to the elements. Yeah, I am probably exaggerating. I do that.

When I got back to my room I noticed that someone, probably my mother, had laid out a suit for me. It was dark grey, double breasted, flannel. There was a pale blue shirt and a red, white and blue striped tie.

Since I wasn't a part of the ceremony I didn't have to wear the hideous lime green tuxedos that Ed and his friends were decked out in. My sister was one of the maids of honour so she had to wear some outrageous off-orange laced sack that I'm sure Mother chose to make sure her daughter looked as unattractive as possible. They could be somewhat competitive about such things.

My wedding duds weren't too bad really. Maybe they expected me to wear the suit to job interviews. That is if I was ever going to get close to one of those occurrences.

Oh, look. Dress shoes. The black leather was soft and the words "Made in Italy" were stamped on the insteps. Heck of a lot nicer than the horrific platform boots the best men were wearing.

I saw a van pull into the driveway. The fact that Rob and the Jag were doing something with Space Truck was making the wedding set up easier.

Audio Transcript:
Rise Up Alberta!, Radio Free Blinn
June 197—

Sound: *Music: Fanfare for the Common Man.*

Announcer: This may be what we will remember for generations as the day when everything changed. At this very moment great and heroic events are transpiring in our community. By this time tomorrow, many truths will be revealed and we will be free to walk forward together into a wonderful and just future.

12:00

High noon at the intersection of Highway Nos. One and Two.

Rob brakes Space Truck to a stop. Two rusting and ragged vans follow suit. He and the Jag get out and wait for the other drivers to join them.

They speak for a time and get back into their vehicles. Space Truck leads the way as they roar towards the P.A. building.

13:00

To be fair, Ed and my mother had recently let up on the harangues about my future.

Maybe they felt sorry for me. More likely they were just busy with the arrangements for the wedding and the (ugh) honeymoon.

There was a knock on my bedroom door.

"Matthew?" It was Ed.

"Yeah?"

Speak of the fuckwit devil.

"Do you need any help with your clothes?"

"I can manage, I think." Just because I never wear suits doesn't mean that I don't know how to put one on.

"Sometimes those ties can be a bit tricky." Which I read as a directive to be sure to put that tie on. Fine.

"My father taught me how to tie ties." Proving once again that in spite of his millions of faults, my dad wasn't nearly as useless as you.

"People are starting to arrive."

At this point I had stripped down to my underwear and was trying on the dress suit.

"So?"

Nice material.

"It would be good if you could go down and do a bit of socializing." Another directive: get your ass down there.

13:30

Very few people know that Progressive Apparatus employed no human security staff during its weekend and evening shifts at its southern Alberta campus grounds. Even during normal office hours there was a minimum of breathing guards on site. This practice is one more organizational expression of P.A.'s desire to reduce as many "variant factors" under control as possible. Some security paradigms see guards as a big risk factor.

On this particular afternoon, the campus grounds were patrolled, as usual, by three-foot high drones. Essentially metal boxes mounted on either treads or small balloon tires, they had a portable TV camera mounted where its "head" would have been and sported a single articulated arm with a multi-purpose manipulator unit at the end. A magnetic holster held a .357 magnum on the side of each P.A. drone. The holster was designed to break away, allowing the drone to draw and aim its weapon. The specifications for the drones stated that it was capable of firing and stopping the equivalent of an eighteen wheeler truck within 3.5 seconds of first sighting the target.

Technically, arming robots with deadly weapons violated just about every gun-control law and weapons-safety regulation in Canada. However, the P.A. drones were viewed as marvels of 1970s technology and no one wanted to stand in the way of progress.

Each drone also had a two-foot antennae on its upper right hand corner which was connected to an internal transmitter-receiver which allowed each robot to communicate with the Progressive Apparatus Mainframe Supercomputer that was housed somewhere deep inside an exhausted coal mine shaft. Or some place equally James Bondish.

These drones were working perfectly as they traced their pre-programmed routes through the campus grounds. The ones with balloon tires were assigned beats either inside the buildings or along the concrete and asphalt walkways. The drones with treads were either rolling along gravel roads or across the short grass of the surrounding foothills.

For the time, perhaps the drones were indeed technological marvels. The Jag referred to them as "fucking nasty pieces of work".

Two drones stopped and watched as Space Truck rolled towards the gateway in the chain-link fence leading to the main entrance to the campus. The cameras on the drones focused on the side door of the car as it opened and the Jag got out.

She removed a yellow plastic punch card from her jeans pocket and pressed it into a metal slot set in a pole next to the gate. It was later learned that the Jag had used a children's mould-making toy to create an unauthorized duplicate of her father's entry card.

The gate swung open but one of the drones picked up its pistol and pointed it at the Jag as she walked over towards it. If anyone had been in the security control to study the TV signal coming from the drone, they would have noticed that the Jag had a whistle in her mouth. The whistle was small, red and also made of cheap plastic. The sort of toy you would find in a box of breakfast cereal.

The young woman, apparently not at all worried being shot, bent down in front of the drone, inhaled and blew on the whistle, which emitted a high-pitch chirping approximately for two seconds.

Again, if there had been any people in the security centre, they would have seen that the TV signal from the drone had just cut out into static. Then they would have heard another high-pitched chirp and seen the other drone's signal break down.

14:30

Even though I was not seated front and centre, I did have a reasonable view of my mother, dressed in her puce wedding dress, stepping out of the rec room, outside onto the patio and down the synthetic carpet they had rolled out on the backyard.

With the patio doors open, the music playing on our stereo came through loud and clear. My mother's choice for the bridal march: the theme to the eternally popular soap opera, *The Young and the Restless*.

I would have gone for the opening music to *The Edge of Night* which was sort of like stripped down Wagner or Beethoven and promised all kinds of suffering and violence. But that was just more evidence of my chronic bad attitude.

My mother certainly seemed to like the music. So did my sister. They were both smiling so hard it looked like their faces were going to break and my sister looked like she might start crying.

I felt like I might start vomiting. But no, that never looks good at any social gathering.

Ed and his two best men were standing at the far end of the backyard facing the minister and not too far from the garden shed. Somehow, with their light green tuxedos and matching shoes they reminded me of gigantic Fisher Price toys. The sort of figures you might push to make them roll back and forth or maybe store in a cartoon version of Noah's Ark.

I, on the other hand, had found a way to rebel with my attire.

Yes, I was wearing my very sensible grey suit. Yes, I had even tied my tie successfully. But those lovely Italian shoes were still in my room. Instead, I was wearing my oldest and most ragged sneakers.

I doubted anyone noticed. I wasn't the object of much attention on regular days, why should it be any different today?

Mother and Ed, the minister and the whole ritual crew were all gathered at the far end of the yard and I couldn't make out what they were saying. Speaking of footwear, the minister was wearing open-toed sandals with no socks. I think he was going for a Jesus of Nazareth look but the effect was more Hobbit-meets-Beast Boy. It shouldn't make any difference but somehow it doesn't seem right that Our Saviour would have big hairy feet.

Hush brain. Stop yapping.

I really couldn't hear the service properly. After the minister spoke, the betrothed read their own wedding vows. In truth, because she was a communication professional, my mother spoke her lines from memory. She used that TV voice that she practised on me and my sister back in Saskatoon and had honed to near-perfection every weekday afternoon for the viewers of Blinn. I couldn't understand a word of it. Maybe it was some kind of psychological block, maybe it was the effects of all that Valium I wolfed down. Maybe I was still worried that I might throw up.

Then Ed said his piece. I could actually make out some of that. He used a lot of sports metaphors. I don't think he exactly said that he was happy that he had been able to "score" with my mother but the analogy sounded disturbingly close. I do know that he likened the marriage to a "field goal at the bottom of the ninth inning" which to an athletically-challenged person like me sounded just wrong.

Never mind.

The ceremony continued. Bright yet ugly rings were exchanged, the minister made an unholy declaration, the couple locked faces for an awful moment and the soap opera music started up again.

"Isn't that sweet?" A blue-haired lady, I think it was Old Man

Erdos' wife, whispering at me. "You must be so proud!"

Please God, deliver me from all of this.

Audio Transcript:

Rise Up Alberta!, Radio Free Blinn

June 197—

Sound: *Announcer hangs up telephone receiver.*

Announcer: I am sorry for the interruption but I think you will find the pause was worth the wait. (clears throat) The time is upon us, comrades. If you venture out into the streets and buildings of your community you will find something remarkable. Something that will point you towards the irrevocable truth that there are forces in your everyday life that—

Sound: *Sharp electronic howl. Fades into static.*

16:20

I was sitting in a folding chair looking at the folding table where the guy from the catering company was running the free bar. In spite of all the activity as the guests were scooping up their containers of beer and champagne, I could also see Ed talking on the phone. He'd been doing that for about fifteen minutes.

Work related call? On the weekend? On his wedding day?

That did not look good.

Again, never mind. Since he wasn't going to ever give me any money, I didn't care if he had a job or not.

Never mind nevermore. I had more interesting things to consider. Like regretting that I didn't pay much attention in my biochemistry class. I really wanted to ingest a large fraction of that bar and get extremely drunk. But I wasn't sure if that was a good idea with all that Valium in my bloodstream. Would the tranquilizers combine with the alcohol and do something inconvenient like inhibit my autonomic nervous system and shut down my lungs? Or would the chemical combination just give me massive diarrhea?

I thought I remembered something like that. Or maybe not.

Maybe I should have six or seven drinks and see what happens. I'd always been a big fan of the scientific method.

"Matt?" There was a big, beefy, sport-carved hand on my shoulder.

"Huh?"

It was Ed. I hadn't noticed that he had hung up the phone and walked over to me.

"A brief word with you."

"Uh, okay."

He was smiling as he led me to his giant rectangular car that he had parked in the garage. We got into the back seat.

"What's up, Ed?" Something cheerful occurred to me. Maybe my mother had appealed to him to give me a big cheque, so I could start out on my own, away from them. Or maybe he had set up an entry position for me at Progressive Apparatus. I preferred the first option to the second.

"So, Matthew…"

Ed punched me in the face. Really hard.

As I blacked out, I couldn't tell if he was smiling or not. But probably.

17:47

When I came to, Ed had the car radio on.

Somebody was singing about tomorrow and why we had to keep thinking about it.

Fuck. Fleetwood Mac. Why couldn't I still be unconscious?

The singer was warning us that tomorrow would be today very soon.

Or dead. I could handle being dead if I didn't have to listen to this song anymore.

The music continued as Ed braked the car by the side of the road.

"Matthew, I would really like to kill you."

He pulled a pistol out from somewhere and stuck it in my mouth. It was obvious that we were going to have an interesting conversation.

Today, tomorrow, yesterday. What was this damn song going on about?

"Blurph?" (It's hard to speak clearly with your mouth full of gun.)

"I would really like you to give me a reason." He took the gun away.

I couldn't think of anything to say, so I just whimpered and looked very afraid. Just for dramatic effect, mind you.

Ed waved his gun in the direction of the car radio. "Turn the dial."

I must have looked really stupid and confused because Ed repeated himself, only louder:

"Turn the dial!"

So I started scanning the radio frequencies. Nothing too unexpected. Pop. Country. Evangelical. Farm market reports. CBC (but very distant and staticky). And nothing else.

"What do you hear, Matthew?"

"R–radio?" Well, that's what I was hearing.

"University students these days really are very stupid." Ed shook his head in disgust. "What *don't* you hear, moron?"

Well, Blinn University Radio was off the air but that had been the case for a while now.

Ed looked impatient. "You won't be hearing from your commie faggot friend anytime soon. Or ever."

Eugene? They'd gotten to him?

"He's off the air."

And who the hell were They?

Ed pointed the gun at the centre of my forehead. "Last chance, you little shithead. You and your pothead friend are completely unimportant..."

Fine, I will be happy to leave and never come back again.

"...but Colleen Jang is a problem."

I could see that. She was on the inside and obviously she had been doing things they did not like.

"Isn't Fleetwood great, Matt? Only group I like better is the

Bay City Rollers." Ed tuned the radio back to the original station.

"Where is she?"

It felt like he was going to perform a lobotomy with the barrel of that gun.

"I—"

"Where is she?"

"I don't know!" I didn't! The Jag came and went as she pleased. She was like the fucking Shadow. Invisible. Intangible.

Ed pulled the trigger.

I pissed my pants when I heard the metallic click.

Ed shook his head and put the gun away. "Now I'm going to have to get the upholstery cleaned."

I was fairly sure that urine would be easier to clean than blood, bone fragments and brain-matter.

Ed sighed and reached into the back seat of the car. "I've got some things for you to sign." He pulled out a metal-sided briefcase that looked a lot like the one that Sue's dope-dealer friend had. "You are now an intern in the employ of the Progressive Apparatus Group of Companies."

I struggled to read the masses of fine print in my lap as Ed started up the car.

"You're giving me a job?"

He laughed. "You'll be working."

"I don't—"

I don't understand. That's what I meant to say, I just didn't understand what was going on.

We were back on the road, very far out of town and heading to a bunker-like structure in the distance.

"Be sure to sign every one of the last twenty pages."

We passed a small shed with a large fire burning in front of it.

"Those are your letters to your mother and me for the next three years."

A group of men in uniform were burning a pile of Capekoids.

One of the men looked like Timmie but I couldn't be sure, because it was kind of hard to look back.

BOOK TWO:
FACTORY ROMANCE

1.
COMMUNIST ALARM CLOCK

05:00

Tick! *Tick! TICK!*

Ring.

The gears on the clock were louder than the alarm.

THUD!

I hit the stupid thing with the palm of my hand. Just like every morning for the last six months. This was not always an act of anger; sometimes you just had to apply a lot of force to turn off the alarm. As usual, the clock hit the concrete floor. It sounded like a brick was bouncing off the bottom of a cave. No damage. My time-keeping device was loud, solid and essentially indestructible.

Stupid communist alarm clock.

At least I assumed that it was a communist alarm clock. The words "MADE IN ROMANIA" were stamped on the back in big ugly block letters. My geography was pretty spotty but the last time I looked, Romania was one of those countries that was seriously hooked up with the U.S.S.R.

Eugene would be so disappointed with my uneven awareness of the scope of World Socialism.

But Eugene and Rob and the Jag might be dead anyway, so it could be that he was beyond worrying about such ideological disappointments. Unless Eugene was in Heaven, looking down on me, which would have *really* offended his atheistic political sensibilities.

Tick! *Tick!*

However, life goes on for some of us.

Unfortunately?

Which brought to mind the questions that I often had first thing in the morning: was I now working for communists? Or maybe I was working for capitalists who knew where to buy really cheap time-keeping instruments (i.e. from communists)? Was there any difference between them really and was it even worth worrying about?

I rolled off my sleeping slab and walked over to the sink. The floor was ice cold.

Typical.

I caught myself before I continued with the internal complaints. Objectively, I seemed to be on some kind of privileged list. I had my own sink which meant that I could wash my face in private. Or perhaps Management just thought I was really funny-looking and people shouldn't have to put up with that unpleasantness as part of their morning routine. Regardless, Winston Smith and I had the same interior decorator.

Objectively, I probably was kind of funny-looking now. My boyish features had never fully recovered from my first encounter with high gravity when the barge launched.

06:00

Next step: find a bicycle.

If you dress and eat fast, you can sometimes score one of the functional ones. If you don't, you're going to be late for your shift because you're going to be walking into the Assembly Complex. And you don't want to be late for your shift because they will dock 500 calories off your lunch allocation. It also means you have to work into the next shift. And that meant that you weren't going to get back until after the evening meal and that meant that you were down another 800 calories at least.

There was some kind of Darwinian selection going on. The

less often you got a bicycle, the more you had to work and the more likely you were to be tired and weak and the more likely you were to miss out on getting hold of a bicycle the next day. Plus: accelerating malnutrition.

Management probably could have dealt with this by putting out more bicycles or upping the maintenance schedule on the bikes we did have; but I suspected that the chronic bicycle shortage was a way of solving another level of problem.

We were working in a zero-sum environment here, there were only so many resources and there seemed to be a constant influx of new interns. From what I remember from all those notes I had to copy down in my intro Economics class, authorities had to create structural reductions on continually increasing demands on finite resources.

Thank you, Professor McBrokenheart.[1]

Like most mornings, I managed to get out there pretty quickly and get my hands on a bike. I was still a little bit One Gravity Tough.

And as with many winners in competitions I had some prior advantages over the losers. I showed up at the Plant with a few extra pounds of energy reserves (i.e. fat) and even though I wasn't hugely into sports or exercise I used to do a lot of walking around Blinn so I was at least a little bit stronger than some of the other interns.

Riding the bicycle towards the Assembly Quad was not exactly an inspiring experience. There were almost no distinguishing features along the giant concrete tunnel—just some lane markings on the asphalt road and row after row of fluorescent light fixtures overhead with tangles of grey pipes and gas meters bolted onto the walls. There weren't many signs to tell you how much farther you had to go before you got to the Lines. You and about a million other people just pedalled and pedalled, and you got to Assembly when you got there. Hopefully, before your shift started.

---

1   See Book One: *Invasion of the Capekoids*, which to my surprise and
    dismay turned out to be a happier time in my life.

Other things contributed to making the daily commute such a grim business. The sounds of hundreds and hundreds of bicycle chains being pushed through those gears, and the thousand plus of us huffing and puffing as we tried to make the best possible time—or else! There was a big rubber seal on the tunnel wall, it had a diameter of about thirty feet and I estimated that it was located about three-quarters of the way into Assembly. I remembered feeling a tiny pang of relief and joy as I cycled past it. Only another (estimated) five miles to go!

One time, about two months after I arrived, some really big guy with excess lung power started to sing while he was pedalling. He was totally out of tune but he sang very simple and cheerful songs—they could have been nursery rhymes in a language that I didn't understand.

The next day a few more people started singing. The next day even more. Some of the singers probably had no idea what were the words they were singing but they seemed to enjoy it anyway. The rides into work were getting a bit more fun.

Then one day, our lead singer and some of his more talented friends just weren't there anymore.

It seemed that Management did not approve of musical bike rides.

No distractions.

Just get to work.

And work.

And work some more.

07:00

Your Shift Card was something you definitely did not want to forget to bring to the Lines at the Main Assembly Quad.

I've been told that by today's standards a Shift Card was laughably crude; back then it was a very exotic techno-presence indeed. It was made of hard plastic, a little bigger and thicker than your average Chargex Card and it was all one colour: yellow for males, orange for females. If anyone in Management thought you might be gay then your Shift Card was coloured dead. I suppose they figured homosexuals didn't work hard enough or maybe Management simply didn't have a category for queer people.

Regardless of the shade, every card was liberally perforated with small rectangular holes—like those old-fashioned computer punch cards.

No.

They weren't "like" those old computer punch cards; they *were* those old computer punch cards.

Each Shift Card had a piece of string attached to it so you could wear it like a necklace while you were riding. After you had parked your bike you could hand the Card to the Shift Administrator who would insert it into the Logistics Clock and then tell you your day's designation:

"Materials Handler."

I nodded when I heard this. Even if I could have, I would not have complained. It was pretty hard work but it meant that you got to move around between at least six different production zones inside the Plant and that was a lot more interesting than just working at one station on the Lines. Plus it wasn't as disgusting as doing Waste Disposal or Nutrition, which were really just different aspects of the same bio-industrial process. It was also kind of a compliment. Not everybody got to handle materials; you had to be at least part of the upper 50% aptitude scale for interns. Which meant that I hadn't sustained serious brain damage. Yet.

Great.

At this point the Shift Administrator had said everything he or she was going to say to me that day (unless I really screwed something up). And now that I knew my assignment I would dial in the five number Job Code on the Big Clock and get my Task Specs:

"Re-port-to-In-Bay-Three. Use-Lo-ader-Bee-twel-ve-to-de-liv-er-stock-seals-to-in-stall-on-Lines."

I'm completely serious here.

The Logistics Clock sounded just like those computers from

1960s Irwin Allen TV shows. Even at the time I thought this was tremendously hokey. However, the fact that I didn't approve of the Plant's production values was irrelevant. Corny or not, this was the reality here.

Let me re-state: I'm not complaining here. The loaders could be fun to work. They were electrically powered forklifts with very cool hand-manipulators mounted on a big dial at the front of the vehicle. They also had these wild padded tires with self-adjusting pressure. These things go like robo-bats out of asphalt-hell and they were almost impossible to tip no matter how much you were carrying and how moronically you were driving them. Pretty entertaining sometimes. And much better designed than what you usually found around here.

The seals we had in stock were fairly lightweight and packed in crates that were easy to lift and unload into the Assembly Line bins. That meant that I'd be able to make seven, maybe eight, runs between the In-Bay and the Lines, which would mean that I'd be able to keep my quotas up, and best of all I'd get to see Angie seven, maybe eight, times before lunch break.

Not that I could actually talk to her.

But we could wave at each other and that was nice.

If I was really lucky the Clock would let me keep working loaders during the afternoon shift. If I was less lucky I'd get moved over to run the stackers in one of the out-bays. They had crappy heating in the out-bays and the seals were prone to leaks, so you might have to wear a breather for hours on end.

If I was completely SOL I'd be working the vats where they mixed the resins and polymers to actually make the seals. It was a lot hotter than the out-bays where the smells were so bad that they threatened to melt your sinuses. If there were any leaks in the vats they could also melt all of you.

Let the afternoon take care of itself. I was going to have a morning looking at Angie and if all went well we'd sit next to each other at food-break.

12:05

"Hey fuckwad!"

Angie dropped her tray down on the counter. The soya-paste slices and yeast cake cubes bounced slightly.

"It's lovely to see you too, dear."

Angle planted herself in the seat across from me. "Stop staring at my tits."

She was right about that, I was definitely taking her in.

"But you have such lovely breasts, darling."

My girlfriend shook her head. "You are *such* an asshole."

'Asshole'. Another one of her terms of affection.

"But I still like your freckles the best."

Maybe that wasn't completely true but I did like her freckles a lot. Angie's fair complexion was her main source of vulnerability; she could never hide it when she was blushing. Strangely enough, I seemed to be the only person who could make her blush.

She was blushing just then. Fortunately, also smiling.

"You have a good shift, jerkwad?"

I smiled back at her while I felt the gentle pressure of her foot on mine. "You know me and the loaders. Zip, zip, zoom."

"Nice sound effects, moron."

"How was your shift?"

"Fucking awful, except for the usual distractions."

It was nice of Angie to mention my drive-by visits but from her tone I knew that this was not a joke "fucking" or a horny "fucking"[2]. It was an "I've got a problem" fucking.

"What's up?" I asked through my mouthful of cubed soybean extract.

Angie seemed to find small lapses in manners reassuring. I think she believed it meant that I was being open and honest with her. And talking with my mouth full was easier to manage than farting on cue.

"Goddamned drivers aren't working right." Angie used her plastic fork-like object to convert her small soybean extract slices

---

2   On reflection, Angie almost never used the F-word when it came to actual sex.

into smaller soybean extract strips.

"The drivers?" I didn't like hearing that.

Drivers were a big deal. They were the air-powered screwdrivers the interns used on the lines to fasten in the different Box components: bolts, seals, plates, switches, wires, etc. Drivers were probably the buggiest important piece of equipment in the entire Plant. Management would never admit that there was any problems with the drivers so they weren't going to tell us why they kept breaking down any time soon. And since there was no official problem, then Management wasn't going to tell us how to solve it.

However.

The "fucking things" (to quote Angie) were breaking down all the time—which meant that the Lines stopped, everything got jammed up and all of us fell behind quota.

Which was both inconvenient and dangerous.

"Anybody get hurt?" I didn't want to ask that question but worker-industrial etiquette required that I ask it anyway.

Angie nodded and put some mini-cubes in her mouth. "Pat got her face bruised and her hand cut."

"Shit."

"Just a couple of stitches." Angie swallowed her cubes.

"Bummer though, she must be behind on quota."

Angie nodded. She always tried to look like she didn't care but I could tell that she was sad.

Some of us used to theorize why the drivers were such a hideous piece of dysfunctional technology. One of the smarter people on my resident block (I think he was a pre-engineering student who flunked out in second year which really must have pissed off his family) had the best hypothesis: he figured that the Lines and the Plant Life Support systems were competing for air. When we had a big run on the Lines, say we got a huge new order for Boxes, it would mean that more gas was getting pumped through more drivers for longer periods of time. It also meant that more interns were working and servicing the Lines… and all of us were inhaling more O_2 and exhaling more CO_2. It seemed logical that all this human and mechanical activity would put a strain on the Plant infrastructure. So it was like the Lines and Life Support were in a tug of war. For a few hours one system would have all the air while the other one sucked vacuum. Then things would switch around.

The ratio would never get so bad that we'd all pass out or (Forbin forbid) the Lines might stop. The truly dangerous point was when there was a sudden surge and the Lines grabbed more than their fair share of air. My neighbour figured that an extra 30% of compressed gas got blasted through the hoses that powered the drivers—and these hoses were much more likely to pop off the end of a driver. Then the hoses would whip around at a speed of what looked like 30,000 miles an hour. The intern who was holding the driver could get beat up or cut up pretty bad by a runaway hose.

A hose usually popped off a driver two, maybe three, times a week. Usually the intern was able to get out of the way before he or she got hurt.

Usually.

"Are you going to be okay?"

Another thing about Angie's complexion was that I could usually tell when she was about to cry. Not that she'd ever do that anywhere near the Lines. I could just tell that she really wanted to.

I really hated the fact that Angie was permanently stationed on the Lines. Unfortunately she had excellent visual discrimination and fine motor skills. Born to drill and drive, one of her Line Captains once said.

"Shut the fuck up, fuckwad."

These were upset "fucks" so I decided to be quiet for a while.

Angie put her other foot on mine so I would know that she wasn't angry with me.

14:20

My shift captain put me on the scrubbers for the afternoon.

Not as much fun as loaders but at least I wasn't surrounded by molten plastic for the rest of the shift. Well, not directly anyway. The scrubbers were these little wheeled remote controlled robots designed to clean out all the ventilation and feeder shafts. Dust and rust and polymer goo would collect in there and the scrubbers were supposed to roll up and down the shafts and sweep/scrape all that crap out of there.

In theory, this was light duty because the training manuals claimed that all you had to do was stand next to the opening to the shaft, look at the signal on a little TV screen and use the remote controls to steer the scrubber as it went down into the shaft.

Like many theories, this scenario failed the reality test on a fairly regular basis. Not only were the scrubbers designed to deal with crap, they also happened to *be* crap. Stupid things broke down almost as often as the drivers. In which case, your mission—and you absolutely had to accept it—was to get in there, crawl down to clean off the scrubber and fix the goddamned thing.

Since most of us interns (me included) only had the most rudimentary technical knowledge, 9.5 times out of ten, once we located the scrubber, there was no way we could repair it. This took you to the next paragraph in your job description—which was to haul the scrubber out and clean the shaft manually, i.e. on your hands and knees with a chisel, a sponge and scouring pad. This process was very uncomfortable, very messy and very time-consuming.

Some of us more TV-literate interns used to call this job "doing the Barney" after the guy in *Mission Impossible* who always seemed to be climbing up elevator shafts or crawling down air ducts. I wondered if Barney suffered as much as we did.

"*Bishop!*"

The Shift Sub-Manager was screaming down the shaft at me.

"*Whaaaat?*"

Then I started coughing. No wonder my scrubber had fritzed out, there was a mother-fucking dune of resin dust in here.

"*Matthew Bishop! Intern Number 802,701!*" Wow, this guy was actually screaming. "*Get your shit-lazy ass out here!*"

"I'm coming!"

I channelled the spirit of Plastic Man and somehow managed to turn myself around and pull my pathetic aching body out into the fluorescent light.

"Hurry up, asshole." The Shift Sub-Manager today was Rogers, actually one of the nicer (i.e. less crazy and abusive) ones. "Don't you think I have better things to do with my time than chase after low-lifes like you?"

"I don't know." I tilted my head and pulled a thin skin of plastic and grime out of my brush-cut. "I didn't see your schedule on the Logistics Clock."

Rogers looked like he would have greatly enjoyed jamming his finger into one of my eye sockets. I wasn't too worried. We interns are classified as Plant Equipment and the rules clearly state that no one, not even a Management toadie, is permitted to damage or destroy Equipment. If any gear, transistor or human organism needs to be retired, Senior Management has formal procedures for that. Nobody knew what that was but we were all sure that there was one.

Rogers fumbled for something in his jacket pocket. "Congratulations, dickhead."

"Hey, don't get too friendly, bud." I could say that because the rules also say that while Equipment can have sex with other Equipment, *Management* cannot have sex or otherwise be excessively familiar with Equipment.

Rogers slapped a palm-sized sticker on the chest of my union suit. It was a big red cross with electrons orbiting it.

"What's this?"

"You're the new Health and Safety Volunteer."

"No way, Richardson's HSV!"

Rogers shook his head. "He got promoted."

That was just crazy talk. "Nobody gets promoted around here."

The Shift Sub-Manager folded his arms. "Richardson got promoted out of here."

Usually it was not a good thing when someone was suddenly "not here" at the Plant. Remember that rumoured formal procedure?

"But…"

I knew fuck-all about safety procedures except the odd PSA we'd get on the big screens like 'Don't set fire to your hair near open buckets of gasoline'.

"But?"

"What if I don't want to be HSV?"

"You get twenty quota points for taking on the assignment." Roger shrugged, a sinister gesture if I ever saw one. "You get minus 2,000 points if you refuse."

"Minus 2,000?"

Cripes! If I lost that many points they'd have me swimming around in the polymer pools for the rest of my life. Which depending on the chemical composition of our resins, would be about three days.

I looked at Roger for a moment. His expression suggested that he wouldn't mind it if I turned down this gig.

"Well," I said finally. "Guess I'm the new Health and Safety Volunteer." My math skills were basic but equal to the challenge posed by this situation.

"Attaboy, asshole." Rogers slapped me, just a little too hard, on my left shoulder.

Then he handed me a dark plastic brick about the thickness of a large-print edition of *The Brothers Karamazov*. "This is your orientation video."

"Where am I going to watch this?" Us interns didn't have access to exotic technology like VCRs.

"Report to the Training Centre right after shift."

Fucking great. I was getting homework.

18:30

The honour of being the new Health and Safety Volunteer was already proving to be a major pisser.

First, and rather important to me, was the fact that I wasn't going to make it back to the cafeteria in time for supper. As far as food was concerned I was SOL until 06:00 tomorrow. Apparently the joy of being able to serve the Greater and More Efficient Operation of the Plant would ward off any feelings of hunger or the symptoms of low blood sugar.

Step One in conversion into the professional paradigm that would allow me to function as a successful and effective HSV.

Second, I had to forego one of the few entertainment experiences available here. I was going to miss Television Night.

Worse yet, it was actually something I wanted to see. Usually the content of Television Night were recycled *ABC Movies of the Week* with the odd segment from *Walt Disney's Wonderful World of Color* or episodes of *The Waltons* and *The FBI* thrown in. One night they actually showed a Clint Eastwood western and the excitement in the Common Area just about blew the seals off the airlocks.

The notice pinned on the cafeteria bulletin board said that tonight's feature was a made-for-TV adaptation of a Theodore Sturgeon novella *Killdozer*. I'd read that story back in the days when I had access to books; what's more, I liked it. Even if the movie was a piece of cheap low-budget shit, I really wanted to see it. I was also curious to how my fellow enrollees would react to what was essentially an industrial horror story. Angie might have some choice words.

Last, and maybe worst of all, I was going to be stuck in the Training Centre and not spending time with Angie. TV nights were always a good opportunity to sit next to each other and hold hands. That was okay if you kept to the back of the room.

Stupid training video. Not the right kind of television.

Although as I watched it, I did discover that the program had a certain entertainment value. The producers gave these workplace scare scenarios a Q & A format:

Question:

"What do you do if there is a resin spill in the plate fabrication facility?"

Answer:

"Immediately seal the processing chamber. Do not attempt to evacuate the interns. Promptly summon new interns to the auxiliary work stations to maintain output quotas. Do not forget to position and activate chamber cameras to make a full video record of all damaged and retired equipment."

Question:

"What do you do if an intern is directly exposed to seal polymers?"

Answer:

"Push the exposed intern to the floor. Remove bandages from the first aid kit and gag the intern. Administer 10 cc of Extract B using a manual syringe into the intern's stomach. Direct replacement intern to vacant work station. Promptly use loader to remove the body of the exposed intern from the production area as the presence of injured and deceased interns can adversely affect morale."

Question:

"What do you do if a pressure hose becomes detached from an assembly line air-driver?"

(Aha! So they do admit that there are problems with those fuckers!)

Answer:

"Above all, do *not* shut down the air supply for the line as this will unduly and negatively impact on all production and personal quotas. Including your own.

Instead, push the intern who is using the affected air-driver away from their work station with one hand and secure the free hose with your other hand. While holding the hose, reach under the station bench and locate the control tap. Turn the tap clockwise twice and counter-clockwise once. This will shut off the air supply for said work station *only*. Re-attach hose to driver and if the intern is not severely injured, direct her to return to work. If there are extensive lacerations, insert new intern at work station."

As you know, this last scenario was my worst nightmare:

My sweet, foul-mouthed Angie is working through her twelve hours on the Line, there's a big puff of air in the system and the hose of her driver blows off and suddenly she's sitting in the middle of a whirling rubber propeller. I could turn down the pressure in less than two seconds if they'd let me shut down the whole Line for a minute or even half a minute. But, no.

I'm supposed to make sure everybody can keep humping away at their stupid little jobs and risk letting the goddamned hose take Angie's (and my) head off.

22:01

"Turn that fucking TV off and get the fuck out of here." The guy on night shift at the Training Centre had turned off all the lights except the one in my cubicle.

"Okay, okay." I leaned on a big toggle and the desktop belched out the big plastic brick at me.

"Fuck man, hurry up!" Mr. Night Shift turned off the lights in my cubicle.

"I'd be a lot faster if I didn't have to stumble around in the dark, you moron." I couldn't see the guy's face but I was pretty sure it was wearing some version of a 'I'd like to beat the living shit out of you' expression.

The Plant was such a happy place!

I decided I would get revenge by getting out of the Centre first and taking his bicycle.

The ride "home" was just weird. An occasional roller would pass me, probably making sure that I wasn't a misdirected automatic loader or some guy high on fumes. Otherwise the tunnel was totally empty. I'd never had such a clear view of all the seals and gaskets that lined those walls. It looked like the same technology we were using to make the Boxes only on a much bigger scale.

Logical in a limited kind of way.

And with no one else in the tunnel I was getting a new sense of just what a humongous construction the whole Plant really was. I hadn't seen that much open space since I'd been escorted out of Blinn.

It was also very quiet which made it easier to think. I tried to do a few mental calculations and work out how much material they'd used to build this place. What methods did they use? Eventually I gave up.

Which was odd because I was getting really good at doing quantity calculations when I was feeding parts to the Lines or picking up packages with the loaders—but anything less concrete just eluded me. Guess I was more of a fingers and toes person than a high-level planner.

I coasted into the Intern Residence Cluster and saw that just about every light was out. The movie must be over and everyone had gone to their rooms to hit the slabs.

Crap.

That meant that the food outlet was closed. I knew this was the case but I hated the confirmation.

Hunger!

I parked the bike in the main communal rack and told my stomach to shut the fuck up. I pushed myself upstairs and opened the door to my room.

Angie was waiting in bed.

This was against the rules but as long as interns did not permanently co-habit, it was a rule that Management decided wasn't worth enforcing. Or rather it was a rule they only enforced if they wanted to get rid of you.

"Hi baby." From her vague tone of voice I could tell that she'd just fallen asleep when I'd walked in.

"Hey sweetheart."

Nice kiss. They usually were. We lay there in each other's arms, me in my coveralls, Angie in her nothing.

We didn't say anything for a while. Then I felt that I needed to say something:

"I don't suppose you brought any food with you?"

Angie shook her head. Even though it was the wrong answer, it was a beautiful process to observe.

"Gosh, I guess I could have done that."

Never mind. More nice kisses were on the way. While we were making love I forgot about the food.

2.
GREAT MOTIVATORS

03:34

I had that dream about the Jag and the Capekoids again. The one where we were having all that sex in the back seat of Space Truck with Capekoid #1 driving.

The last thing I remember were about a thousand Capekoids slowly walking towards some giant aluminum cubes out there on the moon's surface.

Then I woke up.

"Good grief, baby!" Angie was laughing. "Have you been eating oysters?"

"What?" I felt her hand touching my penis under the blanket. "I haven't eaten anything since yesterday."

"Maybe so, but you are definitely ready to go."

06:30

Finally.

Something to eat.

Reconstituted eggs and powdered milk never tasted so good. Even the deep-fried quasi-spam wasn't bad.

"So why are they making fuckwads like you Health and Safety Volunteers?"

Fuckwads? One of Angie's favourite descriptors. She was back in her public persona.

"Dunno." I sucked back on the bag of quasi-coffee. "Maybe I'm the most disposable intern on shift."

Angie didn't smile at my little joke. That meant that she was seriously considering that I really was the most disposable intern on shift. Now I was nervous.

"What have you learned so far?" she asked eventually.

I really didn't want to talk about the contents of the video. "Just that I need you to do me a favour."

"What's that, dink-head?"

"When you get to your station in the morning—" I took Angie's hand and squeezed. I knew that she wouldn't be comfortable with this kind of public display of affection but I really needed to make a point here. "—every morning…"

"What?"

"Never, *ever*, forget to check that the hose on your driver is fastened on securely."

"That's SOP, asshole."

"I mean *really* secure."

Angie's mouth twisted a little which suggested that she was going to give me another smart-ass response.

I squeezed her hand a little harder. "The only thing I want to hear is a direct answer to my next question."

Angie's eyes widened; she was used to being the tough guy in this relationship. I continued: "Now, this morning, when you sit down at your work station on the assembly line, what is the first thing you're going to do?"

Angie took a breath and I knew that she wanted to say a sentence that had the word "fuck" in it at least three times. However, I was pretty sure she could tell I had my eye-phasers set on their "Destructo" setting.

Angie sighed. "I'm going to check that the hose on my driver is securely fastened."

I held on to her hand but my grasp was much gentler.

"You total fuckwit," she said.

"Thank you, darling."

Angie was really pissed at me and maybe she had a right to be. When we were riding our bikes into the Lines, she changed lanes to be with some of her shift buddies. And not with me.

Yeah, Rudy (or was it Rod?) was there in that herd. The guy she kept mentioning was a total hunk.

That was just fine. Angie could be as mad as she liked. She could stay mad all the way to the end of her shift, which she would be able to do because she would be alive.

10:15

Time for more "coffee".

McGowan, the Alternate Assistant Shift Coordinator, came up to me.

"Hey moron, report to the Training Centre in fifteen."

I shook my head. "I was there yesterday. After-shift, even."

"You must need extra orientation." Then he swatted my groin with his clipboard, rather hard. "Because you are particularly stupid."

Ouch.

Great motivators, those Shift Coordinators.

On my way to the travelator I saw Angie heading back to her work station. She noticed that I was not going towards the warehouse and gave me her 'what the fuck is going on?' look.

I shrugged at her which is Universal Boyfriend for 'I don't know what the fuck is going on'. The big conveyor belt whisked me away.

11:00

There were about fifty of us in the big lecture theatre. I recognized half of them as Assistant and Sub-Assistant Shift Managers/Coordinators (i.e. Junior Management cretins) and the rest were material specialists and general interns like me with varying amounts of technical ability (i.e. more or less useful people).

If I was going to be completely honest with myself (rare, I know), I had to admit that all of the interns had more seniority than me—so everyone in the room was, at least on paper, more useful than I was. Which meant that I was probably attending this lecture in my new role as HSV (i.e. industrial scapegoat). I wondered if anyone in the lecture theatre noticed that the temperature in my seat was about 70 degrees higher than everyone else's.

A Senior Shift Manager walked out to the front of the hall. "Listen up, pissants!"

Like most On-Floor Management, every Monday, Wednesday and Friday this guy was John Wayne. On Tuesdays, Thursdays and Saturdays, it would be George C. Scott. He probably thought he was God on Sundays.

"We don't make a habit of wasting time sharing any Big Picture with you grunts…"

Okay, not inspiring but at least honest.

"…but all of you will soon be working with at least three completely new Lines on a daily basis, so out of necessity Management is going to share some background information with you."

Collective gasp in the room.

Partly because we were looking at a huge change in Plant processing and partly because they were actually going to be providing us with *information*.

Information and gravity were the two most controlled and valued currencies in the Plant.

"We have someone in from Central who is going to try and explain all of this to you ungrateful idiots."

Central?

I'd never seen anyone from Central. I always viewed the place as a theoretical or mythological concept like the inside of the box with Schrodinger's Cat or the ultimate value of Pi or the latitude and longitude of Santa's Village.

This session might be more interesting than usual.

The Management people in the audience clapped, but not very vigorously.

The rest of us folded our arms as a young man, about my age, walked up to the front of the hall.

Holy fuck.

When you weren't Management in situations like this, it was best not to give anything away. I had trouble doing that because I knew this guy.

The hair was a little bit thinner, his posture was a little bent and the lenses on his glasses were a lot thicker, but this was definitely the same person I shared a locker with in high school.

Ross.

He was holding a scale model of one of our Box units in both hands. I think it was a Box; there were all kinds of extra do-dads and shit on the sides.

The Shift Manager sat down and Ross put the model on a podium.

"Okay, folks."

I doubt that Ross would have recognized me. My face looked about thirty years older, my hair was cut down to stubble and I was sitting at the back of the hall. Besides, I think he was too much in love with that model to notice anything else.

"This is a very exciting time."

Maybe for you, Ross.

Probably about to become a terrifying time for me and the other interns. Ah, we serfs are so suspicious, aren't we?

"We are finally ready to move into Phase Two."

Phase Two? I hadn't even known that we were in Phase One.

"So far we have been building Boxes for use as test and training modules."

We were? Okay.

"We are now going to apply this educational technology at a level that will fulfill its ultimate potential."

Ross really was ensorcelled. He picked up the model and turned it very gently so we all could see each of its surfaces. I bet he and a lot of other propeller heads at Technical had spent a lot of hours perfecting whatever the fuck that thing was.

"This new generation of Boxes will be an essential tool in the conquest of galactic space."

Is that what we were doing here? Conquering the galaxy?

I suppose it was more interesting than making tractor parts to be shipped to southern Manitoba. I wondered if this was a noble undertaking or just a crazy one.

"The Boxes are the primary mechanism for the advanced program of Operant Conditioning—which in turn is the only way we can be certain of the high levels of competency needed to pilot spacecraft for the centuries needed to reach heretofore unknown destinations."

Operant Conditioning?

I briefly remembered my Introduction to Psychology class and fought the urge to spontaneously piss my pants.

Also *heretofore*? Ross, where did you pick up old-fashioned words like that?

"What kind of spacecraft are we talking about?"

Ross looked up from his model, probably a little surprised that anyone in the room would interrupt him.

Well, it wasn't me! No interns would dare say anything and almost nobody from On-Floor Management would either.

The question came from a guy wearing grey coveralls with a sledgehammer logo on the upper arm.

That figured.

We had a Gravity Worker in the room.

Please note the distinction, the guy was a "Worker" and not an "intern". Also, please note the capitalization. Nobody wanted anything to go wrong, *ever*, at the Gravity Division. Therefore you gave their people all the respect they wanted and you definitely did not mess with them.

Gravity pulled a lot of weight around here.

I know, ha-ha.

Gravity Division had probably heard that Central was holding a big meeting and decided to invite themselves.

The Senior Shift Manager looked like he was going to shit a brick and have a stroke—but he didn't say anything. Ross stood there, obviously thinking very hard about the next best thing to say. This gave me an opportunity to better study my old locker-mate. White short-sleeved shirt, checked polyester pants and suede hush-puppies. Pen protector and a small slide rule in the front shirt pocket. Ross had moved from the GWG jeans and Keep on Trucking t-shirt to the typical uniform for anyone in Technical—Central or not.

Poor bastard.

I looked a little harder and noticed that he had a couple of Rapidograph drafting pens nestled in the pocket protector. That made me kind of happy. Even in high school Ross loved to use good drawing pens and I was glad that he'd kept his standards up.

But he looked a little sad. Older and sad. Was that a bit of white in his thinning hair?

Jesus.

I could relate. I was pretty sure we had both been through rather a lot recently.

My old friend smiled at the Gravity Worker. "That's an excellent question."

What was this? *Friendliness?* With Gravity?

This tactic was either brilliant or insane.

"Yeah?" Gravity Guy's belly was sticking out and his hands were on his hips—like he was threatening to enter Mussolini Mode. All this courtesy-type talk seemed to confuse and annoy him.

"The design of the spacecraft is based on a shared expandable core platform." Ross put his open palms about a foot apart. "There are multi-year and multi-decade configurations for inner and outer solar system exploration." He put his hands about three feet apart. "Multi-century for extra-solar." Then he stretched his hands out as far as they could go. "Multimillenia for intergalactic."

"And all of these will be powered by *our* gravity drives…" The man in the grey coveralls was using his words more as legal claim than as a question.

Ross' arms dropped to his side. "I'm sure you know more about that than I do."

The Gravity Worker nodded.

Okay, asshole. Everybody in the room knows that you and your annoying division are still really fucking important. Now sit down.

The Gravity Worker sat down.

Ross' strategy seemed to have worked. He picked up the model and resumed his lecture: "The Conditioning Boxes are mounted along a central access and supply tower…" Ross pointed to a large black disc on one side of the model. "…this means we have to have an almost indestructible mounting that connects the Boxes to the tower." Ross tapped the disc. "Even more so because the Boxes will be directly exposed to vacuum. There will be no hull covering the nurture zones."

No hull?

I don't know if there was another collective gasp in the hall but it sure felt like it. A no-hull spec sounded completely nuts.

"What about micro-meteors and radiation exposure?"

That question actually came from one of the older material specialists. I guess under times of stress, respect for protocol starts to break down.

"That's why the Box plates are going to be 60% thicker." Ross was a trooper, he was completely calm as he opened up the model and showed us the edge of one of the sides. "The composition of the plates is also getting upgraded so they will function like a polarized plexi that's resistant to radiation and excessive light."

Sounded good.

I wondered if we could actually do it.

"What about the micro-meteors?"

Ross had the good grace to blush, just a little bit, when he answered. "We ran hundreds of thousands of simulations on Central's mainframe and we calculate that there is an absolutely minimal danger from external impact."

Everyone in the room took note of Ross' exact words:

Absolutely. Minimal danger. But not: *zero* danger.

I wondered how the discussion went in the Technical Division when they decided the time and money they would save on not enclosing the Boxes would be worth a certain percentage of blind, mutated or dead human occupants. However, being stuck on the outside of the spacecraft would probably make the bodies easy to jettison, so less bother.

"To cut to the chase, the new Operant Conditioning Boxes represent a complete redesign and re-specification of what we have been producing at the Plant to date." Ross put the model back on the podium so we could all get an unobstructed view of it. "That means new tools, new materials and new processes on every assembly line and at every stage of the manufacturing process." Ross smiled at us. "Explaining the Big Picture for all of this is beyond my pay-grade so the Sub-Director is now going to speak to you."

Ross sat next to the Shift Manager and a couple of interns from Technical wheeled in a big TV set. It reminded me of a big Box with a flickering grey face on it.

The Sub-Director never met directly with anybody below the Most Senior Management Team. Not even with Gravity people. I couldn't understand what the old fart was saying. Maybe because he was referring to things I'd never had access to or maybe because I was doing my best to suppress a panic attack. What I *did* understand was that as the Health and Safety "Volunteer" I was now partly responsible for anything that went wrong with all these new and untested gear and processes. And since it was all new and untested, some fairly serious things were bound to go wrong.

I felt the temperature in my seat rise another 350 degrees.

"We *must* meet this challenge…" The Director's voice had a distant, whisper-y quality that sounded incredibly old. Like his first big project involved constructing stone pyramids in some desert somewhere.

21:30

No Angie tonight.

Maybe she was still angry with me. More so because she knew that I was getting in on something at a level higher than she had access to. Angie was pretty sensitive about access and hierarchy. Maybe it was ego. More likely, it was survival instinct.

I wasn't too worried. She'd probably get over it, especially after I explained that none of this was my idea. So I did what I usually did on those evenings when I was alone and deprived of books, music, television or art supplies.

I masturbated. Probably that was some faint stirring of my survival instinct at work. Pointless expression of eros/expulsion of genetic material, I suppose.

Then I lay on my slab and thought about the past. Sometimes I thought about movie stars or playmates or pets of the month when I masturbated. Every once in a while my old friend Sue would come to mind. When I was in a slightly twisted state of mind, even memories of the Jag would get me off.

I never thought about Angie when I wanked.

I used to feel guilty about that.

Not the fact that I was committing all this self-abuse but that I was mentally cheating on my girlfriend. I was reasonably sure that I did love her—at least in my own special selfish and dysfunctional way; so why was she not the sole object of my desire?

"Will you fucking chill?"

At this point a reality factor (maybe a surreality factor?) would kick in, and whenever that happened the voice in my head sounded a lot like Rob.

His voice was very close, very relaxed, like my stoner friend was sitting at the end of the slab puffing away on a reefer.

"Do you remember your grade twelve biology class, Matt?" Indeed I did. My teacher was Mrs. Davidson, the owner of the best rack in the whole City of Blinn School System.

"Kid, forget those forever unobtainable boobs!" was exactly what Rob would say at a moment like that. "What did she actually say about the baseline differences between male and female sexual processes?"

What the hell was my memory of Rob talking about? I did remember a question the Boobs, I mean, Mrs. Davidson once asked us: "How many reproductive elements does the human female produce every month?"

One of the keener girls, the one who told everybody she was

going to be a nurse, raised her hand:

"One. The egg."

Mrs. Davidson nodded.

"Correct. Now does anyone know how many reproductive elements the average human male produces every month?"

Nobody raised their hand.

"Anyone?"

More dead silence.

The girls in class had decided that we boys were on our own here and us guys were just too ignorant or embarrassed to say anything. It was too much like confession to our teacher how much of our boy-juice we had released as we dreamed about sucking on her nipples.

"Do any of you young men have any idea how many sperm cells you might be generating at this very instant?"

Her tone of voice was not particularly pleasant. But then again, sperm was probably a substance that had caused Mrs. Davidson a certain amount of inconvenience.

"This is kind of important information, folks."

Still nothing.

"One sperm cell? One hundred?"

Mrs. Davidson folded her arms in disappointment. I was disappointed too because she had covered up her chest.

"Try 1500 a second."

That was more than a little startling.

"Each of you young men is producing an average of almost nine billion sperm cells a month."

Gosh. No wonder it got a little tight down there sometimes.

Mrs. Davidson put her hands on her hips. I liked this pose a lot more.

"If our ears were tuned in on the right frequency we would hear a constant doomsday roar of spermatogenesis going on."

Doomsday roar?

Okay, so Mrs. Davidson may have experienced a *lot* of DNA-related inconvenience in her life.

"So why do you figure your teacher was telling you all of this?"

It would have been just like Rob to interrupt my recalled admiration of Mrs. Davidson's waist-to-breast-to-shoulders ratio at that moment.

"I don't know. I think she was trying to tell us that we should use condoms if we had sex but the school board would have fired her if she just came out and said it."

"Very plausible." I remembered how Rob used to gaze lovingly at the glowing ends of his reefers. "But what else can we learn from that interesting genetic statistic?"

"Evolution sucks?"

"Sucks? Very scientific, Matt."

"And that nature is cruel?" That was always a good answer for any situation involving biology.

"Also plausible. But what else?"

"Isn't that enough?"

A stupid question like that would just make Rob sigh because it meant he was going to have to explain something very obvious to me.

"What it means is that you, and just about every healthy person with a penis, is producing a lot of excess sexual energy. Which I guess is another variation of what you said—evolution is a real mother-fucker."

"And love is doomed?"

"*No!*"

I'm sure Rob would have reacted that way. Essentially he was a big romantic.

"No?"

"It means that *real* love, lasting love, has to be realistic. Just because your balls send your imagination into some uncomfortable places doesn't mean you love Angie any the less."

That was a very kind thing for fantasy-Rob to say. It was also a big relief.

"And it doesn't mean that you're going to cheat on her."

Cheat on Angie? When was I going to get a chance to do that? Anyway, god bless you, Rob. Wherever you are.

But of course, those vivid memories of Mrs. Davidson's

gazongas got me all horny again and soon I was back to choking the chicken.

And once I got thoroughly into that, I was thinking about Sue. And pretty soon I was done. And now I was thinking about the Jag again.

"Do you like your father?"

We were in the back of the Jag's Datsun B210 on the way to her studio. She had her legs wrapped around my ass while a Capekoid was at the driver's seat.

It wasn't just nature that was cruel; the subconscious could be pretty nasty as well.

3.
THE BICYCLE GIFT

While I knew that being the Health and Safety Volunteer would eventually lead to me having my head handed to me, it was strangely reassuring that someone in Management was determined that I was not going to be late for their next event.

One morning there was a new bicycle chained to the handle of my room. Someone from Maintenance had even tightened and oiled the chain. Another someone from Management must have decided that I was not going to be late for any of their meetings.

When I got down to the cafeteria they handed me my breakfast chits. They were a different shade of yellow and sure enough I got slightly larger portions of everything.

I offered some to Angie:

"Fuck off, brown-noser."

Ah, my love! You are my constant star.

When I got to the Plant, the Logistics Clock sent me to work the loaders, as it had done for the last two weeks. Normally this would have been great, but whenever I went out to the Lines and waved at Angie, she just gave me the finger.

This was her angry finger and not her "I love you but I'm way too shy to be publicly affectionate" finger.

Our new situation was clearly going to take some work. At morning break I was heading over to talk to her when one of the Sub-Managers tapped me on the shoulder. "Shift Captain wants to see you."

"What for?" There was nothing problematic happening on the Lines or at the warehouses.

"Don't know, don't give a shit. Get out of here. Pronto."

10:55

"The reason we called you here today…"

When I finally found the Shift Captain, he just handed me a Xerox of a document telling me to go to the Training Centre. Twice in two days? More big changes afoot, as if I gave a rat's ass.

The trainer was an old guy. Tall, chrome-domed, grey-faced and with a very deep voice.

"…is to run you through the new Incident Report forms." This guy was obviously Senior Management material who had irritated someone higher up than he was. "With all the upgrades to the Lines and specs, the paperwork has completely changed and Health, Safety and Efficiency issues are no exception."

His punishment must have been to be forced to work with people at grunt level like me. I looked up at what they had put up on the overhead projector. It didn't look all that complicated:

DATE:	TIME:	LOCATION:
EXTENT OF INJURY:		
__ MINOR	__ MAJOR	__ FATALITY
INCIDENT DESCRIPTION:	(Enter appropriate alphabetic code)	
ESTIMATED TIME LOSS:	(Enter appropriate numeric code)	

Like I said, pretty straightforward.

The only things that puzzled me were these codes (because I didn't know them yet) and the fact that he and I were having this meeting in the Training Centre's simulator lab. It would have been easier to get together in Unlucky Baldie's office or if they wanted to be truly efficient, they could have just sent me a memo. I wasn't hard to find.

ESTIMATED PRODUCTION COST:	(Enter appropriate graphic code)	DESCRIBE NATURE OF HUMAN ERROR INVOLVED

"I imagine you've already worked out what the headings mean." At least Baldie wasn't assuming that I was a complete moron. "It's probably when we get to the code specifics that you might run into some questions."

He changed the transparency on the overhead:

GRXS	GRAVITY SPIKE
MCHA	MECHANICAL ANOMALY
ATMD	ATMOSPHERE BREAKDOWN
RESE	RESIN EXPOSURE
RESN	RESIN NON-CONTAINMENT
MISH	MISCELLANEOUS HUMAN ACTIVITY

Mish? As in what happens before mash?

Okay, these were fairly mysterious, but I could sort of halfway work out what these codes and definitions were supposed to stand for. Unfortunately 50% knowing what you are doing on the Lines was definitely going to get you killed at least 90% of the time.

"Now let's go over these codes in order of priority and

likelihood." No-hair walked over to the screen and started pointing at the block letters: "MISH" (he pronounced it 'mish' like 'missed' but with a lisp) "Stuff that people do. That's what's going to happen most often. It's like HAL 9000 said in that movie, just about every serious problem can be traced to human error."

Individual members of Management loved to attribute all fuck-ups to the organic creatures working below them because it was one less thing they could be blamed for.

"We hear you're a very creative kid so you should have lots of fun with that part of the form."

I could see it now. After ten years as Health Safety and Efficiency Officer I could compile all my reports into a best-selling book: *100,000 Different Ways to Describe Maimed and Dead People*. Or maybe a pop-song along the lines of 'Fifty Ways to Leave Your Lover'.

"MCHA." Baldie said it like he was about to spit, then he shrugged. "Very rare. Our Plant has the best technology, the best technicians and the best Management anywhere." (Interesting that he didn't mention that they had the best workers.) "So usually MCHAs (Mechanical Anomalies) can be tracked back to an underlying MISH." He turned and pointed at me. "Think six or seven times before you enter MCHA, then go back and vigorously search for the MISH."

In other words, *never* enter MCHA.

Baldie turned back to the screen and waved in the direction of ATMD. "Now I'm sure you know what that is."

Yup. Decompression. Usual cause was when an environmental seal produced by our 'superior' technology had blown.

Happens every once in a while. It's messy.

"The main challenge here will be staying alive long enough to actually complete the form." No-hair laughed at his own joke for a few seconds. "Sorry, I know it's really not funny but in situations like that you either laugh or you cry."

Or you die.

"Now the new things here are GRXS and the two RES modes."

A door opened at the back of the lab and someone wheeled in

an equipment locker. The someone was Ross.

Baldie continued: "Those codes are most closely associated with the planned Line upgrades."

Ross nodded in my direction which suggested that he recognized me this time.

Or maybe not.

Anyway, he opened the big steel cabinet and removed a large copper plate. Baldie pointed at the plate.

"As you know, Gravity generation has always been an essential part of the Plant's climate and infrastructure control systems."

Well, if I had ever thought about it, I guess I did. It would be another fucking awful reason why the Gravity Workers knew why they were so goddamned essential.

"Some of that has changed now."

Ross set the copper plate up on a tripod on the other end of the lab, then he plugged a set of coiled wires into the back the plate.

"We need to test certain Box components under high and low gravity conditions to ensure they will hold up for long periods in deep space."

Right, because the Boxes on the spacecraft would be interfacing with vacuum. Having Ross in the room must have been making me smarter.

"That means we are going to bleed off some of the energy from Gravity to run a tempering furnace at the end of at least three Lines per manufacturing zone."

What I knew about the use of Gravity was just what I had picked up since I'd arrived here—but I did know that the division generated some pretty powerful shit. Using Gravity on the Lines seemed a little like using plutonium to power your disposable lighter.

"Now we do know how this will work, right?" Baldie looked in Ross' direction when he asked this.

Ross nodded as he started flicking switches and turning knobs at the other end of the lab. The copper plate started to hum and vibrate a little.

Baldie looked at me. "This is a prototypical process and there are likely to be some minor hiccups until everyone is at optimum coordination."

Meaning that they've only got this thing 50% worked out.

"We are aware that there are likely to be some occasional fluctuations in the energy field."

"Is that what you mean by a gravity spike?"

Baldie looked rather surprised that I was actually able to open my mouth.

"Yes. And we're going to show you what can happen when a gravity spike occurs and an object is not properly shielded or fastened down."

Ross took a bolt, about the size of a large marble, out of his pocket. Then he threw it at the copper plate. For the briefest instant it looked like the bolt just hung there in mid-air. There was a high-pitched whistle and I heard something hit one of the walls. I looked in the direction of the sound and sure enough, there was a bolt-sized hole in the concrete.

"Good god, man! You're bleeding!"

No-hair was right. There was a perfectly straight cut, about three inches long, across my left cheek. And it was bleeding.

Ross' face went white, he ran over and handed me a handkerchief. "Sorry, Matt."

So he really did know who I was.

Baldie sat down. There was sweat all over his forehead.

"What do you think the chances of that were?" He laughed, a little pathetically. "Astronomical?"

Once Ross determined that I wasn't going to bleed to death, he walked back to the equipment locker. "Yeah. I told you this was a stupid demonstration."

"Sorry about that, Bishop." No-hair still looked very nervous.

"No harm done." No point in making a big fuss. It wasn't the first time someone in Management had just about gotten me killed and judging from the agenda items for these briefing sessions, it wouldn't be the last.

The old man sighed and looked at Ross. "The next demonstration will be less hazardous."

"At least for you."

Ross put on a thick pair of rubber gloves and took a covered tank of ultramarine fluid out of the locker. "This is the new active compound we are going to use in the fusing resins for the panels."

Ross set the tank on a table and removed the cover. My eyes started to water; the fluid had the sort of smell that threatened to melt your sinuses.

"The odour might take a little acclimatization," No-hair explained.

No kidding.

"The resins are based on a chemical compound that's quite complicated." Baldie looked at Ross. "Could you explain it, please?"

Ross was back at the equipment locker, unpacking more stuff. He shook his head. "No, it's too complicated."

No-hair frowned. Ross held something fat, wingless and covered with tiny feathers: it was one of those High-Density Birds.

"Well, what we can tell you," the old man said, "is that exposure to the new resin compound will lead to some fairly extreme events." He pointed at the tank. "If you don't mind?"

Ross put the HD Bird on the table and shook his head. "No. I'm not going to do it."

Baldie glared at Ross. "We have been specifically instructed by Senior Management to demonstrate the effects of the resin compound on living tissue."

Ross took off the rubber gloves and threw them on the floor. "You want to show him, you go ahead and show him." He folded his arms. "I am not going to put that bird in that tank."

It was hard to feel all that much empathy for HD Birds. When you were assigned to Nutrition they told you that they were a special breed of protein-enriched chicken. Most of us didn't believe that.

Big fat greasy rats with feathers was the most popular counter-theory.

When you worked in Nutrition Processing you saw thousands

of HD Birds bite it every day. Truthfully, you didn't really see them die; you just stuffed a dozen or so of them into a blender-vat, closed the lid, turned on the gas, waited for exactly twenty-two seconds and flipped on the meat-mulcher. I was told that you got used to the sickening growly crunch sound after a while but that was not my experience.

Watching one of them HDC's suffer, right there in front of me, was not my idea of a good time either.

"I am strictly Forms and Communications Training." Baldie's forehead was sweating again. "I am not permitted to perform technical demonstrations."

Ross took a loose feather off of the HDB. He held the feather over the tank.

"One... two... three..."

All three of us (four if you counted the bird) watched as the feather drifted down towards the tank in a series of diminishing arcs. It landed on the coloured fluid, there was tiny crackling sound and the feather disappeared.

I can't say that I was terribly surprised.

Ross dropped the HD Bird into Mr. Baldie's lap. "Enjoy your dinner." He left the lab.

Go Ross.

13:15

I was sitting on the can in the washroom next to the warehouse when I noticed the slip of paper in the pocket of my overalls. Ross must have slipped it in when he handed me the handkerchief. Something on the back of a print-up was written in pencil:

'You're going to see a lot of specs. Be skeptical.'

What the fuck was that supposed to mean?

Thanks, Ross.

4.
OOOOOOOOLLLLAAAAAW

02:47

Couldn't sleep.

I was trying very hard not to think about what I would be getting into with the new Lines and not having much success. While I was never all that supportive of Rob's regular use of wacky weed, I could have done with a few hundred pounds of it at that moment. Or a fifth of scotch or a bottle of beer, or even a series of blows to the head with a rubber mallet. Unfortunately no form of anaesthetic was available so I sat up on my slab and began another imaginary conversation with Rob.

"Pretty wild about Ross, eh?"

It wasn't fair, but the only way I could visualize Rob was him floating six feet off the floor, held up by clouds of sickly-sweet smoke and with a look of profound tranquility on his face.

Lucky bastard.

"He always did have a lot of integrity."

Rob smiled. "I thought everyone in Management was a weasel-faced asshole."

Phantom-Rob was making me a little angry.

"Ross isn't Management! He's Technical."

"There's a difference?"

"*Apparently!*"

Non-existent Rob took a long drag off his imaginary reefer. "Could be good. At least you might have a useful friend."

My old friend Ross as a tool to work the system? That idea did not make me particularly happy. Mostly because I had no idea how to do that.

04:00

At first the hammering of my Made-In-Romania alarm clock made it hard to hear the sound. It was low and constant, creeping its way up the octaves, stopping, then starting again at the bottom of the scale and working its way back up.

I kept hoping that it was just the ventilation system acting up a bit and each time the murmur-howl paused, maybe it might not start up again. That way I could get a little more sleep.

"OOOOOOOLLLLAAAAAW!"

No such luck.

"OOOOOOOLLLLAAAAAW!"

The sound reminded me of the calls the Martian war machines made in that Jeff Wayne concept album.

"*OOOOOOOLLLLAAAAAW!*"

And it was getting louder.

My brain finally suggested that the sound might be some kind of alarm. It didn't sound like the usual klaxons and synthesized tones we heard fairly often when things went wrong in Shipping or the Lines but it was kind of scary.

"OOOOOOOLLLLAAAAAW!"

Therefore probably not good.

Another pause, then a voice:

"Attention!"

The voice was weird, not quite as inhuman as the Logistics Clocks but still seriously distorted by the public address system.

"A-A-Attention!"

All those speakers were creating a weird echo effect.

Now, there was a pounding at my door and it didn't want to stop until I got up and answered.

"Bishop!" Angie stood there, sweating a bit, breathing hard.

"What?" I'm sure the perceptive nature of my response filled her with a lot of confidence.

"You're almost Management now, tell us what the fuck is going on?"

"Ummmm…"

I'm sure that recommendation was very helpful.

"Attention, all interns!"

I looked past Angie and noticed that lots of us interns were coming out of their cubicles and looking in the direction of the nearest speaker.

The Plant's version of the Voice of God continued:

"All shifts in the Plant have been suspended!" Then the voice repeated the message because it was probably sure that none of us believed it: "No shifts until completion of Line upgrades!"

Angie had calmed down some and was standing there, nodding her head with her arms folded.

"All interns will remain in the Residential Complex until further notice!"

Then the public address system went back to the low but rising howls.

Arms still folded, Angie walked into my room.

All was forgiven? Impossible. Some of it was forgiven? Maybe.

5.
Off-Shift Stories

14:20

After most of the first day of hanging around doing nothing, the loudspeakers got around to telling us that this phase of upgrading the Lines was going to take another twenty-four hours. When we all got up at 05:00 and put on our uniforms, we heard that it was going to be another twenty-four hours. After three days of this, they just stopped saying anything.

I certainly didn't object. They kept the food and beverages coming and pretty much left us Interns alone. Nobody in Management thought that they should use the down-time to provide additional training to "volunteers" like me, so there was loads of extra bed time with Angie.

Except…

"I'm kind of bored."

Which I pretty much read as Angie saying, 'I'm getting bored with having sex with you'. Which was understandable because I was barely into my twenties and as far as sex was concerned I was learning as I went.

Dating on the moon can be a real challenge.

"Let's go out somewhere."

Like I said, Angie introduced me to sex; she also introduced me to the Plant "social scene" and now she was introducing me to the pastime of lunar exploration. Interior industrial lunar exploration to be more exact.

There were a fair number of places around the Plant that nobody went into, she explained as we zipped ourselves into our denims. It could be fun to check out spots that Management might not want us to be; that is if they actually knew about them. And not that we posed any kind of danger. Even if we had evil intent, we were just interns who were too dumb to do any real damage.

"I guess this breaks that rule about staying in the Residential Quad." That's me, Mr. Timid.

"Oh, screw that!" And that was Ms. Angie.

So we went walkabout. I kept myself motivated by thinking that we might find some interesting new places to have sex. In the meantime, there was sight-seeing and conversation.

"I can see why the ratings dropped after the first season."

"It does look kinda like a cement quarry in Saskatchewan, doesn't it?"

Angie and I found ourselves trading *Space: 1999* references as we continued exploring.

"Or northern Ontario… where I grew up…"

"Ontario?" Believe it or not, this was the first time that Angie had mentioned where she was from.

"Nowheresville, next to Timmins."

"*Timmins?*" Hey, I was from the west, I wasn't sure what a Timmins was.

Angie and I were in one of the open cubes: big enclosed expanses of concrete that somebody could have used to play volleyball or basketball. That is if somebody ever had any free time in the day to play games. I occurred to me that you could use some of the smaller disc-seals to play a wicked game of Frisbee.

"How far from Timmins were you?" I was just being polite, I had absolutely no context to process Angie's answer.

Speaking of which, there were a few of those discs laying around. No big surprise, whoever built this place left their old tools and materials and crap around all over the place.

"Close," Angie replied. "Just a six hour drive."

"Practically a suburb." Sometimes the geography of our home country seemed to have interplanetary proportions.

"My dad used to harvest trees in the summer and go up to the trap lines in the winter."

"Sounds like a movie." I picked up one of the discs, stepped back a few paces and tossed the grey-black object at Angie.

"Pretty lousy movie." Angie easily caught the disc. "One of those ones made by CBC with the bad sound and washed out colours." She ran for a bit, turned and threw the disc back at me.

"*Not one of those!*" It hurt my fingers when I caught the disc. "You sure you want to remember a childhood with such bad production values?"

I kind of fluffed my return throw and Angie had to run towards me to try and make the catch.

"Why not?"

No way was she going to get that thing.

"Since we have nothing else to do, we might as well suffer."

She caught it! Not too surprising, I supposed. You had to have excellent hand-eye coordination to work on the Lines.

"Was it rough with your dad gone half the year?"

Angie threw hard. "Oof!" The disc bounced off my chest.

"Naw." Angie put her hands on her hips and watched me pick up the disc. "The house was a lot quieter when he was gone and if he had a good season out on the trap line, he could bring in good money."

I peered at Angie and aimed the disc carefully. "So it was all wonderful? Your life in Nowheresville?" She was going to suffer for that last throw.

The foolish girl nodded. "The best part were the book crates."

"The what?" I lowered the disc. I wanted to know what these book crates were before I decapitated my girlfriend.

"There was a huge book depot in Cobalt." I gave Angie a real softball toss. She caught the disc easily. "Every year the people at the depot would fill a furnace box of paperbacks and ship it up to my dad out in the bush."

"What?" This sounded just bizarre.

"To keep him entertained during the winter." Angie threw another finger-burner at me. "There's no TV up there and the shortwave reception was terrible."

I thought about what life must have been like up on the trapline. Five months of nothing but cold and black all around you. Not all that different from our current situation.

"The books kept him from going nuts."

Angie was smiling. I think that on alternate days she kind of liked her father. I, on the other hand, had no idea how I felt about my father. Even now it was hard to work up an opinion of the guy.

"So the best part, *for me*, was that he'd bring a lot of the books home with him."

"That would be good."

"Most of the trappers either sold them back to the depot or just burned them after they read them."

"They *burned* their books?"

Angie shrugged. "Sure, paperbacks make good kindling."

This sounded very practical. Disturbing and quasi-fascistic, but practical.

Something else occurred to me. It probably cost her dad a fair bit to haul those books back south. It suggested that he cared about books. And maybe even cared about his daughter and the state of her intellect.

"Nice of your dad to do that."

"Yeah."

I re-aimed the disc and threw it as hard as I could.

Angie laughed and Wonder Woman-like she knocked the disc off target and grabbed it before it hit the ground.

"Wish we had one of those book depots."

"Dad would approve." Angie made like she was going to throw the disc very hard.

"What did your mum do?" I held my hands up. I surrender!

Angie threw the disc anyway—with a lot of force. "Her job was to be drunk and crazy most of the time."

She missed me (probably because she was being nice) and the disc bounced off the concrete.

"So not a big reader."

"Not really."

6.
NOBODY GETS KNOCKED UP

01:08

Goddamn Mother Nature anyway. Always scheming to get more human DNA out into the universe.

However. Since Angie was a member of that half of the human race that had to manage the manifestation of all this genetic data within their bodies, she was likely to be a lot more cautious about any events that might be happening between my testicles and my prostate gland. What were all those sperm cells planning on doing? Did they have honourable intent? Would they clean up after themselves?

I, on the other hand, wasn't thinking about much of anything. Something big and warm was building up inside of me and how could that not be a good thing?

"You can stay inside if you want to." The first time Angie said that it took me a little time to figure what she was talking about.

Like most males in the sexual act, at the point that Angie spoke up, it had not occurred to me that I couldn't cum inside her. We had some biological dots to connect here. Truth be told, it seemed like the best idea *ever* to fill Angie's womb with as much of my genetic material as possible.

An hour later, and back on Earth, I might feel very differently. You're pregnant? How did *that* happen?!

Nature is so fucking relentless. Or rather Nature encourages us to relentlessly fuck.

Which is why there's so many of us.

Wait a minute.

Why wasn't Angie worried about all my baby makers entering her body?

"*But?*" It was hard to form sentences of more than one word given my state of mind at time.

Angie laughed a little and smiled at me.

"Nobody gets knocked up here."

"Nobody?"

"Probably something in the water."

And so the flood ensued and I ceased to exist for a moment.

Angie kissed good. Being in her arms was sweet.

07:45

We heard the rumbling of the freight rockets shaking up the landing pads and past the warehouses. Something very serious was happening on the Lines.

That was when the whole thing started to get extremely real for me.

I'd been at the Plant long enough to know that not everything that got planned always got implemented or sometimes gets done in various half-measures and half-assed measures that lets Management not change things too much.

Moon or Earth, large organizations tended to be the same. Once they started doing things in a certain way for a certain amount of time they seemed to hate and fear having to do things differently.

I heard that one time we were going to produce double Boxes because someone at Central figured that some of the big ships needed to be run by clone-twins to add a redundancy-safety factor. Easy to say, but really hard to do. Things would have to change.

So, it was, by definition, a bad idea.

So, it never happened. Not that we didn't implement a lot of bad ideas here but they happened for different reasons.

Apparently another time they said they were going to stop making Boxes altogether and dedicate all the Lines to engine components. There were accompanying rumours that they were going to build a whole new Plant down by the South Pole and they'd be making the Boxes there. That gossip really worried me because all us interns could end up working directly under Gravity and I had absolutely no faith in the ability or intelligence of those jerk-wads. We'd all be crippled or dead in two weeks.

A few days after the resin presentation, with everything more or less running the way they always ran, I had convinced myself that none of what Ross and No-hair talked about was going to happen. And maybe after a few months of not much new occurring, they might even rotate me out of this goddamned HSV position and everything would end up exactly like it used to be.

Just like minute twenty-three of every sitcom ever made.

That was me, Mr. Optimistic. Hysterical (and yet pathetic) when you considered my circumstances.

"Assholes."

"Yeah."

"You're an asshole, too."

We were still in bed but Angie was now hugging herself on the other side of the slab. The wonderful sex-glow from earlier on had pretty quickly spiralled down into a black hole of total grumpiness.

So let's get really wild and crazy and Super-Optimistic and think about how I could persuade Angie to stop being pissed off at me. Even if it was only a temporary stop-gap.

"Fucking around with us all the time."

"They fuck with me too…"

Long-term, the only way for things to improve was for me to stop being an HSV and go back to being a regular intern like everyone else.

"I don't know too much about what they are doing but I can tell you what I do know."

"Don't you dare!" She moved further away and hugged herself

tighter.

Okay, no more sex today.

"But I don't mind! Maybe you could help me." I wasn't talking bullshit here, Angie was very smart. Even when she was angry and unreasonable.

"Do you have any idea what kind of trouble we'd both be in if they found out you were leaking?" See? Smart.

"They probably wouldn't care."

"We'd be breaking a rule…"

"When did you start caring about rules?"

"We'd be breaking a *big* rule! Management cares about information security."

In case you were wondering, we were bunking at her cell, so at least I got to study the bootlegged Heart poster she'd adhered to the concrete wall.

"Well, don't say I didn't offer."

"Thanks for nothing, fuck-face." Angie's private language was about as rough as her public voice these days.

In some ways Angie was a total paradox. (Love you/hate you/good fuck you/bad fuck you.) In other ways she made perfect sense (this place is Hell and everything about it makes me mad as hell).

I mentally addressed the big-haired members of Heart: since we're looking at each other and there's been a pause in my real-world conversation, let me tell you about Day One with Angie:

"If you don't stop looking at me that way, my boyfriend is going to beat you up."

This was worrying. There were some pretty big guys here in the cafeteria.

"Who's your boyfriend?"

"You are."

I thought for a second.

"I know how to beat myself off… I'm not sure I know how to beat myself up."

Fortunately, she laughed.

"Okay, boyfriend." Then she looked me straight in the eye.

"From now on, the only time you get to beat yourself off is if I get to watch."

My day had suddenly gotten much better because I had found true love.

I know, respective members of Heart: crazy.

7.
UNCLE CREEPY

13:01

It was the middle of next week and we were still not working. There were distant thuds and thumps at the far end of the Lines Complex but not much else was happening.

Angie wasn't too pissed at me that day and we were out exploring again. She started talking about how she got to the moon:

"Took me about three months to figure out where I was." Considering that we didn't get all that many views outside, Angie's situation wasn't all that unexpected. "What really confused me was just why they had to haul us all the way up to here."

"Yeah." I wondered about that too.

"Still bugs me."

"Didn't seem to make much sense."

"Is that bubble wrap?" Angie pointed over at the far corner of the room.

It was time to shut up and play for a while. As we were both bursting our way through row after row of synthetic boils, I remembered something else that I often wondered about since I first found out that we were on the moon. What about July 20, 1969? The day when Aldrin and Armstrong stepped down on the lunar surface? I remember what I thought was the first moon landing. I was delivering newspapers that day and the six inch letters on the front page made a big impression. So did the select group of people who shut their curtains and locked their doors that day. Somehow they knew that the human race was going to be destroyed by God because we had travelled over from one planetary body to the nearest other planetary body. Apparently this was hubris. Pride.

Which apparently is a really big sin.

On reflection maybe those fearful people had a point. Hubris can be a pretty terrible thing. Witness a number of stupid wars, dictators and why P.A. and the Plant even existed.

Then as the tiny plastic spheres continued to explode (in the cutest way possible) between our fingers, something else occurred to me that bothered me about the whole being on the moon thing. Was Management up here before or after Apollo Eleven?

We ran out of bubble wrap before I could share this question with Angie. Satisfied and exhausted by something other than sex, we leaned back and laughed. Then we went back to my place.

19:35

"That fucker."

Angie was spooning up against me but she did not look at all happy when she said that.

"Who?" I was suddenly worried about what I must have done wrong.

"Not you."

"Oh, okay." I was embarrassingly relieved.

"My goddamned uncle."

"Your uncle?"

"Something made me think of him."

I wondered if Angie had decided to tell me more of the story of growing up just a six hour drive from Timmins. Frankly she could take as long as she needed to, I had a feeling that most of the tale was pretty bad.

Yeah, I know. Admitting that makes me sound like an insensitive asshole. I am an insensitive asshole. However, I like to think that I am not a *completely* insensitive asshole. Maybe only a 2.5 on the A.H.-Richter Scale. It wasn't that I didn't care, it was just that once I knew the full extent of the hurt I didn't know if there would be any way that I could actually help.

So, I knew that I loved her. Yes, I even cared (in my unique and inept way).

And no, I doubted that Angie would ever believe that I loved or cared about her. Or that anyone would ever really love or care about her. If I ever managed to convince Angie that I did love her, that would simply be evidence that I was stupid, insane, and possibly dangerous.

Yeah. Definitely dangerous.

Also, it would mean that Angie would have to trust me; and beyond printed job descriptions, Angie didn't trust anyone. I was pretty sure that her uncle was a big part of the reason why.

Angie went to sleep before she could tell me anything more.

Angie, paradox of my heart.

23:50

I woke up and there was blood all over the blanket.

"Wha—?"

Okay, I admit it. I was surprised and I really shouldn't have been. I was sleeping with an adult female. Although it seemed at the time to be way too much blood for any normal human process.

The first thing I did was check to see if Angie had somehow been decapitated during the night or perhaps someone had snuck into the room and cut one of my legs off.

Nope. No evidence of recent chainsaw use.

"What the fuck?" That was Angie talking this time. At least she was laughing when she said it. "What gives?"

"I don't know." Well, at the time I didn't.

"Looks like it's my period."

"Uhhhh…"

Angie pushed me off the slab and stood up. "You know about

periods, right?" She pulled the half-scarlet sheets off the metal frame. "And where babies come from?"

I guess I really looked very stupid at that moment. "I heard some rumours back on Earth."

On that planet, I had lived with my mother and my sister, both of them apparently women. Over the years I would occasionally encounter bits of menstrual technology lying around the bathroom: pads, boxes, strips of tape, plastic applicators that looked like tiny ballistic missiles. I knew that something was going on but it never got talked about. I figured that it might not exactly be a secret but at least something a bit more subtle. More of a need-to-know thing.

"Are you squeamish?" Angie was soaking the only towel I had in the sink. "Are you going to freak out on me?"

"No."

"You sure? You grossed out?"

I shrugged. "I'm just glad nobody bled to death."

Fortunately Angie laughed again.

"That one was pretty intense." She started wiping herself down with the towel. "Whatever they're feeding us stops our cycles for months and months…"

Probably why the Plant wasn't wall-to-wall with babies, I thought.

"…but when you start flowing, you really flow." Angie started to dry herself with an unstained section of the sheet.

"Do you think that's healthy?" I remembered a radio interview Eugene did with a woman doctor talking about possible health risks of the birth control pill.

"Probably not." Angie threw the damp towel at me. "Sweet fuck all we can do about it, right?"

I used the towel to wipe her blood off my skin as I watched Angie strap herself into her underwear and climb into her coveralls.

"When I first got here, before I knew anything, what they were doing with the additives…" Angie took my toothbrush and started cleaning her teeth. "…I was scared to death."

"Why? I mean, what in particular scared you?" When I first arrived on the moon I was afraid of a lot of things. I still was.

Angie stopped brushing. She spat a huge wad of white goo into the sink basin. "I was incredibly late."

"Late?" I was so dumb.

"Late. I was sure that my asshole uncle had knocked me up."

I sat on the bed and I got to hear the rest of the story.

"Uncle Ted was the Great White Hope of the family."

"He was a boxer?"

"Funny." Angie had come back to the bed and put her arms around me. "No, he had some brains, he'd been to college and he moved down to the Big Smoke."

"Toronto?" I was still naked, cold and still a bit damp. The denim of her coveralls wasn't very comfortable against my skin but I liked the feeling anyway.

"Right, that's where Uncle Ted hooked up with Progressive Apparatus."

Those bozos. "Doing what?"

"Don't know. Nothing very complicated, I figure."

"How do you figure that?" I really should have stopped asking questions. That way Angie would be finished the story sooner and then I could get dressed. Or she could get undressed. Either way was good.

"He was smart, but not that smart. I think he just helped ship electronics out from southern Ontario."

"Do you figure he knew about the Plant? About the moon?"

"Probably not at first."

"But later?"

Angie nodded. "I first met him when I was thirteen."

I remembered when my sister was thirteen; it was a very bad age. She was falling in love all over the place. When the process inevitably embarrassed her, she would yell at me.

"He was like something out of a James Bond movie."

"Suave, was he?"

"Styled hair, and sideburns, tinted aviators, suede safari jacket, black leather boots with zippers on the sides."

"Oh, the Man Who Reads *Playboy*." In other words, a dick.

"He drove around in this weird futuristic sports car. Bright orange."

"He drove a Brickland?" Those were the only futuristic orange cars I knew about.

"Yeah, I think so. He was very proud of it."

"They must have been paying him pretty well at P.A."

"It was incredible. I didn't even know my mother had a brother and then one afternoon this orange version of Thunderbird 2 rolls up in front of the house and suddenly a Roger Moore-in-training is in my life."

"Were your parents happy to see him?"

"My mother was, at least in the sense that she got to be proud of him."

"Proud? He sounds like a dork."

"Successful member of the family."

"And your dad?"

"Not so impressed."

"Jealous maybe?"

Angie shook her head. "That's what Mother said, but no."

"Maybe your dad was a good judge of character."

Angie nodded.

"So, Uncle Ted drives up to the house…" I had to move this along, I was starting to freeze.

"He and my folks sit down, have some coffee and beers and gab for a while. He and I get introduced and pretty soon he jumps back in the Unclemobile and jets back to Toronto."

"That's it?"

"A week later and he's back for another visit."

"And the week after that?"

"Another visit." Angie sighed. "And just about every week after that."

"Why do you figure he kept coming around?" I think I knew why he was dropping by all the time but I also figured Angie felt she should tell me.

"He said he wanted to reconnect with my sister, help us move south where she and Dad could get better jobs."

"Did you believe him?"

"My mother did. The idea of moving to a big city made her crazier than usual, she nearly drove Dad off the deep end too."

"But did you believe him?"

"Dad didn't." For some reason, Angie didn't answer my question. "I think he knew Uncle Ted was coming around to check me out."

"But did you believe your Uncle Ted?" I probably should have just shut up here.

"I wanted to." Angie let out a ragged breath. "He was the most interesting person I knew and he represented a future that didn't involve drinking myself to death in a shack in some frozen subarctic wasteland."

That made sense, but nosy big-mouth me just couldn't leave it at that: "So, were you like… *attracted* to him?"

"No, but—"

"But?" I naively believed back then that attraction was a yes-no binary thing.

"*But.*" From the way Angie spoke that conjunction I should have known that the upcoming statement joined to the previous one was likely not going to be very pleasant.

I continued with my line of questioning: "So that was it? He was just super-fascinating? You loved his flared pants?"

"They were wicked huge flares. At least eighteen inches."

"Jeez. So at least five years out of style."

"And somehow the denim had purple stripes."

"Osmond-worthy. I completely understand the appeal." (Smart-ass!)

"Even so, the George W. Groovy Jeans weren't enough." Angie shook her head a little. "Truth be told, and back then I didn't always tell myself the truth, Uncle Ted was pretty goddamned creepy."

"No shit."

"But he kept coming around."

"So, you couldn't get away?"

Angie rolled her eyes. "Of course I could get away."

This was making my head hurt a little. "You could?"

"We're talking northern Ontario here. I just had to step out the door and five minutes later, I'd be so gone you wouldn't see me for another six months."

"Okay, I'm confused now." And maybe a little pissed off. "If Uncle Turd is the supreme creep, why didn't you just take off whenever the dickmobile rolled around?"

Heavy sigh. Sounded a lot like a large but slow air leak in one of the corridor seals. "Uncle Ted figured out my kryptonite."

"I didn't know you had super-powers."

More eye-rolling. "He knew my weakness."

"Which was?" Ultra-Tough Angie had a weakness? I had to know!

"Music."

Oh, Angie really liked music. I knew that already. Idiot. "Right."

"At first he tried books but that didn't go over very well."

"No?" That kind of surprised me.

"We already had lots of books and the idea of somebody else giving me books really honked off my dad. Books were something special between me and my dad."

I was briefly envious. There never was much special between me and my dad. Even if he knew that I'd left the planet, I doubt that this information would have made much of an impression.

"So the next thing Uncle Ted shows up with are some LPs."

"Long-playing records?"

"Lots of them."

"Stuff like Heart?" I remembered the poster in her cell.

"Yeah. And T-Rex, ELO, Klaatu, Queen, Rush, Neil Diamond, Frampton, Floyd, the Moodies…"

"And you liked that stuff?" This was all too stadium rock for me, but I bet you it was totally cutting edge six hours from Timmins.

"Yeah." Angie narrowed her eyes. "And don't be so condescending."

"Sorry." Guess what? I was still an asshole.

"Getting exposed to all those albums helped me forget how slimy Uncle Ted was."

"There was no alternative source of good music?"

"We didn't even get CBC AM on a reliable basis."

"Shitty and regrettable." Something occurred to me. "So how come your folks let him give you all that expensive vinyl?"

"He said he had a friend who was a buyer for Sam the Record Man so he got all this stuff for almost nothing."

"And that kept your parents quiet?"

"My mother didn't seem to care, and the fact that there was a bargain involved seemed to keep my dad from punching his lights out."

"So he kept giving you records." I stupidly wondered why if her dad was around, how did anything get weird with Uncle Creepy?

"Eventually Uncle Ted offered to take me to a Supertramp concert."

"They toured northern Ontario?"

"Dumbass! They were playing at the CNE."

"CNE?"

"The Canadian National Exhibition—it's a big fair in Toronto. They give big concerts at the stadium."

"Why did your parents agree to let him take you there?"

"They didn't really have a choice." Angie's expression got more complicated as she continued remembering stuff. "Once Uncle Ted said he had the tickets, I was pretty much an unstoppable force of nature."

"So were they a good band live?" Stupid question, given the context, but I was a former DJ and was still interested in such things.

Angie frowned. "It's a little hard for me to separate the experience of the actual concert from what happened afterwards."

"I think I can understand that."

Then she smiled a little. "Even so... it was probably the best period in the lifespan of the band. They were outstanding musicians and maybe they weren't distracted by their success yet."

"Which is why they were playing places like the CNE?"

"Exactly."

"So, from what you recall, you enjoyed the concert?"

There was a bit of a pause. Then Angie spoke very evenly: "From an abstract, totally intellectual, perspective, I can assure you that the concert was *absolutely fucking fantastic*."

"And the rest of the evening?"

No hesitation at all: "Was fucking horrific."

I immediately regretted asking my last question. Angie continued: "It was dark by the time the show was over. I don't remember what time and I'm not even sure how we got out of the stadium and into that car." Angie might have been a little hazy on some of details but it was pretty obvious that she re-lived that night at least five or six billion times. "We were driving up the 427 when he turned down an exit ramp, then drove down a side street and found a spot that didn't have too many streetlights. He seemed to know exactly where to go."

"If it's too hard to talk about…" I was more worried that it would be too hard for me to hear about.

Angie looked thoughtful for a moment. For a second it seemed like she might, indeed, change the subject. Then: "Maybe you should know about this."

I wasn't sure I agreed.

"Somebody else should know about this."

Okay, I couldn't really argue with that. "So tell me."

"It's pretty simple, really. Uncle Ted reached over, grabbed me by the hair and pulled me into the back seat of that stupid car and raped me."

Oh god.

"He raped me in ways that I didn't know were even possible."

God.

"There was some blood."

Fucking hell.

"Afterwards, Uncle Ted slapped me around because I'd messed up the upholstery of his fancy car."

Fucking horrific. Just like Angie said it was.

We sat there for a while. Eventually, Angie said something: "Are you okay, baby?"

She was asking if *I* was okay?

"Yeah."

"You sure?"

"Sure."

I remember something one of my profs said in psychology class about 'emotional intelligence'.

"Okay."

Angie had a lot more EI than I did.

Then she kissed me. My eyes really were tearing up.

Angie smiled but it was a very hard smile. "But that bastard didn't break me."

8.
SHOEBOX

Angie had a slightly sad look.

Since the story of Uncle Creepy, I knew what the problem was. She wanted to be back in the stadium feeling the bass pounding the rhythm through her heart.

The Plant was not the best place for a Rock and Roll Girl. Never mind. It took a week or so but I had a solution.

"Got something for you."

Angie propped herself on her elbows and looked at me. "What?"

I reached under the slab and presented her with the shoebox. Then I handed her a baggie full of AA batteries. She looked a little dubious.

The shoebox contained something that looked like the tricorders that Spock and McCoy used in *Star Trek*. It wasn't a tricorder but it was close. It was a late 1960s era Sony cassette player/recorder—the kind that you would load up with blank tapes and record top ten tunes off AM radio or your favourite TV theme songs off the speakers of your dad's Zenith console set.

That music was important, as was the technology needed to capture it.

Angie gasped. "Where did you get this?" No lie! I managed to impress Angie so much that she actually gasped!

"Asked around." Really, I had no idea how the player managed to migrate its way from some Radio Shack in a strip mall to the moon. Maybe it got accidentally shipped as mis-labelled equipment or maybe it belonged to some unlucky Management or tech worker who owned it and then bought the space farm in one of our industrial accidents.

Maybe it was brought here for a legitimate purpose. Like maybe Management wanted to have audio records of their many (no doubt) fascinating meetings instead of just written minutes.

Anyway.

What I did know was that someone, at some level, lifted the thing from somewhere at some point. Then somebody I knew on the Lines knew that I was looking for something to make my sweetie happy.

It took some creative threatening, bartering with the little spare resources at my disposal and the making of some promises I truly hoped I wouldn't have to keep.

"It's so cool!" Angie pressed the toggles on the recorder as though it was a Fisher Price toy. "But what the fuck am I going to do with it?"

I pulled out another shoebox.

Angie smiled. "You've been busy." She opened the box and then she really smiled. Hell, she grinned. "Is this what I think it is?"

I think it was. And I was never going to tell her how many extra shifts I owed to get it.

The shoebox was filled with cassettes. Rock and roll mix tapes. Lots of rock and roll. Some fan back on Earth had carefully printed out the names of the songs and the bands from Abba to ZZ Top. A music pirate's treasure chest.

No Tangerine Dream or Yes though. Two tracks from those bands could eat up half a dozen tapes.

Yeah, yeah. Apologies to the record companies but this was the only music delivery system in town.

"Happy birthday?"

"No." Angie kissed me. "But close enough."

9.
Same Old

We lay there on the sheetless bed, holding onto each other. Angie was still in her coveralls and I had climbed into mine so that I didn't freeze my ass off.

It felt good but there seemed to be more hurt to explore.

The rest of Angie's story had some similarities to mine. The Monster Uncle took her to his apartment, probably because he needed to sleep and probably because he wanted to rape her some more once he could get it back up again. And probably, and most importantly, because he didn't want Angie talking to anybody.

Frankenuncle did clock out again and when he woke up he caught Angie trying to use his phone to call her dad. So he slapped her around really hard and realized that he could be in serious trouble here. Then he pulled a hypodermic needle out from somewhere and jammed it into the side of her neck and mostly likely made a phone call of his own. Given where Angie ended up, Uncle Ted must have called up one of his friends in the Progressive Apparatus organization.

I could imagine the ad in the back of an old copy of *Tales to Astonish*: 'Does your existence compromise someone who is much better connected than you? *Congratulations!* You have just won a free one-way ticket to the moon!'

Just like Angie and me and most of the interns here.

I could imagine the illustration would render all of us in the same style as those inserts for 'Grow Your Own Sea Monkeys'.

"OOOOOOOLLLLAAAAAW!"

No…

"OOOOOOOLLLLAAAAAW!"

Say it isn't so.

"Attention Interns!"

It was those damned loudspeakers.

"Report for first shift! Report by 06:00."

The Lines were running again.

"We have to get up."

I couldn't believe it. We'd had less than two hours of sleep, we hadn't worked for over a month and Angie was wide awake and ready to start her shift.

At least we were dressed for it.

"But…" Amazing how I could fit that much whining into just one word.

"Really Matt, we gotta go." I didn't like the message, but I loved the medium of her whispered voice in my ear very much. I rolled out of bed even though it felt like my legs weighed about 5,000 pounds each. I had a feeling that Uncle Ted was going to be eating away at my brain for quite a long time.

"Right, right…" I stood up and looked over at Angie. Sometimes, even in the denim coveralls, she kind of glowed. Not in that deadly plutonium contamination kind of glowing, it was more like one of those mysterious organic, I think I will love you forever sort of ways. Why I would love her forever was something I wasn't quite sure of. The fact that I did love her forever was, as my philosophy professor once said, an Absolute Truth.

Angie also rolled out of bed. "What would your shift be?"

"Ducts, I figure."

"You figure?" Angie often found that kind of ambiguity both irritating and dangerous.

"If I remember the averages on the L-Clock right." I laughed. "I just don't like to think about the fact that at the end of the day I will be covered in a thick layer of green slime."

"Okay." Angie looked less intense.

"What's yours?"

"Back on the Lines, same as always."

"Which ones?"

"Two in the morning. Seven in the afternoon. That is if they've carried over the old numbering system." Angie could just about always anticipate what shifts the Logistics Clock was going to give her.

"Using the old drivers? Or do you figure they've upgraded them?" Now it was my turn to sound intense.

"What do think they'd invest in?"

Now it felt like each of my legs weighed 50,000 pounds.

"You be careful."

"I know my way around those Lines." Angie thought for a second and shrugged. "Well, I used to."

Fuck.

14:00

"*May I have your attention, please!*"

I was wrong, I was not crawling around inside industrial duct-works. I was somewhere much worse.

A meeting.

A tall guy with a brush cut belted out the request that was not a request. He was standing at the podium, wearing a Management shirt and pants, but he was twice as high and three times as thick as the average lunar bean counter.

Management needed their enforcers, I guess.

We all shut up, except for a couple of Gravity guys at the back of the room, who kept on yapping.

"*Quiet!*"

The Gravity Contingent went silent.

Finally. Someone in Management who was halfway effective.

"As most of you know, all the test runs on the new Lines have hit 82.7% efficiency and P.A.H.Q. and Senior Management agree that's high enough for us to restore the whole Plant to full operations."

Well, I didn't know we'd reached 82.7% efficiency. I wasn't even sure what 82.7% efficiency meant. But why would anyone explain anything to a meat motor in blue overalls like me? In fact, I wondered why I was in the room at all.

"Projections show that any rate under 90% is likely to result in a higher than usual number of intern incidents."

Incidents? More like injuries and fatalities. So the only reason I was here was because it was going to be necessary to blame someone like me for what was going to happen.

"You people with responsibilities in human resources and redeployment are likely to be pretty busy for the next ten or twelve cycles."

Oh, good. More pain. And at higher speeds.

Progress.

I looked around to see if Ross was around. A supportive glance might be helpful about now.

"Make sure you leave here with additional Incident Report Forms."

But was any kind of support even possible?

I did spot Ross at the far end of the third row, stuck in between a really thin guy and someone with a face like a rat.

"You are definitely going to need the extra paperwork."

Was this the information that Ross had warned me not to believe? Probably not; what brush-cut was telling me sounded more like a (pretty accurate) prediction than any sort of speculation.

"We're running the first two days at half-speed but bottom line is that as of 06:00 day after tomorrow, this Plant will be back up and running." Brush-cut folded his massive arms. "And Headquarters expects us to be chugging out at 110%!"

110%? There's no such thing. And what does 'chugging out' even mean?

Fuckwits.

I was enslaved by total fuckwits. I looked around and hoped my expression wasn't broadcasting my thoughts.

"For the technical portion of today's session, we have someone from Earth-side here." Brush Cut backed away from the podium and someone wearing a zippered flight suit bounded across the stage. Very dramatic.

And speaking of fuckwits…

Ed? Holy shit.

The big guy who was gripping the edges of the podium with strong manly fingers and baring his giant teeth in a truly terrifying smile was indeed Ed. My sort-of stepfather.

A bit greyer and puffier around the edges but definitely the same guy who punched me in the face on my mother's wedding day.

"We're at a milestone in the Project." Big booming, masculine voice. Coupled with his height and steely grey eyes, I supposed that it was only a matter of time before Ed moved up the ladder at Progressive Apparatus. "And I'm sure it will surprise none of you that P.A.H.Q. is expecting even more from this outfit in the coming months."

So what should I have done at that moment? Bellow out a crazed vengeance-cry? Leap up onto the stage and beat the living shit out of Ed?

Not likely. The guy was even more fucking ginormous than I remembered him. Still, even under lunar gravity, working at the Plant had made me a lot stronger and meaner than I was on Earth. I might at least be able to inflict some damage.

Which would be satisfying.

Ed had no idea that he was in any danger at all: "So let's move on to what you need to know today."

No. I decided that the best thing to do was sink back into my chair and hope that Ed didn't notice me. Working on the Lines had not just made me stronger, it had also bulked up my survival instincts.

A big circuit diagram flopped onto the overhead screen behind Ed while a couple of junior techs rolled out a prototype of Box Version Two.

"You've been testing out the superstructure of these units for a few weeks now and based on the quality control reports we've been receiving, you've managed to work out the basic integration issues."

Another, even more complex, schematic appeared behind Ed as he kept on talking.

"We figure you're as ready to go as you'll ever be."

By now, there was a huge pounding inside my head and my eyes were having trouble focusing. Either I was having a stroke or I was extremely upset.

Possibly both.

Extremely upset?

Biggest goddamned understatement of all time!

Life on the moon was hard. Crazy brutal even. But it had self-contained logic; if you kept to the rules and didn't do anything extremely stupid you had a (to use Management's way of thinking) 65%-75% chance of finishing your shift alive. And I had lucked out! I had someone I actually cared about here. That was more than I had back on Earth. If this was what the rest of my life was going to be, then somehow I could cope with that.

But Ed…

His presence on the moon posed a major existential problem. It meant that my old life in Blinn had not been an elaborate and occasionally embarrassing hallucination. My family, my friends, the university, the radio station and my collection of *Famous Monsters of Filmland* were still back down there on Earth.

And if Ed could get up here to the Plant to give us these pointless pep-talks, then he was obviously going to get back home. That meant that, somehow, however astronomically remote, there was a chance that I could get back too.

Seeing Ross here at the Plant didn't bother me in the same way because:

1. I liked Ross.
2. I loathed Ed.
3. Also, Ross being a genuine genius gear-head, it made sense for him to be here.

4. Also, also, Ross was like me. He was more useful, he probably had more privileges than I did, but, like me, he was most likely stuck here for the duration.

"This is going to be the most important thing you're ever going to do…"

I didn't exactly faint but I sure as hell didn't catch much of what Ed was saying about the inner workings of the new Boxes.

"…these units are going to finally allow us to take that last great leap forward…"

So much for those specs Ross wanted me to pay attention to. I did manage to pick up one salient fact and just because it sounded incredibly gross and scary:

"…essentially there are two modalities for the units: a low-level nutrition and subsistence mode and an advanced wetware interface mode."

It didn't sound like it would be much fun to be in one of those Boxes, new or otherwise.

"The second level of operation requires a lot more power which is why the craft superstructure has a lot more buffering than you would expect at the basic level."

As Ed said the words "wetware interface", a scientific illustration of a human brain, covered with electrodes, appeared on the screen.

"It may seem counter-intuitive…"

Would it?

"…but the investment in the extra power and materials is definitely worth it…"

Well for sure, the Plant and whoever was running Progressive Apparatus always did everything as cheaply as possible. Spending more on anything definitely would not come naturally to them.

"Good and cheap."

The first time I heard someone sneer that at me was when one of the Dean-Drive Jockeys was strapping me to the capsule wall before liftoff. Miraculous anti-gravity propulsion or not, every piece of that prison-barge must have been built by the least expensive contractor.

"…but the enhanced computational capacity we get from the organic-electronic link are truly tremendous…"

Organic-electronic link? P.A. had really figured out how to use people's brains as computers? Frankly, I doubted that the cretins who designed the Lines had enough of their own cranial power to do something like that. Maybe they had enough money to hire somebody else to figure it out for them though.

Either way, I really hated the idea that P.A. could now stick wires in your head and make you crunch numbers for them. Ad infinitum. I sincerely hoped these were the specs that Ross suggested might not work.

The disturbing brain picture disappeared and Ed was now standing in front of a huge wall of static.

"That's enough of the preliminaries."

What? There was more?

"Let's get on to the big show."

I looked around and noticed that the guys in the Gravity jackets had their arms folded and were all looking pretty smug. Then it looked like Ed was turning a dial at the podium. A more complex pattern of static fuzzed onto the screen.

"We've got a live feed from one of our satellite cameras…"

Ed kept twisting that dial and we kept seeing different varieties of static. It was starting to feel pointless and I had to stop myself from giggling. I guess I had a bad attitude.

But then regrettably…

The video-projected image was pretty washed out but it was impressive anyway.

It was a shot from space. I figured that it was probably somewhere in lunar orbit. We had a reasonably clear view of three gigantic clusters of what looked like steel girders connecting turbines and drums composed of thousands of tiny glass cubes. I recognized the cubes. I think all of us did.

The giant spacecraft was lined with Boxes.

It was an amazing construct and I am probably not doing justice to the engineering and design involved. Let's just say it looked like someone had given Derek Meddings a shitload of money and gear to make an SFX model that was so incredible that it would have saved Gerry and Sylvia Anderson's marriage.

Holy shit, as they say.

10.
WALKING TOUR

Rules of the Game
Boycotts

1. At any point in the game, the High Roller may initiate a boycott against any one of the other players.
2. A High Roller Boycott starts when the High Roller pays a containment bonus to the other two players to withhold trade from the player who is the target of the High Roller Boycott.
3. The Boycott may continue for as many turns as the High Roller wishes to pay the cooperating players.
4. Alternatively, the Boycott can end when the targeted player has been eliminated from the game or when the High Roller and the targeted player enter a Condition of Truce or a Condition of Conflict. (See section on War)

Ross and I had gone up seven flights of stairs with no sign of stopping.

"So how did you end up here?" I thought some conversation might take my mind off the pain in my feet.

"In Central? In Technical?" Ross turned and looked at me as if I was some kind of an idiot. "I'm talented."

"No, how the fuck did you end up on the moon?"

"How did *you* end up on the moon?" Ross wasn't even winded.

How could a nerd like him be in such great shape?

"I asked first."

We were on the ninth floor and I was really wishing I was back in bed with Angie.

"Okay." Ross looked at me again. "Unlike you, I wanted to be here."

"You volunteered?"

"Came on my own free will."

"How did you manage that?"

We started walking again and reached Floor #10. Actually the walk was getting easier; we were probably at the edge of the building's gravitational field.

Floor #11. Two hours ago, there was a knock on my door and there was Ross, although he didn't exactly say so, what he said sounded like there was some kind of emergency meeting over at Technical.

"To be completely accurate, I wasn't sure what exactly I was joining up for."

Floor #12. I don't think Ross planned on lying to me but he probably got a glimpse of Angie and decided that he'd better sound official.

Floor #14.

Okay, even Technical people could be superstitious.

"I didn't know about the Lines and the interns."

"Glad to hear that you weren't gung-ho about helping to run a lunar forced labour camp."

"I was finishing my accelerated doctorate at M.I.T." Ross was too polite to add 'while you were pissing away your life getting your undergrad degree in Nothing In Particular at B.U.'

"Impressive."

Floor #15.

We were at normal moon weight now. It felt a little like being drunk. Maybe tipsy was a better description.

"Some recruiters from Progressive Apparatus approached me and asked if I wanted to work in the field of Gravity Mechanics."

"So that's what they call it."

Floor #16. My toes were feeling a lot better and we were moving a lot faster.

"I had no idea what they were talking about."

"No?"

Floor #17.

"I told them they must have me mixed up with some astrophysics student."

Floor #18.

"What did they say to that?"

I could see Ross' shoulders lift a little as he shrugged. "They explained to me that I was completely wrong and that it was all very hard core brass-tacks engineering work and that I was going to love it."

"And?"

We stopped at Floor #19.

Ross looked at me and smiled. "They were right, at least partly. I really got into the work. P.A. is doing some really incredible stuff."

"So next thing you knew, you were living in Selenite City helping them make Boxes."

Ross nodded his head a little and opened the door.

Rules of the Game
War

1. War occurs when the two Players In Conflict declare this Condition and roll the die in sequence. First one die, then the next.

2. Seven times the value of the first die is the profit gained for the aggressive or defensive manoeuvre. This number is added to the value markers held by the player.

3. Five times the value of the second die is the cost of making war and this number is deducted from the value markers held by the player.

We walked down a short corridor which took us to another

door. Ross opened that one too.

"So were you, like, surprised when you found yourself living off planet?"

Ross looked thoughtful. "For the first few months at P.A. I was working with specs and drawings of things that could only work if you…"

"Had some kind of anti-gravity?"

"If you could *control* gravity."

"Which they needed to build this place."

"Exactly."

"Holy Cavorite, Batman!"

Ross laughed. Not a gut-busting guffaw or anything but definitely a laugh.

We walked into a room. It was a big room, maybe about the size of the gym at Blinn Collegiate Institute. Ross smiled and put his hand on my shoulder. This kind of surprised me because while Ross always seemed like a good guy, he never came across as particularly touchy-feely.

"So arriving here was probably less of a surprise for me than it was for you."

"No lies, man."

There were two young men sitting in folding chairs in front of a card table. Like Ross, they wore white shirts and ugly checkered pants.

"Larry! Melling!" Ross called out. "This is Matt!"

Rules of the Game
War (continued)

4. The High Roller may initiate hostilities at any time and any point in the game without ensuing any cost.

5. Other players can initiate hostilities only when it is their turn and they must pay 15% of their total value markers as "Armament Costs".

6. Players may cooperate with each other when attacking the High Roller. However, they have to reduce their

overall marker value as a "collaboration tax" and all alliances can only last three rounds of the game table; as such collaborations are inherently unstable.

7. At any time the High Roller can approach a member of an opposing war alliance and "buy them out" of their relationship with the other players. The cost of this arrangement is to be negotiated between the High Roller and the player in question.

The card table was covered with about a dozen sheets of computer print-out paper, all fastened together with clear tape to make a large but flimsy table cloth. At first it looked like a typewriter had barfed out a couple of billion ones and zeros all over the table.

Then I looked a little closer and realized that the numbers made up a huge map of the world; well, *a world* anyway. What was even weirder was how there were different columns where the oceans were supposed to be and there were paper panels with closer views of specific countries pasted onto some of the sheets.

This game was definitely more complicated than Go Fish.

"Sit down."

The guy I later learned was Larry pointed at an empty chair. He had glasses with thick round lenses and a face that reminded me of a sheepdog. That is if sheepdogs shaved, cut themselves with the razor and still had bits of Kleenex stuck to the points of injury.

Ross and I sat down.

Melling (the other guy) peered at me and frowned.

"You sure he's up for this?"

Melling was short, had small sharp features, almost no chin and wore his long, thin, blond hair in a ponytail. He reminded me of a forgotten member of the Partridge Family whose career had somehow gone horribly wrong. No, not the Partridge Family, the Rodent Family. I could tell that he didn't like me and it didn't look like I was very fond of him.

Since I had no idea what I was up for and whether I was up for it or not, I didn't say anything.

"Matt can handle it." Ross took some bolts from an envelope that was sitting on the table. "Really."

Melling studied me again, which made him look even more rat-like. "He's an intern. They have dog-shit for brains."

With that kind of charm, I figured Melling had definitely had the interpersonal skills potential to move from Technical into Management.

I started to get up. Time to fuck off out of there.

"I went to school with Matt." Ross put his hand on my arm. "He has hidden depths."

I sat back down.

"He better." Melling looked down at the table. He probably didn't want a direct confrontation with Ross. "Nobody wants a lame-ass game."

"Yeah, that would be terrible." Larry stood up and walked over to a big countertop. "We sure don't want to be finished play in just two or three hours."

There was a large translucent tank sitting on the counter top.

"You dickheads, I mean, *gentlemen*, will just have to trust me." As memory served, Ross never used words like 'dickheads' unless he was trying to make a point. He started handing out bolts which were painted different colours. My bolts were blue.

Speaking of the colour blue, Larry returned to the table with a tray that someone had probably lifted from one of the cafeterias. He was carrying four beakers filled with clear blue liquid. He handed each of us a beaker and sat down.

What was it with the beakers? If they could rip off trays from the cafeteria they could have gotten some glasses. I bet they drank out of those beakers because it made them feel more *scientific*.

I picked up my beaker and studied the contents.

"What is this?" The liquid smelled alcoholic. Very alcoholic.

"Hyper-Gin." Ross took a drink from his beaker. "Sort of a homemade brew."

This was weirding me out. Back in high school, Ross was never part of the boozer or stoner crowds. It didn't feel right to see him drinking now. Even though it was years later and here we were on a secret moon base and everything.

"We also mixed in some Grape Kool-Aid to give it a little more flavour."

Larry took a very big drink from his beaker.

"Not Tang?"

Larry shook his head in mild disgust.

Grape Kool-Aid? Come to think of it, the liquid was a little more purple than blue.

Melling was watching me. No doubt waiting for me to drink some Hyper-Gin and/or say/do something really stupid.

What the hell.

I took a drink.

The purple-blue fluid had more of an impact than a taste. It felt like someone had poured five pounds of Vick's Vapo-Rub down my throat and decided that it would be a good idea to scrape the insides of my eyeballs with steel wool. But that was okay. Soon I didn't feel much at all in my mouth and throat, and I think that was because my parasympathetic nervous system had gone into shock.

I coughed and spluttered.

"What a pussy." Melling shook his head.

By now, Ross had passed around all the coloured bolts. I had ten blue ones, Ross had ten green ones and Larry had ten red ones.

Melling had what looked like fifty or sixty yellow ones.

I wondered why he had so many more than the rest of us but I figured that this would be revealed when we started playing the game.

Melling picked up a pair of dice and threw them on the table.

"Welcome to the Real World Game, asshole."

And fuck you too, buddy.

But there would likely be time for that sort of discourse later on.

Rules of the Game
Objectives and Priorities

The Real World Game is divided into three phases.

PHASE ONE – involves one player taking control of the entire World with all of its territories, resources and all value markers. The goal is not to eliminate or otherwise destroy the other players (although this may happen) but to place them under the Phase One Winner's absolute subjugation and to marshal all resources held by the other players towards the goals of the Winner.

You will note that the High Roller at the outset of the PHASE ONE game has a substantial advantage over the other players. This strategic "upper hand" is simply a reflection of the way the World works.

Rules for PHASE TWO of the Game should only be read after the successful resolution of PHASE ONE.

11.
PLUTONIUM ENEMA

04:34

Suddenly I was kissing concrete. By way of a preamble:

By the time we'd finished up all the Hyper-Gin and decided that we'd spent enough time trying to conquer that paper world, I was told that I was way too plastered to even consider riding my bike back to the Residence.

"You can stay here." Larry pointed to some folding cots in the corner of the room. "We keep those for marathon sessions."

We'd played for over eight hours. I wondered what constituted a marathon session.

"I got to get back, my girlfriend is probably waiting for me."

The H.G. must have been making me optimistic.

Melling and Larry made whipping sounds but Ross leaned over and slapped my knee.

"That's all right, Matt. I can run you home in one of our drivers."

Like any good engineer, Ross looked like he could handle his lab-synthesized booze, so I agreed to his offer. Of course, like any humanities undergrad wannabe, I had absolutely no tolerance for alcohol so I would have agreed to a plutonium enema at that point.

Fortunately Ross decided that we could use an elevator, so I didn't have to add falling down a stairwell to my day's experiences.

By 04:00 we were in the driver (which was essentially an electric golf cart with really good steering but not so good suspension) beetling down the main access corridor.

"That's a strange game."

Ross smiled as he kept the driver in a more or less straight line.

"You like it?"

"Yeah, sure."

Truth was that I'd much rather have spend the last eight hours naked with Angie but even in my totally pissed condition, I was pretty sure that Ross didn't need to know that.

"You're not bad at it." We hit a small bump. "For a beginner."

I was quite proud of myself because I managed not to puke everywhere.

I did burp loudly, however. "Where did you get it?"

"We invented it."

"Fuck, why?"

"It started out as a training exercise that kind of got out of hand."

"But there were only three of you."

Hey! I could still differentiate between very low numbers!

"Originally four of us." Ross sighed. "Melnyk had an accident last week." Then Ross burped too. "He's not able to play anymore."

"What kind of accident?" It must have been my relatively recent HS&E training kicking in; I couldn't think of any other reason why I wanted to know what happened to some geek I didn't know and probably wouldn't have cared about either.

Ross made a few minor adjustments at the steering wheel which made the driver weave around the corridor like it was having an epileptic fit for a few seconds.

"Woooooooooooooooooooooooooaaaaaaaahhhhhhhh!"

Another wrestling match with my stomach.

"He was reviewing some shop tests of our designs over at Gravity. There was a slight fluctuation in one of the fields."

"A fluctuation?"

"There was an accident."

"You mean he got killed?"

"Melnyk and two Gravity Workers look like pancakes now."

"Holy shit!"

Ross laughed feebly. "It's kinda funny…"

"Fucking hilarious!" Somebody dies and Ross sees the humour in it? My high school friend had changed.

"Well, maybe not funny ha-ha." Now Ross was blinking a bit. "The autopsy said that they were mathematically precise pancakes."

"Mathematically precise?"

"Perfect discs."

"That is just bizarre, man."

Ross shook his head. "It's just the way that gravity fields seem to work—"

It was at that point that Ross steered the driver into the wall and I started making out with the concrete floor.

Not that I am complaining.

Yes, the collisions with the wall and the floor did hurt a lot, but not as much as it would have if I hadn't consumed all that alcohol. Also, it didn't seem that I had broken any teeth. And I still hadn't puked.

"Jesus, man!"

Ross braked the driver to a stop and I could hear the 'scrunch-scrunch' of his Hush Puppies as he ran to the site of my body-sprawl.

Another positive note: I had not become a pancake. Mathematically precise or otherwise.

"You okay?" Ross grabbed my arm and pulled me off the concrete. Normally this would have been pretty painful but the anaesthetic effects of the Super-Gin were still working.

Not too much later we drove up to my building and I rolled out of the driver. Ross called out after me:

"You sure you're going to be okay?"

"Yeah, yeah."

I remembered that I had some ampules of something morphine-like in my HS&E kit. If things hurt too much, I could always shoot up with that.

"Tomorrow? Same time?"

"I dunno, Ross…"

My friend looked a little desperate.

"Don't let Melling get to you. He's just mad because he's not High Roller any more."

Fortunately for me, Larry was now High Roller and that guy was such a marshmallow that he was really bad at pressing his advantage. Even I could see that.

"But I'm just an intern…"

"Please, Matt."

Please?

Nobody said please to an intern. In my fluid-filled brain, the dots were connecting. Very slowly, but they were connecting.

It occurred to me that even if we went to high school together, it was probably a very bad idea for an intern to refuse a 'please' from anyone in Technical.

"Sure, sounds good."

06:13

Still no sign of Angie.

I lay back on my slab. I felt a rumbling sensation and sat up. I finally puked.

Blue-purple barf.

10:32

There was no food left in the cafeteria. Some would appear if I waited around for an hour or so.

I didn't care.

I didn't care that I had missed breakfast and I probably wouldn't care if I missed lunch. I wasn't all that hungry and I did not want a repeat of the barf incident.

Point of interest: when you do not have ready access to a shower, it is not easy to remove the smell of vomit from your person.

Angie was the only other person in the cafeteria. I limped over to her table. (The pain from my foot and my concrete encounter were making themselves known.)

"Hey."

"Hey."

Angie gave me a look that might have had the capacity to reduce me to component molecules.

"How was your meeting? Something important?"

"Why are you sitting out here?" I decided to try the old 'answer a question with a question' technique to try and defuse the situation. "You could have come up to my room."

"I was interested to see if you were ever going to get up."

"You never mind sleeping in when you stay over."

Angie narrowed her eyes. "Are you hung over?"

"There's no booze in this sector." Time for a tactical lie. "How could I be hung over?"

"You *are* hung over!"

I realized that I had just said something very stupid. With her family history, Angie was probably very good at identifying when people were suffering from the effects of booze.

I rested my head on my hand. "It's not my fault."

"*Not your fault?!*"

Angie hit me on the side of my head with the flat of her hand. Not too hard, just enough to make a few thousand stars explode at the edge of my field of vision.

"Are you telling me that they ordered you out to Technical just so they could force you to get drunk?"

"*Why?*" I sounded angry.

"*Why what, you asshole?!*"

This was the second time in less than twenty-four hours someone had called me an asshole. Not that uncommon up here but I still didn't like it very much.

I was also angry. I really don't like getting hit in the head, either. "Are you pissed off that you didn't get invited?"

For a second it looked like Angie might hit me again. Then she just whispered: "You *fucking* asshole."

I gently pressed my thumbs into my eyeballs, hoping that the pressure would somehow relieve the pain. "It's not as though I had a lot of choice in the matter. When Management is not around, Technical and Gravity call the shots."

My (now former?) girlfriend folded her arms and slowly shook her head. "You pathetic piece of shit."

"Thank you, darling. I love you very much."

Since there was no else in the cafeteria, I knew that I was not listening to one of Angie's public bad language displays. She was not showing off, she was supremely pissed off.

"*Shut up, shit for brains!*" Angie stood up.

In fact, out of proportionately pissed off.

"What's happened, Angie?"

"There was a pile up on one of the test lines last night. While you and your big-shot buddies in Technical were getting shit-faced, six interns got cut up!"

She started to walk away.

"Great job, Safety Officer."

Then she was gone.

It was my turn to stand up.

So I did that.

Badly.

Then I wobbled back to my room. Then I puked some more.

12.
DROOL

Rules of the Game: Survivors

If the lower roller players are able to stay in the game for more than 20 cycles of the board, they must pay a 20% "Survivor's Tribute" to the High Roller.

Larry was on the floor. Snoring. Drool was leaking out of his mouth, seeping down his chin and dripping onto the concrete.

Melling, once again our current High Roller and glorious leader of our hypothetical planet, fell backwards out of his chair. After a whimpered complaint, he, too, was on the floor snoring.

Tonight's batch of Moon-Gin was very strong.

"Ross, I gotta tell you…" I was not in very good shape either. "…this game of yours really sucks."

"The real world sucks," one of the several Rosses I was looking at said. I also think one of the flickering faces was smiling at me.

"So what the fuck is your point?"

Maybe it was Ross' Management-trained tone of condescension that pushed me over the edge. I stood up, took a swing at the Rosses and missed all of them. Just to be annoying, all of the Rosses laughed at me.

I decided to do something different and managed to make it to the sink without having to crawl.

"We based the rules of the game on chapters from the Plant Orientation Manual." Funny, how only one of the Rosses was talking.

"That's very fucking creative." I gripped the stainless steel rim of the sink, aimed as carefully as I could and projectile vomited. "And efficient," I said once my stomach was finished.

"Efficient?" There was only one Ross now and he had followed me over to the sink. This must have been the nice Ross who wanted to see if I was okay. I decided I still liked Ross (at least this one) after all.

"Yeah, efficient." I also wiped my mouth with the back of my hand. "You worked with the material you had on hand."

Ross nodded and turned on the tap. "I'm pretty good at that kind of thing."

The water made the former contents of my stomach circle down the drain a little faster.

"You were always a useful person to know, Ross."

He helped me back to my chair.

"So do you know what the whole point of the Game is, Matthew?"

"You're going to tell me, aren't you?"

"The point of the Game is the point of Plant."

"Very good, Ross. Means absolutely nothing but it sounds very good."

Ross sighed and put his hand on my shoulder. "The point of the Game is to teach one very important thing."

"Just one? But it's such a complicated game."

"It's a very important thing."

"Which is?"

Ross looked me in the eyes. "The point is… we are *not* all in this together."

21:07

End of shift. On my way back to my cell, I was giving some serious thought to making a cocktail of whatever interesting meds

I could find in my VHSO kit and sucking it down. I was that miserable.

Not so miserable that I was thinking about offing myself, I was way too much of a chicken-shit for that. No, I was miserable enough that I was just willing to risk death to try and simulate the effects of a quart of Hyper-Gin.

I didn't have a girlfriend anymore. Our romance was dead. Also, she and all the other interns probably despised me. I needed to get hammered.

The hazardous ingestion never happened. I sat on the edge of my sleeping slab, thought about laying down (just for a second) and then it was lights out. Absolute nothingness: no gradual relaxation, no inspection over the events of the day, just bash me on the head with something hard. It was probably some kind of stress reaction.

Yeah. I probably had a big backlog of stress to process. Poor me.

So it was all oblivion for I don't know how long. And it stayed that way until the pounding started. The noise was even louder than my communist alarm clock. There was somebody at the door.

The pounding continued.

At least I didn't have to get dressed to answer the door.

And there he was.

"Ed."

My stepfather smiled at me with those blinding ivory bricks in his mouth.

"Matthew."

"Still on the moon I see."

"Matthew, Matthew." Ed looked at me some more and finally shook his head. "You never write, you never call."

"Communication can be a bit of a challenge up here, Ed."

He belted me square in the face. Hit me hard enough to knock me to the floor. There were twin rivers of blood streaming from my nose.

"Keep up the good work, kid."

BOOK THREE: LUNAR RADIO

1.
THE GERRY AND SYLVIA ANDERSON REVELATION

17:46

"There's still some labour resistance so we're down on the production quotas by least 17.5%."

Another fucking meeting.

The speaker was some mid-level numbers guy from the Statistics Office. "Some kind of testament to the power of human stubbornness…" He wore the usual white shirt, thin navy blue tie and horn-rimmed glasses. "…because we all know that the damage to the equipment on the Lines was minimal. Under normal circumstances…"

Even though the guy looked tediously normal, he sounded rather robotic. Like his voice was produced by some kind of voice synthesizer.

"…any two-digit drop in output would be completely unacceptable."

And his metallic monotone might have been the result of some lingering damage to my eardrums from when Biffo/Roy/Whatever-Angie's-New-Boyfriend's name was insisted that I kiss the floor so intimately.

He put another acetate sheet on the overhead projector and we all got to see the inevitably scary diagram. Yes, there was a sharp dip in the height of the thickest line on the graph and the arrow at its end was definitely pointed in the direction of down.

"It is also true that the new specifications were more difficult for the work force to process and therefore we got greater challenges to our production capacities."

It had been over a week since the latest blow-up and there was no indication that we were getting even remotely close to hitting our targets.

"But that does not change the external factors."

So no improvement—even though we had been threatening all the interns just as hard as we could. Management must have been totally freaking out.

There was a new acetate sheet on the projector.

"Signals Division is also telling us that we now have definite coordinates for the first rendezvous."

We were looking at a black screen with white dots scattered all over it. The darkness was overlaid with a grid and there were cryptic columns of numbers spread in various points on the grid. Made absolutely no sense at all to me.

Oh, wait a minute, it did! It was a shot of space with some kind of map, maybe something from a radio telescope. Maybe I was a little bit smarter than I thought.

"Signals Division is certain that we won't reach this point if we aren't flight-ready on schedule."

Some people in the audience were muttering something. Probably some assholes from Gravity.

"And we won't be at departure point if we don't make the production quotas."

So the whole Project was in trouble. Therefore all of us were in trouble, and as usual, the people at the bottom (us interns) were in the most trouble.

About four hundred middle and low level supervisors had been taken off shift (so we were probably falling even further behind schedule) just so we could all be officially informed how bad everything was. This must have set some kind of record for Corporate Panic.

"We could be looking at a total failure scenario."

I suspected that I had been invited to this bureaucratic anxiety-fest because as a designated Volunteer Health and Safety Officer, it would be important for me to have up-to-date information when any interns decided to beat me up again.

"We must get the Lines back on target." The speaker turned off the projector. "There simply is no alternative."

"Gentlemen… and…?" The man who replaced Mr. Normal who was really a robot, wore a black military style shirt and a marine's haircut. He peered into the audience. "…and ladies?" Apparently he was trying to ascertain if there were any vaginas lurking out there. Could be dangerous, I suppose.

Blackshirt wasn't wearing a name tag or any kind of badge but the guy's look practically screamed some kind of new Security and Enforcement Unit. The guys looked like they could be the last people you were going to see. Ever.

"There are some new guidelines regarding personnel and discipline procedures on the Lines."

I bet that even the Gravity bullies were scared of this S&E type.

"We should go over these." Even without my ear damage, this guy would have sounded like a killer robot.

I could see Ross over at the other side of the auditorium and I was pretty sure he could see me. It would have been pointless, maybe even dangerous, for us to acknowledge each other. The last thing either of us needed was some snoopy type to start wondering how he and I might be acquainted.

The rest of Mr. Blackshirt's presentation was pretty grim and focused on the following key points:

1. We had to get production on the Lines up by at least 29%.
2. This had to happen by the day before yesterday at the latest.
3. We were to improve productivity by inducing the interns to work much, much, *much* harder.
4. Everyone in the room was directly responsible for all this inducing. Therefore, we too were expected to work much, much harder.

5. We were also expected to work *smarter*. Most of our jobs were designed to be performed by a mentally challenged monkey, so I wasn't sure how we were going to do that or even what the point of that would be. I guess I was too dumb to figure out how to work smarter.

6. We are also expected to work meaner. That wasn't hard to understand at all. There would be even fewer restrictions on the application of force and other forms of abuse by supervisors. For me, that meant I would be dealing with more interns in pain.

7. There was, however, one primary rule we couldn't break. We couldn't deliberately go out and just kill somebody. This was not for humanitarian reasons but because there wasn't enough time to transport and train very many replacement interns.

8. Great. Just fucking great.

Mr. Blackshirt finished talking and some other types came up and said more stuff; I don't remember exactly what. As far as actual things that were in our power to do and change, none of it really mattered. I suppose if it made some people on the other end of a TV monitor back on Planet Earth feel a little better, it wasn't a completely pointless exercise.

Eventually the presentation was over.

The big take away was that we had to get back on schedule because the Big Fucking Immovable Deadline was looming. We miss that target and we were all screwed.

Of course for some of us, making that deadline was going to kill us, so we were screwed anyway. As we all started to rise and slouch out of the auditorium, I was genuinely curious as to how all of this was going to turn out.

"802,701?" One of the few women in the group was standing next to me.

"That's my number."

Like me, she was wearing intern coveralls. Probably, also like me, she was some poor sap Volunteer Health and Safety Officer.

She handed me a moderately thick padded envelope:

"This is for you to deliver."

The word 'LOGISTICS' was stencilled on its surface. When I looked back up from that word, my poor sap counterpart was halfway to the exit.

Good idea.

We were all going to have to move pretty fast these days.

However, there was no delivery time or individual name or position on the envelope, which was both annoying and dangerous. Ambiguity was not what I needed just then. I didn't know if this package was hideously urgent with all kinds of life or death shit associated with it or if it was just some random afterthought that nobody gave a crap about but somebody needed to get off their desk anyway.

I was just egotistical enough to figure that if someone took the trouble of giving me this package then it probably wasn't completely trivial. Even so, you never knew around this place.

After that session from Management, I was pretty sure that all departments would now be running 24/7 so I could jump on a bike, take a spin after my next shift, and give the envelope to whoever was on duty at Logistics.

Maybe.

Whomever?

21:06

There was another problem with this stupid package. I mean, who exactly wanted it and was I going to get into serious trouble if they weren't the first (and maybe only) person to see it? Would the person working the front desk at Logistics even know what to do with the thing?

I was now very aware that I had absolutely no specialized training or insight into the highly complex field of intra-organizational communications. I was only an adequate materials handler and not really a competent health and safety officer. So, of course I was going to be a terrible courier.

Up until that evening, after my shift, I had never been over to Logistics. At least they had bike racks.

The building looked slightly newer and was set a little bit lower than the Main Management complex. No signs of Security at all. When I got inside, there was someone sitting at a big half-moon desk just by the main entrance. I walked up to him, fumbling with my card just in case I had to punch in some data into some device or other. I mean this was Logistics, it made sense that they might have a Logistics Clock around.

Nope.

Just this guy, hunched over a CRT monitor with a big FORTRAN binder opened up next to him. He was not smiling, which was not surprising because computer languages in those days hardly ever made people smile.

"Hey." (Well, I had to say something.)

"Hey." Oh, good. We at least had one word in common.

I held up the envelope. "I'm supposed to drop this off."

The guy looked at me and didn't seem to be particularly interested. "Right." He nodded, pointed his thumb over his shoulder and resumed pecking at his keyboard. "Room 105."

"Thanks."

I walked in the direction of his thumb. Seems that they weren't too formal here in the Logistics Division. Not that my presence had much chance of disturbing any members of Management. Aside from Captain Fortran, the place seemed deserted.

So much for that 24/7 commitment.

Room 105 wasn't hard to find. There was a corridor at the far end of the lobby and the correct door was located conveniently between Room 104 and Room 106.

Remarkable, that.

I quietly turned the door knob and discovered that the door wasn't locked. I probably should have knocked but I didn't. My reasoning was that since the place was down to minimum staff there was likely nobody in there. I could just leave the package on a desk, get the hell out of there and never have to think about what this was all about ever again. It would be much safer that way and I wouldn't have to go to all the tedium of actually speaking to anyone.

I opened the door.

And immediately wished that I hadn't.

Melling, my occasional game-playing associate, was in the room. His feet were up on the desk and he was holding a magazine in one hand and holding something that the cognitive processing centres of my brain do not want to acknowledge was his penis in the other.

Melling was masturbating.

"Shit, man!"

Or rather, he had been masturbating. At that point it felt like that old sitcom *Bewitched*. With a twinkle of a pretty witch's nose, whatever Melling had been fondling seemed to magically disappear. Or at least get a lot smaller.

"Sorry."

"Christ, Bishop! Don't you believe in knocking?!"

"You got transferred out of Technical?"

"Yeah."

Melling's normally pasty complexion went beet red and there was a little zipping sound as he re-arranged himself into a more family hour condition.

"Thought you'd all closed up for the day."

I tried not to smirk as I walked across the room and put the envelope on his desk.

"Dickhead." Melling picked up the envelope.

"Don't worry if you think I don't respect you anymore, Melling, because I never have."

"Never have what?"

"Respected you."

"Sit down, dummy."

Sure, why not? From my new vantage point I got a good view of the magazine that Melling had been jerking off to.

"*Gent: Home of the D-Cups!*" I laughed, trying to sound as though this was the lamest possible smut ever; however, back on Earth I was more than mildly familiar with this, and similar, publications. "How did you manage to get porn up to the moon?"

Melling snorted as he started to open the envelope. "There's loads of girlie magazines up here. 70% of Management personnel are engineers."

I nodded and started to page through the copy of *Gent*. There was a pictorial titled 'Keep the Faith' which was about 42DD Dody, an organizer for the British Labour Party who explained that her astonishingly massive Anglo-rack was probably the result of a decade's worth of regular visits to the pub for pints of bitter. Dody also urged us all to stay true to the egalitarian Post-War values represented in social democracy. As I admired a picture of this politically aware babe dreamily sucking on her own nipple, I had a sudden vision of H.G. Wells, looking a lot like Benny Hill, chasing a corset-clad Rebecca West through a 1904 Fabian Society conference. Fast motion, and with that silly saxophone theme of course.

I closed the magazine and resolved that somehow, someday, I was going to lift this from Melling and get it back to my room. All in the cause of Interplanetary Socialism, of course.

"This is great!" Melling grinned and poured the contents of the envelope out onto the desktop. What the proverbial fuck? It was the parts of one of those travel chess sets you get for road trips and camp grounds.

"Now we can play!"

"Someone had me bring this so you could play chess?"

"Ross did. He said you knew how to play."

"But *chess*?"

"I like chess."

"But I don't like you, what makes you think I'll play?"

"Because Ross wants me to bring you up to speed." Melling smiled a little and made his beady little eyes even smaller. "And this is my price."

"Up to speed about what?"

"Choose a colour: white or black?"

So Melling and I were playing games again; at least we had a very interesting conversation while we did so. I do have to admit that unless you were there, it is going to read like having to swim through a vast and muddy sea of exposition. You might stop listening to my story and then where would I be? Unfortunately, if I don't share what Melling told me then you may get confused by what happens next and that would very reasonably annoy you, which would also make you stop listening to my story. And then me, all my problems, all the people I care about (as far as I'm capable of caring about anyone), the whole damned thing, would just vanish from your consciousness. It would all just disappear. Like it never mattered.

And damn it: it does matter.

Therefore, towards the aim of informing you, dear reader, while at the same time maintaining your interest in an engaging, entertaining and yet period-appropriate manner, I am going to interpret what Melling told me (because Ross told him to tell me) in the form of a television script inspired by Gerry and Sylvia Anderson's classic sci-fi/disco inspired programs such as *Captain Scarlet*, *UFO* and *Space: 1999*:

EXTREME LONG SHOT. EXTERIOR. THE INFINITY OF DEEPEST OUTER SPACE.

The great black expanse is sprinkled with millions upon millions of stars. The CAMERA TILTS AND PANS DOWN to reveal a grassy hill upon which rests the stately white dome of an observatory. Next to the dome is the massive wire concave dish of a radio telescope. We realize that we are now on Earth and, like the astronomers inside the observatory, we are studying the night sky.

We hear a SHARP DRAMATIC/POMPOUS BLAST OF ORCHESTRAL MUSIC – which is the extremely unsubtle cue to the audience that they are about to witness some momentous events.

CUT TO:

INTERIOR OBSERVATORY.

Two men (we know they are scientists because
they wear glasses and white lab coats) stand
next to a computer; its massive magnetic tape
reels slowly, spinning as it collects data
from the stars. The radio astronomers watch
intently as an automatic printer scrolls out
column after column of dot-matrix numbers.

> ASTRONOMER #1
> This is incredible,
> Professor.

> ASTRONOMER #2
> Yes, it certainly is, Doctor.

Astronomer #2 takes out the pipe that all
1960s TV scientists carry in their lab coat
pockets and sucks on its stem thoughtfully.

> ASTRONOMER #1
> Conclusive proof of extra-
> terrestrial life.

> ASTRONOMER #2
> Not just life…

> ASTRONOMER #1
> No, you're absolutely
> correct.

> ASTRONOMER #2
> …but the signals clearly
> indicate *intelligent* life.

> ASTRONOMER #1
> (Excited)
> Yes! *Highly* intelligent life!

Astronomer #2 gestures at the computer's
slowly turning magnetic tapes.

> ASTRONOMER #2
> In fact this "Cosmic
> Encyclopedia" could only
> originate from a vast
> Galactic Super-Culture,
> billions of years ahead of us
> in science and technology!

Now Astronomer #1 takes out his pipe and puts
it in his mouth. Nobody knows why really.

> ASTRONOMER #1
> This is the most profound
> discovery in the history of
> science!

> ASTRONOMER #2
> In all human history!

> ASTRONOMER #1
> When the world learns of
> this, everything, *absolutely
> everything* will be different.

> ASTRONOMER #2
> Hmmmm. Yes.

> VOICE
> (Off-Screen)
> *Which is* **precisely** *why the
> World must never know!*

We hear ANOTHER THUNDEROUS STING OF ORCHESTRAL
MUSIC and FROM ANOTHER ANGLE we see the owner
of the voice: a Spy. She is dressed in a
tight-fitting, many zippered, all black
leather jumpsuit. She also wears wrap around
sunglasses[3] and holds a long-barrelled pistol
in one hand.

---

3   I know, it doesn't make an awful lot of sense for this character to be
    wearing sunglasses at night, but this story is supposed to be a Gerry and
    Sylvia Anderson production where things don't always have to make
    sense just as long as they look cool.

> ASTRONOMER #1
> What the--?!

> ASTRONOMER #2
> Good grief!

The Spy fires twice and the bodies of the astronomers fall to the floor.

FAST CUT TO:

EXTERIOR, NIGHT.

The observatory, a few moments later. There is a series of massive explosions which rips open the dome and causes the radio telescope to collapse into a pool of flame and melting metal.

ANOTHER FAST CUT TO:

EXTERIOR, NIGHT.

A deserted highway, another few moments later.

TRACKING SHOT.

Of a very sleek, very futuristic and completely impractical car racing through the darkness.

EVIL MUSIC PLAYS. THE ORCHESTRA IS JOINED BY A VENTURES-STYLE ELECTRIC GUITAR which emphasizes the covert and conspiratorial nature of these events.

CUT TO:

INTERIOR OF THE MOVING CAR: A TRAVELLING MATTE SHOT THAT IS NOT ENTIRELY CONVINCING.

The Spy, still wearing her sunglasses, sits at the steering wheel. The CAMERA TILTS TO A CLOSE-UP of the passenger seat. There is a

THROBBING SHOCK OF THEREMIN MUSIC as we see what is next to the Spy: reels of computer tape.

CUT TO:

OPENING CREDITS: THE EOS PROJECT!

MORE THEREMIN MUSIC FOLLOWED BY THUMPING BRASS AND HYSTERICAL STRINGS.

FADE.

Wow, did I ever miss real TV.

Meanwhile, back at the chess game, I was trying hard to process what Melling was telling me.

"So how do you know all this?"

"Everyone on the moon knows about it."

"Everyone? How come I missed that memo?"

"Everyone important, that is." Melling shrugged and moved his rook to a place he would really regret in two moves. "It's on pages three to fifteen in the EOS Project Orientation Manual. Not for interns, of course. Need to know and all that."

"Right." Interns didn't need to know? I was really going to enjoy nuking Melling's piece.

"They even got Jack Kirby to draw some of the illustrations."

"Kirby? No way!"

"Way."

Melling went on to make another bad move while proceeding to tell me some more interesting things.

23:32

On my way back to my cell, I decided to stop at what Melling told me would be a pneumatic message point.

What kind of messages, I asked.

"Messages." Melling shrugged. "That's all Ross told me and I don't care much."

I turned my bike down a sub-corridor and saw a thin tube

leading to what could have been mistaken for a fuse box. I braked to a stop and pried open the slightly rusty panel at the front of the box. There was a little brass tube waiting for me, and inside the tube there was a piece of paper with cursive writing on it.

'*Sorry but no more time for Real World Games now.*'

Well, given that we were all missing our targets, that was no huge surprise.

Ross' message continued: '*Pretty incredible, isn't it?*'

From anyone else, that sentence would have come across as a little stupid, or at least pointless. But with Ross, he was probably just trying to confirm that what Melling told me about EOS and the whole ET signal was true.

Okay. According to Ross (via Melling), we were all here on the moon building spaceship components (which I, and just about everybody here, already knew) so some P.A. people can go out and meet the Incredible Space Gods (that part most interns did not know).

Sure.

Fine.

I took out a treasured pencil stub and wrote on the blank side of the paper:

'*Given the context… not really.*' I guess you get jaded up here at the Plant. '*And how about some more context? We could all use some of that.*' Never hurts to try to get more information. Well, maybe it does, but I wanted some anyway.

I wrote a few more rude and impractical things, put the paper back in the tube and put the tube back in the hole in the wall. Ross was going to have more to think about now.

There was an inevitable sucking sound.

The worst thing was that Ross was the closest thing to a friend I had left and now it was more of a long-distance relationship between unindicted co-conspirators. Worse yet, the only way I could complain to him (because that's what you do with your friends) was through those back-and-forth exchanges of those pneumatic tubes. It took so fucking long!

But if you compiled a series them you sometimes even got

something resembling an actual conversation between human beings:

ME: Help me, Ross! They're going to kill me!

ROSS: You have to expect the interns to be angry when there are accidents.

ME: Yeah, but I'm the target! There's going to be another "accident" and it's going to happen to me!

ROSS: I suppose that's one of the occupational hazards of being the Volunteer Health and Safety Officer. On the up side, maybe that's what's keeping you alive. Nobody wants to be the next VHSO.

ME: Great! So I'm the permanent scapegoat! At least you could invite me up to Technical for a game night once in a while.

ROSS: Sorry, no can do. Melling's still re-assigned and Larry and I are pulling double and triple shifts. Looks like the Real World Game is off, at least for a while.

ME: I can't seem to get any kind of a break here.

ROSS: Personally, the game was getting kind of boring. Don't you think?

ME: I had a friend named Eugene from Blinn U— Alberta's biggest Trotskyite—he would have made for some pretty interesting games.

ROSS: I'll be sure to invite him as soon as he arrives.

So there you have it. I didn't even have the questionable comfort of some fascist strategy board game. More importantly, no Hyper-Gin.

2.
BLUE BINDER INSTRUCTIONS

05:15

Knock-knock.

Today was not beginning with tick-tick.

Damn. Any deviation from routine was usually bad.

I didn't bother to put on my coveralls before I answered the door. If Biff/Happy was back to beat on me some more then he could do so while basking in the glory of me in my underpants.

It was not Angie's latest boyfriend but another BFG (Big Fucking Guy) who was standing at my doorway. He was wearing that vaguely military and definitely scary black shirt. A smaller rat-like figure was standing next to Sergeant Hulk-Out.

Melling again.

"He got your message."

"My what?" My message to Ross? This was an interesting development. Worrying but interesting.

New BFG handed me a blue binder.

"Instructions for the day."

06:40

"Okay folks!"

I was in the cafeteria, standing on a table, facing about a hundred interns who were trying to grab some food before they went on shift. I was holding that blue binder open in my hands.

"I have some important news for you!"

"Fuck you!" Somebody needed coffee.

"*From Management!*"

"*Fuck them too!*" That voice sounded like Angie, or at least someone a lot like her.

Never mind. If my job was to going to be the Moon's Designated Asshole, then I was going to go all the way with it:

"Listen up and be sure to tell anyone who isn't here what I am about to say."

"We said *FUCK YOU!*"

Someone threw a tray. Since it was still pretty early in the morning, they managed to miss me by a pretty wide margin. I figured my best survival strategy was to try and sound positive while speaking as quickly and clearly as possible:

"First thing: Management says that Line Quotas have been rolled back by 20%."

There wasn't exactly a gasp. It was more like a confused collective intake of air. It had been so long that the interns had heard anything even remotely resembling good news that they just didn't know how to react.

"*For how long?*"

That definitely was Angie and it showed the expected healthy suspicion of Management. A good sign, I might be able to work with that attitude.

I held up the binder. "At least until we get all the bugs worked out of the new Lines." My statement was probably a lie but to my credit, I really wanted it to be true.

There was a fair bit of muttering and whispering among the interns. This was even more apparently reasonable information and they still seemed to be having trouble processing it.

"But it's still regular quotas for today's shift, right?" Oh, the working classes are so suspicious. With good reason, mind you.

"Well, yes… you have to put the time in today." I kind of half-nodded and half-shook my head. "But no, the quota roll-backs are immediate."

There were definitely happier sounds of escaping human air in the audience.

"The lower quotas are still real targets. We do need to do our best to meet them even under these circumstances."

Now I heard lots of animated muttering. Dangerously, the interns' minds were starting to engage.

"*Second thing!*" I made my voice as loud as I could manage. "When you get back from shift you might find a bigger screen up in the common area!"

That announcement just got silent stares. No one was sure if that represented good or bad news.

I gave them all a great big smile. It hurt, because this is not a natural expression for me. "*Because Management is ramping up to three movies a week!*"

Some of the interns actually clapped and whistled. I guess these poor saps missed TV almost as much as I did.

"*But...*" I held up the binder and everyone went very quiet again, as if waiting for the Big Bad News Shoe to drop. "Management wants everyone to bunk down and get to sleep as soon as possible after the show."

An amazing level of applause.

"We need you all to be as rested and as sharp as possible for the next shift."

Wow. Most of the interns were happy for the first time in I don't know how many cycles and they would think I had something to do with it.

I was the biggest sack of shit ever.

20:06

Courtesy of Management, there was a special feature before we all got to watch TV sexpot and former genie Barbara Eden in *The Stranger Within*. The short was on a pretty beat-up 16 millimetre print of a film that Progressive Apparatus must have used to brief new Management personnel on their new careers on the moon.

P.A.'s movie pretty much covered the same ground as what Melling told me in his masturbation chamber (office) but as you no doubt appreciate, my Gerry and Sylvia Anderson reinterpretation was much more interesting and had way better production values. The short feature had stock footage and royalty-free music while my version had giant screens with insanely complicated oscilloscope patterns pulsating with weird space-knowledge watched by sinister shadowy figures sitting around massive chrome boardroom tables that could only be housed in the cavernous 007 hangars at Pinewood Studios. SPECTRE couldn't use the room *all* the time.

I even thought about adding an evil hunched shape seated at the head of the table who would be softly, yet menacingly, stroking his pink-eyed pet iguana with his clockwork brass and plastic hand. But that seemed a little too derivative and Progressive Apparatus would never be able to produce anything that interesting.

And yet, considering the subject matter of this little orientation, the actual film was pretty pedestrian. Like I said before, they used that generic sort of music that you usually heard in those Encyclopedia Britannica slide shows from middle school and the narration was by that usual nondescript Caucasian male baritone that you heard when your local board of education decided it was time for you to know all about parallel parking, voting in municipal elections, or the miracle of the menstrual cycle.

Yeah it was tedious, but the P.A. movie seemed to do the job and even dropped in a few details that Melling had either skipped over or forgotten:

Soon after World War II, the human race, or at least a small segment of the human race, had established contact with an extraterrestrial civilization. More like civilizations in the plural sense: a big whack of cosmic societies. Like I said earlier, the Galactic Super-Culture.

I looked around the cafeteria to see how my fellow interns were reacting to these revelations. Their eyes were wide open and they were very quiet. My reading of the crowd was that they were interested but pretty much taking it all in stride. Same reaction as me. Remember: context.

A year or so earlier, a lot of us were back on Earth, working at our jobs or going to school or looking for a job now that we were out of school. The most exciting thing that might happen to us down there was getting to see a better than average movie at the local cine-bunker or scoring some weed and smoking up with your friends.

Approximately 365 days later, we are all stuck on the moon, running around in tubes, pushing buttons and pulling levers and making these crazy-ass complicated Boxes all day.

Now Management tells us that somehow aliens are involved? Sure! Why the fuck not?

Near the end of the movie, the production values got a little better: there was a brief animated sequence explaining the design and operation of our Boxes (the old version though) that were edited in with kind of cool paintings illustrating where the boxes fit into the overall EOS spacecraft design. Ultimately they were going to be hooked up to "neural materials" and installed en masse into the infrastructure to serve as the primary and back-up organic supercomputers on the EOS.

And what was EOS supposed to be?

A multi-generational spacecraft capable of sustaining a crew of over one thousand and powered by engines supplied by the Gravity Division. Control of gravity being one of the first things that a select and very smart few had been able to figure out from the Galactic Super-Culture messages. How P.A. got involved was a total mystery to me though; they seemed to be allergic to intelligence.

When they got to the detailed illustrations of the EOS spacecraft, they really did look like they'd been done by Jack Kirby. Reminded me of the *2001: A Space Odyssey* comics that Marvel published for a while. I could not believe that Kirby would knowingly ever work for a bunch of assholes like Progressive Apparatus so maybe that's what the King of Comics thought he was drawing. Or maybe the engineers at P.A.'s aerospace division stole the design motifs from Kirby's work at DC and Marvel. I could definitely see that happening.

Anyway, according to the movie, EOS was already being built somewhere in orbit over the moon. Apparently it rolled over top of the Plant on a fairly regular basis. Not that us interns would ever see it. The spacecraft was going to take decades to finish and its journey to wherever it was going in the galaxy was going to take centuries. More like millennia, I guess.

There was a big swelling of music—not nearly as good as the Barry Gray soundtrack in my imaginary movie—but the stock orchestra did the job of signalling that some very important information was about to follow. The generic narrator now delivered the revelation:

"Even though our heroic enterprise could very well stretch out for thousands, perhaps hundreds of thousands of years, the processes and technologies that make it possible are based on the most exact and precise calculations imaginable. There are only the most infinitesimal margins for error and approximation."

The was a slow montage of the sorts of clunky machinery you would see in a really good issue of *The Fantastic Four* as the narrator continued:

"It is therefore *absolutely critical* to keep *all* project production inputs running at their optimal delivery targets."

Now even for someone like me who used to read a lot of social science texts, that was a really obtuse and horrible sentence. However, I and probably most of the interns were able to figure out what the narrator was baratoning at us and how it related to what we were all doing at the Plant:

1. We were making Boxes.
2. Boxes were important to the successful operation of EOS.
3. Other parts of the spacecraft were being built at other Plants. They were not really our problem unless for some reason they held us up in finishing our work.
4. EOS needed to be ready to go at a very specific time if it was going to get to wherever it was supposed to.
5. EOS also needed to get there because the crew would receive something from the space beings that Would Change Everything for Everybody. Maybe even interns but if you thought about it for more than two seconds,

probably not.

6. Therefore, it was essential that all of us working the Lines meet our target quotas and deliver functional Boxes according to the Master Schedule.
7. Therefore (cont'd) what we interns were doing was a major factor in the success of the entire project.
8. Therefore (cont'd, cont'd) we interns were actually worth something.
9. The two 'therefores' were unstated in the film but pretty easy to figure out.

All of this was rather helpful for the interns to know. However, sharing this kind of datum, particularly information that implied that people were anything more than cogs in a big machine, was completely antithetical to the culture at Progressive Apparatus. Hell, I'm sure that nine or ten of their senior people probably pulled their own heads off when they found out that they were going to show an orientation film to the interns. The idea that workers might actually know what their work meant must have been an absolutely terrifying concept. The fact that they were actually doing it—sharing knowledge, sharing power—must have been an indicator of how truly desperate they were.

Eventually the slow and oddly sensual dissolves of all the cartoon space-tech faded into a shot of a radio telescope sitting on that hill under the night sky, not completely unlike the one that I had so beautifully blown up in the pretend-in-my-head TV show.

The music got all big and cheesy and it sounded as though the narrator was finally going to sum all of this up for us:

"We are confident that we will overcome these challenges and the apex members of our species will fulfill Mankind's destiny among the stars."

Okay, that just confirmed all the messages I picked up while playing the Game with Ross and his associates. Only a most elite group of people were going to get to join Club Interstellar.

Music ends. Credits roll. Nobody I'd ever heard of but I did recognize the Progressive Apparatus logo next to the words:

'Temple of Mentotechnics'.

Who the hell were they?

Probably didn't matter.

Time for the main feature.

Barbara Eden was hot, even pregnant. Movie made me wish that I was an alien baby.

After the show I stayed around and watched the interns as they got up and headed towards their cells. Yeah. Maybe they did look a little happier than before the movie. At least a little bit less miserable.

I mean, why not? For the first time since they got to the moon, someone had respected them enough to tell them what was going on and then they had almost an hour and a half of something similar to dramatic entertainment.

There were even a couple of smiles. Not huge grins or anything, but still.

"This is complete fucking bullshit. You know that, right?" Except for Angie.

She was standing over me and definitely not buying into any of it.

"Maybe." I wasn't going to disagree with her. Too much hazard involved.

She shook her head in disgust. "How can you be a part of this?"

"Part of what? This is good news."

I thought for a second she was going to spit on me. "They're going to sucker us. They always do."

We just weren't going to get into that. Even back when Angie had liked me I knew that she had no patience for me explaining that I had no choice. I used to wonder if she was genetically programmed to think that there was always a choice. Bit of a paradox given our current address.

Instead I tried to change the subject a little: "Maybe if we all cooperated more we might get some better movies."

Angie turned and started walking away. "Asshole."

Of course.

"Complete asshole." Amazing how sound could carry in the common area.

3.
BETTER MOVIES

10:15

The next week was pretty tame.

Nobody died anyway.

Also, I didn't actually see anything or anybody out of the ordinary but I was reasonably sure that Management was watching what was going down on the Lines very closely. Also, also, I think they were watching me very closely.

It was mostly just a feeling but I was sure that some guys wearing black shirts and no smiles were going to show up at my door and firmly escort me out the nearest airlock. I liked to think that Ross would try and warn me before that eventuality happened but maybe he couldn't. Maybe Ross had already gotten his own walking papers onto the lunar surface. I could totally see rat-face Melling selling him out.

No.

Stay positive, Bishop. There'd been four days of completely flawless shifts and considering how badly designed the new Lines were, that was really amazing. Also important, judging from the fact that I was taking at least one, sometimes two, extra pallets of Boxes to shipping per shift, it looked like productivity was up. There were 30 Boxes to each pallet, up from the usual 26-28. That meant we not just meeting quotas. We were exceeding them.

That, however, was just informal observational and anecdotal evidence which was often re-labelled under the heading 'Wishful Thinking'. Management would want hard quantifiable numbers and they were completely capable of fudging those if they felt like it.

Whatever. I had Boxes to get to Shipping. I noticed one of the supers watching me as I lowered a pallet onto a conveyor belt.

"Hey, Bishop!"

The super called out to me as I backed my forklift away from the belt. I took my time because he knew he wasn't allowed to interrupt me while I was working.

"What?!" I exercised my unwritten right to sound as peevish as possible. "I've got quotas here!"

Peevish was better than terrified.

"Someone to see you." The super pointed his thumb stage left. "Line Office #12."

I parked my forklift and sincerely hoped that whoever was waiting for me was not wearing a black shirt.

When I opened the door to the corrugated aluminum room, there was a rat face waiting for me.

"Melling."

He was holding a clipboard in one hand. There were lots of columns of numbers on the top page. "I'd ask you to sit down but there's no room."

"No problem." I was just grateful that he wasn't masturbating at me. "So how are things in Logistics these days?"

"So great they bumped me down to bird-dog you moron interns down at the Line-level." He flicked the page on the clipboard angrily.

Those columns were significant. Numbers meant some form of quantifiable data. Must be make-or-break time.

Probably break because Melling was here. "You're in luck, Bishop."

Luck? Melling might be here to explain that they were going to kill me relatively painlessly.

"How so?" Might as well get it over with.

Melling sort of waved the clipboard at me. "Quota number hits are up."

Management noticed? And they believed the figures? Fortunately my relief was not so extreme that I took a dump in my coveralls but I did smile more than I wanted Melling to see.

"That's good."

"Noticeably up." Melling flipped the last sheet on the clipboard. "But the numbers have to be even better."

Well, of course.

I just shrugged.

"Logistics is interested in what you can suggest."

Management was asking *me* what to do? Well, fuck a duck and my great auntie too.

"Does this mean I'm up for a promotion?"

"You're an intern." Melling smiled and shook his head. "It means you get to keep breathing."

So much for meritocracy. I sighed and leaned against the rusty wall.

"Bishop? Ideas?"

"How about showing better movies?"

"What's that?" Melling looked horrified. Like I'd just dropped my pants and took that hypothetical dump on his desktop.

"Yeah, something better than an in-flight movie that you'd walk out of."

"You interns are lucky we show you anything at all."

This time my shrug was a lot more confident. "We interns are the Masses. We need better opiates."

Melling didn't say anything for a second. It looked like he was *actually thinking* about my last statement. Maybe he took a couple of political science classes at engineering school and understood my reference. Then he shook his head.

"Where would we get better movies?"

"Are you telling me that you types at Progressive Apparatus can build moon bases and starships but you can't score a few decent films?"

It was Melling's turn to shrug. "We can't be good at everything."

It occurred to me to wonder if P.A. was truly good at anything, but I decided not to explore that thought with Melling. I guess I was going to have to solve this one for them, too:

"I know a guy in Blinn you can call who books films for university film societies and the oil rigs."

Melling clicked the end of a ballpoint pen. "What's his number?"

4.
ENTERTAINMENT UTOPIA

20:00
Tonight's feature:

The Stranger (1946)
Starring Edward G. Robinson, Orson Welles, Loretta Young
An agent for the United Nations War Crimes Commission (Robinson) hunts a fugitive Nazi who has assumed the identity of a school teacher (Welles) in an American town and has married the beautiful daughter (Young) of a Supreme Court Justice. Welles' third completed film as director.

Thank god, my father bought me a copy of *Movies on TV*—which at the time was the thickest paperback that I'd ever seen. Even thicker than the Ace edition of *Dune*. *MoT* was one of the most used books I owned; back when you were lucky to have two (maybe three if the reception was good) television channels coming in on the rabbit ears and you didn't live in a city with an arthouse or second run cinema, you needed guidebooks like that if you wanted to find anything that wasn't complete crap to watch.

In the broadcast only (view what we give you) era, it was actually kind of a treasure hunt—a cinema collecting exercise. I would carefully review the films in the local newspapers' TV listings and then check them out with their ratings and summaries in *MoT*. Anything with three stars or more was going to get some consideration. After that I'd have to coordinate the transmission time with my personal schedule. It wasn't that unusual to cancel a date or miss out on a party if they were showing a Stanley Kramer film or even one of Hitchcock's lesser thrillers on a Friday or Saturday night.

Years later, Eugene and Ross explained the emergence of things called Pay-Television and video stores. Those stores sounded amazing: places where you could just walk in, find a taped recording of a film, rent or buy it (must have cost a fortune!) and then go home and play it whenever you wanted to on your own TV in your home.

Astonishing!

Ross said that sometimes he would even rent several movies and schedule an entire evening of his own television. It was like having a library or a bookstore for films that you could use to operate your very own personal cinema.

Entertainment utopia!

We would have none of that up here on the moon, but now at least I could make things a little bit better. Before our meeting in the tin shed ended, I made sure Melling left with a list of movies. I took his clipboard and wrote down whatever three and four star films I could remember from *MoT*. There was no time to think too much about content or any unifying themes that might govern the spontaneous film festival I was creating here. I just wrote down whatever flicks Mr. Maltin seemed to think were not a waste of time.

The Stranger was probably not one of Orson Welles's best films but fortunately it was oceans better than anything we'd seen before and it seemed like most of the interns enjoyed it. Besides, if we'd started with *Citizen Kane* or *The Trial*, they might have found it a little heavy going. Also, the bad guy (played by Welles) is destroyed by the good guy (Edward G. Robinson) at the end of *The Stranger* and it felt good for us to see that.

5.
TENNESSEE WILLIAMS

20:30
Tonight's Feature:

Suddenly Last Summer (1959).
Starring Elizabeth Taylor, Katherine Hepburn, Montgomery Clift.
In this southern Gothic mystery, a wealthy woman (Hepburn) bribes a surgeon (Clift) to perform a lobotomy on a young socialite (Taylor) in an attempt to conceal the details of the woman's nephew's death. From the play by Tennessee Williams.

I had no idea I would enjoy Tennessee Williams so much. I remember watching the made-for-television adaptation of *The Glass Menagerie* back in grade eleven and while I thought it was well done for a TV thing, mostly it made me feel uncomfortable. Maybe domestic dramas about abandoned mothers who were eternally disappointed by their sons was just a little too close to home (if you will excuse the expression).

Hepburn was even more interesting in *Suddenly Last Summer*. There's a scene where she sits in a wheelchair and descends an elevator into a conservatory that looks like something out of a Bond movie. Blofeld's great aunt I guess.

What really got me was the scene where Liz Taylor talks about how her brother coaxes her into the ocean even though she is only wearing a very sheer white bathing suit which gets more and more transparent with each wave. None of this is actually shown on screen, it's just Taylor's character talking, but is one of the most erotic and disturbing experiences I've ever had at the movies.

Yeah, I might be getting a bit bent up here. What with no more girlfriend and everything.

6.
THE TOAD MEN HAVE LANDED

12:14

One lunch break, she just up and sat next to me.

"Where's the Incredible Hulk, Angie?"

She was by herself.

"Grow up, Bishop."

"Is the Abomination on the loose? The Leader and the Toad Men have landed?"

Angie looked annoyed and shook her head. "Rod and I are taking a break."

"A break?"

"Yeah, as in not hanging out together for a while."

"So, like separate vacations? Him in Mexico? You sailing on the Sea of Tranquility?"

Angie's eyes narrowed. "Do you always have to be a complete dink-head all the time?"

"It's probably genetic." I then regretted the separate vacations remark. "Or maybe my upbringing." It was mean and maybe Angie was thinking about the two of us getting back together when she sat down at the table.

And pigs wear jetpacks.

"Sorry."

"S'ok, Bishop. Guess you can't help the way you're wired."

Angie being conciliatory was confusing. I took a drink of 'nutritious' skim milk to buy some thinking time. "So…"

"What the fuck do I want?" Ah, the good ol' f-word. Now we were back in familiar territory.

"You've never been big on small talk."

"Well, excuuuuuuse me."

"Not a criticism, just an observation."

Was Angie actually smiling? I checked the urge to look around for orbiting porcine species. I was mystified but her expression was nice anyway.

"Matt." Angie pushed a piece of paper across the table in my direction. "People on the Lines have been enjoying the new movies."

"Why are you telling me?"

Angie looked at me with a 'great real' expression.

"Okay."

I wondered what was on the piece of paper. Something like I (heart) you in grade four girl cursive writing? No, not her style. A love note like that from Angie would at least have the words "nail" and "me" in it. And it would have been all caps in big block letters. And the note would have been addressed to someone else.

I unfolded the piece of paper. The note was nothing emotional at all. It was a list.

"We put together some suggestions."

- *The Other Side of the Mountain*
- *Julia*
- *The Turning Point*

Figures, girl movies. Oh wait, there was more:

- *Annie Hall* (sort of girlie but funny)
- *The Towering Inferno* (not girlie at all!)
- *Earthquake* (I didn't know if Management would be comfortable with the Sensurround)
- *The Apple Dumpling Gang* (What the hell?!)

Jeez. Some of these were not even particularly good movies.

"We all know what we've been seeing lately is way better…" Angie was trying even harder to sound reasonable which must have been very difficult for her. "…but every once in a while it would be good to see something in colour."

I nodded and tried not to let my feelings get hurt. Angie had a point: with all the concrete corridors around the Plant, the occasional visit to the brighter ends of the spectrum might indeed cheer a person up a bit.

I held up the list. "What makes you think anyone's going to listen to me?" I guess I wasn't completely able to suppress my involuntary asshole reflex.

"Because it's so fucking obvious that the new films were your idea." True to form, Angie wasn't buying any of my bullcrap.

"Oh, yeah?" The innate drive to be a prick is indeed a powerful one.

"Yeah, and if Management is listening to you, then they must be absolutely fucking desperate."

"So why is it obvious?"

"Only you would think that getting better movies would improve production!"

"Hey! It's working!"

Angie grinned at me. Oops. She had tricked me.

"Maybe."

For just a second the bullshit barrier had been lifted and it was just her and me again.

"Yeah, maybe."

It was nice. Wasn't going to last for more than another 4.3 seconds but it was still nice.

"There's something else."

See?

"What's that?" To my credit, I tried really hard not to sound too suspicious.

"You know those mix tapes you gave me?"

"I do." That was not what I expected to hear. I'm not sure what I thought Angie was going to say but old cassettes was not it.

"Turns out that there's a lot of those around the Plant. Maybe more than you think."

"So?" I mean, sure, if I could score some bootleg music up here then it was probably pretty easy for other people to get tapes too.

"Just about all of us share them around."

"Great." I guess…

"It's not very efficient. There's only a few tape players."

"I guess they would be harder to stash in a shipment."

"And they keep wearing out."

"Well, Radio Shack…"

"But the Plant has a PA system that goes everywhere."

"Yes it does. So what?" I'm reasonably sure that my mind just didn't want to make the next connection.

"So we want you to do something." Never mind, Angie was going to connect the dots for me whether I wanted it or not.

"What?"

She took my hand and looked me in the eyes. "We want you to get Management to set up a radio station."

21:32

I figured the fastest way to get moving on the interns' suggestions was to just walk up to the Logistics desk and ask to see Melling. I thought about involving Ross and sending some cryptic note upstairs via pneumatic tube but that would have just added another layer of Management-level mysteriousness onto everything. And all I'd be doing was giving my old friend a heads-up about something that probably wasn't going to happen anyway. However, there were risks associated with going directly to Melling:

1. Cutting out of a shift early so that I could get to Logistics before they closed.
2. Getting there without an appointment might mean that Melling might not be there when I arrived.
3. Without pressure from Ross (if Ross could indeed exert any pressure on Logistics), Melling might say no. Or even

worse, someone with authority over Melling might say no which could endanger the movies we were able to show already.

4. Melling might be masturbating. I never wanted to see his penis again.

All of these seemed like acceptable risks to me. The worst they were likely to do to me was haul me up for missing an hour of shift work and maybe a protocol breach but given the labour shortage, nothing they'd space me for. Also, I could truthfully tell Angie that I had personally done everything I could. She'd be pissed but probably nobody was going to hurt me.

Besides, someone had finally done something nice for the interns and in return they were working their asses off on the Lines. I owed them this.

Since the Plant was back on normal working procedures, I knew that they weren't going to let some intern waltz in, even if he could flash a Health and Safety ID at them. I thought about giving them some bullshit story about how some other department had sent me to see Melling but there was always the risk that there would be some keener working the desk who would try and check out my complex tapestry of lies.

Lurking.

That's what I ended up doing.

When I got near the main entrance, I sort of hovered outside, trying not to be noticed and trying to notice when the receptionist wasn't at his desk. Since interns are semi-invisible to anyone who isn't working the Lines, this was actually pretty easy. Sure enough, I watched the receptionist empty a mug of something into his mouth and after about fifteen minutes get up to relieve his bladder.

When the washroom door closed, I walked into the lobby wearing an expression of 'of course, I'm supposed to be here', turned down the appropriate corridor, found door number 105, and stepped into Melling's office.

"Fuck, Bishop!"

Yup. He was choking the chicken again.

"New issue of *Gent*?" Didn't this (serial) wanker ever do any work?

"What the hell are you doing here?"

"I have some new ideas to exceed quotas."

"Yeah, right." His manhood shamed and wilted, Melling looked despondent as he zipped himself back together.

"That's right." I sat down, handed Melling the list of movies and told him about Lunar Radio.

Melling didn't even think for a second before he replied: "Forget it."

"But we'd just be tweaking something Management is already letting us do."

"There are no performance indicators that prove that what you're doing is having any effect."

"We're hitting all our quota targets, aren't we?"

"Maybe that's just because the interns are getting more experienced with the new equipment on the Lines."

"Are you willing to risk a drop in productivity if we stop showing movies?"

Melling didn't say anything but his face pretty much broadcast that this was a scenario that he did not enjoy thinking about. Good. I had a knife into him. Now to give it a twist:

"You figure Management will be happy with what happens to our quotas then?"

"Okay." Melling sighed and put the list in his shirt pocket, right next to his calculator. "We'll find a little more money and get some of these movies."

"All of them. You can use the same distributor."

"But this radio station idea is never going to happen."

Now it was my turn to sigh. "We already have the content and the delivery network in place."

I kept on talking even though Melling had the amazing ability to say 'so what' without opening his mouth. "All we need to do is find a decent cassette player and there are a couple of dozen of those kicking around the Plant."

"Equipment is not the problem." Melling shook his head. "But you're going to need people to run the thing. We can't spare anybody from the Lines."

"We can plug in really long tapes and get people to come in and switch them over between their shifts."

"Sweet Mary Martha Mother of God," Melling whispered under his breath.

"It's simple!"

"So what?!" Now Melling was actually speaking the phrase, probably indicating that he was really losing patience with me. "So people get to hear music while they work on the Lines. What the hell difference does it make?"

"It makes the interns happy!"

"Who the fuck cares?!"

"When people are happy, they are encouraged to work longer and harder."

Melling, being the Child of Management, did not look terribly convinced.

"It's called morale!"

"It's just wish-wash, Bishop."

"Plus we can add safety and motivational messages. Get the interns to work smarter, reduce time lost through accidents and extra maintenance."

"We're talking interns here, they don't get motivated. They barely have higher brain functions."

"Fuck, man!" Melling was sparking my inner working class hero. "If a piece of equipment is busted or if an intern is hurt, they can't be working the Lines, right?"

Hesitantly: "Right."

"So it's harder to meet quota, right?"

"Right." Melling was silent for a moment. Then: "What kind of messages are you talking here?"

"Well… say… remember to clean out your work station at the end of shift or be sure to re-calibrate your driver pressure every two hours or letting people know when they've hit quota for the day."

Melling snorted. "Deeply inspirational."

Time to give the knife another couple of twists: "Or suggesting that there's no need to mention that your supervisor is jerking off in his office all the time."

Melling went beet red and stared at me for a bit.

7.
PEOPLE AND FEELINGS

18:37

Not that Ross was out of the picture in this situation. Which is one reason why the latest message I sent inside the pneumatic bullet read: *'Help me out here!'*

I wasn't sure how much influence Ross actually had with Management, how much he could help, but it was worth a shot. But Ross being Ross meant that he was obviously going to be incredibly useful to Management—which was why they probably seemed to tolerate his occasional attacks of ethical behaviour.

It was also why Ross seemed to have access to more inside information than most of the Engineers up here. That might also mean that he had the ear of someone(s) with a Yes/No Factor several degrees more powerful than bozo time-wasters like Melling.

I heard that familiar sucking sound and imagined that little brass projectile rattling its way to some slot at Ross' drawing board.

I know.

Lots of speculation in all of the above, but like I said: worth a shot. Worse comes to worse, Ross might think I wanted him to come down to Internland and give me a foot massage. Which I'm sure we all agree, no one wants him to do.

What I did want Ross to do was find some way around Melling who was being a real knob about some of the details regarding the Lunar Radio set-up.

We'd had a minor dust-up at the corrugated tin love-nest at the last lunch break.

Melling looked even crankier than usual. "If you want this thing to happen then you are going to have to be the DJ."

DJ? Would you listen to this guy? Two weeks ago, I bet Melling didn't even know what a radio was.

"People don't want to hear from me."

"How do you know that?"

"I'm the voice of Management." That thought made me sick. "Your voice."

"Sounds good to me. You tell the interns what to do, they do it."

"Fuck, man! We have to take a subtler approach!"

"Subtle?" Melling gestured at the miles of concrete and pipes that surrounded the work shed. "Does anything about this place look even a little bit subtle to you?"

Okay, score that one for Melling.

"The interns are going to pay more attention if they hear a voice that they trust." I tried to execute a Hollywood shrug. "Me? I'm the Moon's Designated Asshole." I really should stop thinking of myself that way; the truth is not always a healthy thing.

Melling sniffed and threw my talent list on the desk, because he was one of the Moon's Actual and Full-Time Assholes.

"We are not going to take anyone off the Lines to host radio shows. The numbers you've got down there are some of the most productive units in the whole assembly process."

Numbers? Units? Melling, like most of Management, still really hated to suggest that any of us interns might be human beings. However, this was not a good time to strangle him.

"But it's an investment!"

"An investment in what?"

"In productivity. The time you lose from the people doing DJ duty will be more than compensated by the additional, and more accurate, work you'll get from the interns who are still at their work stations."

"This is more of your morale theory?"

"Yeah, as in people feeling better about themselves and life in general."

"Feelings?"

"I'm sure you've heard about them at some point."

"Let me tell you about *feelings* and *people*, Bishop." Melling leaned back in his chair and put one foot up the desk. If he had a big cigar at that moment, I'm sure he would have lit it and blown smoke at me. "Around here, there are those in Senior Management—"

Melling briefly lost his balance and almost fell out of his chair. I don't think that was the effect he was looking for. Even so, I decided not to laugh.

"Yes? What about Senior Management?"

Melling gripped the sides of the desk and put both his feet on the floor.

"Around here, we are basically building glorified Skinner Boxes. You know? Operant Conditioning? Stimulus response? Dogs drooling? Getting the pigeons to drop pellets into slots?"

"I remember my Intro Psych class."

"You interns are the pigeons." Melling smiled. It was one of his really shitty smiles. I knew he was about to say something really unpleasant and he really liked having the power to say it: "Some of Senior Management don't believe that you interns have any inner life at all."

"Inner life?" I was pretty sure what Melling was getting at but I wanted him to verify that he was a complete and utter bastard.

"That when you cut through all that mental monkey chatter that rattles around inside your heads, that it's all just stimulus response."

"Nice."

"Eat, drink, work, sex, sleep. Repeat until dead."

"Really nice."

"The job for people in my position..." Melling looked like he might try putting his feet up again, but seemed to change his mind. "...is to expand the 'work' phase of that sequence for as long as possible…" More of that self-satisfied grin. "…while reducing the other stages to the absolute minimums."

I would have loved to smash Melling's face in just then. Instead, I did what my kindergarten teacher told me to do and used my words instead: "Well, if my morale did exist, I think we could agree that it could be higher right now."

"Try to imagine how little I care."

"What's your point then, Melling?"

"My point is that even though production is up, some of the people with actual decision-making authority think that setting up a radio station up here is about as useful as investing in a fairy dust mine."

"So prejudices continue in spite of evidence to the contrary." I probably shouldn't have said that.

"Don't push it, buddy. If this thing is going to happen, it's going to be Station 802,701."

My I.D. number. Cute.

Melling pointed his finger at the door.

"You better get back to the floor before you start missing quotas."

Help me out here, Ross.

8.
GREY OPS

Let's everybody hold on tight to their dreams.

Okay, I admit it. Starting the first broadcast day with ELO was, for me, a bit of a flashback to Blinn U and programming by Timmie the Wonder Creep. However, there was a logic to my selections here:

As I thought about the events that led to my tenure on the moon, I started to think that Timmie was probably some sort of covert agent from P.A. to help make the population of Blinn somehow more pliant to their operations there. Given that Progressive Apparatus was a vast and monstrously disorganized organizational entity, "Project Timmie" was most likely a very vague and poorly conceived initiative with no measurable indicators of effectiveness. But who said that evil conspiracies are run any better than any other corporate initiative? I was just hoping that what I was suggesting sounded familiar enough to other P.A. Grey Ops[4] that they might approve it out of a sense of habit.

Related to the above point, my proposal also had to sound like it was another form of morale-boosting calculated to improve

---

4   Grey Ops is a term I think I made up. It is a secret mission that is not exactly evil (a Black Op) nor is it particularly good (a White Op). It just is and the organization responsible does it because while it may or may not have any useful outcome they figure they ought to give it a try anyway…

intern efficiency just like the enhanced movie program. If movies once a night made workers work faster and more accurately, just think of all the quotas we're going to bust if we entertain interns every second they are working the Lines.

The next song I played was by Fleetwood Mac. It was the one I heard Timmie play while my new stepdad was having me driven off to my disappearance. I needed that for a bit of closure.

Because yesterday was, indeed, very gone.

19:00

Unbelievably, Management and I reached a compromise. I would put in at least four shifts as DJ and be spelled by other interns on their off-shift time. Probably they wanted to make sure I still got some time in on loaders and scrubbers because I was pretty good with those.

There were six people on the DJ list I gave Melling. Angie was the one I picked and she selected the other five based on the playlists we'd worked out.

I need to assure you that I was not sucking up to Angie when I asked her to be the lead DJ Okay, you know me better than that by now; I wasn't *just* sucking up to Angie when I chose her. There were some very valid and useful reasons for getting her on-board:

1. When it came to music, Angie totally knew her shit. She probably wouldn't even be up here if she hadn't been so much into her music.
2. She had a good speaking voice, very clear and even pleasant to listen to. Especially when she wasn't saying 'fuck you' or calling you an asshole.
3. The other interns trusted her. I wasn't BS-ing Melling when I was making this point. Angie wouldn't say something if she didn't believe it and most everybody on the Lines knew this. That meant if she announced some new safety procedures, the interns were going to comply

without asking too many questions or if we really needed to make some higher quotas for some reason—the Lines were going to roll until we hit them.

4. The risk here was that if you pushed Angie to say something she thought was a lie or a mistake, she would very likely get on the air and say exactly what she did think. (Note to self: never push Angie to lie on the air.)

5. I, also, could trust Angie (see above).

And since we are being painfully honest here, I am a fool and deep down I was hoping that if she and I spent enough time in each other's company we might get back together. The rational part of my brain was deeply skeptical about this scenario. One of the reasons you could always trust Angie was that she was more like an arrow than a boomerang. Once she made a decision she tended to keep moving forward. She rarely changed her mind or wanted back on anything.

Still, hope springs eternal and in one-quarter Earth's gravity it can spring a lot higher.

Stupid phenomenon, that.

The rational part of my brain also had its hypothesis confirmed when about two weeks after the launch of Lunar Radio I was scheduled to meet with Angie after my shift to review the upcoming weekly schedule. It seemed that my desperate little note to Ross had produced even more results. All six of the people on my talent list had spots and Ross had even managed a shipment of new tapes from Earthside.

Mostly Greatest Hits that weren't all that great and K-Tel compilations. It looked like someone at P.A. had knocked over a couple of Woolco's and Kresge's because their store stickers were still all over them. In my old days at university radio I would have rejected most of this content as way too 'Timmie' but for our purposes on Lunar Radio, it was perfect. Lots of material, mostly high-energy (something you can dance to!), cheerful or hideously sentimental.

Yeah, I know. Audio narcotics.

However, applied responsibly, painkillers can really help a person. Timmie and his friends from P.A. were pushers. Angie and our team were going to be healers. At least that's what I liked to tell myself.

At the very least we were going to program this stuff in some interesting ways. Yeah, we were mega-pop, but good mega-pop. The best M.O.R. radio ever. Okay, maybe the best M.O.R. radio on the moon.

Vintage Harrison was coming out the cafeteria speakers when I sat down with my little notebook full of song titles and ideas. Angie wasn't there yet. She wasn't late, I was just early because I was eager to see her. I know, pathetic, right?

"Hey Matt."

I didn't recognize the guy she showed up with. Unlike Rod (a.k.a. Biff, Bluto, Bumpkin, Natty-Bumppo), this guy was of normal human proportions. He also had corn-silk blonde hair (lots of it), coke-bottle bottom glasses and a goofy grin that somehow failed to make him look stupid.

"This is Trevor," Angie explained as they sat down in front of me. "He's new here."

"My condolences." It never seemed right to welcome people to the Plant.

"Thanks, I guess."

Yeah, he got it. This one was smart.

"Trevor used to draw for Marvel Comics."

"What?! Like *Howard the Duck*?" I checked the urge to nerd-swoon and ask what Steve Gerber or Don McGreggor were like in real life.

Trevor shook his head. "I just did a fill-in feature in a *Giant-Size Tomb of Dracula*."

"That's something," Angie insisted.

"Mostly I did a run on *Captain Canuck*."

"Oh, yeah. I know that one." If this was the Trevor I thought he was, then he was a pretty good comic book artist.

For a Canadian, I mean.

Angie had some ideas: "I was thinking that if we could set up

Trevor with some pens and paper, maybe we could do a newsletter for the station."

"Cool." It was a good suggestion. If we could print schedules, do some reviews and intro pieces of the shows and DJs, we might have a serious audience going.

Angie and I got down to looking over the playlists and while she was very focused and business-like, it was obvious that there was some kind of vibe going on between her and Trevor.

1. Shit.
2. Sigh.

Which were the sounds of me being disappointed.

I couldn't believe that I was back at the suck-and-blow tube two hours later, asking Ross if he could score some extra stationery from the Drafting Office.

9.
GLOW AND PLUNDER

04:10

During last night's late shift, the radio was playing something about glowing women and men who plundered. When I went to bed, I had a dream about Australia. I blame that silly song.

Or maybe it was the movie we'd played earlier that week:

The Last Wave (1977)
Starring Richard Chamberlain, Olivia Hamnett
Sydney lawyer defends Aborigines accused of ritual murder while struggling with premonitions and nightmares depicting the end of the world.

Okay, the dream wasn't just about Australia. It was also sort of like that Robert A. Heinlein novel *The Moon is a Harsh Mistress*. And really it wasn't about Australia or that book, it was about the Plant and the interns and me.

And Angie. Of course, it was all about Angie.

So I dreamed about the Plant somewhere between 25 to one million years in the future. Except that it didn't look very much like the Plant anymore. It was a lot like the inside of Moonbase Alpha in *Space: 1999* with all those clean lines and monorails taking people all over the place. There were still some bicycles rolling about but they were all electric and much cooler looking.

There was also more colour and plants scattered around.

Plus:

Kids.

Quite a few kids really. That wasn't all that weird; I mean we were all having a fair bit of sex in our off-shifts and maybe they ran out of whatever Management was using to prevent babies. What was weird was the fact that the kids didn't seem to be working. Everyone worked at the Plant in real life. But in my dream they were just hanging out, running around and generally having fun.

Come to think of it, a lot of the adults were just hanging out too. Like I said, weird. Really weird. Because what I'd learned in the last two years was that the moon was all about work. Really hard work.

So my dream-brain decided that obviously I wasn't on the moon anymore. The view proved me wrong though. There was a big glass geodesic dome overhead and through that I could see the Earth, clear and blue as anything, rising over the lunar horizon.

I could see?

We could see.

We was me and Angie. We were sitting in a park watching the Earthrise. Maybe a couple of those kids playing out there belonged to us. Our children. Our grandchildren?

This was a dream, right? So I was seeing through my eyes and I was also looking at us from the outside.

Angie still looked incredibly hot but we were both older. I did not look nearly as good as she did. Not as fossilized as Kerr Dulleau was in the hotel room at the end of *2001* but not too far off. Maybe this was my subconscious exploring the possibility that instead of dying young at some point after I'd missed my 10th quota I might end up living a long and happy life up here on the moon.

Where interns like me and Angie weren't interns any more. We were people and while we still had to work, we also got to do things like fall in love, have families, read books, run around parks and enjoy the view of the universe all around us.

Sounded good to me!

The dream also suggested something else to me. Angie and I were what? Retired? We didn't have to work anymore? We just got to enjoy being alive?

I know. This dream was heavy-duty, hardcore science fiction. No, this was more than sci-fi. We were talking high fantasy here.

And true to these genres, this is the point where everything stops and we all slog through a big passage of exposition so that we know what's going on.

This is also where Australia comes in—while I saw the different living and working spaces in the Plant it looked like the world rebuilds sequence in that 1930s movie *Things to Come* (except that it was in colour). Things were progressively getting bigger, better and safer. The dream logic told me that while we were still assembling starships—somehow—like Australia—we evolved from a penal colony into an advanced and beautiful human community. While that was happening, we interns started doing the kind of things that people living in safety tend to do. Instead of just existing like quantified units in some industrial process that none of us had a full understanding of—we lived. We flourished and prospered. And did good and cool things.

Somehow the interns, Management and P.A. managed to get together and bring out the best in each other.

Okay, it seemed pretty unlikely that there was any good, let alone "best" on the other side of the table, but this was a dream, okay?

The very process of reaching out to the stars was what was allowing us to evolve. It was just the *possibility* of the Galactic Superculture that spurred us on. If we actually got to meet them— that would just be gravy.

So maybe my dream wasn't that much like *The Moon is a Harsh Mistress* after all. That book is an amazingly good read and if we ever get a copy up here, I figure it will shoot in and out of the intern cells at something approaching Mach Seven. *MiaHM* is about a lunar penal colony becoming an independent democratic state but it's done through a revolution. The inmates end up taking up arms and taking over by force. That's where I can't see how that applies to us. At least my subconscious didn't seem to buy into it.

The balance up here is just too delicate.

And there was no real chance of returning to Earth.

So.

If things were going to get better for us…

TICK.

…it was going to take a while.

TICK.

…and we were going to need some help from Management…

TICK.

…which meant all the persuasion we could manage and all the deception we could muster…

TICK.

…and at this point that meant stuff like movie festivals, radio "stations" and (ugh) even newsletters designed by stupid new boyfriends.

Ring.

Time for another day.

05:00

My communist alarm clock still seemed to be the most reliable piece of technology on the moon. As usual, it was the primary tool for getting me off my slab, washed, into my overalls and out the door on schedule.

Lunar Radio was already up and broadcasting: something about holes in Blackburn, Lancashire.

06:15

The trouble with oldies but goodies was the fact that the source tape must have been played over 150,000 times before it had even left the Earth, so there was a fair bit of sonic deterioration. In this case it sounded as though John Lennon was wobbling back and forth on a giant spring and singing with a mouth full of lime green Jell-O. Even so, one of my favourite songs.

The morning DJ came on: "It's a completely cloudless sky and the temperature outside is an even minus 243 degrees. Great day for a picnic, right?"

Groan.

Then she started making some community service announcements: "There's still a few spots in the Bike Repair Club. It's really useful work and if you've been listening to Lunar Radio here, you already know that the Club is a great place to hang out with old friends and maybe even make some new ones."

The Bike Repair Club was a spontaneous thing that was making life better for a lot of interns. The handy-minded among us (not me) were getting together and fixing up bicycles as they broke down. They were even doing some maintenance to prevent problems before they happened and they'd even taken some spare parts and assembled a couple of completely new bikes. They were weird looking but still more or less functional.

The result was that we now had more than enough bicycles. So no more Darwinian scrambles for transportation before First Shift. Also, breakfast was less tense and (although I was one of the few interns that knew this) the a.m. production run on the Lines were up. Significantly up.

At first Management thought we were making mistakes—or even fudging the quota numbers—until someone apparently wasn't afraid to make the obvious point that the extra bikes meant that more people were arriving on time for the First Shift. In fact, the more physically fit interns were actually able to start work a few minutes *early*.

Another song came on and I sat down to a mug of something brown and kind of warm and a plate of quivering cubes. I knew it wasn't Soylent Green because it was brown.

We really needed to do something about the food part of the equation here.

10:25

Working my loader, coming up to my morning hot brown

fluid break. Yes, Mr. Bachman, I was taking care of business.

As usual, lots of Boxes were coming off the Lines and most of us knew by now that there were far fewer defects showing up. That meant that the shipping pallets were filling up a lot faster and that meant more stuff for me and the other materials handlers to move around. As far as I was concerned, that was just fine. Made the shift go faster with far less aggravation. From the increasing number of complaints from my fellow workers that I *hadn't* been hearing, I think I wasn't the only handler that felt this way.

Forward. Stop. Lift. Turn. Forward. Stop. Forward. Turn. Stop. Lower. Reverse. Turn. Forward. Stop.

Repeat 500 times.

Then park.

Time for fluid management, i.e. washroom break and coffee.

Luchavich, one of the other handlers, sat next to me.

"Super was around here."

"Yeah?" Management interest was still rarely a good thing.

"He said he was looking for you."

"He say why?" Not good at all.

"Says you're late with your Health and Safety Report."

"I'm not late." I put my mug down.

"No?" Luchavich didn't look convinced. Or all that interested.

Still, I had some professional pride to defend. "Got nothing to report."

Luchavich nodded and drank from his own mug of brown liquid.

What I said was true. We hadn't had an injury or an accident in over a month.

Not even a little one.

12:00

"It's an incredible downer."

"Not every movie has to have a happy ending."

"Newman is fantastic in it."

The Super did manage to find me when I was sitting at the picnic table with my co-workers. Lunch, you know.

In between mouthfuls of soya and potato chip sandwiches, the crew was busy analyzing last Monday's movie: *Cool Hand Luke*. I had forgotten what a good film it was and for what was a relatively older work, it was interesting to see how many of the interns could relate to it.

"The egg-eating contest was hysterical!"

That particular scene was, in fact, brilliant.

A lot of us up here could probably identify with Luke—who ended up on a chain gang doing hard labour for "cutting the heads off parking meters". Most interns got our one-way lunar vacations for equally world-endangering offences. We also seemed to be surrounded with a great many "failures to communicate".

"Way better than *On the Beach*."

Everyone, except me, groaned. *On the Beach* was one of my major programming failures. People really hated that movie. Even though most of us had reconciled ourselves to the reality that we weren't ever going back to Earth, we still liked to think it was still down there. Safe, or at least intact, and waiting for us if only we could get there.

Or maybe they simply weren't all that keen on black and white films. Even so, I was still going to try *Dr. Strangelove* out on them sometime.

The cinema talk seemed to be winding down and it didn't seem possible to credibly ignore my supervisor any longer. I walked over to him, held out my hand and he handed me a clipboard.

"Busy shift, Bishop?"

"Usually are."

I took out my ballpoint pen (they work just fine in one-quarter Earth gravity), located the appropriate box on the form on the front of the clipboard and wrote in a very large "0".

"Really, Bishop?"

"Really."

I found another box on that page, printed out my name and number, added a slash and dropped in "H.S.V" in even larger capital letters. Then I returned the clipboard.

"Thanks, Bishop."

"No problem."

He thanked me? It was nice but a little unbelievable. I'd kept my super waiting for this report for over a week. Even though it was obviously nothing but a formality, filing this kind of pointless paperwork was the sort of stuff that those inhabiting the lower ends of the Plant Org Chart existed for. Six months ago this guy would have screamed at me, belted me in the mouth and dragged me in the direction of the nearest airlock.

Now he was being nice? It was disorienting but I liked this culture change thing.

"Just a minute."

I knew it, too good to be true.

The super flipped to the last page on the clipboard, pulled out a print-out and handed it to me.

"What's this?" I suppose I could have just read the thing but a guide to Management's between-the-lines messaging was often helpful.

"Dunno." The super shrugged. "Something from Central Evaluation, it looks like."

"But Evaluation?" Never a fun department.

"But it says you get to book off shift early tomorrow." The super started heading towards his tin shed.

"Great. Thanks!" I called out after him.

He waved back at me. And smiled.

All this niceness was just getting too weird. But it was a good weird.

15:15

No time to stop and ingest any more fluids, warm, brown or otherwise, this afternoon.

They were playing more BTO on the radio. Somebody must

have been remembering a road trip.

I was just going to have to unwrap a carob-flavoured powdered milk bar and suck out the various surfaces, as I drove my loader around with more parts for the Lines. People were working hard and fast today and nobody needed the hassle of running out of the necessary components.

I was moving at a pretty high speed between each work station, trying to drop in as many parts as possible and scoop out any wastes and defectives. Mind you, I was going fast but I was still within the safety limits. I didn't want to write up an accident report on myself.

Then I saw Angie packing up at her work station and yes, I was experiencing a completely company-boy sense of satisfaction—observing that everything she did was systematic, careful, efficient and completely regulation. And she wasn't following procedure like she was some kind of Capekoid drone. Angie was doing things right because she understood that her work was important. That *she* was important.

The satisfaction was a little more personal these days because I had recently pushed some safety improvements from the interns up the chain—like extra clamps on driver hoses—which Management had actually incorporated.

"*Hey radio star!*"

I probably shouldn't be yelling stuff like that out on the Lines where everyone can hear, but an intern cannot live by procedure alone. Besides, it was fun. I knew that Angie was leaving a little early because she needed some extra time to set up for the end of afternoon shift drive time spot.

"Hey, yourself!" She shot a big smile back at me. Which was really nice. "Got a second?"

"Yeah, but just a second." I braked my loader and scolded myself. You are not entitled to hope for anything, buddy. "Can't let any of the work stations go dry."

"Where are you with the supplies for the newsletter?" Angie, intelligent person that she was, picked up on my cue and went right into all-business mode. "We gotta get those."

The newsletter didn't seem all that essential to me but maybe that was because unlike Angie, I didn't need something interesting for my new boyfriend to do. It would have been shitty to say that and since I was trying hard to cut down on that kind of thing, I didn't. Instead, I said:

"I'll ask again." And I probably would. I could stop in at Logistics on my way to Central Evaluation.

Angie shut the hatch to her station and fastened some bicycle clips to the ankle cuffs of her overalls.

"We've got some new clubs going and we need the newsletter to get the word out."

"New clubs?" More and more I seemed to be falling behind on things.

"Hydroponics for one." Angie was already heading for the bike racks.

"Hydroponics?" She was already out of earshot.

As in growing things? I revved up my loader and headed for the next work station. Maybe my dream wasn't that far off after all.

Back to work. More business to take care of.

18:55

I walked my bike down that familiar corridor and stopped at the iron rectangle. A message from Ross was waiting for me:

'Pens, paper, stencils and gestetner. All will be left at the studio door tomorrow.'

This was good news, I wouldn't have to do advanced level begging to Logistics after all. There was more to the message:

'Officially, none of these materials exist and you didn't get them from me. Unofficially, nobody's looking these days so don't worry about it.'

Don't worry about it? Wow. When was the last time anyone said *that* to me?

20:30

I had almost forgotten the movie that night. Would have been nice to have a date with me—even for just for a bit of company and light conversation. It would have even been okay if Angie brought along the BF. However, when I found Angie and told her the news from Ross, she and Trevor went "squeeeee!" and went off somewhere to plot something creative.

Cinema stag night.

The speakers were thumping out a song about a full moon over Memphis, which quickly faded away as the lights darkened.

Tonight's Feature:

American Graffiti (1973).
Starring Richard Dreyfuss, Ron Howard, Charles Martin Smith.
As the summer of 1962 winds down, teenage friends listen to DJ Wolfman Jack play rock and roll as they cruise Main Street in a small Californian town. A comic and touching end of innocence story for America and its youth. Zeotrope/THX-1138. George Lucas directs.

I had completely forgotten that I'd booked this one. Universal Studios logo—the Earth from space which always made me smirk, the green lettering and sound of someone tuning through the AM dial in a car radio. That made me smile too. Opening shot of a drive-in restaurant at dusk. Bill Halley and Comets start playing.

Then, and very suddenly, absolute darkness. Before I, and the rest of the audience, could figure out if this was supposed to be a part of the show or not, a loud electronic tone sounded and a voice, not one of my DJs, boomed out over the PA system:

"There-has-been-an-unscheduled-power-reduction."

"What about the movie?" someone cried. Speaking for all of us really.

"Go-to-your-quarters-immediately-until-further-notice."

The artificial voice of the Logistics Clock was bossing us around. So much for culture change.

10.
A Much More Interesting Question

"Gravity did it." Ross was with me in person for a change, standing right next to me, in fact.

"How could they blow out a whole power grid?"

Ross shrugged and looked at the inside of the warehouse. For some reason he had a Polaroid camera hanging around his neck.

"How is easy. Gravity has priority access to all the power they want."

I was a lot more interested in the whole lot of stuff that was sitting on the floor. I didn't get out to this part of the Plant as often as Ross.

"I guess that makes sense."

"You might be surprised." Ross shook his head. "*Why* Gravity blew the grids is a much more interesting question."

"And by interesting, you really mean scary. Right?"

"Right."

"So is this the stuff that's supposed to be scary?" I felt like a hand-puppet asking Mr. Rogers or Mr. Dressup what he'd just taken out of the Tickle Trunk.

"Part of it." Ross softly kicked at an oddly flattened copper cylinder with the toe of his Hush Puppies. "It's part of one of the drive shafts that was supposed to get hooked up to the EOS. They do specialty fit-ups over at the Gravity hangars." Ross waved at the field of twisted metal laid out in front of us. "It's all junk now."

"Okay." First I'd heard of any of this but it made sense, more or less. "So what happened?"

"They got careless." Ross walked down an aisle of shredded wires, aimed the camera and hit the flash. "They were working too fast and overloaded the power grid."

He kept on taking pictures of the wreckage while he slowly walked further away from me.

"So what's the rest of the scary part?"

Ross turned and pointed at half a dozen oversized glass jars at the far end of the warehouse. They were filled with dark brownish red goo.

"That's the Mechanics Team over there."

21:56

Before we left the warehouse, Ross was pretty specific about what he wanted me to check out and what sub-basement I could find it on.

The thing looked pretty old—like a Mercury or Gemini space capsule from the early sixties. There was something like a big gun-metal grey plate wrapped around its ass-end. I figured that it was either a giant hot plate or some kind of gravity generator.

A lifeboat?

Yeah, the capsule was a lunar lifeboat. It must have been left over from the early construction phase of the Plant. No doubt there were enough around here for Senior Management to bugger off if something went seriously wrong.

Ross' directions about the wires looked pretty accurate. A couple of heavy electrical cables between the generator plate and the mains in the tube walls were not connected. Maybe the contractors had forgotten to hook them up or maybe some particularly (and uncharacteristically) diligent contractor had unplugged them to save power.

Didn't matter, I supposed.

I re-connected the jacks and plugs and to my relief, the plates didn't spark, sputter and/or burst into flame. Nor was there any explosion in the silo that would spew out smoking debris and my mangled corpse onto the lunar surface.

So that was good.

Instead, the plates started quietly humming away like their batteries were charging up. I pressed my nose up against the capsule porthole and I could see the rows of dials on the control panels start to glow with a hard neon red. Man, there was a shitload of readouts in that thing.

So that was good too. The thing still worked, right?

Maybe. On both counts.

11.
CARTOON HEROES

20:30

The movie that night was Brian DePalma's *Phantom of the Paradise*. Even if you're not a big Hitchcock fan and somehow managed to miss *Psycho*, the shower scene is one of the funniest things ever filmed. At least I think so.

I had such a good time that I stopped worrying about the little adventure Ross had sent me on, which was still a lot to process.

The film's combination of musical comedy and Gothic horror went over pretty well with the rest of the audience as well. There was applause as Paul Williams' voice started singing and the credits started to roll. Angie turned around and gave me a thumbs up.

That was definitely good. Maybe she'd want to talk about the movie with me for a while.

Then Trevor, that talented jackass, walked up to me.

Bit of a buzz-kill there.

He had an intense expression on his face and was holding a cardboard tube in one hand.

"We need to talk."

Aw fuck. Was he feeling jealous like Angie's other ex, the Incredible Bulk? Was Trevor going to hit me with that compressed paper cylinder? I doubted that he could hurt me but the experience would be embarrassing for both of us.

I looked around for Angie. Maybe she could shame her idiot

lover into behaving better.

Nope. No sign of her.

"Matt."

Oh, there she was. Right next to me.

Angie gently pushed me back into my chair while Trevor pried the plastic top off the cylinder. I could make out a large block of text as the page uncurled in front of me:

"MR. OBLIVION"
PAGE ONE: SPLASH PANEL

The artwork depicted a man wielding a bulky futuristic pistol in one hand. His other hand (fore-shortened, of course) was reaching out to grab something that is just out of view, or just isn't there, but enhances the drama of the figure's pose. Classic Marvel Kirby/Steranko inspired stuff. Not that I was dissing Trevor for that; if you were going to steal, steal from the best.

"Mr. Oblivion?" I looked up from the page. "A superhero? Like Mr. Miracle or Mr. Terrific?"

"No." Trevor half shrugged, half shook his head. "Well, sort of."

"Sort of?"

"Keep looking."

"Sure." Please note, Trevor said 'looking', not 'reading'. This was definitely a visual guy here.

The background behind the running man was frankly much more interesting. It looked something like a cross between illustrations by Moebius, Chris Foss and the designs from Fritz Lang's *Metropolis*. Not only was there a lot of structural detail but Trevor had managed to blow up much of the urban technology apart in a series of fascinating fractal patterns. I doubted that real detonations were as aesthetically pleasing, especially if you were in the middle of one, but this was a comic book and sometimes you needed the ol' Kirby Crackle to motivate your audience.

I turned to the next page and saw a horde of humanoid robots swoop down and capture the still-running man, who I figured was Mr. Oblivion.

"Origin story?"

"Necessary evil."

I was already picking up an anarchist vibe from the story. Which was giving me some idea how this seemingly harmless boyfriend-illustrator managed to get himself exiled to the moon.

"He starts out as an ordinary tech-drone… until the Master Control System decides to wipe out his community as part of a surprise urban renewal project."

"So all the people here who are getting blown up and plowed under, they're like sub-normals or deviants or evil mutants or some such thing?"

"Nope, they're just in the way."

His explanation impressed me. Trevor had a clear understanding of how social structures and complex political processes worked. To quote my sociology professor.

"He's the only one who survives."

The central panel showed the androids really whaling on our protagonist.

"This is survival?"

"It's the most realistic thing in the comic."

Trevor indeed had a dangerous way of looking at the world. I don't think I would ever like him but I might find myself admiring him at some point.

Welcome to the moon, buddy.

The last page wasn't completely penciled in yet but it looked like the soon-to-be Mr. Oblivion was getting sucked into what looked like a giant vacuum cleaner. That is if Douglas Trumbull and Boris Leven were designing horking huge home appliances.

"As a stray human, he gets reconditioned to be an object for a secret government program."

Trevor had talent. Actual talent. And he was intelligent. No wonder Angie liked him better than me.

Fuck.

"Have to admit, the drawings are great." I handed the pages back to him. "But…"

Like many creative people, Trevor's Artist's Spider-Sense activated when there was a danger of rejection.

"…we could print this."

"But?"

I could practically see the wiggly lines squirming out of one side of his face.

"But I don't think we'll be able to properly reproduce all the detail you've got here."

Trevor sighed. "The detail is the whole point."

I could only sigh back at him. "I kind of figured that."

Angie, on the other hand, was just getting mad. "You mean you aren't even going to *try*?"

Argh. I hadn't seen Angie pissed off for a while and I was out of practice about how to deal with it. "I guess I could see if they'd let us use some of the big photocopier machines over at Technical to print these pages."

This was a long shot but I was frightened.

12.
GOOD AT SCHEDULING

After lunch there was another meeting. Wonderful.

The guy from Gravity was talking about some structural mods they wanted in some of the periphery buttresses to prevent meltdowns like the one they'd had in the hangar. As usual there was an overhead projection with a blueprint image whose primary message seemed to be: "This is so fucking complicated that there is no chance in hell that you peasants will ever understand it."

They were right of course (damn it) so I didn't try.

Instead I was bothering Ross with my whispers.

"I just need to get up to your section for an hour. Two hours, tops."

Ross, because he was always practical and good at scheduling things, rolled his eyes. "You're going to need more time than that."

"No, no." I had anticipated his assessment. "I can make the editions with the comics into limited runs. 250-300 sheets a shot."

"What's the point of that?" I could tell that Ross was starting to lose patience with me. His fault though, he had decided to sit next to me, probably not believing that I had the nerve to bug him about something so dumb.

"The newsletters with the comics will be special."

"How can they be special?"

"Like collector's editions."

"So people are going to fight over them?"

"You sound like Melling."

Ross looked a little hurt. I just waved his expression off. "People will share them and if they have to wait a little bit before they can read the comics, they'll appreciate them more."

Was this a true statement? I had no idea. Maybe. Sounded plausible at least.

Ross shook his head (a reasonable response). "Could you at least try to pay attention to what the man is saying? It's kind of important."

"What? Really?" I mean, this was a presentation from Gravity. Normally, it was a safe to assume that whatever was being said was pointless and irritating. Or at least 85.4% incorrect. The speaker changed the overhead and the insanely complicated diagram was replaced by a slightly less insanely complicated diagram.

"*Yes it is!*" Amazing how Ross could yell in completely hushed tones.

Aha!

That was why Ross sat next to me in the first place. He wanted to make sure that I actually listened to this guy.

"Okay…" I squinted at the diagram. Gravity Guy might as well have been speaking in Ancient Venusian, but I decided to at least try to care: "Looks like they want to make parts of EOS… simpler?"

"They do."

"Why? Engineers hate simple."

"They do, but they have to catch up with the outputs on the Lines."

I couldn't help but smile at that. The idea of us lowly interns making those dickwads in Gravity sweat and scramble was totally delicious.

"Is that good?"

Ross shook his head. "These are not good shortcuts."

I didn't like the sound of that. "Is this going to affect anything we're doing in the Plant?" It didn't take much for my mind to start connecting dots. Were there going to be shortcuts on the Lines? Were they going to be less safe?

Ross shook his head again.

"So far this is going to be Construction's problem. Especially for the EVA crews."

"So what?" I wasn't disrespecting Ross (well, not very much) but if the situation didn't involve the Lines then there wasn't a hell of a lot we interns could do about it anyway.

"Thanks for the FYI." I hoped I was sounding positive.

Ross closed his eyes as the speaker kept droning on about deadline updates.

"Yeah, my pleasure."

"So, can I use your photocopier?"

Ross managed not to scream.

"Be done before the start of first shift and stay out of everybody's way."

13.
MAGNETO, TITANIUM MAN AND SIGNS OF SUBVERSION

06:34

I could hear Paul and Linda McCartney singing happy songs about super-villains as I walked over to the aluminum shed.

It didn't take long before getting Mr. Oblivion out on anything resembling a schedule got to be a major pain in the ass.

First there was getting the camera-ready art printed. Sure, I was able to finagle access to better photocopiers but that meant that once (sometimes twice) a week, I had to get up three hours early to cycle out to Technical, load up the heavier stock paper and churn out a couple of hundred inserts.

Then the next day, I had to get the damn pages stuffed inside the centre crease of the newsletter. Sometimes I could get Angie and some of her friends to help with that end of the operation but sometimes not. We were ahead of schedule on the Lines but not so far ahead that people could disappear for whole shifts. Plus Ross was still sending me updates and diagrams via copper cylinder express, and these (frankly) seemed to be making less and less sense.

So far it looked like I had a two-thirds complete map of the first phase of the Plant's original transportation and emergency response system. I mean, thank you for the history lesson, Ross, but what the fuck was I supposed to do with all this? Maybe all the tension between Technical and Gravity was starting to get to him. Ross was one of the sanest, stablest people I'd ever known but that was then and this is now. Maybe he was finally cracking up. The rest of us were pretty much nuts up here, why not him too?

10:00

Speaking of going crazy, Melling called me off the Lines one shift so we could talk about Mr. Oblivion.

Apparently he was not a huge fan: "Some in Senior Management are worried about what the interns might be reading into that science fiction thing of yours."

Melling had the latest page spread out over his desktop.

Asshat had spilled coffee on it.

"Some in Senior Management are probably worried that the interns can read at all." Okay, maybe not the smartest thing for me to say but I'd been working on 00.76 hours of sleep per twenty-four hours for the last three weeks. I was a tiny bit grumpy.

Melling showed uncharacteristic restraint and just studied the artwork for a while. "So…" he said eventually. "You're trying to start some kind of revolution or something?"

I invited myself to sit down in the chair facing the desk. "That's just bizarre, Melling. It's a comic strip, not *Das Kapital*."

Even though I'm pretty sure Melling had never read Marx, his question was not stupid or even bizarre. But it was a good idea for me to act as though it was.

"Do you actually read what you're publishing here?" He just wasn't going give up on this.

Of course I'd read Mr. Oblivion, and pretty closely at that. Standing there by the rolling blue light of the photocopier, it was interesting to speculate as to where Trevor was going with it all. As the storyline unfolded, it did turn out that our drone-like protagonist was most definitely re-programmed into some kind of operative/agent provocateur code-named (surprise, surprise, surprise) Mr. Oblivion. He got some weapons (not all that many really) and some spy-tech (which was unusually retro and included stuff like super-powerful suction cups for climbing those cool complicated skyscrapers as well as infra-red goggles that doubled as microcomputer read-outs that let him peer into myriads of databanks). (The goggles as a concept weren't that retro, but Trevor drew them like they were designed for the 1936 Norwegian Olympic Ski Team.)

Mr. Oblivion's wardrobe was another thing that made me grudgingly admit that Trevor was probably some kind of creative satiric genius. Mr. O wore the exact opposite of James Bond's Knightsbridge bespoke three-piece suits or Nick Fury's skin-tight rubber-zippered kinkster leotards.

Instead, our hero wore denim jeans, a bomber jacket and a very working class tweed brimmed hat. In some of the action shots, Mr. Oblivion looked like Andy Capp with a jet-pack.

Worked for me.

Back to the latest Melling debate:

"Yeah, I do read it." Even with the nicer photocopiers at Technical, we still didn't have the capacity to produce colour illustrations but I thought the half-tone black and whites looked pretty damn good. "Given my current postal code, I thought I might not be up for more science fiction but I really do think it has a certain appeal."

In the last panel on Melling's desk, Mr. Oblivion was taking out a hostile twelve-foot industrial android.

"A certain appeal?"

Appealing like genital warts, Melling was probably thinking.

Mr. O didn't have the martial arts skills of a Magnus Robot Fighter, so our intrepid hero had to improvise and was therefore was using a long-bladed screwdriver to pry off the machine man's metal head.

"Yeah, it's fun."

"Fun?" Melling snatched the comic page away from me. "It's subversive!"

Had to admit that Mr. Oblivion's screwdriver did resemble the air-drivers we used on the Lines. From a certain angle anyway.

"It's just an action-adventure story."

"It's telling interns that they need to bust up the Plant!"

I shook my head, probably not as convincingly as I needed to be. "The story is set on a future Earth, not the dark side of the moon."

The problem (which we both knew) was with the premise. Mr. Oblivion wasn't just a government secret agent. He was working for the Ministry of Policy Impediment and his job was to be a legally sanctioned saboteur—seeking out and destroying other government programs and corporate entities. Not all of them mind you, just the ones that had gone seriously wonky. Not such an unusual idea for a science fiction story, I remember similar stuff from Spinrad and Herbert and even Van Vogt. And some of those stories were even reasonably entertaining. When I agreed to take on the strip, I had decided to avoid thinking about some of the libertarian potentials of the premise, figuring if Trevor started veering off into John Birch territory I'd just stop printing the thing.

Melling was gazing at one of Trevor's fantastically detailed future city-scapes, unable to conceal his admiration. "So you're absolutely sure there's no secret agenda here? No hidden meanings in the story?"

Now I was starting to admire all that linework, artistry that still managed to survive our cheap photocopiers. "You see any signs of subversion?"

"That's the trouble with subversion, it's often hard to notice."

I looked at Melling. "How much higher are the production numbers?"

14.
THE BEST SURPRISE

14:17

I was sort of enjoying my visit to Central Management. The furnishings and rooms were much nicer than anything I'd seen at regular Admin or Technical, where I'd be meeting with the likes of Melling or Ross (on a good day). And absolutely everything was much, much, much nicer than anything you'd encounter in the Interns' Block. Central Management was like somebody had put the best stuff in a higher-end Holiday Inn into a big box and shot it into space.

There was this cozy plush beige-ish carpet on the floor of the meeting room they'd put me in and the walls were covered with these (most likely faux) oak panels and they had these incredibly comfortable padded swivel chairs. Also, I don't know how they did it but the ceilings had fluorescent tube fixtures that actually weren't: the illumination was soft, diffuse and kind of pleasing to the eye, like they'd found a way to install spokes of warm, gentle sunshine into that pressurized room.

If I didn't know that this was where Management was very likely about to do something really awful to me, I probably would have very happily hung out there all shift.

The door swung open.

Fuck.

Something awful was definitely involved.

Ed walked in. On the moon again and wanting to see me.

This could not be good.

Ed sat down in front of me and folded his hands on the (also probably fake) oak table top.

"Matthew." Ed shook his head. "Matthew, Matthew."

So he could still pronounce my name. "Hey, Ed."

"What are we going to do with you, Matthew?"

"Send me home?" I probably shouldn't be cracking wise with him, but unlike the Rules and Regs people, I didn't seem to respect Ed enough to fear him.

"Uh, no, Matthew."

I was pleased to see that Ed looked a little older and a lot fatter than the last time I'd seen him. Hopefully he was under tremendous pressure from his masters at P.A. and was coping by drinking vast amounts of booze and eating lots of unhealthy foods. Could be good, he might die of alcohol poisoning or a heart attack.

"How's Mom?"

"She never mentions you."

"Oh, really?"

"So she's good." Ed gave me another one of his famous shit-eating grins. "And for such an old skank, she's still a pretty good fuck."

You can only shake your head when you hear shit like that. "Ed, you are such an inspiring father figure." If he figured he was going to shake me up with this kind of talk, he was completely off base.

"I'm working on your sister and pretty soon I'll have some younger pussy to fall back on."

That statement was also disgusting but predictable, he wasn't going to get much of a reaction with that one either.

"So, sooner or later, she'll be joining me up here."

Ed looked a little surprised but then he laughed. "You figured out our career recruiting strategy."

I laughed back at him. "What can I say, Ed? I'm a genius."

"Far from it, Matthew." Ed shook his head. "However, some misguided people seem to be over-estimating your value to the company."

"Progressive Apparatus thinks I have value?" I'm sure I looked rather surprised at that moment.

Ed nodded. "Others think you are indeed a genius."

"A genius?"

"One of those evil geniuses."

"Evil?" This was just surreal. "Are you sure they don't really mean inconvenient?"

Ed nodded again. "That what I told them, but based on what's been happening on the Lines lately, one scenario is that you're setting us up somehow."

"Me?"

"I know, stupid, but some people are convinced you might be an agent provocateur."

"What?!" Really surreal. "How the hell do you figure that?"

"Your girlfriend at Blinn University, the Jag."

"Colleen was not my girlfriend."

"Okay, so you never got to nail her…"

"*Gah!*" Ed was a true moron. No wonder my mother fell in love with him.

"Your so-called Jag is still at large."

"At large? Like she's causing trouble for you jerks?"

Ed's eyes narrowed. "Possibly."

"I'm not surprised. She really is a genius." Maybe even an evil genius, but in her case it was the right kind of evil.

"She hasn't had any real impact on our plans." Knowing the Jag, I was hopeful that Ed was operating in one of his usual modes, i.e. lying his ass off. "However, we need to know if you're still working with her."

"Ed…" I couldn't decide whether to laugh or cry, so I did neither. "In case you haven't noticed, my current mailing address is the goddamned wrong side of the moon!"

I had to admit it though, idiotic as his line of questioning was, Ed did not look embarrassed. "You must admit though, you are associated with some major changes at the Plant."

"People get more productive and Senior Management thinks

there's a conspiracy?"

"We both know it's beyond your capacity to cause changes like that, Matthew."

"You people are truly crazy."

"Are you working with Colleen Jang?"

"No!"

Ed sighed and tapped his finger on the desktop. This interview was going to go on for quite a while and we both were wondering if it was going to involve Ed punching me in the face.

15.
DR. BAUMANN

08:43

"You and Dr. Baumann will be spending a lot of time together for the next while."

The middle management drone, who once must have fancied himself to some kind of silver fox, led me into the Training Centre meeting room where the doctor was waiting for me.

Baumann sat at the table, hair so short it was almost impossible to tell what colour it was (dirty blonde I think), ram-rod straight back and heavy black-rimmed glasses. She was wearing a dark grey zippered coverall and I had no idea what division of P.A./the S.S. she was from.

The ex-fox grinned at me. "Dr. Baumann is a physician…"

Oh, she was a medical type doctor! No wonder she didn't look familiar; as a designated HSV, I noticed that we didn't have too many of those up here at the Plant.

"…she is going to walk you through some new health and safety intervention procedures."

And exit Ex-fox.

Dr. Baumann pressed a switch that was set into the table and a light at the far end of the room revealed half a dozen crash test dummies, all dressed in denim union suits, sitting on some folding chairs.

The dummies reminded me of my old Capekoids.

"As a Volunteer Health and Safety Officer, you are often the first on the scene of unplanned industrial events."

I just nodded, not really sure where all this was going.

"Your ability to apply what I am about to show you could save the Company significant amounts of time, materials and money."

Dr. Baumann stood up and walked over to a wheeled metal cabinet.

"I am going to simulate a number of scenarios."

Sure. Baumann was going to show me how to save time, materials and money. Not lives. This *doctor* was definitely working for P.A.

She slid open a drawer at the top of the cabinet and removed a ball peen hammer. Then she took a moment to get a good grip on the handle and swung the hammer into the head of the nearest dummy.

"*G-AH!*"

That was me making a completely involuntary noise.

Dr. Baumann was not an excessively large person, nor was she obviously very muscular. However, she must have been pretty strong because she made quite a dent in that dummy. Maybe she was thinking about somebody she didn't like very much when she brought that hammer down.

She looked over at me.

"Could you please come closer, 802,701?"

I really didn't want to comply with that request, most likely because she was still holding the hammer.

"Uh…"

"Please."

The way she said 'please' didn't mean please. It meant 'obey'.

I obeyed.

"Notice the impact area on the cranium."

About one-third of the dummy's head was a cracked crater.

"Are you looking carefully?"

"Yes." I didn't add my thoughts about horrified fascination.

"Can you please tell me what kind of equipment or process failures on the Lines might cause an injury like that?"

My first impulse was to suggest a psychotic doctor wielding a metal hammer, but that event seemed pretty unlikely outside this room. I tried hard to think about this objectively. Logically. Think like a Vulcan, Bishop:

"It would have to be something at least the size of a fist… travelling at high speed…"

Dr. Baumann nodded as I spoke.

"…so it would likely be a compression breach or container breakdown."

"Where is that likely to happen?"

Okay, detective time. This was getting more like *Columbo* than *Star Trek*.

"Up around the Final Assembly Area is where you'd find the hard couplings that would be about the right size and weight to be a suitable projectile."

Dr. Baumann smiled and put the hammer back in the cabinet.

I smiled too because I suddenly felt in less danger.

"So you will know that you can only expect this kind of head injury at specific phases in the production process."

That made sense, but it seemed like a pretty pointless observation to me. If some intern had that sort injury there was S.F.A. (Sweet Fuck All) that Mr. Health and Safety could do to help.

Dr. Baumann took the damaged head in both hands and twisted it off the body. "That prior awareness may save you a few seconds, because while the regions around the injury will be of no use to us, the other hemisphere of the brain—if you can isolate the cranial bleeding and not bruise the tissue too badly during the removal process—can still provide some useful neural matter."

"Useful neural matter? You mean like brains?"

The doctor responded with a condescending smile and took a felt pen from a zippered pocket and started drawing dotted lines on the broken head.

"These are the points where you want to make the incisions."

After a few more observations, Dr. Baumann put down the damaged object and used a range of hammers to smash more dummy heads from a variety of angles. While she did this, she explained how each injury type presented different harvesting opportunities. Apparently it was particularly important to try and keep as much of the frontal lobes and hypothalamus as intact as possible.

"Some cortical structures offer more potential computing power than others."

Right. Makes total sense. Waste not, want not.

Eventually Dr. Baumann took out a machete and approached the next to last dummy:

"We don't simulate blood because that gets so messy that you can't see the separation points caused by the occurrences."

We certainly didn't want any mess if we could possibly avoid it.

"Now if we get a driver detachment at the same time as a pressure surge…"

Fuck. My nightmare scenario with Angie on the Lines.

Dr. Baumann held the machete with both hands and swung the blade through the dummy's neck. Could have been made of butter.

"You would think that a neat decapitation would be an ideal injury for a full-brain harvest…"

An *ideal* injury?

The dummy's head bounced off the floor.

"…however, there is still the potential for force trauma, and the tissue around the brain stem can bleed out and dehydrate surprisingly quickly…"

The head rolled to the far end of the room and came to a stop.

16.
HAZARDS AND HELPFUL HINTS

HEY READERS![5]

Just a quick word of explanation (and sort of an apology) for the sudden change in format.

From this issue forward, and for the foreseeable future, we are shrinking the size of our ever-popular comic strip *Mr. Oblivion* to half a page. We're truly sorry that we have to do this because the feedback we've been getting is that a huge horking majority of you really love Trevor's amazing stories and illustrations. Imagine how great they'd look in colour.

Someday, fans!

Anyway, we're knocking down Mr. O to a more compact size *not* because Trevor is having trouble keeping up with his deadlines. The guy is a freakin' dynamo of creative energy. You won't believe what's coming up next![6]

---

5   I resisted the urge to start the article with "Face Front, True Believers" because I was worried that the long legal arm of Stan Lee and Marvel Comics might even extend to the moon.

6   In truth, Trevor never was more than two pages ahead so I had very little idea what was coming down the pike.

No, no. Mr. Oblivion needs to go on a print diet to make room for a new regular column by Matt Bishop[7] who some of you may know is one of our Volunteer Health and Safety Officers. Anyway, the name of this column is "Hazards and Helpful Hints" (I know, Matt thought of it all by himself!) He promises that it will be much more interesting than it sounds and who knows, it might even save your life one day.

Take it away, Matt!

How To Do Stuff at High Speed While Standing Perfectly Still

Let's get started on the right foot: I have to say that from a health and safety perspective, just about all of you are doing a really terrific job. In the last three months there's been a 44% drop in work related accidents throughout the whole Plant and an almost 79% reduction on the Lines themselves. That means just two recorded injuries and no fatalities. Think back to that week just after the new Lines opened up.

Phenomenal.

So, **CONGRATULATIONS**!

However: things can always be better. Anyone who's been hurt on the job can tell you that. They call them *accidents* because something happens that you weren't expecting. And usually these unexpected events are something bad. Whoever heard of someone talking about an enjoyable car crash? This was true back on Earth and it's even truer here on the moon.

The only way to prevent these unexpected events is

---

7   Yeah, it felt weird to write about myself in the third person.

paradoxically to expect them and take steps so that they don't happen at all. Sure, things are great these days, but it's exactly when you start taking things for granted that something goes wrong.

Another *however* for your consideration:

The Lines are, and probably always will be, powered by high-pressure gases. If those gases get loose or interface with our tools in the wrong way—something might fly off and cave in your head or maybe slice you in half.

I'm writing to you out of my own self-interest because as your Lead Health and Safety Officer, I will likely be the first one to deal with what's left of you. I am not looking forward to having to deal with that mess.

So, now that I have grossed out enough of you to have your undivided attention, let's review the basic coupling systems on your drivers…

06:35

'You get so busy making Boxes that you don't let yourself think about what they are going to put in them.'
Brains.
Ross' message was really irritating because it was so completely true. The Boxes were designed to contain and connect human neural tissue. Living tissue, apparently.
Ah, denial.
Organic mental components that, once linked up, would form an incredibly powerful calculating and control network for the EOS Onboard Supercomputer. Something huge and complicated like a multigenerational(?)/sleeper(?) starship was bound to need some seriously heavy thinks to keep all those guidance, life support and propulsion systems going. Plus there probably was a whole bunch of other stuff that EOS had to do that hadn't even

occurred to me. I was just bird-course boy social science major, how could I be expected to understand such things?

I had paid just enough attention in my third year psychology 'Brain and Behaviour' class to know that the human brain, to quote my professor, was: "the most complex configuration of matter in the known universe." So it made sense that P.A. would want to tap into all that smart for the EOS onboard. Relatively small and lightweight, simple to feed in those little nutrient fluid tanks and reasonably easy to obtain in our frequently recessed economy. There were also lots of savings in labour costs—much easier to handle your work force if you found a way to dispose of those pesky bodies that kept insisting on eating, sleeping and all kinds of other bothersome biological processes.

Plus. Unlikely to unionize.

Just plugging a bunch of brains together was also way easier than trying to design and build an artificial intelligence when you could get some natural intelligences and manipulate them in a cheaper and lighter artificial environment.

Now, to be honest, I was indeed aware of Management's wetware strategy for a while before my head-bashing exercise with Dr. Baumann. Melling and Larry would sometimes joke about it back in the days when we were drinking all that horrible Hyper-Gin and playing that stupid board game.

Whenever one of us (usually Melling) would make a particularly stupid move, someone else (usually not Ross) would say something like: "I think that brain is safe" or "defective neural component at work". Then we'd have a good laugh because ripping someone's brain out of their skull and plunging their consciousness into endless sensory deprivation was just so funny.

I mean fucking hysterical, right?

Wonder why I avoided thinking about it until recently.

That is the danger of "not my department" thinking. Sometimes something really nasty suddenly becomes your department. And if you applied P.A.'s relentless utilitarian logic, things continued to make more insane sense:

1. The brains had to come from somewhere: people.
2. These people had to be ones that no one would miss and/or people that other people would rather see gone.
3. i.e. these were the same sorts of people that P.A. needed to use as interns.
4. Here we encounter the human resources/economic crunch point: you can either use interns (a.k.a. prisoners) as physical resources (i.e. workers at the Plant) or as mental resources (a.k.a. computational components, i.e. brains in Boxes).
5. This might be a serious problem because: a) it means that you have to find more unwanted people to subdue and transport to the moon; and b) it might be that some guys in authority who weren't working for P.A. and who were reasonably decent human beings (I prayed to God that there were at least a few of them still around) might start noticing all those people who were regularly disappearing.
6. Furthermore, they might appreciate that people have a right not to disappear, regardless of whether they happen to be inconvenient, obnoxious, or otherwise unusual.
7. So body work or brain work? Guns or butter? You needed both. Exploiting accidents on the Line was a way of avoiding this difficult decision. You got a handy little butter-gun or a delicious new flavour of gun-butter. If you were going to lose a certain percentage of intern bodies through routine industrial mishaps, why not reduce the number of brain-owners you had to vanish by harvesting intern neurons before you threw away their broken/bleeding bodies?
8. Like I said, tired and true utilitarian logic.

The only significant hiccup was that some poor schmo had to be there to cut out the brain cells at the incident point while everything was still juicy and fresh. We were looking at a pretty serious sharp end here and yours truly, as "voluntary" Health and

Safety Officer, was sitting right on it.

The only way for me to get my soft little ass off that razor's edge was to do everything possible to prevent any and all future accidents. Hence, my column in the newsletter.

My plan was more probably more pathetic than brilliant. Sure, nothing bad had happened lately, but all Senior Management had to do was speed up the inputs on the Lines by 50% or 60% and screw-ups would start happening as the interns struggled to keep up with the sheer flow of parts. Like that old Charlie Chaplin movie but much more horrible.

Not that Management would ever do anything to deliberately damage their own infrastructure; on the other hand, tweaking speeds and quota levels across different sectors of the Plant?

Exactly the sort of thing that gave Senior Management huge administrative erections.

Time to stop thinking and get to work.

18:10

"Can we talk movie choices?"

Angie sat down at my table in the cafeteria. There was something different about her. Something was missing.

"Sure, Angie."

"Good."

Ah, yes. "Where's Trevor?"

Angie shrugged and smiled (sadly). That wasn't good, it meant that she missed him and therefore still cared about him.

"He's drawing up the latest instalments."

"He's two pages ahead." Yeah, I was being a bit of a shit here. "He could take a break."

"What can I say?" Angie shrugged again. "He loves the new inks you got him."

Yeah, I did good on that one. Ross had squirrelled away a few bottles of colours that the Drafting Section was never going to use because they were now doing all their specs as computer print-outs. Useless to DS but they'd look absolutely great on a comic book page. Not that we were anywhere even close to being ready to printing in colour.

"It was all part of my brilliant plan."

The full colour artwork was just for the edification of Trevor and those of us on the editorial team.

"Plan?"

And Angie of course.

"To get him out of the way."

Angie laughed. "Celibacy has turned you into a genius."

More stupid genius talk. I narrowed my eyes.

"Sorry!" Angie held up her hands in mock self-defence. "Besides, I hear that you have a new girlfriend now."

"What?" New one to me.

"An older woman, the rumours report."

"Baumann?"

More laughter.

Time for a subject change. "Did you say you wanted to talk movies?"

My ex wisely nodded. "There's some science fiction thing the new interns say we have to show."

"What's it called?"

"**Not** *Logan's Run*." Angie really hated that movie for some reason. "I forget the title. *Star Trek*?"

"That's a TV show."

"Maybe they made it into a movie?"

"That kind of thing never happens."

"I don't think that was it anyway."

"Who's in it? Star power can be a factor here."

"Star Power? That's not the title either."

"I meant what actors star in it?"

"Nobody I know. Harry Fisher?"

"Who?"

"Mark Ford Jones?"

"Doesn't ring any bells."

"Oh, I know!" Angie snapped her fingers. "The English actor!"

"Oh, *him*! The one with the accent."

"Alec Guinness." Now it was Angie's turn to narrow her eyes at me as her cinematic IQ suddenly doubled. "He was in that war movie by David Lean."

"*Doctor Zhivago?*"

"Yeah but also a different movie; the one where they're all POWs."

"*Bridge on the River Kwai?*"

"That's the one."

"Forget science fiction, let's get that one." It was a hell of good movie.

Angie shook her head. "Might be too close to home."

"Hmm." I had a sudden and awful flash of insight. I was the Alec Guinness character in *Bridge Over the River Kwai*. In the interests of maintaining POW morale, he helped the Japanese to build a bridge that would carry weapons and supplies that would be used against the Allied forces. I was doing the same goddamned thing—setting up newsletters and radio stations—just to make life slightly less godawful and keep things running smoothly. My dream about us interns and Senior Management somehow hooking up and exploring the universe together was as delusional as Sir Alec's belief in the over-arching virtues of discipline and fair play.

Fuck, now I hated that movie.

"You okay, Matt?"

I'm sure I must have turned about three or four shades of pale while I was having my big cinematic/moral revelation.

"Yeah, yeah. I'm fine." I wiped my eyes because they somehow got a little watery. "The thought of collapsing erections[8] always makes me cry."

"Right. Mr. Sentimental, that's you."

"Anyway." I smiled a little. It was Angie's turn for a revelation. "The film you're talking about is *Star Wars* and according to the blurb in the catalogue, it was the mega-hit of the age and yeah, I'm trying to book it for next month."

---

8   Spoiler alert: that bridge gets blown up.

"Matthew." Angie shook her head in a way that was wonderfully familiar. "You are such an asshole."

More than you know, my love. More than you could ever possibly know.

17.
Star Wars. No, Really.

06:50

'Publish or perish.'

Were the only words that Ross had written in today's bullet. Even so, the brass container was crammed full of folded pages. Each sheet had maps of unused levels of the Plant.

And of course.

No explanation.

Ross was probably assuming that I was almost as smart as he was and so he didn't need to give me the background on obvious stuff like that.

Big mistake there, buddy.

On the other hand…

By the time I was pedalling my way to the Lines, I think I knew what Ross might be getting at. Why was I somehow suddenly less stupid?

Maybe I had absorbed some additional brain matter through my fingertips during my remedial training sessions with Dr. Baumann.

I parked my bike and walked over to the forklift.

Once my shift was over I was going to have an unscheduled editorial meeting with Trevor.

12:00

Star Wars.

Yeah.

Booking the stupid thing was getting to be a hassle.

When it first showed up in the catalogue, it looked like any normal Hollywood movie as it finished its first run and was getting ready for drive-ins or art houses. It would be available as either 70 mm or 35 mm prints that could only be shown at regular commercial cinemas, then it would be distributed on 16 mm or 3/4 inch video cassettes so that non-standard venues like oil rigs, church basements, Antarctic outposts or secret moon bases could show them. Then a year or two later, depending on how many bookings they could milk from these third and fourth runs, the movie would be up for the TV networks and super stations to bid on.

S.O.P. for the cinematic ecosystem with price ranges to match. Except when you had a serious 'sleeper' hit, i.e. a flick that the studios and the distributors weren't expecting to do all that well but ended up doing very well indeed. While Senior Management was not in the habit of shipping copies of *Variety* and *The Hollywood Reporter* up to the Plant, from what I could figure from the prices and available dates (or lack thereof), *Star Wars* was doing phenomenally well.

First the catalogue sheets said the 16 mm and video copies would be ready to go in one to two months. Then they said it was four to six months. Then the notice was just: "LATER".

Also the price for renting the film doubled. Then it quadrupled. Finally the sheets announced: "UPON SUCCESSFUL NEGOTIATION".

The price was my main problem. We could run other movies while we waited as long as we knew that the thing was coming eventually. But dealing with the higher rental cost?

"That's a shit load of money, Bishop!"

And I was just estimating it at eight times the usual rental fee.

"A fucking shit load."

Melling didn't want to pay it and part of me could understand why.

"The interns keep asking for it though." And they deserved it.

"So what?"

"They hear it's really great."

"It's just a stupid movie."

"*Really* great."

"If they're so desperate for sci-fi, why not show *Logan's Run* again?"

"Because they are sick of it."

"Or that one with Yul Brenner and Peter Fonda?"

"*Futureworld*?"

"Yeah, that one. It's cheap to rent."

"It's also so terrible that it makes your eyes bleed."

"You get to see Jenny What's-her-name's boobs in *Logan's Run*."

"Only good thing in the whole movie." Well, maybe Peter Ustinov, too. His acting, not his breasts.

"What about that Evel Knievel documentary?"

"What if the audience rises up and kills us?"

The situation was really confusing Melling. In the old days, the interns were happy to have a refrigerator light bulb on so they could make some shadow puppets on the wall before bedtime. Now they wanted the same entertainment options that they had back on Earth.

"These are premium prices, Bishop." Melling, eternal asshat that he was, shook his head again. "I am not going to go to Management to beg for extra cash just so the grunts can see the latest hits."

"The interns really want to know what all the fuss is about." That included me. I remembered that strange novelization and I was very curious about how all of that would work on the big screen.

"Then the only way we can book it is if we drop three, maybe four other films from the schedule." I noticed that Melling's math skills always seemed to improve when it came to cutting budgets or taking things away from people. "How do you think your precious interns will like a month of no movie nights at all?"

Not very much, I suspected. I told Melling that I'd ask around and get back to him. It turned out that I didn't need to do that. Our good friends in the Gravity Division were about to resolve our dilemma for us.

18.
OFF-LIMITS MAPS

05:50

'It's Showtime!'

Gah. Even more Rossian Mysteriousness. My friend was making me crazy these days. I'd responded to his last message by insisting that Trevor incorporate maps of some of the unused levels into the last instalment of Mr. Oblivion. In the spirit of Ross' preferred means of expression, we weren't being all that obvious—but if the reader looked closely they might see something on one of the computer monitors or on the circuit pattern of a robot drone or maybe even the logo on Mr. O's girlfriend's t-shirt. Although, to be fair, Trevor hadn't revealed if Mr. Oblivion's girlfriend was actually his girlfriend or if she was just a more sisterly girl who was a friend to this alienated loner hero.

That last point might seem a little precious given the wider context of the potential life and death shit that might be going down but we had a comic book to get out there and I supported what Trevor was trying to do with the storyline. Romantic frustration and other delays in consummation were classic Lee-Ditko/Peter Parker-Betty Brant narrative fuel. In the case of Mr. Oblivion, his love interest just might be a member of a secret government cell with a competing agenda, who could be ordered to kill him and all other operatives from the Ministry of Policy Impediment.

All good storytelling fun but in terms of my need to covertly/publicly display Plant access and egress routes—essentially irrelevant. I was happy that Trevor gave the girlfriend a more normal figure than the hyper-voluptuous women characters who had been creeping into Marvel and DC ever since the Comics Code Authority started relaxing its standards on sex, drugs and violence. We didn't need any D-cups distorting the maps. And as much as I loved boobies, I somehow found them embarrassing in my science fiction diet.

Anyway, it was all getting out there for any interns to see when they had some off-shift time to figure it out. I was pretty sure that Management types like Melling, being the one-dimensional types they were, would be focusing on the details of the plot and dialogue and totally gloss over the pictures—so they'd never pick up on what we were doing.

And so what if they did?

None of these areas were off-limits, at least not officially. They were just ignored because they were irrelevant to current operations. If the interns showed up for their shifts on time, did Management really care that much where they might be wandering? It wasn't as though any interns were going to go strolling off the moon.

I would just plead petty subversion if we got caught. I even kept the mark-ups I'd made on the original art so that Trevor could (quite truthfully) claim this was all my idea.

09:25

My pettiest subversion was the fact that I never did tell Trevor to make any storyline changes to Mr. Oblivion—instead I allowed myself to have a lot of fun by making up bogus examples of how our hero's exploits were promoting the P.A. party line when I reported to Melling:

"The device that Mr. Oblivion uses to fly out of range of those missiles?"

"What about them?" If you looked up 'Infinitely Bored' in the

Oxford Interplanetary Dictionary you would find a line drawing that exactly matched the expression on Melling's face.

"That's a demonstration of how great our Gravity Technology is."

"Right." Melling now had another dictionary expression: 'Vast Apathy'.

"And that giant robot that Mr. Oblivion dumps in the nuclear furnace?"

"Yeah?" Back to Face #1.

"That's a critique of poor work habits and the dangers of absenteeism."

Melling pointed at one of the drawings: "Doesn't that guy Oblivion is blowing away look just like Van Dusen?" (One of our least loved Line Supervisors.)

I nodded. "It's irony."

"Irony?"

"Really challenging an acknowledged authority figure would be stupid and crazy."

Melling nodded.

"So it's obviously done for humorous effect."

"Yuck. Yuck."

Melling never seemed all that satisfied with my interpretations of the Mr. Oblivion subtext, but he let them pass. Like most of the middle management drones, Melling seemed completely mystified and frequently intimidated by most forms of creative expression. It must have seemed crazy to him that people would risk so much embarrassment by just going out there and making stuff up in public. Also, it would have been rather humiliating to him to admit that there might be something going on in a silly funny book strip that he didn't understand.

So I got to have a little fun.

None of any of this was going to solve my *Star Wars* problem. Everybody really wanted to see it. Unfortunately there was no way we could afford it.

Then there would be a chain reaction of bad shit happening:

1. Collective disappointment leads to lower productivity levels and decreased quality control.
2. Which means fewer units, more of which will not work properly.
3. Senior Management will, of course, panic and pump up the quotas and force everyone to work even faster.
4. Which will cause more mistakes at every point along the Lines.
5. Which in turn will result in an exponential rise in industrial accidents.
6. Which means that yours truly (if he isn't offed in an accident himself) was going find himself spending most of his shifts pulling brains out of the bruised, broken and bleeding bodies of his fellow interns.

I really didn't like this chain of cause and effect and I needed to find ways to prevent it from starting up in the first place.

Fuck. This stupid place was making me think like a manager.

19.
A Paradigm Shift of Cosmological Proportions

12:12

So here's how my entertainment/morale problem resolved itself.

Melling called me back into the Line Shack the next morning shift: "You're going to have to tell your radio friends to announce that we're scaling back movie night to once a week."

"That's bullshit, Melling!" I was somewhat upset by this news but not as much as I was making out. It was just fun to aim some harsh language at this bozo.

"That's what's going to happen."

"But why? Is S.M. mad at the interns?"

Melling shook his head, a little like he couldn't quite believe what he was about to say: "Exactly the opposite. Senior Management has decreed that the interns deserve to see the results of their work."

There was dead silence for a second.

I really couldn't think of what to say. S.M. actually might care about what the interns felt and thought? That we deserved anything except to toil and sweat for them until we died?

Incredible.

Possibly a paradigm shift of cosmological proportions.

"The infrastructure connected up really well yesterday and they are going to do some trial accelerations."

"Cool." I couldn't help it, this really was pretty cool.

"They're going to make some runs with EOS over the Plant." *Showtime.*

"And we all get to watch?"

Fuck, I blew it: I was grinning.

Melling nodded.

Hot damn! All we needed now was Walter Cronkite and Arthur C. Clarke for colour commentary.

"They've scheduled the manoeuvres for after the main day shifts so the interns and techs can watch them on the screens in the common areas."

"So we can't run any movies after dinner?"

"Viewing the trial runs will be the entertainment. Except for one night a week." Melling seemed mildly annoyed that he had to explain all this to me. He also probably didn't like the fact that it was going to be really fun to make this announcement over the radio.

Then something else occurred to me.

"That means we don't have to rent as many movies."

Melling shrugged. "Yeah, I suppose."

"That means we can afford to book *Star Wars*."

Melling sighed.

This time I liked my grin.

20.
Mouhammad's Adaptive Skills

Mouhammad was one of our vets. Been here way longer than me. Nixon was still in office, crikey, Trudeaumania was probably happening when he arrived.

Mouhammad was obviously an excellent survivor and a reasonably nice guy. I didn't mind it when he sat next to me at the cafeteria. With a bit of luck, he might have that little chess set of his with him. One of Mouhammad's adaptive skills was the fact that he didn't win all the time.

"Take a look at the screen, Matthew."

Okay, no chess.

I was not expecting to hear him say that because when I got to the cafeteria for dinner, they were just showing live feed of EOS in stationary orbit with a couple of tethered EVA-workers doing some kind of assembly on the outer hull. Mouhammad did not have a reputation for wasting people's time (another survival skill), so I checked out the screen.

"Hey…"

I could see two very large structures moving towards the main axis of the EOS.

"What's on those? Boxes?"

Mouhammad nodded. "Connected into clusters, they tell me."

The configurations reminded me of fat, overstuffed Plexiglas

Christmas trees. Even so, at that scale, they were more spectacular than ridiculous.

"Are… are…" I thought I might really hate the answer to my question but I still needed to know. "Are the Boxes empty?"

"I guess so." Mouhammad shrugged. "Maybe?"

God, I certainly hoped they were. You'd have to scoop out a couple of thousand heads to fill all those Boxes.

"They must be just testing out the connections between the configurations and the central hub."

"Looks like."

Was that a look of pride I saw on Mouhammad's face?

I felt it too.

Had to admit it, the EOS was a tremendous achievement.

And even with the illegal imprisonment and slave labour, we interns were a big part of that accomplishment.

Someone up on the EOS moved the spotlight and we saw something else coming into view at the perimeter of the spacecraft. It was even more enormous than the Box configurations: rectangular, like a vast flying slab of Brutalist architecture with massive bevelled holes drilled deep into its surfaces. This new thing was moving towards the end of the Main Axis.

"Bet that's what they've been building over at Gravity," Mouhammad observed.

"You figure those are the primary engines?" Profound fuckwits that they were, I had to admit that Gravity had managed to deliver something pretty amazing.

"That's what I figure."

All very impressive stuff up there on the screen. It reminded me of the expression Alvin Toffler coined in *Future Shock* to explain the merit of space exploration:

Global Space Pageants.

Was that what Ross meant by 'Showtime'? Watching the engines dock with the aft section of the EOS—I just wasn't sure.

Most formidable.

Then I remembered my conversation with Ross in the

warehouse. Should I be looking for something wrong? Or was this just my perpetually bad attitude manifesting itself again?

Fuck.

23:50

I couldn't sleep, so I jumped on a bike and took a ride to the drop box. And wish I hadn't:

'The titan is unstable.'

I really hated this new message from Ross. Not because it was cryptic, I was getting used to that. This time I hated the words because I was pretty sure that I knew exactly what he meant. What I didn't know were the consequences of the message. Mostly likely though, they were going to be pretty goddamned unpleasant.

EOS was unstable?

That couldn't be good.

Like I often said: fuck.

Probably the rush job and dumbing down of the specs had compromised the design somehow. Ross and his associates at Technical must have spotted the problem but they would have no clout with Senior Management to do anything about it.

Unstable. Also probably unfixable.

Fuck a duck.

And it was all the interns' fault. My fault really if you drilled down into the situation. We were working so much faster and smarter on the Lines that we kept forcing dinosaur divisions like Gravity to seriously haul ass just to keep up. And they weren't able to, really. Keep up, that is. Maybe they were doing stuff that was way more complicated and difficult than we were. Maybe they were just a bunch of arrogant, incompetent, fat-ass morons. Could be both.

The outcome was the same either way.

So what happens if EOS has a major systems failure?

Fuck, who knew? Maybe Ross and a few other bright lights in Technical knew. Not me.

One thing I was absolutely certain of though: we interns would be punished for it. Sure, our main failing was the fact that we had all become too good at our jobs. Didn't matter. Interns had the least amount of political power in the Plant, so we were the easiest to blame and to hurt.

How the hell would S.M. hurt people who already had almost nothing? Dead cert that all the fun stuff, the radio station, the movies, the newsletter, the comic strips, our whole little experiment with creative expression would vanish.

All that would be unpleasant but it wouldn't be enough. Too survivable. We would have to be made an example of. I had no idea to whom we'd be made an example of to, but maybe that wouldn't matter either.

I folded my arms and leaned against the concrete wall, watching some interns on the late shift bike home, and kept on worrying about the implications of Ross' message. I was also thinking about all those Boxes that needed to be filled with fresh brains. Maybe S.M. would try and kill two birds (and a few hundred interns) with one stone.

Ugh. Yeah. Definite possibility.

Senior Management really liked that kind of thinking.

I kept watching interns roll by. Some of them looked really happy.

Damned easy to shut down that happy though.

All Management had to do was up the quotas and harvest the nervous systems of those interns who missed their new targets.

What's that I was seeing now?

Hugging and kissing?

A couple was tucked away in the shadows of another alcove. Nothing too serious or non-family friendly, just a bit of spontaneous loving.

But…

Public displays of affection in the corridors?

Outrageous. I should fill out a form and send it to Melling's office ASAP.

Fuck that. There were other things to worry about.

Math was never my strong subject but that didn't stop me from attempting a few calculations: so… per shift… killing one to three people… so reduces the workforce on the Lines by 15%? 20%?

More ugh.

…compensates for the accelerated outputs from the terrified remaining interns by what percentage? Fuck, I don't know.

Ugh. Ugh. Ugh.

Ross could probably figure this out no problem.

No wonder he was getting all weird on me these days.

I had another cheerful thought: what if EOS' breakdown caused some major catastrophic event? Like rumours about how the Soviets accidentally blew up their own moon rocket? Something like that, with a big enough boom, would kill most, if not all, of us. That wouldn't be great, however, it had the virtues of being very final and hopefully much quicker.

Plus, while it was happening, we might get some really spectacular television.

21.
THE PRESENCE OF LIGHT

07:15

"If circumstances permit, it is very important to check for pupil dilation."

"I beg your pardon?"

"Check to see if the intern's pupils react to the presence of light."

"So I shouldn't try and harvest if the pupils are still responsive?"

Another training session with Dr. Baumann:

"Oh, no!"

"No?"

"Responsive pupils means that you *must* harvest as quickly as possible!"

"But brain activity—"

"Yes, a still functioning parasympathetic response means that there's a minimum of trauma."

"But doesn't that mean the intern might recover?"

The doctor shook her head and smiled at me condescendingly (as usual). "It means that we have access to very high quality neurological material."

At that point it occurred to me that I should ask why did we wait for accidents to happen? Why not just remove people's brains before they sustained any injury at all? That would be primo grey matter. I decided not to say anything, best not to give Dr. Baumann and her bosses any ideas.

"It also affects your choice of storage solution." Dr. Baumann gestured at a tray of cylinders of coloured fluids. "With less damaged neurons you should use a higher level of nutrient." She picked up one of the tubes. "You don't even have to waste time reading the labels, just grab what looks like some lime green Jell-O." She smiled. "Yum!"

Dr. Baumann was trying a slightly different tone today. Her understanding of informal and friendly.

"Yum."

I really hated it.

"I've got some homework for you, Matthew."

Baumann handed me a thick binder. I opened it and flipped briefly through the pages. Masses of dot matrix print and lots and lots of ASCII diagrams of brains. A horking shitload of different angles of cerebral cortexes, most with dotted lines suggesting possible accessways for removing them from their owner's skulls.

"There will be a quiz." Dr. Baumann smiled at me. Which was really creepy. She continued: "I'm heading Earthside in two weeks, so you will have to train the other Volunteer Health and Safety Officers."

"Okay…"

"I hear that you have some communication skills so I'm confident you'll do an effective job."

Somebody thought I had a talent? A skill? That was a shame because it meant somebody was also paying attention to me.

"Thanks."

Dr. Baumann walked over to a wall-seal and pulled it open.

"Now it's time for some practical work."

We stepped through the opening and entered another lab.

Argh.

I was afraid of this.

There was a dead chimp laying on an operating table.

This was going to be the point where Dr. Baumann and Management were about to discover the basic flaw in their brilliant plans involving yours truly. I was a complete and total chickenshit when it came to the use of needles, scalpels and any other devices that involved the cutting open, or penetration of, organic matter.

Back at Blinn Collegiate Institute, I could only just manage the basic dissection assignments in biology class. When we had to open up those poor crayfish and frogs, I got my lab partner to do all the cutting and tweezering and labelling.

By the time we got to doing the cow hearts and fetal pigs, I was a complete basket case. I suspect the prof gave me a passing grade just to get me out of the lab.

And now here we were.

Still on the fucking moon.

In a pressurized experimental chamber.

Standing in front of poor dead Bonzo and studying an array of stainless steel knives and hand saws.

Dr. Baumann looked at me. "Matthew?"

"I'm not sure I'm ready to do this."

"Why don't you at least try?" There was that creepy smile again.

"Try?"

"Yes, you might surprise yourself."

So I tried. At first by willing myself to pick up one of the surgical tools.

Nope.

Absolutely no muscle movement or motor function at all.

"Matthew."

Dr. Baumann frowned, which was kind of good because it made her look more normal.

"Yes?"

"Here are some things that you need to think about right now."

"Yes?"

"Number one: we are not going to replace you. At least not right away."

"You're not?"

"So, number two: you *must* do this."

Oh, I was being *compelled*. Like that never happens up here.

"Therefore, number three: if your subject is capable of feeling pain, then they will feel a great deal more if you attempt this procedure without a certain amount of practice beforehand."

"Yes."

Ah, the lesser of two evils. More of the kind of thinking that P.A. did so enjoy.

"Plus, number four: your preparation will mean less damage to the brain tissue. So all this fuss and bother won't be for nothing."

"That's very important." I meant my statement to be all ironic and insulting but it seemed to please Dr. Baumann.

"Therefore and in conclusion, point number five: it really is best that you try this."

About fifteen seconds later I had something with very sharp little metal teeth in my hand and another ninety seconds or so later, I had managed to get the top of Bonzo's head off. We now had all that greasy grey goo exposed to the air, waiting for me to collect.

In just under an hour, or 3,600 seconds later if you prefer, I had most of the chimp's brain and brain stem inside three plastic jars.

"That wasn't too bad, Matthew." Dr. Baumann looked at the floating tissue samples. "A little sloppy but I'm sure you will improve with some more trial runs."

She opened up a freezer which I was pretty sure was filled with Bobo, Cheetah and a few other of Bonzo's unfortunate friends and relatives.

It was at that point that I threw up.

22.
A Few Hundred Extra Helpful Hints

03:35

I couldn't sleep for some reason.

Even though I was incredibly tired.

I decided to keep myself busy by writing another two dozen or so health and safety columns for the newsletter.

19:10

Speaking of the newsletter…

"You feel like telling when you're going to wrap up the latest plotline?"

Not that it mattered all that much, but if Trevor was going to run short of material, I now had a huge back-log of helpful hints.

"Two more pages."

"That's all you need?"

Trevor nodded. "Mr. Oblivion breaks into the hidden processing complex and discovers that robots have been stealing people's brains to use in the City's central mainframe."

"The way Trevor draws how they drill the wires into the brains?" Angie grinned. "So gross!"

Gross? Yeah, and not hard for me to imagine. I must have turned about 9500 different shades of pale, although to my credit I didn't scream and/or vomit all over the table. Instead I spat out words: "*You have to change that!*"

"Why?" Trevor did not seem to like my suggestion.

"Yeah, why? It's great!" Angie was now in faithful girlfriend mode, defending her lover's creations.

"I'm sure it's all fantastic." I nodded, then shook my head. "Change it."

"There's an important statement here!" The red in Angie's face was starting to obscure her freckles. "How machines can be abused to exploit the living!"

Trevor looked a little surprised at Angie's interpretation of his work. He probably hadn't thought of the story that way until now.

"Doesn't matter," I said.

Senior Management would have their own interpretation of the storyline too. Especially if they were aware of what Baumann had been prepping me for.

"You still have to change the story."

"Why the fuck should we?"

Interesting how Mr. Oblivion was obviously a collaborative project between Angie and Trevor. It was so very much not any of my business but I really didn't like how close those two were. "Sooner or later, it is very likely that you will know."

However, all that time of Angie being angry with me was turning out to be useful right now. I knew I would be able to withstand her wrath, at least for short periods.

"*Oh yeah?!*"

"If you want us to have a newsletter, and if you're remotely interested in us staying healthy, then you will change the story. No ripping out brains."

Angie and Trevor looked at each other for a moment. Finally, Trevor spoke: "How am I going to do that?"

"You're the creative one." Wow, I was getting a headache. "Figure something out."

Maybe *I* should have my brain removed.

"You know, Matthew, sometimes you act like you might be a halfway decent human being." At that moment it was a little hard for me to read Angie's expression.

"Okay?"

I knew that she was going to qualify her statement in some way.

"Then you go and do something that reminds everyone that deep down you really are a total asshole."

"Thanks, Ang."

The lights flickered a little as I watched them leave the common area. No big problem probably, just those morons in Gravity messing around with something.

23.
LETRASET PATTERNS

19:34

"Where is it?"

"Top of the screen."

"Where?"

"Far left."

"I still can't see it."

It only took Angie and Trevor twenty-four hours to cool down and devise an alternate approach to the Mr. Oblivion storyline which involved some evil hypnotic ray. Trevor liked this even more because it let him try out some strange Letraset background patterns that we'd found in a drawer in Technical.

Now the three of us were sitting at one of our usual tables in the common area watching, or trying to watch, the evening's fly-by.

"There!"

"Where?"

"It's like a big silver star."

"A big what?"

"But it's moving."

"Nothing's moving!"

"Give it a second, it'll get more obvious as it moves closer."

"What's taking so long?"

Believe it or not, this was the first time Angie's shift let her see this.

"What's taking so long?"

How could you tell?

"Just wait…"

"I thought this thing was supposed to move fast."

"It is moving fast, but you have to consider that we're talking huge distances here."

I'm not sure exactly why I felt I had to make excuses for what the EOS was doing, but there you go.

"But come on!"

Maybe I was still conditioned not to like it when Angie was uncomfortable.

"Patience."

I had to stop feeling that way.

"This is boring."

Had to admit that I was starting to agree with her. It had gotten to the point that watching them assemble, fly, then reassemble and re-fly the EOS for the last couple of weeks was getting about as exciting as watching the TV coverage of the Apollo moon missions from number 14 on.

Even though I had been a huge space nerd with as many Matt Mason action figures as my allowance would allow, those marathon TV sessions with commentators and the silly demonstration models and fleeting shots from space so blurry and so black and white that they could have been taken by your local flying saucer believer got pretty tedious after a while. Almost as mind-numbing as curling or, god forbid, *golf* on television.

I remember about how some of my more paranoid friends, like Rob when he'd smoked too much bad weed, used to talk about how those Apollo missions were all faked. Well, the Plant was pretty clear evidence that my friend was incredibly mistaken.

I do think there must have been some sort of conspiracy associated with NASA and the Apollo program, just not the one that people suspected. Progressive Apparatus sure as hell did not want some civilian government agency poking around lunar space while they were trying to get stuff done. And the Apollo 13 accident just confirmed that human stubbornness endures, and that some of us will just dig in and carry on in the face of crisis and adversity.

That ruled out P.A. just nuking Cape Kennedy. Those crazy Americans would just build another, even bigger facility. Besides, that kind of event might cause World War III and even P.A.'s Most Senior Management team probably needed a planet to live on. At least for the time being.

So the trick would be to get the Americans to stop going to the moon on their own. The USSR manned lunar program had blown itself up on the launch pad (although who knows, maybe P.A. did have something to do with that). The strategy for dealing with the Americans was to transform the idea of exploring the moon from an incredible heroic enterprise to an enormously uninteresting waste of time and money.

The TV coverage of the landings did an excellent job of making space travel as unsexy as possible. From "Astronaut Tough" to "middle-aged virgin stamp collector" in less than two seasons of television.

By the time we got to the last Apollo, Number Seventeen, even with the gorgeous night launch and the amazing colour transmissions, everyone but me in my family would have watched a test-pattern or had root canals rather than tune in.

Sitting there in the common area, I wondered if Senior Management was trying something similar at the Plant. Right now, morale and productivity (on the Lines anyway) were still pretty high—probably because we interns still had some pride in ownership of the now visible EOS. However, if Senior Management could get all of us *really bored* with the whole project, then positivity would drop and so would productivity—maybe we'd be looking at more accidents and deaths. That would give those slack-ass divisions like Gravity some breathing room to catch up and maybe there'd be some bonus brains to harvest.

If my theory sounds like the ravings of a deranged, drunken mind, then you are completely correct. I conceived my "Conspiracy by Tedium" under the influence of some blue Hyper-Gin that somebody, most likely Ross, left by my door.

Since I was drinking alone, my hypothesis was unlikely to become a part of lunar urban folklore anytime soon. I also didn't think it was a good idea to mention my theory to Angie or Trevor.

"Once they get the engines working at full capacity, the EOS will be able to travel at almost the speed of light."

That little bit of techno-optimism was from Trevor, which seemed a little surprising to me. Based on what Mr. Oblivion was up to these days (a particularly dark storyline that seemed heavily inspired by *Soylent Green* and Jell-O Pudding ads), I figured Trevor loathed everything about what we were doing at the Plant.

"Do you think they'll ever be able to pull it off?" That was Angie, as usual asking questions, always trying to figure out what was real. She had the best mental health quotient of the three of us.

Trevor nodded. "They've gotten this far."

Maybe he, like me, was just trying to cheer Angie up.

What did I need his help for?

I know, really mature. Not competitive at all. Time for a subject change. "I booked *Star Wars* today."

Oh boy, wide eyes and big smiles. Little kids opening birthday presents.

"How did you—?"

I explained about the surprise budget surplus and felt very clever and useful indeed.

The TV feed on the big screen changed to an onboard camera.

"The light saber fights are really cool."

Trevor had seen the movie just before they'd escorted him to the moon but he'd been very careful about not telling anyone what happened in it. His restraint suggested that he had both:

a. Discipline (because I'm sure he'd been under masses of pressures to spill); and
b. Faith (because he didn't stop believing that I would find some way to show that movie).

No wonder I didn't like this wholly admirable and talented young man.

"Hey…"

On the big screen we saw what I think was an aft view from one of the EOS exterior cameras. It looked a lot like an oil refinery or chemical cracking plant—but somehow out there in space.

"Hey…"

A spherical pod, nothing that looked too major, started shaking. Next, one of the larger tanks, situated right next to the pod, started to shimmy. Then both structures twisted a little, then a lot, and finally flew off into the wild black.

"Did you… see… that…?" Angie's voice was tentative, like she wasn't sure what had just happened.

Then another tank tore off the main infrastructure.

"Yeah, I did." Trevor's voice was quiet too.

"Me too." Well, I didn't want them to think I wasn't paying attention.

Another tank started to vibrate.

The other interns were starting to whisper.

Then the big screen went blank.

"Do you think that was supposed to happen?"

Angie and I looked at Trevor and shrugged.

"Don't know."

Well, we didn't know!

Everyone in the common area was looking around and talking to each other. It looked pretty serious and the loss of signal was not very reassuring either. Even so, there were no flashing lights or alarms. Not even urgent voices from Technical telling us what to do.

So maybe everything was okay.

Maybe those tanks weren't anything important and we'd just seen a regular SNAFU.

Just a little SNAFU. Yeah, that's the ticket.

"That didn't look good." Thanks for reminding us, Angie. Just when I'd managed to forget all those obtuse warnings from Ross.

"Guess that's why they do all these tests."

"Bet somebody's going to be in trouble for what just happened."

"Someone is always in trouble around here."

What could I say? When Angie was right, she was right.

23:00

So everybody got up and did what they were supposed to.

Trevor had a late shift doing tests on the latest Box seals and Angie was going to put in a few hours on the radio station before bunking down. She was in possession of some new tracks by Klaatu and Dire Straits. I was a little skeptical of DS because like the dreaded Bay City Rollers, they were from Scotland and that culture had also invented bagpipes. Angie promised that I was going to love the Dire Straits so I was going to do my best to stay awake and listen in.

I was officially off-shift which meant that Dr. Baumann expected me to be studying up on high-speed surgical techniques and cranial anatomy. Now that was not going to happen. I might, however, write another health and safety column for the newsletter.

Get some sleep, Bishop.

24.
PLAUSIBLE SCENARIOS

04:23

It was no good. Not only couldn't I sleep, I was completely blocked on my latest column.

And the lights kept flickering on and off too. They were burning the midnight oil somewhere at the Plant. The idea that some engineers somewhere were having a really miserable night too did offer me some comfort.

I was even debating if I should just get out of bed, climb on my bike and check if Ross had any more messages for me. Before I could make that decision, I heard something.

At first I thought it was something gone wrong with the residence HVAC, it was a sort of low vibration, and on a regular pulse. Like some big motor or generator was starting up.

Then the sound got louder. Much louder.

Then I realized it was a completely new sound. Someone was pounding on my door. Whoever it was, it seemed like they were pretty upset about something.

I wondered if it was Angie's other ex-boyfriend (not me, the current ex-boyfriend) or Ed coming around to punch me in the face some more.

Plausible scenarios.

Both sets of hammering continued.

I thought about ignoring whoever was harming my door but that would probably just make whoever it was even angrier.

Besides, I still had a new batch of painkillers in my first aid kit, my visitor could whale at me for a little while anyway. I braced myself and opened the door. Turned out that it was Larry, the other guy from the Real World Game.

Bit of a surprise but maybe not a horrible one; I figured I could take him out in a fist fight if I had to.

"Starting up a new game?" It was the only reason I could think that Larry was slumming here in internland. "Kinda late, isn't it?"

"*Shut the fuck up!*"

At that point I noticed that Larry was breathing hard and sweating like a pig wearing a parka in a sauna. Techies were usually pretty out of shape.

"I wasn't saying anything before you got here."

Larry was still struggling to breathe.

"T-the o-only reason I'm here is that I owe Ross!"

"You do?"

"*Big time!*"

"You and me both, buddy—"

Larry didn't wait for me to finish what I'm sure was one of the best sentences that I was ever going to speak. He just stuck something in my hand and fucked off out of there at very high speed.

I was left with one of Ross' brass bullets in my hand. The message inside read:

"Three important things, Matt:

1. *Tonight it will all go to hell.*
2. *You must get the word out. Tell everyone what's in Mr. Oblivion.*
3. *Then get out of here. ASAP. You know how."*

I did? What was I supposed to know?

Next thing, there was a vast, low sound. I didn't just hear the sound. I felt it.

05:00

"Hey."

"Hey."

Angie was kind of standoffish for some reason.

"Are you okay?"

"These power fluctuations are screwing up my playlist, otherwise yeah—" Angie stopped herself, realizing that I asked that last question way too seriously. She didn't say anything and took quite a while to cue the tape to the first track of Supertramp's *Crime of the Century*.

"What?" she finally asked. And reluctantly at that.

"Something very bad is going to happen to the Plant, Angie."

"What? Where in the Plant? How bad?" All good questions.

"The whole Plant. And real bad." I sighed. "Maybe terminal."

As I expected, Angie responded by looking unconvinced. "Even if that shit's true, what the fuck can we do about it?"

"We need to leave."

"Oh and how are we going to do that? You got a rocketship in your pocket?"

More vibrations. I took a deep breath.

"Sub-basement #4, Stairwell D. Third hatch on the left."

"What about it?"

"Escape pod."

"But—"

"Fuelled up and I think the automatic guidance system is still functional."

"You are totally fucking crazy, Matt."

Alarm bells. Distant. *Finally!*

"You have to go there while I get on the radio and give people directions."

"What directions?"

"To the other escape pods. There's almost thirty of them in working order, some interns might get to them in time."

"I'm not going to leave you here!"

"I will be there just as I get the word out." I actually meant that last statement. I had no intention of dying on the moon if I could possibly avoid it. "You need to get to the Lines and get Trevor to come with you."

I had no idea where that idea came from because I had no idea that I cared that much about Trevor. Or, aside from his ability to generate cool illustrations, at all really.

Anyway, what I said seemed to have an impact; Angie stood up from the console, paused as if she was going to say something, didn't say anything, and left.

Hopefully eventually heading in the direction of Sub-basement #4.

05:05

"Attention shoppers…"

Even with the alarms now going full blast, you had to lead with a joke, right?

"…you might have noticed a bit of a break in our routine."

I decided to keep on playing some music in the background: Lennon's 'Imagine'.

"This is your Volunteer Health and Safety Officer speaking."

The tape was handy and I figured it would discourage panic.

"The best thing you can do is stop whatever you're doing and check out the bottom panels in the *Mr. Oblivion* comic for the last three issues of our newsletter."

I figured out what Ross was getting at in the second point of his message. The details he asked me to put into Trevor's art. An option in case Australia wasn't going to happen.

"Those squiggly diagrams and designs are maps of the outer levels. Once you see where the escape pod closest to you is located, proceed there as quickly and as safely as you can."

Maybe hearing music telling you that there's no heaven wasn't much of a comfort at that moment. Or maybe it was a good motivator. Could go either way.

"If you see anyone in distress and you think you can help, please do that. Senior Management may cut in with more information and we'll keep on the air as long as we can to keep you up to date."

'Imagine' was fading out. What else did Angie have here? Heart? Maybe not the best time for 'Crazy on You'. Credence? Klaatu?

Sure, Klaatu. 'Calling Occupants' or 'Hope' would work in a strange sort of way if I could find the right tape.

"Uh… so… check those maps in the comics…"

I tried not to do the math in my head. What was a reasonable capacity for the pods? How many were actually working? Would there be enough time for anyone to actually get to the sub-basements?

Don't quantify. Any numbers that I might come up with would not look good.

The one true thing was that there was a chance. At least for some of us. That's all I needed to think about. Plus if I kept things approximate, my chances of not losing it on the air were much better.

A few minutes into side one of "Hope", Ross called me on the studio phone. EOS was seriously breaking up almost directly over the Plant and one of the main propellant units hit the Gravity Complex square on. Unfortunately, the impact didn't completely take out the field generators which meant that we were getting G-fluctuations throughout some of the levels. That and giant pieces of spacecraft crashing down all around us made the whole Plant an extremely dangerous environment.

This was indeed a catastrophe. Big one. Way beyond the job description for a Health and Safety Volunteer.

For some reason I wasn't dead yet. Maybe the accident didn't seem so bad because it seemed to be happening in slow motion.

"You should get out of there, Matt."

"I will, Ross."

"So why are we still talking?"

"I will once I figure the interns have had time to clear the Lines. There's a video feed here, maybe I can tweak the directions on the map."

"No need, Matt." Ross' voice cracked a little. "There was a big feedback effect about five minutes ago. Most of the Lines are flatter than a Saskatchewan pancake."

The Lines were gone? I just sent Angie down there.

"Hang on, Ross." I put the phone down. "This is a message to Angie…" I was just about eating the microphone at this point. "…Trevor is already waiting for you at your pod, so you just head on down there."

Total lie. But lying is what total assholes like me tend to do.

BOOK FOUR
MR. OBLIVION

THERE'S NOTHING TICKING SO I must still be sleeping.

I'd really like to wake up now.

Karxday

IT IS ALSO ELEVEN noobles past plotnick o'clock.

Please don't tell me I don't make any sense and don't waste time arguing with me. This is my world now and I get to decide how I'm going to measure time. Perhaps the word "measure" is too strong a term, also it may be a less than necessary concept. Let's all just relax and agree that it is now my job to deal with the whole sequence of events thing.

Today (whatever the hell *today* is) I will spend time working on the Lunar Excursion Vehicle. No, it is not the latest generation of Apollo landers (cute as they are). No, the LEV is essentially a fat-tired tricycle with a pressurized pod that lets me ride to places in the Plant that have gone all vacuum-y and/or are too far away for me to get to on foot. The tricky part is finding some seals and gaskets for the LEV that maintain a controlled internal environment while leaving enough clearance to pedal the stupid thing. Using the LEV reminds me of those crank-operated submarines from the Civil War. At first I was pretty dubious about the whole thing but Ross assured me that I could put all this together from odds and ends in my quad of the Plant.

"Why can't I just wear a suit?" That was me, Mr. Low-Hanging Fruit, always on the lookout for the easiest possible solution.

"It won't work." Ross' answer was a little slow in coming. I wasn't sure if it was extra signal lag or if he was choosing his words very carefully. "You'd have to wear a standard suit for that distance and they're so bulky that you won't be able to work up any speed."

"How fast do I have to go?"

"Depends if you want be able to breathe on your way back."

Don't believe all those fun scenes in the movies where you see the spacemen bouncing around under lower lunar gravity. When you're in a Standard Suit you might as well be hiking up the side of Mount Everest. And if you're wearing an Emergency Pressure Suit, you ought to keep your movements to a minimum. Otherwise you might just pop. Fragile balloon-y things those EPSs, they are.

Even so, I did not want to believe what Ross was telling me. But what we did agree on was the fact that sooner or later—I preferred to think of it as an undefined number of noobles—graffaws and trubbles—I was going to have to get out to Quads Three and Four, and check out what was left of the EOS crash site.

My visit to Ground Zero was way overdue.

—◆—

I found a large pile of unscrolled paper on the floor of the Radio Room. Ross had been very busy. I picked up some of the paper and studied the fresh printing: lots and lots of instructions with columns of specs for me to work with.

Lots and lots. Enough to keep me hard at it until next Bloomsday. That is unless I decided to change the name of the day.

Before the evacuation, everything at the Plant was driven by those Logistics Clocks. Every micro-second was identified, scientifically measured and strategically deployed to most effectively and efficiently meet that day's production quotas (at least in terms of how Senior Management defined E & E). Even when I was asleep I could sense the regular and systematic elimination of my existence through the gears of those clocks.

When I first arrived at the Plant I was surprised that they didn't run full evening and night shifts. Almost all the time pieces in the

Plant were twenty-four hour clocks, so why not drive us Interns 24/7?

I didn't bother to ask any of the other interns about this. It was pretty apparent that most of them hadn't much of a clue of how things worked at the Plant and even less of an idea of *why* they worked the way they did. The few interns that did act like they knew something were not going to waste their limited time explaining stuff to some newbie-pleb like me.

We all had quotas to meet.

Eventually I came up with a credible theory.

Management needed to shut the lines down for a few hours every day to allow the infrastructure to cool off, settle down and let the sweepers, scrapers, suckers and lube-jobbers roll around and clean/fix everything up. Much of this gear was automated and the few people who were controlling them were likely to be from Technical so us lowly interns would never see them. Sort of like tooth fairies with automatic wrenches.

Some bright light in Technical had probably done some calculations on their big mainframe and figured out that any time and productivity lost by shutting down the Lines and letting the interns sleep would result in a net increase in output because the off-shift maintenance would reduce breakdowns during the day and extend the lifespan of any mechanical or electrical equipment. It really didn't compute that Management gave a flying fig-handle about the well-being of its human equipment, but if we interns wanted to sleep during our downtime, then fine, Management would turn off the lights for us.

Lovely people. Fun times.

It did not take very long for me to start hating those Logistics Clocks even though they did have the cool Irwin Allen robot voices. I wasn't alone in that sentiment. Everybody who worked shifts came to hate those clocks.

Angie hated them because she didn't like being pushed around, especially by machines. Most of the Interns hated the Logistics Clocks because they feared them and they feared them because the devices were a constant reminder of the fact that if an Intern paused, just for a few of those relentlessly measured microseconds, that Intern was in danger of missing his or her quotas. And if you missed enough of your quotas, soon or later you wouldn't be around to be measured.

I had my own special reasons for loathing the Logisticals. I hated them because of the fact that they had absolute control of all time, everywhere in the Plant. How they divided time into tiny, tedious units that were all exactly the same and how these units were always sequenced one after another, after another and after another.

So tediously linear!

That was not the way it's supposed to be. Time needs to be more dynamic, more creative, something you dive into and play with. At the very least it should speed up when you're having fun and slow down when you're getting a root canal.

Now that I was master of this pressurized universe, I was making sure that time was a lot more fun! God knows, I have enough of it on my hands.

———◆·◆———

"Today is Valentine's Day…" Eugene's voice whispered out of the receiver speakers.

Maybe on Earth it was Valentine's Day. I sat down, opened a can of water and turned up the volume. Here on the moon it was still Karxday. Why? Because I say so.

"…As we do every Valentine's, we will be playing Gay-Lesbian and Transgender folk music for the next twelve hours…"

I was pretty sure I remembered the concept of "twelve" (because I needed it to understand Ross' specs) but I refused to recall those things Eugene called "hours".

"…but first I have a lecture on tape from the University of East Berlin on the commodification of desire and the use of sexuality as a tool of global economic exploitation."

Commodification of desire? That Eugene. He was becoming a real romantic in his old age.

"The lecture is entirely in German and even if you don't speak the language, I'm certain that if you listen very carefully you can deduce the essential meanings from the speaker's very distinct patterns of vocal inflection."

Regardless of how I defined it, I had the feeling that the waves of time were going to pass over me very slowly for this particular segment of Karxday. I took a sip of water and started to study Ross' paper transmission.

An unfamiliar voice in an unfamiliar language started talking:

"*Ihre tiefe lust…*"

MOOMDAY

"BIT OF NEWS FOR you, Matthew."

Angie's voice was crackling out of the speaker.

"News can be fun." I know, my reply reeked of naive optimism.

I sat there and waited for the 1.5 second lag as the transmission signal worked its way through space. This effect was always explained to me as an inconvenience but I liked the fact that there was a tiny silence between our statements. It gave me a little extra time to consider the shape of a conversation and maybe do some course correction by thinking more about what the other person was saying and responding with a statement that was slightly less stupid than what I might normally say.

What kind of stupid thing would I say without the interplanetary sound-gap?

I miss you, Angie.

I still love you.

I will always love you.

You're the only thing that's keeping me alive, Angie.

If I wasn't such a lunar chicken shit I would just open an airlock and take a big breath of vacuum—since I'm never going to see you again and there really isn't a compelling reason to keep on living.

Yeah.

That is the kind of moronic shit I would be screaming into the microphone if I had to endure the burden of instantaneous communication.

"Your mother and Ed are getting a divorce."

Even without 240,000 (give or take) miles between us—there would've been a pause in the conversation at that point. I just didn't know what to say. Finally: "Now where did you hear that?"

Good move, Matt. When you don't know how to feel, request some irrelevant data.

"Ross' mom is friends with a friend of your mother." Okay, we have just established for the 15,000,000th time, Blinn, Alberta is not a particularly large community.

"Any idea why they split up?"

Did I actually care? Not really but it was good to keep Angie talking.

"Not really."

More static.

I wondered if it was the time-lag or if Angie was doing some conversational course-correction of her own, trying to think of the best thing to say next.

"But I do know that Progressive Apparatus is pulling out of Blinn. Maybe Ed's going with them."

"Makes sense."

Yet more static.

"Are you upset, Matthew?"

I thought for a minute.

"No, I'm good," I lied.

I guess I was a bit sad. Not that I gave a rat's ass about Ed and I was feeling not all that connected to my mom either these days.

"You sure, Matt?"

"Sure, I'm sure."

I suppose I did feel badly that my mother would be alone again. I know that's not an easy thing.

Geebleday

"It should work."

"But these are Plant seals we're talking here, they're probably total shit."

"But these are very basic seals."

Was that a sigh of impatience from Ross? Or was it just the static?

"Not even P.A. could mess these ones up."

"Really?"

"How long have you been up there? Three years?"

"Three years, two months and four days." (So much for my theory of subjective time.)

"Have you noticed any doors or windows blowing out on their own?"

"Maybe we're about due."

"You're stalling, Matthew."

Yes, Ross was definitely losing patience with me.

"Are you afraid?"

"No." I looked at our creation. Balloon wheels mounted on a big aluminum gumdrop. Essentially a human-powered lunar rover. "I'm fucking terrified. If those seals and gaskets go while I'm pedalling out there I won't be talking to you anytime soon." There was another one of those distance-enhanced pauses. "Or ever," I added.

Eventually: "I suppose that's true."

"Thank you for pointing out the obvious." Now I sounded impatient.

"If it was me, I wouldn't want to go out there in that thing either." Ross was cheating by being unexpectedly sympathetic and reasonable. "But there isn't a lot of choice here. You've just about exhausted all the supplies in your quadrant."

I knew what the choices were…

"You have to roll over to Q3, seal it up and get that stuff."

…suffocation/decompression and/or starvation. I looked over at a tin-headed, denim clad figure sitting in a chair across from me.

"I don't suppose I could send a Capekoid instead?"

Ross laughed. "Angie said you started making those things again."

"I can't rely on you for all my companionship."

I had been making Neo-Capekoids for almost two years (18-21 ooblogs MNVST (Matthew's Not Very Standard Time)). I had also been searching the far sections of Q1 and Q2 looking for food concentrates and any stray electronics that might fill up Ross' spec sheets. I did manage to locate some of that kind of stuff but I also found the entrance to a rest and rec room that some Gravity workers and techs must have used when they were between shifts. There was lots of stuff that was only useful for making fake androids.

———◆—◆—◆———

The window had ice crystals on it and the seals were jammed up tight around the edges of the door; a reasonably clear indicator that the room had been depressurized for quite a while.

Ross and I had worked out a routine for this situation about a week (Non-Subjective Time) into his first broadcast on Eugene's transmitter:

1. Locate the nearest Emergency Pressure Suit.
2. Check for leaks and faulty seals. If the Suit is undamaged, put it on and inflate.
3. Waddle over to the depressurized area in question. (You had to waddle because an EPS was essentially a big

translucent balloon with rubber feet and a fishbowl helmet.)

4. Contain adjacent areas and equalize pressure (i.e. let all the air out).
5. Open area in question. Waddle inside.
6. Determine if area in question can be resealed. If this is possible, do so and re-pressurize because then you can take off your EPS, which makes all subsequent steps a lot faster and easier.
7. Whether you are in or out of your EPS, reconnoitre the area in question and locate any:
    a. Food.
    b. Useful materials or technology (Ross' spec sheets were a good guide for doing this.)
    c. Bodies.
8. Load items #a and #b onto a handcart, backpack, big burlap bag or whatever you have handy for humping things around in.
9. Initiate burial procedures for anything falling under category #c.

There had been quite a few smaller explosions after the last of the evacuation pods pulled away from the lunar surface. Maybe the big booms were caused by ruptures of the infrastructure as various bits of EOS hit the Plant or maybe Senior Management decided that it was a good idea to try and destroy as much of the Plant as possible just in case somebody else came back to the moon and tried to figure out all the weird and naughty things they were doing up here.

If Option A was the case, then rube Plant was probably built worse than Management thought; if they were going for Option B, then the construction of the Plant was likely better than they expected.

Whatever. The net result was the same.

About 30-50% of the Plant, or at least the Quads I had access to, was more or less intact. I had a pretty big place to live and for better or for worse it looked like I was here on my own and in relative comfort. Provided I managed to stay alive.

On Impact Day, when the first after-shocks hit, I found another evac capsule and crawled inside. Its propulsion system hadn't been hooked up which was probably why it hadn't been moved into a launch tube. Never mind, I was able to pressurize the thing, which meant that I had a place to breathe just in case the main seals blew. The seals did just that. Just about everywhere in the Plant. All the Interns, Techs and Junior Management personnel who hadn't been classified as essential experienced a rapid deterioration of the conditions of their employment.

As in total vacuum.

As in they were S.O.L.

As in Shit Out of Luck.

For once, we were all in this together.

--------◆◆--------

Task #9 was complicated and I am not going into how it broke down into a lot of sub-tasks, except to say that I was supposed to check the bodies to see if they had any items in categories #a or #b and that at the end of the procedure the human remains were to be clothed in clean, white re-purposed sheets and I would then roll them out to the Plant Mausoleum.

Originally it wasn't a mausoleum, it was a storage hangar for stuff that could survive in a vacuum. That and the cold were the best means available for preventing bodies from decomposing and once I had cleared off all the shelving I had a clean and reasonably respectful place to keep all the deceased. I never seemed to find any people who I were sure were Management, which was good because I wasn't sure what I would have done with them. Probably something not very respectful.

Speaking of respectful, or at least trying to be, every time I placed another body on a shelf I would stand there, protected in my big balloon EPS and experience a moment of silence. Then I would sing a hymn.

The song was Angie's idea and it was a compromise. At first she wanted me to say a prayer.

"I'm no good at that sort of thing."

"You have to say something."

"Don't you have to believe in God to say prayers? I won't sound very sincere."

"If you don't say something they you're just saying that you agree with Management."

"How the hell do you figure that?!"

"You have to acknowledge that the deceased was a human being—not just a piece of busted equipment that you're throwing away."

Fine.

She was right. Damn it.

So we did some more talking and we agreed that I would sing a hymn.

But which one? We needed something simple that was pretty, easy to remember and within my limited vocal range. For a while it looked like we were going to go with 'Jesus Wants Me for a Sunbeam' but I always started giggling halfway through the chorus. (It's a silly song!)

Eventually Angie found the right hymn. It was called 'I Know That My Redeemer Lives'. It was not from Handel's Messiah but was written by some guys called Lewis and Medley from the hymn book for the Church of Jesus Christ of Latter Day Saints. The lyrics were a bit 19th Century but simple enough for me to remember.

"I didn't know you were a Mormon," was what I asked Angie the first time she sang the song and made me write down all the lyrics.

"Fuck, yeah!" Angie's voice chirped out of the speaker.

"And did you pick up that kind of language at Sunday school?"

"Matt, I haven't been to church in about 800 years."

Even across the vast ethereal void of space I knew that Angie was blushing.

Now back to that particular vacuum filled room on that

particular (or rather approximate) day:

Three bodies. Two men. One woman. One of the men was a Gravity Worker, the woman and the other man were dressed in the light blue coveralls of Techs on day shift. Techs on the night shift skeleton crews wore yellow coveralls, maybe to make them more visible? Given that the Plant used to have a constant level of artificial light at all times in all public spaces, I was never able to figure out why that was a concern.

They were reasonably polite corpses. While they didn't exactly clean up after themselves, they hadn't left much of a mess either. And it wasn't too difficult to figure out what had happened here; I saw a fist-sized hole in one of the walls and constant points of starlight beyond. Something (probably a bit of flying spacecraft) shot through the plating and blew out the atmosphere. Poor saps were probably dead before they even saw the hole. At least I hope they were.

It was also pretty easy to make the room more or less habitable. Just apply some plastic goo, duct tape and a portable seal. After that I turned on the oxygen taps, dialed up the heat and I was able get out of my EPS and get to the serious work of bundling up these people.

I had to work fast because now that they were out of vacuum, they were going to go ripe pretty quickly.

Note to those of you who may have seen different scenarios in science fiction movies, rapid exposure to vacuum does not do very many horrible things to the human body. I mean aside from killing it. Your eyes don't pop, your head doesn't explode and your guts don't boil off into space.

I found a few nasty remains in the Plant but most of those were the result of deaths caused by direct impact or Plant machinery going wonky. The majority of the dead people here were covered with a thin layer of ice crystals and looked like they'd been rapidly freeze-dried. Which, of course, they had been.

The crystals were like fairy dust which made the bodies look sort of Christmassy. Not that Christmas showed up on the Contemporary Bishop Lunar-Centric Calendar.

The biggest problem with these recovery missions was when the bodies just wouldn't bend. As an experienced materials handler, I can assure you that irregularly shaped cargo is a real pain-in-the-ass to transport.

Fortunately these three, after a certain amount of pulling and pushing, were pretty pliant. It didn't take long to get the sheets and cords over them and pack them into the cycle trailer.

With luck, in less than an hour I would be back in my suit and commence singing hymns in the hangar. By this time I had figured out that some of the souls I was commending to the afterlife might not be Christians. So when I finished singing I usually whispered an apology and concluded with a statement like "this is just an approximation, okay?"

Buck Rogers Memorial Day

EUGENE WAS PLAYING SOME pretty weird music to help me honour my recently declared Interplanetary Holiday.

The last of the "*huh! huh! huhs!*" faded out.

I wasn't sure if I was hearing static or if Eugene was just breathing a little heavier than usual.

"So?" he asked eventually.

"Yes?" I responded right away.

"How much did you hate it?"

"Try not at all." I laughed. "It's neat." (I bet only people on the moon said that things were 'neat' these days.)

"Really?" Eugene sounded a little suspicious.

"Really! It's the first interesting electronic work I've heard since Syrinx and TD."

"That's true." Eugene was still hesitant. "Although some people wouldn't say her work was strictly electronic music."

"It sounds like she's being really creative with a very retro synthesizer and the vocal manipulation is super cool." I felt an evil smile creeping over my face. "And I liked the implied political message."

"I suppose…"

"You suppose? What's the issue here, Gene?"

Eugene didn't like being called 'Gene'—I really had to stop twisting the knife in.

"Frankly, Matthew." There was a heavy sigh that you probably didn't need a radio transmitter to hear. "It's the nature of that message."

"What about it?"

"It's too ambiguous."

Bingo! Eugene was about to demonstrate the central problem with his entire life.

"You need to have it all spelled out, Gene? Have to know the chapter and verse of the Party line?"

Static. Static. Static.

Now I was worried. I was being a real asshole here. Eugene was trying to make me feel less lonely and I was offending him.

More static. Finally.

"Yes."

"Yes?"

"I'm not sure if the song is a libertarian anthem to elitism or a progressive critique of the nuclear arms race."

"So what part is tripping you up?"

I promise, I had stopped being nasty thirty seconds earlier; I just wanted to know what was bugging my friend.

"I'm troubled by the popularity of the artist."

This was a weird answer.

"You mean it's a problem because people like her music?"

"They're playing this song on AM radio!" I could feel an ocean of disgust buoying up Eugene's words.

"Dear god! Not Timmie Territory!" I pretended to be horrified.

"She was even on *Entertainment Tonight*!"

"What's that?"

"Something too awful to discuss." Another interplanetary pause. "And I watch it every night."

"That sounds..." I dug very deep for the most accurate and diplomatic description. "...a little pathological, Eugene."

"I know and I deeply regret it."

In spite of his automatic acceptance of orthodox far-left ideology, Eugene was being very brave and honest with me and he totally deserved 35 out of ten on the Friendship Scale for that. Now it seemed astonishing to me that he even played the song for me in the first place. So I asked him: "So, why that song, Eugene?"

I could sense that he was relaxing a bit. "Oh, Angie thought you might like it."

Eugene really was all right. I mean for a commie stooge.

"What else have you got for me, buddy?"

Eugene chuckled. "Are you ready for the Safety Dance?"

I didn't laugh. The title reminded me too much of my old job.

Assembly Day

I WAS FEELING NAUGHTY and I felt like I was surrounded by the spirit of Timmie.

I'd found one of the mix-tapes we'd made up to cover air time while the DJs were between shifts. Usually they were nothing but Top 40. My nemesis from Blinn U would have been delighted. But oddly enough, so was I. I think it was because much as I appreciated my friends on Earth's efforts to anticipate my tastes, it felt good to choose my own music once in a while. Even if Timmie might have liked it.

Supertramp, slightly distorted, whined and pulsed out of the loudspeakers I'd wired up in that quadrant. That was just fine.

I started the day with good intentions. I took some manuals with me to the launch tube where the Escape Module was located and tried to do a preliminary systems check—hoping to pin down what was working and what wasn't. The sort of thing Ross would do and what he definitely wanted me to do.

I got most of the lights on the main panel to light up (which I think was a good thing) and it looked like the controls for the gravity unit were undamaged (as far as I could tell). Couldn't get a peep from the guidance computer and that made me very nervous. For some reason I was not crazy about catapulting off into the infinite void and having absolutely no idea of how to steer my way home.

For about ninety minutes I searched the manuals looking for something to help wake up the tracking systems but no joy. Boredom and frustration set in, so I put the manuals down and climbed out of the module. I got on my bike and pedalled towards the laundry to the sound of BOT once again telling me to take care of business.

Right.

Definitely.

There were more interesting things to do.

<hr>

As you can probably guess, securing the ingredients for my latest creation was dead easy. I took the first pair of coveralls I could find and took them back to the radio room. I might like to have my project close at hand when Team Earth started calling.

The chicken wire was also pretty easy to find. Whoever built the Plant used the stuff to reinforce the concrete they used in the corridors and there was masses of it laying around for repairs. Then I shredded up Management documents and print-outs to fill out the body. There was probably some kind of political/artistic statement in that but I wasn't sure exactly what it was.

The hardest element to find was an appropriately sized empty aluminum can to use as the head. There were plenty of containers to be found around the remains of Moonbase Omega (a.k.a. The Plant) but as befits their name, these containers were usually containing something. After spending a few hours rummaging through various janitorial closets on various levels, I managed to find a bunch of cans that said they were full of petroleum spirits. Happily, one of the cans was not full of anything, and so Bob's Your Uncle and I had one perfectly good Capekoid head.

For the feet I got a pair of EVA boots and likewise I got a moon-suit glove for the right hand. For the left hand I used one of those needle-nosed oil applicator cans. That seemed about right because this Capekoid's function was to be a social lubricant, i.e. someone for me to talk to that didn't involve the use of large transmitters.

It took a little under eight hours to assemble the Capekoid and position it in a chair next to the Radio Room microphone.

When I sat there, gazing at my creation, I did not feel like screaming: "It's alive! It's alive!"—but he/she/it definitely felt like it was there.

I was pleased.

Now.

What to name today's Capekoid?

Frankenstein's Monster?

That seemed unfriendly and just asking for trouble.

Robbie the Robot?

Implied greater technological sophistication than was the case.

Thing #15.

Yes.

Simple. Direct. Elegant.

And as all good Seussians know, make a Thing #15, that means you have a Thing #1 and a Thing #2 and so forth up to Thing #14. And why would you want to stop there?

Angry Goat Day

"You've got to take your situation more seriously!"

"Sorry."

"Don't say sorry, Matthew." Ross was the closest to angry that I'd ever encountered. "You're the one who's still marooned up there."

"Right, I get it."

"Maybe it seems that you've got lots of time but you have finite resources." Eugene the dialectical materialist was always looking at things from an economic angle.

"I think I understand that." I was answering in my most respectful indoor voice.

Now it was Angie's turn: "We're trying to help you, Matthew, but you have to do your part."

"I really appreciate everything all of you have done." Well, I did. Sort of.

Team Earth was very upset with me which was why this evening's broadcast had turned into less of a conversation and more of an intervention. And as with most interventions, everything was, indeed, all my fault. Earlier that day, I had been trying to boot up that pesky guidance system and instead I shorted out most of the instruments on the main board.

"We just want you to come home," Angie continued.

"Safely," added Ross.

"Alive at least." Eugene's voice was off in the distance. He'd probably been banished to a far corner of the room because he was smoking one of those horrible black cigarettes of his.

As if the minor electrical fire wasn't bad enough (good news, the module's extinguisher works), the shit really started flying when I reported the problem to Ross. He started asking all kinds of complicated technical questions and it became apparent that I had not mastered as much of the manuals as he thought I had.

"Gosh darn it, Matt!"

This was pretty harsh language for my friend.

PLATOPORKDAY

No, I don't know what it means either.

It just kind of popped into my head as I rolled off my slab and it was kind of fun to say.

It wasn't even a particularly special day. Just more humping around corridors looking for dead people and potentially useful stuff. Or was it potentially useful people and dead stuff?

Probably didn't matter.

Corridors. You may have heard me go on about them before but they are a still a big part of the landscape of my life.

Usually my days involved walking, riding, crawling or hopscotching (if I was feeling a bit silly) down some corridors. I think because I was spending a lot of time in corridors and I happened to be on the moon and all, I started to, once again, think about all the corridors I had seen in different science fiction movies and TV shows.

Corridors were usually very important set pieces. They helped establish where and when the story was taking place, they often established tone and ambience—were we in an interstellar or future Earth place? Was it a utopia? A dystopia? Alien? Technophilic? Technophobic? The corridors would signal all that.

Corridors were also interesting places to be because a lot of the scenes where the main characters ran around, hit each other, shot at each other and explained things to each other—all of it happened in corridors.

Corridors were also an immediate indicator of how much

money the producers had and if they were complete morons or not. *Star Trek* and *Westworld* had acceptable corridors given their limited budgets. Now *Space: 1999*. Silly scripts but really great places to walk around in. *Logan's Run*, given all the time it had spent in development, had surprisingly disappointing corridors—especially considering all the running around and shooting that happened in them.

Ross and Angie assured me that *Star Wars* had excellent corridors. I had to take their word on that one.

For a place that actually existed, the Plant gave pretty good corridors. All the seals and gaskets were a credible techno-presence while the deteriorating pipes and concrete walls generated a somewhat exotic 'lunar noir' look to it all.

As I was walking down this particular corridor, it occurred to me that I might not want to think about those particular deteriorating pipes and walls in any terms other than their aesthetic properties. If they were going to start cracking and rupturing out into the vacuum, there wasn't an awful lot that I could do about it.

But the really fun part of the day was the fact that this was an "unknown" corridor.

I shit you not.

"I don't see it anywhere on my maps!"

When we were talking earlier, Ross was getting pissy because I presented him with conflicting and ambiguous data: "Computer says it's there."

I had recently figured how to get some of the terminals to display things and I was feeling rather proud of myself.

"I guess it could be a plan for something they intended to build but didn't get around to."

"Or maybe your Earthside map is out of date."

"Maybe."

I could almost feel my receiver warm up with Ross' mad-on. He wasn't crazy about obsolete information.

I pressed a toggle and a screen full of green numbers replaced my illuminated map. "System monitor says there's power and air in there."

"If there is a there, there."

What a cranky engineer!

"So what's the problem? I go down and check. If there's nothing there, then I go look somewhere else." I was enjoying this conversation because it was giving me the illusion of autonomy. "If it is there, then I do some hunting and gathering, just like always."

"The problem is that you might walk into a zone that's incomplete, damaged or otherwise unstable."

"I haven't forgotten how to put on an EPS, Ross."

"Then you had better get off your lazy ass and go."

Ross just needed to be annoyed at me.

He probably would be more surprised than annoyed when I told him what I found at the end of this 'unknown' corridor: big, but not particularly massive seals and a circular hatchway at the end. The hatchway was plugged in with explosive bolts to allow for rapid removal and thick coiled hinges for when you wanted to open it in a more controlled manner.

Looked like some kind of launch tube entry to me.

I walked up to the hatchway and wiped the crystal off the porthole.

Of course.

A launch vehicle.

Another one. Just a small one and it looked pretty dead.

As a consolation prize, there was a utility closet and I found three pairs of overalls.

Good Capekoid material.

Geebleday

"I HEREBY DECLARE 1982 to be the Year That the Future Began." Eugene made this declaration with the confidence that characterized his usually mistaken statements.

"Is that what year it is?" Well, I was a little curious about his opinion.

Ross kept mentioning the actual date on Earth but who could remember crap like that when I had all those spec sheets to go through?

"Hell no, 1982 was eons ago."

"*What?!*"

I panicked as thoughts of time distortion and protracted suspended animation flashed through my mind.

"Sorry, sorry. I just meant that 1982 was a while back."

Eugene had been playing me John Williams soundtracks. *Star Wars*, of course. Then *Close Encounters of the Third Kind* and then some stuff I didn't know: *Raider of the Lost Artists* and something called *E.D.*

If Angie was Bad News Girl, then Eugene was Mr. Entertainment, which seemed surprising for a soon to be middle-aged Marxist but true even so. As these movies came out, Eugene did his best to explain them to me. He said he liked *The Empire Strikes Back* for its "revolutionary zeal against Imperialist Oppression" but he didn't seem too keen on most of the movies that were coming out in the 1980s.

"So why did the future begin in 1982?" asked the kid who had been stuck on the moon since the late 1970s.

"For one thing, all the major films that summer were some kind of science fiction movie."

"So what?" I mean, people paid too much attention to what they did in Hollywood.

"Twenty years before that, the most popular films were westerns, war movies or some sort of historical drama."

I briefly considered the subject matter of just about everything I'd ever watched on the late movie on CFAC. I realized that Eugene was right.

"So what?"

"American films have shifted their focus from a celebration of false histories to adventures in futures that can never be realized and realms that can never be reached."

That Eugene. Always had to be the killjoy, even when he was the showman.

"So you figure we'll never explore space, Eugene?"

"Afraid not."

"So what am I doing up here on the moon?"

There a pause, slightly longer than the usual 0.4 seconds signal delay.

"Exactly my point, Matthew."

Time for another pause.

"Yeah."

"Sorry."

It was time to talk about movies again: "So I guess quantity is more important than quality or novelty?" I was slipping into student mode. It felt kind of nostalgic.

"Not necessarily, why?" Aha! Eugene had just stepped into my trap.

"Then I would say that we all started living in the future on May 1977 when the first *Star Wars* movie was released."

"That's a good point, particularly since you haven't seen any of them." Eugene could be a gracious debater. "However..."

Wait a minute... "However, what?"

"There are other factors involved."

"Like what?"

There was another one of those long pauses.

"I've been wondering how to accurately explain this when the subject came up."

"What subject?!" I suddenly felt myself feeling very angry and very helpless. "Are you guys all flying around in your personal ornithopters? Have the giant crabs crawled out of the sea and taken over the government?" Back there on Earth, life was going on, things were changing. And without me! It just wasn't fair.

"Nothing quite so obvious." The signal distortion of Eugene's voice made him sound a little like an anemic robot for a moment. "But I suspect that the consequences will be far more profound."

"So enlighten me." For fuck's sake!

"Did Ross ever mention that he owns two computers?"

"Two computers?" I glanced over at the feebly blinking lights on one of the mainframe terminals. "He doesn't have that kind of money!"

When Ross wasn't sweating away his nights on Operation Rescue the Idiot on the Moon, he was teaching first year electrical engineering at Blinn Community College. I had a pretty good idea what he was pulling in.

"The computers cost him $400 and $600."

"Bullshit!" The word just popped out of my mouth. I thought for a minute and added: "So he bought a couple of build-it-yourself kits. They're just toys."

"Each of those home computers has at least twice the power of your Quadrant's Mainframe."

"The Mainframe has almost no power!"

"I mean when it was working properly. I mean, that's what Ross tells me."

Wait a minute. *Home* computers? *Powerful* home computers? *Useful* home computers? These were all pretty staggering concepts.

"Okay, so now the 0.0001% of the human population consisting of geekazoid engineers and scientists can now own their own computers."

I had a feeling that Eugene was smiling when he made the next statement. Which was odd because back in the days when I could see his face, Eugene didn't smile that much. "I have my own computer, too."

"You mean you own an abacus."

"It's got a screen and keys and electricity and everything."

"A pocket calculator, then."

"It's about the size of an Etch-A-Sketch and I write my editorials on it when I ride the bus into town."

After Eugene spent the next two hours telling me about all the incredibly cool things he could do with his Tandy Model 100, I had to sign off and go make some more Capekoids.

A computer that you could write your own stories with? That corrected your spelling mistakes and typos? Like something Commander Koenig might tuck under his arm between crisis meetings on Moonbase Alpha and stealing glances at Dr. Russell's (somewhat conical) chest?

I was so jealous.

Bloogday

Time for the Angie Show.

Another thing I discovered about my ex-girlfriend, now that I wasn't trying to have sex with her all the time, was the fact that she had evolved into a closet classical music fan. When we were together the only music she talked about were power ballads and Stadium Rock. Maybe she was embarrassed by her love of high culture. "Did you like it?"

Angie had just played me Beethoven's Seventh Symphony.

"Yeah. It's beautiful." (Just like you, Angie.)

I recognized some of the music from that wonderfully dumb science fiction movie where Sean Connery wears red diapers. What was it called again? *Return to Witch Mountain? The Apple Dumpling Gang? Zardoz?*

"How about something a little more upbeat?"

And how is it that with over a quarter of a million miles between us I could still tell that something was bothering her?

"What did you have in mind?"

Eventually she said: "How about the Beatles? You like them."

That was true, I used to sing selections from *Sgt. Pepper's* and *Abbey Road* when we were in bed all the time. Angie seemed to like it but I guess you had to be there to understand.

"Sounds good."

She played "Let It Be".

Argh.

Inspiring? Maybe.

Touching? Absolutely.

But upbeat? Not so much.

There were also some personal associations with that song that I don't think I'd ever mentioned to Angie. These involved the only serious theological discussion I remember ever having with my mother.

Back on Earth, a sliced fruit logo was rotating on my stereo turntable.

"Turn that off!"

My mother opened a door and poked her head inside my bedroom.

"What?"

I immediately knew that it had been a mistake to use the speakers instead of the headphones.

"Why?" That was also a dangerous question to ask my mother, but this was the Beatles here!

"*It's blasphemy!*"

Mother had been dating some Born Again real estate agent. For the last few weeks whenever she got out of his Thunderbird with the "I Found It" bumper sticker, she entered the house with some freshly recycled moronic sales ideas crudely disguised as religion.

"How do you figure that, Mom?" Was I crazy? Asking that question was just asking for more grief.

"He's singing about the Virgin Mary!"

"What's wrong with Paul McCartney singing about the Virgin Mary?" If I kept this up I might be meeting the Virgin Mary soon.

"It's a rock and roll song! You can only sing about things like that in hymns!"

With the Idiot Perspective Revealed, my mother turned and left the room.

Don't get me wrong. My mother was not an idiot. In her own (possibly completely irresponsible way) she was pretty smart. She was just impatient and she liked to put lots of new things in her head, regardless of their accuracy. Sort of like an ideological explorer-sponge. She was probably just trying on this new form of Christian Fundamentalism in the same way she might try out a new pair of shoes. I knew that if I just kept my head down and my mouth shut, this would all blow over and she would take up some new enthusiasm like Existential Aerobics or Vaginal Yodelling. Usually this involved getting a new boyfriend as well. Mom was just like Toad of Toad Hall but she was more attractive.

But dammit, this was the Beatles!

I cared about these guys. Their music had improved my life and helped me see the world in better ways. They were a good thing to put in your head and in your heart.

I did some research at the university library and found an interview with McCartney in a back issue of *Rolling Stone* where he talked about the inspiration for the song.

"It's not the Virgin Mary McCartney is singing about," I later explained over a bowl of Shreddies.

"What?" My mother looked up from her half grapefruit.

"'Let It Be'."

She nodded. "That evil song."

I shook my head. "He's singing about hearing the voice of his dead mother."

I saw my mother's eyes narrow from over a mug of coffee. We were now officially at Family Defcon One.

She set the mug down very carefully, probably so that her rage did not cause any brown stains on the tablecloth. "Well, it certainly *sounds* as though he's referring to the Virgin Mary." Her voice was calm but trembling just a little. Most likely caused by the building righteous fury.

"Why's that, Mom? Because it sounds respectful? *Sort of* like a hymn?" My sister was right, I was really an incredible smart-ass sometimes.

Speaking of which: "It's a very spiritual song, Mom." My sister decided at that moment to disengage from her Special K and contribute to the discussion. "It's very beautiful, really."

"*OH!*" Mother picked up her car keys, marched down the corridor and slammed the front door on her way to the driveway. The sound was not beautiful, nor was it particularly spiritual.

The song on my hyper-radio came to a very peaceful close. "That was very nice, Angie."

Now my ex-girlfriend and I were going to talk for a while. I was a little worried about the direction this conversation might take.

"I'm glad you liked it."

"But it wasn't very cheerful."

"I know."

Oh dear. I had just figured it out. Angie was about to turn into her alter-ego: Bad News Girl.

Sure enough: "I guess I wanted to play you something that was a bit more appropriate."

"Appropriate for what? We broke up years ago."

"Please, no jokes, Matt." I was definitely talking to Bad News Girl. "Please."

How bad could this news be?

"Do you remember Sue Robinson, the friend of yours you told me about?"

"From university, yeah." Oh, hell. I really wasn't going to like this information.

Angie choked up a bit. I'm pretty sure there were a few more tears on Earth at that moment.

"The police found something."

"Something? The police find somethings all the time."

Angie rushed into the next sentence: "They found some human remains on the river bank. They must been washed up."

Human remains? No! *Fuck, no!*

"They had probably been at the bottom of the river for at least four years." Another pause. "They're pretty sure it's Sue's body."

"*That's bullshit!* How could the cops know it's her after all this time?"

Angie sobbed. "They have dental records, Matt."

"And how do they know they have the right records?"

Here I was, acting totally true to type. Denial was a river in Egypt for me and it flowed right to my doorstep.

"Matt." Now Angie's voice was infuriatingly calm. "They don't make mistakes like that."

"*But why?!*" I gasped and it felt like the tears were sort of exploding out of my face. "Why would anyone want to kill poor Sue?"

At that point I was pretty much a heaving, blubbering mass. "Nobody may have killed her."

At that moment I had a sense that Angie was wondering if that piece of data was going to help or not.

"W-what do you mean?" My voice sounded like a siren in a lot of pain.

"If she was depressed she might have wandered off into the foothills and got confused…"

At least Angie didn't come right out and say that Sue might have killed herself. Those words would have sent me completely over the edge.

I was crying and I was pretty sure at the time that I would continue to do so for the next two or three thousand years. A part of me detached itself from the rest of my consciousness and positioned itself in a very small and still part of my brain. That little bit of me observed the rest of the grieving tear and snot-generating maelstrom that was Matthew Bishop.

And it wondered if my reaction to Sue's death was a bit strange. For the past few months I had found, prepared and stored hundreds of bodies. By the time I finally cleaned up the Plant, I must have dealt with over a thousand corpses. Quite a lot of dead people really.

So why would hearing about just one dead person bother me so much? I mean, she was my friend and she was a girl, but she wasn't my girlfriend.

Wail, wail. Boo-hoo, boo-hoo.

Get a goddamned grip, Bishop.

Nope.

Still crying uncontrollably.

Maybe because Sue represented the end of one more link to my old life on Earth. A life that wasn't tremendous but it wasn't that bad. I was happy sometimes and I wasn't so alone all the time.

Maybe it was because even though I hadn't seen or talked to her for years and years, I found the idea that she was still down there doing Sue-stuff very comforting. Or the fact that she was now no longer down there doing Sue stuff was deeply distressing. Maybe I was just really, *really* sad that my friend was dead.

They found her body at the bottom of a river. What a lonely death.

My death was going to be pretty lonely too.

"I'm so sorry, Matt. We all are."

"I-I know."

Eventually I had to stop crying. It was either that or hyper-ventilate and pass out.

"We wondered if we should tell you—"

"N-no." My voice was still all weepy-wobbly. "I-I'm very grateful that you did." In the same way you're grateful to your dentist for doing that root canal, but even so Angie, Ross and Eugene were my only connection to any kind of human reality; the last thing I wanted was for them to start lying and withholding things from me.

"Is there anything I can do, Matt?"

"Yeah."

I sniffed and wiped my nose. Oh great, more snot all over my sleeve.

"You can play 'Hey Jude'."

Definitely Laundry Day

Perhaps the title of this entry needs some clarification. While the housekeeping standards of Hotel Moonbase Omega could definitely use some improvement (yeah, I need to run the dishwasher this morning), I do want all of you to know that I still bathe, shave and trim my nails on a reasonably regular basis. I was not going to devolve into some shaggy, snarly, smelly mess with masses of keratin curling out of the ends of my fingers and toes.

I'm not particularly ashamed of the fact that I'm slowly going nutsy-coo-coo (I believe that is the correct psychiatric term) but I do want to maintain pride in my personal appearance. So these days, I lean towards a brush-cut (because that is the extent of my hair-styling skills) and I did power up a couple of washing machines and dryers to make sure I'd always have clean clothes on hand.

Frankly, getting off my slab to do some household chores was the only thing that kept me going some days. That and the prospect of the next broadcast from my friends on Earth.

No, I dubbed today "Laundry Day" not because it was time to scare up some detergent and load up the washing machines, but because I'd made a major find in one of the sections that I'd managed to power up.

More on that later. Back to those life-sustaining signals from Terra. Ross was on mic duty, playing some tracks off Tangerine Dream's latest albums. Eugene was on a TD strike; he'd decided that my favourite synth band had generated too many movie soundtracks and was therefore making "significant contributions to cultural capitalism and mindless consumer culture."

Fun guy that Eugene. Still.

"Matthew?"

The last track was fading off into interplanetary hiss.

"Ross?"

I was fairly sure I knew what Ross was asking me about and I now wondered if there was an ulterior motive for Ross playing Tangerine Dream. These were twenty-five minute plus tracks and they delayed the moment when he was going to have to raise a difficult topic.

Difficult for him, I mean. After the news about Sue, not too much seemed to bother me.

"What are you doing about reviewing the specs I sent you, Matthew?"

"Not a lot, Ross."

"Damn it!"

Although I didn't enjoy upsetting my friends.

"Sorry, I got distracted."

"*What?!*"

Ross was probably thinking: what the hell could be distracting this moron up there on the moon all by himself?

The Unified Earth Front (i.e. Ross, Angie and Eugene) had decided on a rescue strategy but an essential element of this plan was that while they could provide me with information, I had to pretty much rescue myself. Maybe that was the problem?

"Yeah?" I had fallen behind with the specs and exploring in the sections that I'd opened up.

In the broadest terms, Team Earth had gifted me with a simple plan. However, in fairness to me, it was just when you dug down to the next level of thinking that this strategy became both insanely complicated, profoundly suicidal and way, *way* beyond my core competencies.

Team Earth's solution to these challenges was predictable: more education. Ross also pointed me in the direction of the various maintenance manuals for the Escape Modules. That was pretty easy because this place was knee deep in boring documentation and since I had a module without any obvious holes in it, the expectation to master all this technological information was getting pretty intense.

Which you could not really fault my friends for. All they wanted was to get me home. Then we could all get on with our lives.

"Matthew?"

"Yes, Ross?"

My lack of enthusiasm puzzled even me but there it was. From the outset I had been skeptical of the plan and these days, what I was doing to cooperate was just to keep them happy.

"Did you find anything potentially useful?" That was typical of Ross, always trying to find something positive in the situation.

"More like interesting than useful." I wondered if Ross could hear the smile in my voice.

I could certainly hear the frown in his. "Do tell."

"I think it was the main tailoring facility for the Plant."

"How do you figure that?"

Ross, like me, probably had no idea where all our clothes came from when the Plant was up and running. Maintenance Interns, mostly because there was no way for them to contribute to any quotas, were probably very nervous and always seemed to keep to themselves.

"Well, I found about 8,000 racks of clothes."

"Clothes?"

"Intern coveralls mostly. Folded and hung up on racks that filled up three warehouses. "

"So?"

"Capekoids?"

"So what?"

"It was just something that came to mind."

"Sure."

Bit of a pause in the conversation. Fair enough, what do you say when someone says 'I just found 10,000 denim coveralls'.

"Listen, Matthew..."

"Yes?"

"Angie wanted me to play you the soundtrack to *Star Trek: The Motion Picture* before I signed off."

"Who's the composer?"

"Jerry Goldsmith."

"Great!" (Well, Goldsmith is great.) Plus *STMP was another movie that I'd missed*. It bugged me even though I had no idea how they could adapt a TV show to the cinema screen. I mean, where would they put the commercial breaks?

"But we need to review a few more chapters from the manuals tomorrow."

"Of course." Truthfully, I could feel a different project taking shape.

Bad Slacker Day

Soon, Team Earth assembled and harangued me for about an hour. Couldn't blame them, my slacker mode is very well-practised and I'm sure that them not being able to take direct action was very frustrating for them.

Eventually the three of them seemed to calm themselves and Eugene, who was now the closest to the mic, spoke: "We've got some new records here, do you want to hear them?"

"What do you have?"

"Syrinx and two solo albums by John Mills-Cockell."

Some tasty classic synth work on those but I looked over at my main Capekoids: Things #1–#6. There had to be at least six Capekoids to have quorum for any official meetings. I was willing to stick around and listen to tracks but it didn't seem like my tinheads were all that keen.

"Maybe later, Eugene."

"Are you sure?"

"Yeah. We're going to turn in early."

"We?"

"Sorry, me."

Revelation Day

WHEN YOU'RE AN ADULT, sometimes you can lose a friend but the process is so subtle that it's almost imperceptible. You stop inviting each other over for dinner, movie times never seem to work out right, you never seem to get invited to the same parties anymore, and you gradually stop calling each other on the phone.

Or your trans-lunar radio exchanges get shorter and shorter.

And unlike childhood relationships, once a mature friendship is broken, it's gone for good.

"You sure, Matt? It's still pretty early."

Angie was offering to play all three discs of the *Yessongs* album.

"Yeah. I'm really beat."

"Okay…"

"I'm just going to turn in."

And I really wasn't interested. My increasingly poor attitude was not going to be improved by over two hours of Jon Anderson vocals.

However, it was not a good idea to make Angie suspect that I was angry so we agreed to check in later in the week to "give me more time to study up on the module specs" (which of course I was not going to do). Then we signed off and flipped off the appropriate switches.

Of course I wasn't going to bed either. I'd made some interesting new discoveries in the kitchens and chemistry labs which inspired a new side-project. It was recipe time:

1. Three measures of alcohol (very large).
2. One half pouch of grape Kool-Aid (artificial flavour).
3. One quart distilled water (no metrics on Moonbase Omega).
4. One eighth pouch of orange Kool-Aid (also artificial flavour for an added aroma and tribute to Tang, the Breakfast Drink of Astronauts).
5. Mix together in large glass flask (or bucket if nothing so elegant is available).
6. Stir with anything (that won't dissolve).
7. Refrigerate (if you have any patience).
8. Pour into laboratory beaker (it is vital to do so, otherwise the alcohol will have no effect).
9. Drink as desired (or as medically possible).
10. Pray that you don't die (or go blind).
11. Hello, Hyper-Gin! My old friend and frequent downfall.

After two and a half beakers of that stuff, I was doing more than a fair share of falling down. In fact, pretty soon I was laying flat on the radio room floor, thinking about firing up the transmitter and telling Team Earth exactly what I thought of them and their dumb-ass rescue schemes. However, this course of action would require some fine motor skills, which might present a problem.

"You there."

Then I noticed Thing #1 bending over me. Since I neglected to give him any eyes it was difficult to tell if he was looking at me but it seemed pretty likely.

"Bishop."

My creation seemed to be talking to me as well.

"What?" Hey, I could still make words.

"Matthew Bishop." A very deep and serious voice rumbled inside the aluminum tin can that served as Thing #1's head.

"What?!" Good god, it hurt to talk. I'd forgotten how efficient Hyper-Gin was at generating hangovers.

Thing #1 gestured at four other Capekoids who were

occupying the radio room. "We have a message for you, our creator."

"Huh?" I know, some higher agency was reaching out to me and I was almost completely inarticulate. Not cool. Hyper-Gin, you are a false friend indeed.

Thing #1 didn't seem to notice my condition, which may or may not have been a good thing.

"We must speak to you of your mission."

What followed was essentially a one-way (and very probably imaginary) conversation.

POST-REVELATION DAY #1

THE ABSOLUTE WORST THING about a Hyper-Gin hangover, aside from the fact they last for weeks and weeks and weeks, is when you can't tell if something is:

1. Real.
2. A dream.
3. A full-blown Sensurround IMAX-powered hallucination.

Hours later, as I continued to lay on the concrete, aching everywhere, and with the walls of the radio room slowly circling around me, I decided to go with Option B because that one worried me the least. Option C would suggest some sort of neurological accident or psychotic break and I didn't need either of those. Option A could only be real if the Capekoids were animated by a distant alien intelligence or perhaps possessed by the dead souls of Plant personnel. Both Option A scenarios stretched definition of "reality" far beyond my comfort level. And the ghost option gave me the creeps.

I turned my head slightly so that I could check to see if Things #1-4 were still positioned where they should be.

Yup. Also, they weren't talking among themselves. Which was mildly reassuring.

Another after-effect of consuming that amount of Hyper-Gin (i.e. any amount) was severe memory black-outs. I would have welcomed a few of those regarding the events of the night before. Unfortunately the recollection of last night's events was all there, clear as the moon floating in a vacuum.

I turned my head in the other direction to see if I'd done any damage to the equipment in the radio room during my intoxicated state. Just in case I wasn't remembering absolutely everything.

Nope. All the gear looked just fine.

Then I threw up.

———◆———

It wasn't until almost lunchtime that I finished cleaning up the floor and myself. Maybe I could have finished the job sooner but I wanted to be thorough. In situations like mine, once you start letting your personal hygiene slip, you were starting to get yourself in really serious trouble.

While it was soon noon, it was lunchtime only in theory. My head was still pounding some and my stomach was uncertain, so I wasn't going to even try and eat.

As I carefully walked towards the door, I wondered how long it would take to find Trevor's sleeping quarters. I had a rough idea where it was located but there was quite a bit of wreckage between my realm and the old dorms. Even so, Trevor's crib was likely to be the easiest place to find what I needed next.

———◆———

Art supplies. Paper, pencils, pens and inks.

I was going to start the next phase of my project by getting a god's-eye view and start mapping the whole thing out. Fortunately, Trevor's room was full of the drawing tools that I'd cribbed from the Drafting Department for him, and also fortunately not occupied by a dead Trevor.

Back in my room I picked up one of his 2H pencils and started drawing big circles on a sheet of newsprint. Immediately I became aware of the following as I struggled to make some recognizable shapes:

1. My drafting skills needed a lot of work.
2. Thing #1's proclamation in my drunken state made a bit more sense: "When they arrive, they will need some stories."

⁕

I finally managed to eat and there was nothing but static on the radio receiver. Team Earth was staying silent; so no lectures, no scolding. The Capekoids were behaving themselves and not doing, or saying, anything.

All good.

Maybe a few more hours of drawing up plans and then off to bed. Perhaps the sleep would provide more inspiration. Even better, I might wake up with a renewed sense of responsibility and practicality. That would make Ross happy. Maybe I'd like it too, my biggest problem these days was not a lack of energy or ideas but having so many ideas that I didn't know what to do with them, i.e. stop assing around with all this arty stuff and focus on getting yourself back home.

⁕

I lifted one of my hands out from under the blanket and studied it: four fingers. One thumb. All bendable and reasonably limber. But still pretty useless. Couldn't draw, handwriting was absolute shit, couldn't type, or (as much as I loved music) play an instrument. If the Neo-Capekoids weren't dead easy to make, I would have been totally screwed as far as my project was concerned.

Flexible fingers? Bah! My hands might as well have been a pair of stainless steel hooks. No, that wasn't fair to all those amputees out there. I'm sure that all of them were much more skilled artisans than me.

"Oh, boo-hoo, Mattie."

It looked as though my old stoner friend, Rob, was sitting at the far end of my slab. Guess I must be asleep.

"Doesn't matter if you're dreaming or not, buddy." Rob took a long drag off his phantom roach. "We're going to have a conversation."

"Are you going to lecture me too?"

"Far from it." Rob smiled. "I'm here to provide guidance and support."

"So you're with Thing #1?"

Rob took another drag. "Poor guy isn't as articulate as he needs to be sometimes."

"Never did get the hang of making them mouths."

"No worries." Rob exhaled. "I'm here to help."

"What do you have to tell me?"

Inhale. Exhale. Repeat. This dream was getting a profound sickly sweet smell.

"For one thing, stop whining all the time." Through all the reefer smoke, Rob was starting to look like that caterpillar from *Alice in Wonderland*.

"Whining? Whining?!" I toned it down at bit when I realized that it did kind of sound like I was whining. Even so, I continued: "In case you haven't noticed, I'm marooned and alone on the moon, I'm slowly losing my mind and I'll probably be dead from hunger, thirst, suffocation or explosive decompression any time in the next five seconds to five years."

"Everything you just said is true." Rob coughed and offered me his roach. I shook my head. Real grass never did much for me and I imagined that lunar dream weed wouldn't make me feel much better either.

"But consider this, Matthew: you are finally doing something nobody's done before."

I was about to reply with something rude but I stopped myself. Rob was right. This was a completely unique situation. True, I would soon be crazy and/or dead, but I will still be first.

"You're a pioneer, Matthew."

"A pioneer of epic misfortune."

"But still…"

I sighed and leaned back into my pillow. Actually it was four standard issue pillows that I strapped together until they were just about comfortable. "If anyone returns to the moon and they find the Plant and find me, it will definitely get their attention."

"You'll be one of those historical curiosities, Matthew."

"An unsolved mystery?"

"Maybe Leonard Nimoy will host an episode of *In Search Of* all about you."

I laughed. "Immortality awaits."

Rob laughed too. "Or at least celebrity."

I was starting to enjoy this conversation. "Was there anything else you wanted to tell me, Rob?"

"Yeah." Rob's expression got more serious. "You need to stop thinking that you're not creative."

"But I'm not!" It felt like I was sitting up. "Even back in Blinn you had me figured as a total poser."

Rob shook his head. "Everybody's a poser at one time or another."

"Really?"

"At least to some extent."

"I never thought you were such a cynic."

"I'm not." Rob took another drag. "I'm just aware that people are vulnerable and sometimes do silly things to protect themselves."

It was hard to disagree with that statement.

"Okay, so I'm a creative genius." I never could win an argument with Rob. Not even an imaginary dream Rob. "What am I supposed to do with my mighty talents way the fuck up here on the moon?"

Rob didn't hesitate for a second when he answered me: "You and your friends started a story."

"We did?"

Rob coughed and his voice was rough from the pot-smoke.

"You did."

I think I knew what Rob was talking about but I thought that I had better check. "Are you talking about Mr. Oblivion?"

Rob nodded. "Don't you think somebody has to finish it?"

"I guess." I shook my head. "Although it's not as though anyone even remembers it."

"That is irrelevant." Rob jammed what was left of his roach onto my blanket; for some reason, it didn't catch fire. "Don't you think you just need to get down to doing the job?"

This was getting unreasonable. "How can I do that?"

Rob was gone. So was the reefer-cloud. Maybe he thought it was getting too boring to stick around and keep answering stupid questions.

Eventually I fell into a more confused than troubled sleep. Maybe in the morning I'd try to get Thing #1 to explain more things to me.

POST-REVELATION DAY #4

I SPENT THE NEXT few "days" in a bit of a haze, trying to figure out those manuals and spec sheets, looking around the quadrant and pretending that I hadn't had some religious experiences with one of my creations and an old friend who wasn't there. I knew I was probably crazy but that was little too crazy even for me.

As I woke up on this particular day, however, I very clearly remembered what I was talking to Rob about. And it didn't bother me. In fact, it made me kind of happy.

Mr. Oblivion.

It was a continuing story but the Plant blew up before Trevor could finish it.

I sucked back on a carton of UHT milk and wandered into the radio room. There was no incoming signal but Ross had sent me a message that had curled out of the teletype:

'Suggest you locate and inventory all portable oxygen supplies. Will be needed after lift-off. Also, check all connector hoses on the module.'

I noticed that he hadn't suggested a date or time for our next conversation. He (and probably Angie and Eugene) were still pissed off at me.

Fine. I wasn't all that happy with them either.

I noticed that Thing #1 was looking at me with great meaning. Yeah, there was some merit to Ross' suggestions. You never knew when some extra O_2 would come in handy and checking for some was not only smart, it was also dead easy. Even I could handle that one. Dead easy.

Ah. Now I got it.

Ross was giving me an easy job to do. To build up my confidence. First step in getting me re-engaged in that whole jump in a bucket and die on the way back to the home planet project.

Trickery!

Thoughtful and kindly trickery mind you, but it wasn't going to work. However, for the time being I would pretend to be a good boy and play along. It seemed pretty likely that there'd be some oxygen bottles in the medical supply lockers in Quadrant #3. My discussion with Rob also gave me some reasons of my own for checking out that part of the Plant.

Artistic reasons.

Post-Revelation Day #22

Another message via teletype. This one was from Eugene:

'Transmission at 20:00 your time. Got the new TD album.'

Well, I wasn't going to miss that, was I?

20:05

"The title is White Eagle." Eugene was briefing me on the album art and notes before we got into the actual music.

"What does it mean?"

"Who knows?" Eugene sounded a little cranky. "Those Germans can be so precious and obscure sometimes."

"Isn't that part of their charm?" This was weird, Eugene was a dedicated World-Stater, he usually didn't grouse on about specific nationalities.

"Humph."

As I noted earlier, I suspected that Tangerine Dream might represent a problem for my friend. He liked synth-driven music almost as much as I did but TD was definitely on the wrong side of the Berlin Wall for Eugene's tastes.

"Have you listened to it already?"

Plus the fact that the band almost never had lyrics that could be politically evaluated also might bug him.

"Of course."

Instrumental music would be more of a challenge to reliably place in an ideological category.

"So?"

"So what?"

Now Eugene was just being awkward.

"So what did you think?"

"I wouldn't want to influence your pure aesthetic experience."

"My what? My fucking what?!"

"It's better for you to make your own determination."

That was way too freedom of choice for Eugene.

"For cripe's sake, Gene! I'm a big boy now!"

"You sure about that?"

"I can make my own opinions, regardless of what you say."

"So why do you care what I think?"

Argh.

"Because I do."

"Okay." Then Eugene sighed. "Better than *Exit* but not as good as *Ricochet*."

"Really?"

"That's what I think."

Hmmm. *Exit* (which they'd played to me a few months ago) was a good album. The tracks were a little shorter than I liked but there was some innovative sound work in there. *Ricochet* (which I played constantly on my headphones in my bedroom in Blinn) was one of the greatest pieces of recorded music in the 1970s. At least I thought so.

"So B plus, A minus?"

"I would say that was accurate." I heard a soft crackle as Eugene placed the needle on the revolving vinyl. "You might think something completely different."

Enter lonely notes and synthesizers.

Afterwards.

Eugene cleared his throat.

"Well?"

"A worthy effort."

"Yes?"

"And I agree with you completely."

"But?"

I wondered if Eugene could somehow sense that something

was bothering me.

"Well…" I was about to say something I was reluctant to admit. "It feels a little like already explored territory."

"Wouldn't argue with you there."

"Maybe they need to explore a new sound."

"Who knows what the future will bring."

What will the future bring? Probably me sitting around in this room until the last of the atmosphere distributors in the Plant give out and I die. I didn't think I needed to bring that scenario up with Eugene just then.

"Right. Who knows? Whole worlds of possibility."

There was a scratching sound as Eugene finally took the needle off the record. That was odd, Eugene was usually pretty steady with his gramophone movements. Maybe he was nervous about something.

"So Matthew…"

I knew it! Here it comes.

"…before we sign off, there's a few things we should discuss."

"Sure. Shoot."

"How's work on the module going?"

"It's not."

"No progress at all?"

"I've decided to start a new project."

"Did I hear you correctly?"

"Yeah. I think I'll be working on something else."

"What can be more important than getting back to Earth?"

"Maybe I can explain later." Or not. Because if I did tell them what was on my mind, they would all think I was indeed completely nutsy-coo-coo. Which I probably was.

We had another thirty seconds of that embarrassing inter-orbital static.

"Maybe that's just as well," Eugene said eventually.

That was a surprising observation. It seemed sensible to shut up and let my friend continue:

"You won't be hearing from Ross for a while."

"What happened? Is he okay?" My heart started to race. The

idea of Ross being gone was pretty disorienting. Like someone had cut the tether to the space capsule.

"Ross is fine." Eugene sounded… angry?

"Fine?"

"As far as these things go."

Why would Eugene sound angry? And… uncomfortable?

"So what the hell happened?"

"Ross and Angie split up."

That was a shocker. On 0.3 seconds of reflection, maybe not.

"Split up? Why?" A rush of conflicting feelings made me feel guilty. Sure, I was upset that there was pain and discord among my closest (and only) friends. But also: hot damn! I was totally excited because Angie was now available. Did I finally have another shot? Who knows? They say that some long distance relationships can work, right?

"Why?" Eugene was in that condescending tone that he used whenever he explained to you how everything you know is completely wrong, like when he tells you that capitalism might not be the greatest thing since inflatable shoes. "Because these sorts of things happen between adults sometimes, Matthew."

I wanted to tell Eugene to fuck off, which is what I used to do when he sounded like that. But I had to get real careful here. Ross was my main source of technical advice. I might need him at some point if I wanted to stay alive a bit longer.

I re-calibrated and continued: "Why can't Ross come to the studio when Angie isn't around?"

"Matthew. Matthew." More big sighs from Planet Earth. "Angie's living with me now. So she's almost always at the studio."

Fuck a duck.

So she wasn't available after all.

Still…

The idea of Angie and Eugene was simply insane. The universe must be about to end soon.

"So, you two are an item now?" Well, I had to ask.

"Yes." Pause. "No." Another pause. "I really don't know."

That certainly cleared up nothing. "I see."

"I wish I did."

Should I pity or envy Eugene?

Static. Static. And more static.

"Do you want to hear more music, Matthew?"

I knew that Eugene was probably just trying to change the subject but it was still a considerate gesture.

I took a deep breath. "Got any Hawkwind?"

"No."

"That's good."

Laughter across the void.

POST-REVELATION DAY #31

IT'S NOT THAT I didn't at least try to work in a less cumbersome medium. There were lots of pens and paper laying around the Plant and with the imaginary encouragement of Things #1 and #2, I set myself up in one of the Engineering offices, taped some sheets onto a drafting table and attempted to draw the concluding chapters of the Mr. Oblivion saga.

Attempted. I certainly was no Trevor. Even Thing #1, who was the big advocate of this approach, had to admit that my efforts at illustration were at the level of a mimeographed fanzine. At best.

No. If I was going to make the grand narrative statement, I was going to have to use a medium I was experienced with.

Capekoids.

Post-Revelation Day #35

My excursion to the Engineering Office was not a complete waste of time. I found some photographic equipment that turned out to be very handy in what would become the prologue section of my installation.

I went ahead and made slides of every page of Trevor's comic and was going to set up projections of each instalment of Mr. Oblivion along the main access corridor leading into the Administration Complex. I even pulled out some chairs and benches and set them along the walls at strategic points so that any non-existent visitors could rest while they were reading the text panels and word balloons on the walls, ceiling and floors. An immersive experience like that needed a soundtrack so I found some instrumental tracks from Alan Parsons and mixed them into a two-hour running loop. Ideally I would have liked some way to run the music on a continuous basis, but that would have hopelessly distorted the magnetic tape in less than three days. I had to settle for a basic on-off switch that I'd hit whenever I went down there. The overall effect was still pretty good.

Post-Revelation Day #102

"Turn on your monitor, Matt!"

The voice was echoing out of the radio room's speakers. A voice that I hadn't heard for a while. Well, actually I hadn't heard any voice for a while. At least not with my ears.

"Wha?"

I know, not me at my most articulate but I hadn't spoken out loud for over two months so I was a little out of practice.

"Matt!" The voice barked out of a few more speakers. "*Focus, you fuckface!*"

That was definitely Angie.

"Ah. Um." More brilliant conversation. "Okay."

"Turn! On! A! Monitor!"

"Why?" This was a fair question. None of the exterior cameras had worked since the Big Crash.

"Humour me. I'm trying something."

"Okay, okay." I remembered that it was usually just a good idea to do what Angie told you to do, even when she was 240,000 miles away. I flipped a few switches that hadn't been switched for a while and I heard that soft, low buzzing sound you heard when you turned on an appliance that you'd been storing in your attic for the last few decades. There was always this nervous pause while you waited for the device to either start working or start issuing plumes of smoke.

Three video screens in front of me flicked and started to form an image. That was a relief. Any kind of fire, electrical, chemical or otherwise, would pretty definitely kill me.

The image broke up into static, then I got some horizontal bars, then bouncing vertical bars, and then: Angie. Her face was in black and white on two monitors; in colour on another one. A little fuzzy on all three.

"Can you see me?" Angie peered into what must have been the lens of a video camera.

"*Yes!*" This was, in truth, pretty damned thrilling. I'd never expected to see Angie's face again. Or anybody's face.

"Excellent. Most excellent."

The colour monitor blinked off into some very dark static. Maybe its electronics were just too old and beat up to handle the incoming signal.

"How did you pull this off?"

Angie smiled, obviously pleased with the technological breakthrough.

"The AV department at Blinn Collegiate was selling its old equipment and Eugene got lucky."

"Who would have have thought that a life-long communist would be such a good shopper."

Angie laughed. Good, she still liked some of my jokes. "Bargain hunters of the world unite."

"Did Ross help upgrade the transmitter? I'm impressed."

Now Angie frowned. "Bite your tongue, buddy. I did that myself."

I was smart enough to try to not look surprised. I was, however, not smart enough to remember that it didn't matter if I looked surprised or not. There was no camera moonside.

"Nice work, Ang."

"You didn't think I was capable of setting this up?"

Gah. Still defensive after all these years.

"No, I guess I was just thinking that the three of you were back working together."

Angie shook her head. "Ross has left town."

"Left Blinn?"

"Yeah, he was getting bored out of his mind here. Since P.A. pulled out, most of the suppliers have shut down and there's not much for an electronics engineer to do."

"Where did he go?"

"Ontario." Angie must have converted to the Albertan faith because she pronounced the name of the central Canadian province as though it was located somewhere just past the River Styx. "Doing some work for the computer science department at the University of Waterloo."

"Really?" That sounded pretty dull.

Angie must have picked up on my tone: "Not exactly reaching out to the Galactic Superculture, but the last we heard, it sounded like he's enjoying himself."

"That's nice." Actually at that moment, I felt pissed and abandoned. And deep down, I really didn't care if Ross was being fulfilled in his new career or not. Selfish me, as per usual.

"Yeah, it's fucking terrific."

Bless you, Angie.

"So, it's just you and Eugene these days?"

Angie looked at the floor and sighed. "Not exactly."

"No, really?"

"At least not for very much longer."

"I'm sorry to hear that," I said, not feeling very sorry at all.

"Don't be." Angie smiled but it was kind of a sad smile. "It was kind of inevitable."

"Inevitable?"

"And at least Eugene is being a lot nicer about breaking up than Ross was."

"He's probably just grateful for the relationship while it lasted."

"What?" Angie looked puzzled and not entirely happy.

"I know I was."

I couldn't be sure but I think I saw a slightly faraway expression on Angie's face, like she was filing her feelings away for analysis at some future date.

"Look Matt, before Ross left, he said some things that I think you might like to know."

"Why didn't he tell me himself?"

Angie frowned. "Maybe because he couldn't bring himself to."

"Okay." This sounded like it could be pretty heavy news. "I'm all ears." I laughed. "And eyes, thanks to you!"

My ex-girlfriend smiled for a second and then went back to frowning. "It's about the escape module."

Oh god, that stupid thing! "What about it, Ang? And before you say anything, I've got to tell you that I haven't been near the pod in quite a while."

"Maybe that's a good thing."

A good thing? What the fuck was going on here?

"How so?"

"Ross said he'd changed his mind."

"Changed his mind? About what?"

"That's not the best way of expressing it, it was more like he's re-evaluated the metrics of the scenario."

"What metrics? What scenario?" What Angie was saying sounded like Ross, but either I couldn't, or didn't want to, understand the message.

"The getting back to Earth scenario." Angie looked at me like I was being incredibly stupid, which was fair enough because if you thought about it for more than two nanoseconds, what the hell else scenario was there?

"What about it?"

"Ross doesn't think you can make it back in the module."

"Holy shit!" So Team Earth was really, truly giving up on me. "Ross actually said that?"

"He said that even if you could completely reactivate the D-Drive and successfully regulate the internal environment, it's probably completely impossible to properly program the guidance system."

"So no direction home?"

"That's what he said."

"Why? The electronics on my module are essentially the same as the one you got back in." It wasn't that I was disagreeing with Ross' conclusion but I was at least mildly curious about his reasoning. Ross was smart and it might be entertaining.

"Something that Ross found out from locals that lost their P.A.

contracts. None of the escape modules that got back actually used the internal guidance systems."

"So why aren't you calling me from Jupiter right now?"

"The return coordinates were beamed in from a satellite network that P.A. was running to support the EOS project." Angie frowned. "That network isn't there anymore."

"How would anybody know that?"

"Because we got a letter from the Jag a couple of months ago."

"Colleen?" Jeez. I was surprised and a little pleased that she was still alive and possibly causing trouble somewhere.

"She says she's still tracking Progressive Apparatus."

"I'll bet."

"She says they're still into all kinds of shitty stuff but they don't seem all that interested in space or the Superculture anymore."

"Those are pretty big things to give up on."

"The Jag says that P.A. is extremely economically rational."

"Probably true."

"Which is why they are so incredibly evil."

"Also probably true."

"They probably just figured that they'd missed their window of opportunity and moved on to the next items on their agenda."

I thought about all the suffering that we went through to meet their quotas and deadlines at the Plant. Fuck a duck. All for absolutely nothing now.

"The Jag's probably right."

Angie continued: "When Ross heard that, he connected the dots and figured that P.A. had already shut down that satellite network."

"I bet it would be very expensive to maintain something like that if it had no purpose."

"Exactly."

"Good reasoning there."

"Sorry, Matt."

I just sat there for a while, softly rocking back and forth on the wheels of my chair. I looked over at Thing #1 and Thing #2. The fluorescent lights on the ceiling reflected off their rectangular aluminum heads in an unmistakable 'I told you so' sort of way.

"Gosh," I said eventually. "Now I don't feel so badly about being lazy."

"Listen, Matthew." Angie leaned towards her camera. "Your situation is not hopeless."

"How do you figure that?" My question just sort of popped out; I didn't mean to sound like a self-pitying dork.

Angie didn't seem to notice anyway. "There's always a chance that NASA will return to the moon and find you."

Angie was usually the one with the stronger reality orientation but maybe it was my turn now. "I don't think so, Angie. From what you guys have been telling me, it sounds like the Americans are more interested in making movies about exploring space than actually exploring space."

Angie seemed to shrug my rather perceptive observation off. "Fine, the Soviets then."

"Even Eugene thinks that the commies don't care about the moon."

Angie didn't seem to be able to stop herself from nodding. She's probably had that conversation with her soon-to-be-latest ex-boyfriend more than a few times.

"So as far as getting back to Blinn, I figure it is kind of hopeless."

Angie shook her head. She just wasn't going to let this go. "Maybe Progressive Apparatus will come back looking to reclaim some of their investment."

"What isn't broken up here will be obsolete by the time they have the resources to get out of Earth orbit." Me and the Things thought this was the most unlikely of the scenarios we'd discussed so far. "And even if P.A. did come back, they'd probably shoot me in the face rather than give me a ride home."

Angie was now so close to the camera that her face was almost completely out of focus. "Then you have to convince them that you've learned something useful."

"Such as?"

The face on the screens was starting to break up.

"Matt, my angle is going, I'm going to have to sign off."

"Okay—"

"Just remember—"

Now there was just a soft hiss and lots of spots and sparkles on the monitors. However, Things #1 and #2 agreed that Angie's half-statement did raise a really interesting question:

Just what had I learned on the moon?

Taken from a strictly narrative perspective, the transition from the Tunnel of Sagas to what scholars and folklorists have labelled 'The Labyrinth' is fairly smooth, taking the visitor from one chapter in the tale to the next. At the end of the Tunnel, our culture hero leaps down a vast metal-clad ventilation shaft that takes him into the bowels of the Central Control Complex.

Those of you familiar with Joseph Campbell's mono-myth will recognize this as the Descent of the Hero into the Realm of the Underworld. While perhaps familiar, there is nothing mundane or predictable about the barrage of sensory inputs and sheer dimensionality when one crosses the existential threshold from the Tunnel of Sagas into the first of the Labyrinth's chambers.

from *Wonders of the Moon: A Visitor's Guide to Important Lunar Heritage Sites* by D'Arcy Christopher Blake, Senior Selenitic Museologist

Post-Revelation Day #114

AN EARLY CHALLENGE WAS to find a credible way to destroy Mr. Oblivion's hat. For some reason Trevor felt that it was important to give our hero some distinctive visual element, like the bat symbol or Nick Fury's eye patch. Trevor's answer was giving Mr. O that classic flat cap that looked like it was made out of tweed.

When I saw the first sketches I told Trevor that I didn't think the hat was particularly futuristic, but he didn't seem to be all that interested. What kept Mr. Oblivion from looking like an Andy Capp swipe was a pair of high tech goggles with automatic zoom lenses, micro plasma screen displays and fat, complicated face-hugging straps. Those were wickedly futuristic. I suspected that Trevor booted up their techno-quotient just to make me happy.

Trevor had an artistic ego but he wasn't stupid.

Anyway, Mr. Oblivion's cap did seem to have that iconic quality. Whenever I thought of the character I thought of that cheese-cutter headgear (and maybe those huge honking goggles).

The eye-wear I could manage because I found about five hundred pairs of protective lenses in one of the maintenance shops which I could use on as many figures as I wanted.

However. That stupid damned hat!

There was nothing like it anywhere in the Plant. So I had to get some inks from Drafting and dye some denim. Step two was needle and thread time. The result was pretty distressed but still recognizable as something resembling tweed.

The next problem was that it took me almost a week to make

just one, barely acceptable, flat cap. There was no way I would be able to reproduce however many dozen I might need for all the tableaux. I'd be doing nothing but making bad hats.

Ergo, Mr. Oblivion's hat must die.

Also, I'm sure some of the more alert readers among you will have asked yourselves: what tableaux? More on that later.

Probably too much more.

All of this is a rather backwards way of explaining how I was going to finish the storyline that Trevor started in the Intern Newsletter. I got the idea when I was poking around the Administrative Complex looking for more office supplies that I could re-purpose as art media. Frankly, this was another one of those tedious and time-consuming tasks. Not as boring or as thumb-endangering as trying to sew a hat together, but pretty close.

Exploring the Admin Complex without the clutter of human beings gave me a very different perspective on the interior architecture. It felt like a combination of rats' nest/beehive with decor by Franz Kafka. It was incredibly, and needlessly, confusing to find your way around—and it seemed to take forever just to get in and get out. True to P.A.'s organizational philosophy, the very idea of installing anything as sensible and democratic as an orientation map was completely out of the question. It was important to build in as much inconvenience and inefficiency into daily operations as possible. Designing these flaws right into the architecture probably made it easier to blame everything on the interns.

As I was trying to navigate my way around the offices, I tried to create my own mental map of the place. It became quite an adventure in visualization: if I could just strip off the ceiling and levitate myself about one hundred yards off the lunar surface, I could look down and get a nice overview of the entire Complex. Eventually I could hold that image in my mind and add in what details of the rooms and corridors that I could remember.

Then something occurred to me as I considered my mind map: all those spaces and rectangles… if you looked at them from that God's Eye POV, then the whole Complex looked like the panels on a comic book page.

Great. Another revelation.

The image of the undrawn panels on a page pretty much infected my brain. Soon I knew what I had to do and thanks to my work on my unwitting (at least to me) prototypes Thing #1 and Thing #2, I was fairly sure how I was going to do it: a walk-in comic panel rendered in life-sized 3D. Which became my basic strategy for the treatment of all the rooms in the Admin Complex, i.e. tableaux.

For the first panel/room, I wanted something that would be kick-ass but not too kick-ass. I needed to signal that we were entering a new phase in the story, keeping the action going while generating some tension and emotional connection to the climax in the last scene at the far end of the Complex.

Mr. Oblivion activates his anti-gravity jump belt (direct swipe from early Buck Rogers) to avoid the barrage from the particle beam weapons from the Master Computer's synthezoid guards.

I needed fifteen Capekoids, including one representing Mr. O—these were dead easy to do because mostly all I had to do was to stuff one blue and fourteen olive green union suits with paper and wire mesh and angle them in the proper positions. Plus I'd already made the flat cap and I had that in the process of partial destruction by a charged ion blast. Goodbye, stupid hat. Bliss, bliss, bliss.

The major technical challenge was fabricating all those weapons and frankly that wasn't all that difficult because I raided one of the workshops and found some heavy duty voltage meters that looked way more dangerous than they actually were.

Post-Revelation Day #182

"I'M IMPRESSED THAT YOU got the video transmission up and running." We now had two-way face-to-face communication.

"I'm not as smart as you, which is probably why it took me so long."

"Yes, that's probably it."

Okay, I'd walked into that one.

"Anyway…"

"Hey!" Angie smiled. "You look better than I expected."

"Health benefits of staying busy."

"Sounds like."

"I'd like to show you something."

"Is this going to get dirty?"

Now where did *that* come from?

"I'd like to show you what I've been working on."

Angie shrugged. "Too bad they don't run the bus lines that far."

It was my turn to smile. "I'm just going to switch the feed from this camera to the video tape player…"

Angie actually looked impressed.

Way, way back at Blinn Collegiate Institute, my grade eleven media arts class was abruptly gifted with the capacity to create our own television. Sort of; we could produce black and white moving pictures but it could hardly be called broadcast quality.

Even so, I thought (and still think) that the Sony Port-A-Pack one-person mobile video camera/recorder was the coolest, most magical piece of technology that I'd encountered in my seventeen-odd years. My joy was tempered somewhat by the main lesson I learned from the Port-A-Pack: just how difficult it was to produce anything that looked half as good as the worst-made episode of *The Trouble with Tracy*[9]. Also, although technically portable, the unit weighed about a tonne.

After months of fiddling about with the contrast controls and figuring out how to thread the magnetic tape on those reels and then nagging kids from the grade ten drama class, some of us managed to piece something together that presented itself as a sketch comedy show—you know, something like *Laugh-In* or *The Smothers Brothers*. We tried to get some musical numbers in there but the logistics and the lack of access to talent were just too much of a nightmare.

We had a hockey player on our team, Mike, I think. It was pretty obvious that he was in search of a bird course, and he got interested in the Port-A-Pack because he figured he could get his girlfriend to make pornos.

Boy, was he surprised!

Mike claimed that the two of them eventually decided not to do it because they didn't like the fact that they could only tape in black and white. The rest of the team figured that it was because the girlfriend worked out that the boyfriend was going to let his horny creep friends watch the tape.

Actually, it was the Port-A-Pack's monochromatic imagery that resulted in the only footage that I was really, truly happy with. That semester, the grade ten drama class was doing a stage

---

9 There is a saying among some creative professionals that something can be produced according to the criteria of "Fast", "Cheap" or "Good" but you can only chose two. Based on this paradigm, *The Trouble with Tracy* may have been the fastest and least expensive television program ever produced.

production of *Macbeth* and I caught the lead actor running through his lines at the same moment that I had finally cued up the tape. So I persuaded him to sit on one of those folding chairs while I cut all the lights except a single overhead spot. My actor had a surprisingly big voice for a fifteen-year-old and when he did that "tomorrow and tomorrow and tomorrow" monologue, it sounded pretty impressive.

It looked good too; had a kind of a *Chimes at Midnight* feel to it. Which, incidentally, was one of the least well-received movies I'd booked for the Plant, even less popular than Lindsey Anderson's *O Lucky Man* which I thought was going to get me lynched. Sometimes people can be such philistines.

Speaking of which, the ultimate use of the Port-A-Pack at BCI was to serve as a delivery system for pirate tapes of such classic adult films as *Deep Throat, Beyond the Green Door* and *The Devil in Miss Jones*. Most of the audience consisted of the football team and their girlfriends at after game parties. Mike and his chums didn't seem to mind the black and white picture so much after all.

Assholes. Of course, on the other hand, maybe I was just jealous.

On the other, other hand, maybe that wasn't the last of the Port-A-Pack. Maybe that was the unit that Eugene bought from BCI and Angie ended up using to transmit her face to me.

Probably not, but I really liked the idea.

The Optics of Confrontation

A serious scholar never wishes to descend to the often-trod or cliche in their writings, however, one is still undeniably obligated to address the readers' expectations. Especially when they are so entirely justified. I shall therefore refer to one of the best known anecdotes and quotations of the later 21st Century.

When exo-philogist and space explorer John Colarusso first viewed the penultimate tableau, the system was still operating on its original mechanical motive power. A wonder that Dr. Colarusso felt compelled to comment on:

"It felt as though I was standing at the top of a vast shadowy tower, viewing the scene through a cosmic camera obscura— and I was helpless to intervene as an insanely intricate clockwork hell wound and unwound itself below."

The restoration of the scene has only intensified the ghastly truth of Dr. Colarusso's observation.

—D'Arcy Christopher Blake

Post-Revelation Day #253

FOR THE LAST SETTING we were back into the realm of full-sized classic Capekoids. And I needed to make a hell of a lot of them. Because of the way the story went, I didn't have to dress them in the same uniform, which eased things up some on the costume front. Even so, at the end of the last installation I think I must have used just about every spare scrap of cloth left in the Plant. I'd also created a not-so-small toxic waste dump outside the Quadrant Two structures because I had to empty a lot of aluminum cans to use for Capekoid heads. Fortunately there's no lunar water table to contaminate.

The biggest challenge was installing all those figures in and around the main impact crater. This required hours and hours and hours of working in an EVA suit which meant that I consumed almost all the easily portable oxygen.

The up-side of this was that I was able to use some of the empty tanks as Capekoid heads, so less fumes and toxic waste. The downside was that there was now no way to provide an atmosphere for the Escape Module even if I could get it to work. I had essentially placed myself under permanent house arrest. As long as the Plant's air-generators were still working I'd be okay, but unless I wanted to deeply inhale some vacuum, I was stuck in here for the duration.

Post-Revelation Day #300

For some reason, Angie had lots of music to play. Much of it was new to me. Artists who appeared after my departure from Planet Earth.

Tears for Fears?

Erasure?

Depeche Mode?

Who on Earth were these people?

I think Angie chose them because there was lots of synthesizer tracks, even though most of them had much faster, much pop-ier beats than I was used to. Even my favourite band didn't sound the same anymore. With classic '70s Tangerine Dream, you have these monstrous 345 minute tracks which needed to be listened to while on either LSD, hashish or Valium (so I was told) and you'd go semi-comatose, lay back and let the waves of sheer cosmic weirdness wash over you as your consciousness slowly melted its way into infinity. Mid-'80s Tangerine Dream had shorter, more radio and cinema friendly tracks and what those beats were doing was encouraging you to scarf down new kinds of drugs and get up and dance. Admittedly, it would be some kind of extremely cool and sophisticated Euro-Germanic dancing, but these were not the psychedelic techno-hippies that gave me so much comfort in my youth.

Can you say 'Space cadet glow'?

All of this was to try and explain why I was having some pretty conflicted reactions to Angie's broadcast that day. Novelty, anything new, was very welcome. I mean, I was stuck up here on the moon. If you didn't stay active, you start to notice how barren and boring this place is and then you will go seriously nuts in some way that will completely incapacitate you. Hell, if Timmie suddenly cut in and played me some new Bay City Roller tracks, I would have happily sat through them.

Alternatively…

…I was really uncomfortable with the way all this new music was making me very aware that the world had the nerve to change in my absence. I didn't have any context to appreciate most of what I was hearing.

It was damn disorienting and it made me feel even more incredibly lonely. Unlike my usual state which was just profoundly lonely.

"What do you think?"

Angie had just played some songs by something called Duran Duran.

"Great," I lied. "Really great," I continued to lie. There was no way I was going to let her know I was anything but absolutely thrilled with her choice of music.

"I'm really sorry I can't show you some of their videos."

"Yeah, too bad."

Videos! What were these music videos that Angie kept talking about? It sounded like every tune that came out had to be accompanied with a miniature TV show down there. Pretty stupid idea if you ask me.

"Maybe if I catch some of their videos on MuchMusic I can tape them and rebroadcast."

"Uh, sure."

Wasn't the music enough these days?

"Got another album for you." Angie was smiling, like she had a box of spudnuts for me. "Canadian synth band."

"Not Syrinx, is it?"

"Who?"

Wow, it never occurred to me that Angie might not have heard of them. Then something else did occur to me: "Listen, Angie, before you play that, I need you to tell me a few things."

"Okay." Angie's expression got more serious. With good reason, really. Usually when we talked about anything but movies and music, things got pretty difficult.

"Were you able to make a tape of my broadcast of the installations?"

"Yes, I did." Angie waved a black plastic rectangle at the cameras. "Right here on Beta."

Beta? I could have asked what she was talking about but it didn't seem all that important.

"Any interest?"

Angie looked like she trying not to shake her head. "Not yet."

"But you did show it around?"

Angie did nod her head. "Some newspaper and TV people I know."

"So what did they think?" It seemed ridiculous that Angie hadn't mentioned this earlier. And it seemed incredible that media types wouldn't be all over that footage.

"They thought some of the installations looked pretty cool."

Some? "But?"

"They had trouble believing that any of it was shot on the moon."

Fucking morons! "But what about the establishing shots I took of the lunar surface?"

"They were impressed by the special effects."

"Special effects?"

"They were particularly impressed with the models."

"Models?! They think all of this is a bunch of models?"

"That was the general consensus."

"You've gotta be shitting me!"

"The TV guy complained a little."

"Complained?"

"Yeah, she said that at least *Space: 1999* was in colour."

"Fucking morons!" I was starting to really hate that show.

Angie gifted me with one of her wry smiles. "I'm still waiting to see if the Jag writes me."

"You'd think she'd be interested."

"Anything P.A. does interests the Jag." Angie frowned. "Unfortunately I have no idea if her last address is any good."

Or if those assholes had finally caught up with her. I didn't need to say that one out loud either.

We were both quiet for a moment.

Eventually Angie smiled again. It was a pretty lousy smile but I appreciated the effort.

"You're going to like Strange Advance, Matt."

"Who?"

"The band I was talking about."

"Oh, right."

"I should play them."

Maybe she was right, I could get back to work later.

The media techniques employed in the so-named "Tunnel of Sagas" draws on the classic 20th century stagecraft referred to as Somini Lumiere or Sound and Lights shows—where large scale projects and ambient sound effects, quadraphonic stereophonic music and theatrical narration combine to animate settings and structures such as castles, pyramids and even Grand Canyons and volcanoes. This technical artistry is in the service of telling the great stories, legends and myths associated to a site of great historical or natural importance.

In the case of the Tunnel of Sagas, we find more of the creative and adaptive re-use of period technology to relate the adventures of the Lunar Culture Hero and his struggle for freedom and the deliverance of his oppressed industrial tribe.

While this crude but sometimes ingenious equipment has been replaced by more contemporary plasma-cloud image rendering, great care has been taken to reproduce the eccentric angles, strange focal ranges and almost ethereal colours of the original optical transparencies as they were discovered by the earliest selenite archaeologists.

—D'Arcy Christopher Blake

POST-REVELATION DAY #322

TO RETURN TO THE subject of friendship[10], when I was a kid, I noticed that these relationships were fragile and they were gooey. That is to say, you might lose your best friend in less than two seconds by things as unimportant as cutting in front of him in line or refusing to trade one of your steelies for three of his cat's eyes, or mentioning that *2001: A Space Odyssey* was a really dumb science fiction movie because it didn't have any monsters or ray guns in it.

So one minute little Ronnie was the most important human in the universe, the next thing you two were scheduled to pummel each other senseless in the playground at the next recess.

Snap! Biff! Pow!

But the situation could reverse itself just as quickly. You might remember that you both hated the same girl in Health class (and neither one of you could figure out why you both seemed to be looking at her all the time). Or you might have picked up the latest issue of *Prince Namor: The Submariner* with that fantastic John Buscema cover and Ronnie was desperate to read it. Suddenly the two of you are friends forever again.

Splong! Squish!

Like, I said. Childhood friendships are very gooey.

Now when you're an adult, it is still possible to abruptly lose a friend, but mostly the process can be so subtle that you hardly

---

10 For fairly obvious reasons, the nature of friendship was almost as important to me as knowing how much oxygen was available.

notice it. Friendships could still be fragile but they were more spindly and hard to see—breaking one was like walking through an old spider-web that you hadn't noticed until it was gone.

Ross was gone. Eugene was gone. How long would it be before Angie was gone?

<hr>

"I like to think that he made it back somehow."

The miniature grey face on the tiny screen looked wistful. We were talking about Trevor.

"Don't you think he would gotten in touch if he had?"

Angie nodded. "You'd think so, wouldn't you?"

"But nothing?"

"Maybe he wants to keep a low profile."

"Maybe." I really didn't think so.

"We did hear from some of the others who made it back."

It occurred to me as rather bizarre that I never thought much about other possible survivors. Life alone at the Plant must be narrowing my horizons.

"How many?"

Angie almost smiled. "More than you might think, thirty-five, maybe forty. They kind of straggled in. In dribs and drabs."

"Flotsam and jetsam." But forty? Nice of Team Earth to mention that! However, it made not much sense to get angry about it at this point. "The evacuation system must have been built better than I thought."

"You and Trevor saved them. Ross too."

There was that. Our plan hadn't been a total waste.

"Anybody I knew?"

"Nobody mentioned you."

"The result of my charming personality, no doubt."

I think Angie decided that this was a good point to slightly redirect the subject matter of our conversation:

"At first Eugene tried to get all the returnees to take some kind of united action."

"That sounds like Eugene. What specifically did he want to do? Unionize them?"

I guess Angie decided to ignore my joke. "He wanted all of us to go public, or at least take some kind of legal action against Progressive Apparatus."

"That also sounds like Eugene."

"Like a lot of Eugene's ideas, there was some logic there, but somehow it never happened."

"So you all figured that nobody would believe you?"

Angie nodded. "That and the possibility that we'd all wind up with P.A.-shaped bullet holes in the back of our heads."

"Always a possibility…" I nodded too. "…with that wonderful organization." Still, Eugene was not one to give up on causes easily. "What about subversion and sabotage?"

Angie frowned and looked at her hands. "Everyone agreed that something like that should happen but ultimately we ended up doing nothing."

"Didn't people at least want to get revenge?"

"Yeah, yeah. At first maybe." Angie closed her eyes. "You have to understand."

This was just weird. "Understand what?" If you put Ed three feet in front of me, I'd remove his fucking esophagus. And I thought Angie was the direct one here.

"Once everyone got back…" She shook her head again. "…it all seemed so incredible that a lot of us seemed to think that none of it ever happened."

"You're shitting me, right?" Actually this account was just stupid enough to be true.

"I shit you not, Matthew." It looked a little like her eyes were tearing up a little. "It was so discouraging, maybe that's why we never wanted to mention it to you."

I leaned back in my chair, looked at Things #1 and #2 and wished that I had the luxury of denial like I did back on Earth.

"What about the rest of you? The non-delusional ones?"

I got one of Angie's 'be careful not to piss me off' looks but she gave me a straight answer: "It got hard to keep it together. People just wanted to get back to their old lives."

Now I was the one who couldn't think of what to say.

"Can't argue with that, I suppose," I said eventually.

Angie sighed. "They all sort of stopped coming around… and gradually drifted away."

"Like Eugene and Ross." Wow. I was still using my nice indoor voice but I was incredibly angry. "Maybe that's what you want to do." Incredibly angry and incredibly stupid.

Angie might have reacted with a huge 'fuck off and die' and flipped off her transmitter. I wouldn't have blamed her. To her credit, Angie just sniffed and wiped her nose.

"Yeah, like that."

Maybe it was time to step back from the cheap shots. Maybe this was a good juncture to get back to the original point of our conversation: the person that she actually loved.

"So none of the survivors had any idea what happened to Trevor?"

Angie just shook her head and I felt like a grade-A first-class shit. I was pretty sure what happened to Trevor. When the EOS shit-storm started, he got caught up in that gravity field and was turned into a perfectly symmetrical pancake. I had to sing that hymn over some of those too.

POST-REVELATION DAY #323

AS I DECIDED WHETHER I was actually going to get up at all today, I realized that I could smell something. I couldn't believe it.

Weed.

That familiar sickly sweet smell that permeates everything. The odour soon got a lot stronger until it felt like getting sprayed by a psychedelic skunk. Not that I had conflicted views on the subject of cannabis or anything, right? Since I'd sworn off Hyper-Gin about a hundred or so days ago and was also trying not to go off my nut, I was, if anything, even more puritanical in my views about any mind-altering substance.

Anyway, how could there be weed up here at the Plant? On the moon, for god's sake?

I rolled off my slab, opened the door to my room and started sniffing—seeking out the location of the mystery dope-cloud. A part of my brain, possibly one of the more sensible portions, wondered if this was indeed Maryjane smoke at all. It might be some electrical wires overheating and slowly sizzling away—and maybe it just kind of smelled like burning reefers. I wished that part of my brain hadn't said anything. A fire in a pressurized high O_2 atmosphere would not be a good thing at all. And there would be very little that I could do about it.

I started walking and kept on sniffing.

After turning a few corners it seemed like the hemp odour was getting progressively stronger. Really did smell a lot like weed. Which at one level was reassuring because it suggested that this was not an Apollo One scenario and I would not be in the middle of a raging inferno any second now. On another level it was less reassuring because it suggested that I was losing my mind at an even faster rate than I thought.

It would not have really surprised me if somebody tried to smuggle dope up here. That type of entrepreneur was usually very persistent and resourceful and there was definitely the need for some narcotic relief from the grind of the Lines. Not that any of that kind of stuff would ever percolate down to the Intern levels. It was very important to keep us labourers clear headed and feeling optimum pain at our work-stations at all times.

On the other hand, a total lack of dope was also conceivable. There was Hyper-Gin, which met middle-management's need to periodically obliterate their consciousness/consciences.

The smoky stuff seemed to be coming out of some metal vents set at the base of the floor. I had a sudden random thought: pest control seemed to be one of the few things that P.A. seemed to be reasonably good at. I had never seen a bug, a rodent, or any sort of varmint in the Plant. Given the sheer volume of cargo they were pumping in and of the place when it was operational, you'd think the odd little beastie would have stowed onboard.

Maybe some had and none of us interns had noticed them.

There was a lot of toxic shit used on the Lines and maybe the creatures just died off and dissolved before we saw them. So maybe there was the odd rat up here. Or maybe even more likely: raccoons.

The smoke was getting pretty thick now.

I had just now developed a new theory about the phantom stoner. Some raccoons had made their way up to the moon. Only the most intelligent and athletic raccoons would have survived up to this point because they would have had to have been able to avoid the Plant's janitorial systems and all those pesky explosive decompressions.

I opened a big bolted door and found myself inside one of the bigger loading bays. Months ago, after I'd cleaned out any useful supplies, I tended to stay away from places like this. Loading bays, and airlocks and observation bubbles, had direct access to vacuum and I really didn't want to be around when some hinges or panels finally decided to buckle.

Still, I needed to know where that smell was coming from.

To continue with my latest (stupid) hypothesis: raccoons have a much shorter life span than humans (don't they?) so the ones on the moon have been evolving away for a few decades and because of their cute little dexterous hands, have turned into a full-blown tool-using species. So the Smart-Raccoons work hard, play harder, get bored and like many sentient creatures have the urge to get high once in a while.

Those darned raccoons were the moon's secret potheads.

I wondered if after I met these frisky fur-criminals, if we would become friends. I could introduce them to Hyper-Gin; they might enjoy that. Or maybe they would just throw me down and eat my face while they were in a crazed drunken stupor.

Wait a minute. Phantom stoner?

Of course.

There he was, floating up in the far corner of the bay.

"Hey, Matt!" my friend giggled.

"Rob." He was back.

Not exactly, mostly likely I was either dreaming or hallucinating. I preferred the former over the latter.

Rob inhaled deeply on whatever it was in his mouth. "Love your digs here."

"Thanks."

When Rob exhaled, he propelled himself about six feet to the left. The effect was a little disconcerting; maybe a bit too Disney.

I got over my unease and Rob and I started talking and pretty soon I had an idea. It was a complicated idea so it took about two hours to explain it to my astral friend.

To his credit, Rob managed to look at least a little bit interested: "So why the change of pace at the end?"

I couldn't believe I was shrugging at an illusion. "You have to punctuate these things, right?"

"Why go from life-size to miniature? Big change of

perspective, don't you think?"

More shrugging. "I got the idea from a documentary I saw on the CBC back on Earth."

"God bless the Canadian mother-corp." Rob, who was suspicious of all organizations consisting of more than four people, was of course speaking with a certain amount of irony.

"What was the show about?"

"This miniature village in Ontario that some landscape outlet had set up."

"Oh, fun!"

"Apparently it's one of the most popular private attractions in the province."

"I bet, little models are fun."

"I tried to recreate all the mechanically animated effects they had."

"Clever." Rob gazed out a porthole and seemed to study the lunar landscape. "So small is beautiful?"

I shook my head. "Small is the only way to portray the sheer complexity of the setting. Beauty has nothing to do with it."

"Hooray for Modernism." That was true to type, Rob used to occasionally drop little philosophical observations like that.

This illusion was not going to distract me though. "The last instalment of the comic we printed was at the point where Mr. Oblivion is about to try and destroy the Master Control Construct."

"Yeah, that figures."

"I need to give the audience an overview of the sheer scale and complexity of the place."

"Lot of work to realize somebody else's vision."

Perhaps Rob, or my subconscious, was getting perceptive.

Annoying.

"It will also be a recreation of the whole Plant," I said softly.

"What was that?" Rob was just being awkward here. Since he was really some expression of me, I knew what I meant to say even before I said it.

"I want to make some kind of representation of the Plant—what it was like, how it works."

"Why, buddy?" Rob was smiling at me, another one of those sad smiles. "You know all that shit already."

"It seems important."

"Important to who? Who's going to know what it means? Who's even going to see it?" Real Rob probably never would have been so brutal with me.

Even so, I grinned at my friendly hallucination: "I'm working on that."

Regarding the content of the Tunnel, art historians and scholars of the last century's popular culture are more or less completely bemused. While the panel designs and illustration style is typical of the so-called 'comic books' and graphic novels of the time, there is no evidence of any character called 'Mr. Oblivion' in any media on Earth. Yet it seems almost inconceivable that such a richly realized figure could simply spring into existence independently on what must have been an almost completely isolated colony.

And perhaps it is this mysterious aspect of the character's origins that have contributed to Mr. Oblivion's emergence as one of our generation's most prevalent heroes. Certainly an essential element to the Mr. Oblivion mystique is the identity of its creator or creators. Did they somehow return to Earth and obscurity, would we find their bodies among the unmarked mummies in the site's strange mausoleum? Or did they meet some other unknown and unknowable fate?

—D'Arcy Christopher Blake

—→ END ←—

Three-time Aurora Award nominee, Hugh Spencer has been writing science fiction and cultural commentary (popular and otherwise) for longer than he cares to admit. He has been published in *On Spec*, *Interzone*, and *Descant* magazines, and has also been included in various anthologies. He also writes for radio and the stage, and has collaborated with Shoestring Radio in San Francisco, Praxis Theatre, and the Scripted Toronto Festival. He also occasionally contributes his alleged wisdom to the Gernsback Continuum, the podcast for *Amazing Stories* Magazine. Hugh's collaborations with Brain Lag Publishing include the novel *Extreme Dentistry* and the collections *Why I Hunt Flying Saucers and Other Fantasticals* and *The Progressive Apparatus and More Fantasticals*.